Benign Dystopia

Elder's Vault: System Lord Book 1

Benign Dystopia

Elder's Vault: System Lord Book 1

By Kody Killam and Aaron Harvey

ISBN: 978-1-957195-00-1 (Paperback)
ISBN: 978-1-957195-01-8 (Hardcover)
ISBN: 978-1-957195-02-5 (Electronic)

Library of Congress Control Number: 2022902341

Front & back cover by Kody A. Killam & Aaron B. Harvey
Book art & design by Kody A. Killam & Aaron B. Harvey

Killam Publishing First Edition 2022
Published in the city of Fredericksburg, Virginia.

www.EldersVault.com

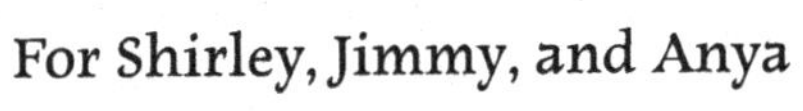

For Shirley, Jimmy, and Anya

Table of Contents

♀ Part One: The Watcher

"Every portrait that is painted with feeling is a portrait of the artist, not the sitter. The sitter is merely the accident, the occasion. It is not he who is revealed by the painter; it is rather the painter who, on the colored canvas, reveals himself." – Oscar Wilde, *The Picture of Dorian Gray*.

♀ Red Dust

⊖ 1

A black saucer nearly disappears against the moon's dark sky as it lands onto a bay outside a dome structure. Above the structure's stone body hovers a sign reading, Stet's Place, in an intoxicating purple glow. The bay's dim white lights come alive tracing its square outline, welcoming the ship's descent.

The saucer touches down gently while the sign's violet light illuminates it and the dust covering the ground. A dark ramp extends from underneath the ship revealing Jadecan, an Akiko who walks to the radiating ground at its end. He steps out onto the moon's surface and glances up at the slowly rotating sign. Mountains fill the dark landscape, as a few common large dragon-like sitadoom fly overhead within the endless star filled sky.

His faded pale white skin blends into the moon's environment, it's as if he belongs here. Which of course, he does. He stops to listen for a brief moment feeling his surroundings while his elbows' large protruding curved bones cut the sweeping wind. They, as well as his snake-like eyes, extremely sharp serrated teeth, and unnaturally wide smile, are all well known and have a bit of a reputation on Niushki.

He's dressed ragged but conventional, wearing nothing but a pair of black pants and footwear, as always. He intensely stares at Stet's Place with his narrow yellow eyes. The planet Vyn is visible on the moon's horizon as usual, it's a permanent fixture, a constant onlooker.

The Akiko strides to the familiar dome structure while nodding at the couple of insect-like Scuts guarding its entrance. A howling wind rolls through, as he stops briefly in front of Stet's Place. Niushki's white dust dances around his legs while he stands still, allowing the moon's cool aroma to penetrate his nostrils. It's been a long while since he's seen Stet, looks the same since last he was here. A strange feeling being back, but as it is, Baby believes the Balgorex is their best shot and who was he to disagree. She's never been wrong before, so why would she be now? The wind subsides, and he begins again, heading for the dull colored complex.

The structure's sliding door opens as he nears, revealing the violet light saturating the large room behind it. He walks through its glowing entrance and stands while the door closes behind him. The same old wooden tables were here before Stet killed the original owner and still populate the quiet open room before him. Sitting about the area are a few more of the insect-like henchmen. The Scuts look up acknowledging his entrance, they're common fodder in places such as this.

Each of them wear a large set of goggles, completely covering their eyes. Their entire body wrapped from head to toe in dark cloth, with only the two antennae on top of their heads visible. Alone they were worthless, but together they could become a force to be reckoned with. Used to be a strategy unique to them, until the Reogki arrived and did it better. The hairy faced bear-like boss of the complex stares from across the room within a circular enclosed bar. A heavy and impervious hat wearing Balgorex, by the name of Stet.

"Jadecan, it's been a while. How are things?" he shouts, with both arms raised.

Jadecan saunters through the tables in between them, while the Scuts watch his every move. Stet stands inside the steel bars and stone counter encircling him, as an oval shaped shelving unit stretches to the ceiling behind his hefty body. His four brown eyes lock upon the approaching Akiko.

"Things are fine," Jadecan answers. "How are you?"

"Good, what brings you in?"

"An energy cell," he answers.

"Ah... I see, quite the find."

Jadecan sells items he scavenges from the moon's surface regularly here. This time however, he was looking to buy. The Balgorex are dangerous but honorable, and like Jadecan, kept their word. Stet's always been good to him, no matter the situation.

"Do you happen to have one?"

"Oh... well, this is a surprise, I just might," Stet chuckles, and answers intrigued. "It ain't an easy item to come by. Let's say uh, 100 units."

An energy cell is rare, but one-hundred units rare? No. Stet's reputation as a black market dealer's well known, and his prices are usually reasonable. Anyone else could, and would, have gone elsewhere, but trust is a luxury in a place like this. And Jadecan... he isn't just anyone.

"I do not have those kinds of units," he says.

"Have you considered salvaging the corpses?" Stet slightly chuckles, knowing very well of the bodies Jadecan leaves behind. "I suppose I'd be willing to hand it over, for a favor, of course."

"What kind of favor?"

"Retrieve for me an item," Stet says, as if it's no big deal. "Return to me with it, and I'll give you the energy cell. Simple."

"Why not retrieve it yourself?" he asks, annoyed at Stet's proposition.

"Are you interested?" Stet asks. "I'm sure the Reogki would be happy to accommodate your request," he adds, aware of the Akiko's reliance on him.

Jadecan contemplates the proposal and chuckles amused at the thought of asking the Reogki. "Where is the item?" he asks.

"You know the old Reogki outpost?" the Balgorex asks. "The one just before the cliff?"

"Yes, what of it? It has been abandoned for quite some time."

"Well, it has a secret," Stet says, with a bit of a smirk.

"What kind of secret?" Jadecan peers across the stone counter enticed.

"I think you may find all of it… intriguing," Stet answers, with a mischievous smile while placing a small metallic sphere in front of him.

"What is this?" he curiously asks, while picking up the sphere and inspecting it.

"A key," Stet answers, while Jadecan studies its mysterious engravings. "Just give it a slight squeeze while inside the outpost."

"Is that all you have for me?" he questions. "To squeeze it?"

"Pretty much."

"Typical," Jadecan states. "Whatever, seems easy enough," he asserts, smiling.

"Be careful, old friend," Stet warns, as the Akiko turns to leave.

With a simple thought, the sphere fades from Jadecan's hand in a flash of blue light, as it dematerializes into his molecular inventory. He laughs under his breath amused by the warning, then leaves the same way he entered, with his every move watched by the Scuts. Stet is never alone and rarely accompanied by anyone other than his own thugs. You didn't just show up here, well one could, and it has indeed happened. The poor souls, they didn't leave, well not alive anyhow. The Akiko would know, for there was a time you could've seen him sitting at those tables, same as they do now. That time was long ago. He did not miss them.

The door slides shut as Jadecan stands just outside. The moon's dust lingers in the still air, refracting the purple light of Stet's sign. With its black body covered in the moon's dust, he looks upon the saucer parked on the bay in awe. Baby, he called her. A gust of wind rolls through as Jadecan walks toward her. His thoughts ponder the quest ahead as her black ramp extends out to him. He paces up entering into her command deck, and as he sits before her viewpoint a blue screen projects out in front of him.

"Went well?" Baby asks, as he sits staring out at Stet's Place.

"Indeed," Jadecan answers, retrieving the small sphere from his inventory. "I believe he may possess what we have been searching for."

⊖ 2

Baby lands in a clearing next to the cliffs, near one of Niushki's many rocky outcrops. Within the side of the rock face sits a relatively small and worn down ancient stone outpost. The holographic projection within her command deck disappears as Jadecan lifts himself out of the black seat. He stares out at the abandoned outpost, then makes his way to the rear of the saucer and strolls down the ship's ramp, silent as always.

The swift wind kicks up the moon's dusty surface as he steps gently onto it. He ambles toward the decrepit outpost and glances up at the twinkling stars. When he was much younger, many decades ago, he would stare at them admiring their beauty. It's been a long time since he's done that. Every now and again, he thinks back to before the Reogkis' arrival, and the destruction that followed in their wake. There was once a time when Niushki was the Akiko's hunting grounds. Those times were long ago, forgotten by most, being but a distant memory to himself.

He approaches the outpost's broken door and walks through, entering the dark room waiting within. A bleak dust covered room greets him, it looks to have been untouched for quite some time. The small sphere reappears with a flash of blue light within his hand, he pauses, looking over the tiny dismal area as the wind howls behind him. He steps further into the compound and stands briefly, then begins to squeeze the sphere. The cracked floor before him slowly fades, revealing a stone staircase in its place. Different, can't say floors normally do this, but here we are.

Torches line the walls of the stairway. At its bottom resides a cobblestone landing, in front of it stands an immense ancient wooden door. To the landing's right is a compact patio, upon which sits a slightly raised circular platform. Its metallic silver color, coupled with its unusual appearance among the dull worn stone, calls for Jadecan to investigate.

The flames of the torches dance as he progresses down the stone stairs. He steps onto the landing as a white hologram of a small hooded individual appears on the platform. The hologram stands about half of Jadecan's height and speaks in a language somewhat familiar to him.

"spuwrho shgow rihshmuhrawshdrng shmuw rhoshduh woytuwroh shfharih shghorngshfuwrow shkuhwoytuw woh shduwruh tuwryu shkuh rawshduh rehshfowrow shfowrawsrng shbowwuhshmrngshbow ruhtuw waw shkuhruw shgowwow srng shkow rihshghorng shduhwoh shgah rng sfhawuhshbuh wyu shkuwrow shbuh reh tuwrho shfha rahshkuwwoytuw wohshduwruhtuw rheshkuh wowyho shnohreh"

The small figure abruptly disappears as the large door shutters awake slowly, yawning open before him. He watches as the stone passageway it has kept hidden unveils behind it. Jadecan walks through the open doorway, and as the door begins to close behind him, he notices at his right an empty pedestal. A colorful mural depicting a winged beast within a star rests upon the wall behind it. He gazes upon the painting but for a moment, then ventures down the dungeon's waiting torch lit corridor.

The crackling of flames echo as Jadecan walks beneath the walkway's curved ceiling. An ivory statue stands watching from within the heart of a grand chamber presenting itself at the hall's mouth. Jadecan admires the sculpture's marbled texture as he sets foot within the big room. It resembles the hologram who greeted him in the dungeon's vestibule and stands brilliantly holding a sphere within its outstretched hands. Just below where the dome ceiling meets with the room's wall, a ring of torches now blaze, illuminating its entirety. Jadecan continues around the effigy and discovers at its back three separate rectangular corridors. Above each sits an engraved glyph, reminiscent of the etchings seen on the sphere. He stands before the center pathway deep in thought at the obvious puzzle before him.

At each of their ends the same open grassy scenery looks back. Midway up the corridor on the right, a decomposing torso lies face down, its legs nowhere to be seen. Deciding against it he peers through the center, then over at the left. Although both were painted with blood, they seemed reasonable, but he knows they are likely to be filled with traps.

After a few moments of pondering he shrugs, and says to himself, "Guess we are going with the left one."

Just as he comes to its middle, the end of the path seals rapidly. The floor below him splits in two, folding inward. He turns and jumps up swiftly, running along the wall back toward the chamber as the ceiling begins to lower at an unnerving pace. A spike filled trench begins to ascend from the blackened depths below. He leaps off the wall and stretches for the floor's edge. He grabs hold of the edge and notices what appears to be Scut bodies decorating the darkness below.

The light from the torches reflect off the glistening back of the sculpture as he hangs for a split second at the chamber's entrance. He nimbly pulls himself up and rolls away as the descending ceiling of the corridor passes by. He pauses glaring at the solid wall before him as the stone block stops moving with a reverberating crash. The Akiko vaguely smiles as he looks over at the center corridor.

"Looks like the sensible option."

He stares through the entrance upon the green grass at its resolution, then glances around the large room and journeys inside. His shadow takes shape behind him as he treads carefully down the corridor. Three rotating blades swing out, emerging from the walls at his back and race for him. He promptly picks up pace, as a duplicate set of blades appear at the mouth of the hall before him. Jadecan jumps forcefully into a tight spiral between the spinning blades barely missing them. He rolls out of the passageway into the lush pasture unharmed headfirst as the blades retract back into the stone walls and disappear. The Akiko peers back at the now empty corridor. An odd contraption, he's never seen such a device before. Weird, well this entire place is weird.

He stands in the meadow's rolling terrain. A beam of sunlight streams from a blue sky through a jagged crack in the ceiling above him, as the sound of flowing water resonates. It's clear, he's no longer on Niushki. A bright orb levitates overhead, its pulsating light mesmerizing. This must be the secret Stet was referring to. Jadecan steps deeper into the grassland when the green hills vanish. An endless void now encompasses the small area around him, as an unseen light dimly illuminates it.

A pair of glowing red eyes pierce the darkness before him, as a blood-curdling scream bellows, accompanied by the sound of chains. The monstrosity responsible for the hollowing sounds slowly creeps out of the shadows, revealing its hideous ghoul-like face. Its deathly foul breath sweeps through like the winds of the moon. Its torn wings flap, sending Jadecan sliding backwards in a gust of stale wind. The beast swipes out with one of its long forearms, barely missing him as he leans away just in time. Its other scaly hand slams down as it roars, cracking the dark stone between them. It drags its long black claws back along the cold floor as the chains attached to its collar rattle. Finally, a challenge worthy of the Akiko, this is going to be fun.

"Threatening me with a good time," he whispers, grinning.

With a twisting jump Jadecan lunges toward it. His blades slice the still air as he twirls in front of its growling black face. The monster leaps back as one of its many long whip-like tails lash out in an attempt to wrap around his spiraling body. Jadecan's blades slice it away from the beast and as it cries out in pain he lands perfectly before it. Almost as soon as his feet hit the dreary stone, he's swiftly backhanded and sent soaring into the shrouded wall encompassing them. With a deafening whack he collides with it and falls nearly lifeless, meeting the eerie ground beneath him with a resounding thud. The back of his head bounces off the stone floor from the sudden impact as the monster stands roaring into the blackness. The creature looks down upon Jadecan as he slowly picks himself up. Blood flows from the gashes left upon his body and bald head, dotting the black stone. He grins at the challenge present before him.

"Not impressed," he states, staring into its red eyes.

The beast charges with its wings fully open behind it. It closes in quickly, and lunges at Jadecan. The Akiko jumps up at the creature's throat dodging its dagger-like teeth and spins becoming but a blur within the darkness. In a spray of blood, his twirling blades paint the obscure walls red as he almost decapitates the creature. The soft terrain of the meadow welcomes him as he lands back within its sea of grass.

With his hand upon its soft ground, still crouched from the landing, he glares around the peaceful rolling hills with the monster nowhere to be seen. Blood drips off him onto the lush grass staining it. He stands as the glowing orb slowly descends and comes to a stop floating just above the meadow. The orb's glow illuminates his face, and while a blue moonlight shines through the chasm's jagged cracked ceiling, he crouches at its side. He reaches out and plucks the orb from its suspended state, then admires it briefly before scanning it into his inventory. Sensing an-other's presence, he watches as several armed Scuts walk out from the corridors onto the moonlit ground.

"Betrayal it is then," the Akiko mutters.

Jadecan observes a few Reogki among the goons as they gather across the large pasture before the corridors. Of course the four fingered green skinned invaders of Niushki would be here. Stet sort of had to send more than just Scuts. He smiles recognizing them from the lobby of Stet's Place. No matter, they're just as dead as the next. No one but the Akiko was going to get out of here alive, and there's no way the Balgorex thought any differently.

Jadecan strafes off to his left at a walking pace while activating his white holo-weapon. Its energy fused body materializes from his molecular inventory forming within his right hand. The goons open fire as they advance toward him. Raising the now solid holographic weapon, he fires back in stride, mowing down most of them almost instantly. With only a couple remaining, he finishes them off, coming away from the fight surprisingly untouched. Angry and annoyed with Stet's lack of honor and traitorous ways, he treks back to the corridors fed up.

"I am coming, Stet."

Just before entering the passageways he notices a Reogki, pulling himself slowly along the ground, leaving a trail of blood streaked grass behind him. Jadecan strolls over to him and stands for a moment at his side before flipping him over. The thug coughs rolling onto his back as blood streams from the corner of his small mouth, his clothing drenched in blood. Jadecan watches as he struggles to breathe, then points his weapon at the Reogki's bald head and pulls the trigger. He stands for a moment and watches the life fade from the thug, before slowly returning to the corridors.

The dread once occupying this trap-filled corridor is no longer foreboding, as he deactivates the weapon and strolls for the main room. He flows into the chamber once again, then saunters around the statue's base and comes to a stop before its outstretched hands. He retrieves the orb from his inventory while admiring the one within the effigy's hands.

What is so special about this orb? He ponders.

With one final look upon the statue he scans the orb into his inventory and turns away, heading back to the ancient door. He summons the silver sphere and slightly squeezes it as he nears the entryway. The Akiko then stands before the pedestal admiring the mural, wondering if what he had just gone through was pictured within, while waiting as the large door opens. After a few moments he ascends the torch-lit stone stairs leaving the dungeon's meadow of death behind him whilst the wind of the moon sweeps through the open doorway of the outpost. Jadecan chuckles quietly, happy to be home.

He emerges from the complex and takes note of a lone Reogki next to a hovering exo-craft, apparently in wait for the others' return. Jadecan glances around and quickly notices Baby's absence from the silent environment. The waiting Reogki is much younger than the others and cowers as the Akiko approaches. The young thug shakes in fear as Jadecan stands before him. In one swift movement, the Akiko relieves the Reogki of his head. The Reogki's body stands headless momentarily, then crumbles as Jadecan makes his way toward the craft.

The planet sits on the horizon as a mysterious entity watches him board the vehicle. It views from a distance unnoticed as Jadecan speeds off in the exo-craft. Behind him a cloud of dust bellows, fleeting away from the Akiko and the death following within his wake.

⊖ 3

Jadecan arrives at Stet's Place and takes notice of Baby on the landing pad. He hops out the open-top craft and upon contact with Niushki's surface the moon's dust rises up to meet him. The two Scut guards at the front door of the complex approach the Akiko, who looks up grinning. They open fire as he dodges rolling in their direction and then jumping up he spins, cutting them both in half. The Scuts have never been a match for the Akiko, they weren't before the Balgorex, and they surely aren't now.

The exo-craft at his back begins to smoke from the stray shots of the Scuts' onslaught as he makes his way toward Stet's complex. He glances over at the black colored saucer as the building's door opens signaling his approach. Upon stepping through the entrance the few Scuts within the room look over at him, their weapons already in hand. The room's violet light saturates them as his holo-weapon takes form.

"How is everyone?" he whispers, under his breath.

They begin to fire laser bolts at Jadecan hitting him a couple of times as he marches into the room with his weapon blazing. Closing the gap between him and the stone bar ahead, he advances without pause while picking them off one after the other. Within moments the room becomes quiet as he wades through the tables unfazed by his minor bleeding wounds. Stet is absent as he prowls around the circular enclosure glaring through the steel bar barrier above its dull counter.

"I take it Stet is busy, not surprised," he remarks.

A locked wooden door leading into the enclosed bar is present on its far right side. It would appear as if it's the only way in. Strolling over, he forcefully kicks it down and steps inside with his weapon still in hand. He examines the oval shelving unit completely consuming the entire center of the room, and then walks the narrow aisle around it searching for the energy cell. Browsing its numerous shelves and inspecting the items upon them, he examines most everything. Dominating its shelves are primarily dusty glass bottles of alcohol. Outside of a few other insignificant items, there is nothing to write home about.

With no sign of the energy cell he deactivates the holo-weapon whilst standing where Stet had stood during their exchange around a cycle ago. Frustrated and disappointed he stares at the countertop that separated them and then smiles chuckling to himself.

Of course not. Why would it be here? He thinks to himself.

Jadecan gazes through the violet light as it floods the complex's main room, with his eyes intensely focusing upon the structure's entrance. After a moment of thought he sighs and turns his attention to the empty counter before him. He rummages through the cubbies below hopeful and determined but comes away none the better. Peering inside, he notices a very intriguing button located underneath its stone top. Upon pressing it the shelving unit behind him splits, gradually sliding away from one another revealing a hidden stairwell beneath it. The Balgorex have never concerned themselves with hiding anything well, and to be honest, they have no reason to.

"Simple," he states, grinning eagerly.

The Akiko takes note of the Reogki voices resonating from the room below and reactivates his weapon while standing at the head of the stairway. The intense light shining from below illuminates a fourth of the stairs as he descends the steps anticipating the skirmish surely awaiting him. Walking into the light through the rectangular doorway and emerging from the darkness, he manifests before the Reogkis' eyes. The area is reminiscent of the violet one above, only much smaller. The Reogki stand around a couple of wooden tables in front of the dark archway lying within its back wall, awaiting the Akiko.

"Why hello," he says, under his breath as he raises the holo-weapon, sending a barrage of energy projectile bullets into the room.

After a few moments he relaxes and slightly lowers his weapon, examining the now mute room. The sound of gunshots reverberates within its stone walls and as a bullet ricochets penetrating his shoulder, he almost immediately returns fire. The Akiko's shot strikes the Reogki's round head who stands within the confines of the walkway, killing him instantly. It is not often he's caught off guard.

The thug's body falls as Jadecan gravitates over to the corridor while muttering in irritation, "Seems about right."

The Akiko looms at the hall's entryway briefly before advancing forward and stepping over the Reogki's body just within. The corridor sharply turns after a couple dozen paces blindly to his right. Strolling over to its edge, he stands with his back upon its wall annoyed with the small space of the passageway. He peers around the corner and quickly withdraws as shots echo from its end striking the stone before him, causing a thin cloud of dust to linger.

He exclaims calmly once the firing ceases, "I am going to kill each, and every one of you."

"Jade? Is that you?" Stet sarcastically yells from down the hall.

Jadecan turns into the hall firing his holo-weapon, killing the few Scuts who were trying to walk stealthily up the corridor toward him. He stands fully exposed at the pathway's head, while staring down at the doorway of the room Stet hides within. The entry is a dozen paces away towards the end of the hall's left wall, he begins to trek in its direction.

"I suppose that is a yes," Stet sighs.

Jadecan watches as one of Stet's thugs takes up position inside the entryway facing him. He fires a fatal shot in stride as the goon situates himself, killing him instantly. Continuing without pause he makes for the entrance and once there notices a lone Reogki standing within. With the goon's eyes fixated on the Balgorex standing with his back against the wall in front of him, the thug fails to notice the Akiko now standing outside the doorway.

"I take it you've managed to retrieve the dungeon's secret?" Stet asks loudly.

"Yeah," he answers, raising the holo-weapon, and as the thug looks over at him in surprise, Jadecan pulls the trigger.

The wide-eyed Reogki looks down at his bullet littered chest as his clothing soaks in blood. With a shocked expression worn upon his face, the thug looks up at Stet who sighs shaking his head, and as the goon's eyes roll back he collapses onto the floor. Stet slowly turns to face Jadecan who stands just outside the perimeter of the room's entrance.

Jadecan stares up at Stet who chuckles and casually says, "You'll earn yourself a mark for this." And after a few moments of silence the Akiko violently slices his throat with a quick twist of his arm.

"I do not care," Jadecan says, walking past Stet and deactivating his holo-weapon.

The Balgorex falls to his knees holding his throat, and as he keels over onto his face, the Akiko studies the small cubical enclosure. Jadecan takes notice of a young turquoise skinned Cerulean female leaning on the wall across from him, as well as an iron door to his left. She's clearly being held as a prisoner, sitting on the concrete floor with her hands chained above her horned head to the room's stone wall. Bruised and beaten, she looks up smirking at him. He glances at her then makes for the iron door, as Stet's twitching body quiets behind him. Upon reaching the grey metal door he grips the handlebar above its dead bolt and attempts to pull it open.

"Thought as much," he whispers, as if expecting to find it locked.

The Akiko peers over at the Balgorex's motionless body then back upon the door. In hopes of it possessing the key, he leisurely sets for the corpse. The Cerulean's light purple eyes watch as he kneels next to the body and rummages through its pockets a few paces from her. Jadecan removes his hand bearing a key within his palm, then briefly looks over at the prisoner before calmly wandering back over to the door.

He inserts the key into the dead bolt and turns it, then easily pulls open the door revealing the compact storage closet behind it. A light flickers a few times soon after, before fully lighting up the packed, small space. Jadecan steps inside and examines the overflowing cubbies and shelves surrounding him. The prisoner observes him combing the depository as he searches casually without a care in the world. After what felt like an eternity he emerges from the storeroom and peers at the Cerulean, then grins at the energy cell within his palm.

"All this, for that?" the female prisoner asks bewildered.

"Yes indeed. For the most part," he answers, admiring the energy cell.

"You gonna kill me too?" she asks tartly.

"I am still deciding," he states, as the energy cell disappears with a flash of blue light.

He strolls over and crouches in front of her grinning widely. The Akiko briefly contemplates killing her right there simply because he can, before deciding instead against it, in light of some entertainment. Who knows, could be fun, and if not, what of it? With his menacing gaze locked upon her, he holds out his hand in the space between them.

"What can you tell me of this?" he questions, as the glowing orb materializes within his raised palm.

♀ Dark Terrain

⊖ 4

An A.I. piloted small Olensi transport flies silently through the vastness of space while the surrounding stars reflect off the shuttle's silver body. The planet Vyn and its moon lie in wait in front of the oncoming craft as a Cerulean by the name of Amelia sits looking out at them from within its main cabin.

A pair of dark horns curve away from her forehead whilst flowing through the black hair hanging down and covering her breasts. She's dressed quietly upper class as always, wearing a white blouse, sable sweatpants, and hiking boots, nothing too extravagant. It's her go-to attire for occasions such as this. Her lavender eyes migrate down to the handheld device within her light blue hands while she swipes through images of dark skinny figures known as "Watchers" upon its screen.

She turns her gaze to the green planet, as the ship heads for its white dust covered moon. It's not often the Cerulean ends up in situations like this, and when she does it's normally her own doing, as this time is. Even so, she's not happy about it.

Why do we have to meet on Niushki? Why a moon? She mentally frets.

An arm-like robot with a large blue eye at its end, moves busily along a track on the cabin's ceiling. Most everything's done in one form or another by artificial intelligence. With that being said, the technological singularity, as it has been so dubbed, has been aggressively avoided with prejudice for obvious reasons, and successfully so. With a cybernetic tone the cabin bot speaks as it briefly comes to a stop focusing upon her.

"We are within proximity of our destination. Please prepare for atmospheric entry."

Amelia watches as the bot continues along its course, pausing at each monitor and storage unit along the ship's walls. Although rather active now during free space travel, the cabin bot is mostly inactive for the majority of the flight in hyperspace. She returns to the ghastly mysterious figures inhabiting the screen inside her hands and then sighs while looking at the dark moon through the circular window.

Why not on a pretty planet? She ponders irritably.

The spacecraft enters Niushki's atmosphere, en route to a nearby terminal, and within moments it is gliding above the rocky surface. The transport begins its landing sequence almost immediately and gradually slows as Amelia surveys the moon's endless wasteland.

"We will be landing shortly," the cabin bot relays, passing by.

The ship decelerates to a smooth halt outside the fully automated terminal and begins to descend at a regular pace above one of its many landing pads. Touching down softly, the vessel powers down as a small ramp extends from an open doorway connected to its elongated body.

"We have reached our destination," the bot states, positioning itself beside the door inside the craft's cabin.

Amelia stands and walks down the short aisle passing in front of the robot as she exits. She descends the ramp of the transport onto the railed metal path and follows it away from the landing pad toward the illuminated main building. The entire structure's supported by a solid steel frame while its large slate roof overhangs its glass walls. Vyn looms on the horizon as a subtle breeze rolls through and the cooling smells of the white landscape arouse her senses.

It's beautiful, she thinks in awe, while dreamily wandering below the moon's star rich black sky. "This was unexpected... wow."

A sphere of white light swallows the entire structure as each of its landing pads glow on their own around it, fading into the endless darkness beyond. She approaches and peers through the clear walls of the square building. A ring of several kiosks encompass a silver circular platform in its center, the terminal's intelligence portal. Of typical Cerulean design, it shares an interlinked intelligence database with others of its kind. Each adding their unique knowledge to the collective forming the Olensi Galactic Network, or the OGN for short. The same connection Amelia's data-pad uses.

The sliding glass doors of the complex open upon sensing Amelia's approach and close behind her entry. She walks to the room's center and activates one of the kiosks surrounding the platform. It scans the Cerulean with a wave of blue light. After a moment or two, it ends as a white hologram appears and addresses her.

"Hello Amelia, how may I be of help?"

"I'm to meet with Stet Stal. Do you know where I can find him?" Amelia asks.

"Stet Stal," the hologram says. "Ah yes, resident of colony 208, owner of the local stop, Stet's Place. You will most likely find him there."

"Thank you," Amelia says graciously.

"You are very welcome. Is there anything else I can be of help with?"

"What can you tell me about Stet?" she asks curiously.

"I only know what is public on the OGN, for my program has not met him," the hologram states.

"I understand. I appreciate your help," she says, heading to the back door of the terminal.

"You are very welcome," the hologram says, then disappears.

Amelia walks through the terminal's back door and stands upon a large rectangular terrace extending the width of the complex, the terminal's holo-deck. To her left she notices a blueprint kiosk and ambles to it. She activates the console's blue projection and scrolls through the exo-craft options available within its database. Upon choosing a vehicle the blue screen disappears, and she is once again scanned. The scan completes and Amelia observes as the craft's printed by laser into existence behind the kiosk. Within moments, it is hovering above the platform in front of her. She walks past the console and boards the open-top vehicle, then ventures away from the terminal into the moon's dark terrain.

⊖ 5

Amelia heads for the violet sign of Stet's Place glowing in the distance. She arrives and parks the exo-craft to the side of the dome complex. She walks around to its only entryway in front of its dimly lit landing pad and enters the structure. The Scuts inside stop and gaze at her standing before the doorway. She had heard of these insect-like creatures before, but had never actually seen one.

So these are the infamous Scuts? She thinks curiously.

"You must be the Cerulean I've been waiting for," Stet comments, from the enclosed bar.

"And you must be Stet," Amelia says.

"I am."

Amelia strolls through the tables over to the stone counter he stands behind. She peers up at his four eyes through the metal bars and questions him.

"So, you have information about the Watchers?"

"I may," Stet answers, shrugging with a slight tilt of his head.

"I didn't come here because you may have information. You either do, or you don't," she states with a bit of sass. "I was told you have information."

"I may have seen a Watcher nearby."

"Where?" she asks demandingly.

"An abandoned outpost 'round the way," he answers calmly. "I could take you if you'd like."

"Lead the way," she states, gesturing to the door.

- ⊜ 5 -

Stet leaves the enclosed bar through its side door and heads for the exit. Amelia follows his large body as the Scuts begin to file outside in front of him. They amass outside the stone complex into two groups and board separate exo-crafts. Amelia and Stet get into the same one along with a few Scuts. And after a few moments of staring awkwardly at one another, they speed off to the abandoned outpost in a cloud of dust.

"How far are we going?" she asks.

"Not far," Stet answers. "Relax my dear, we'll be there soon enough."

The drive wasn't all that bad. It was mostly quiet, 'cept for the remark here and there, mainly made in an attempt to make small talk. No one however, was very talkative. Amelia spent the bulk of it admiring the serene Niushki landscape and creatures flying within its dark sky. They arrive at the rundown shack relatively soon, as Stet said they would, and exit the vehicles.

"That Watcher of yours, was right up on the cliff there," Stet says, standing in front of the hovering crafts and pointing to the top of the rock face ahead of them.

"What was it doing?" Amelia asks, looking up at the empty cliff.

"Standing, just standing, and watching," he answers.

"What else can you tell me?"

"One of the Scuts found this here sphere in the outpost," he says, revealing a small silver sphere covered with inscriptions. "Other than that, not much else."

"Interesting," she says, taking it from his hand. "I recognize these symbols. They appear to be a part of the ancient writings I've been researching. You said they found it here?" she asks, quickly gesturing toward the decrepit outpost.

"Yes," he answers.

She rushes to the shack's broken entry as the hefty Stet and his thugs follow casually. After entering through the doorway she stops abruptly and scans the small desolate dark room before her.

What does this sphere symbolize? What does it say?

She sits deep in thought, as Stet and his goons file inside behind her. She retrieves the pad from her molecular inventory and searches for her notes on the language hoping to at least partially translate the sphere. Glancing back and forth between the pad and sphere she begins to squeeze it out of frustration. The floor before them fades, revealing a stone staircase leading down to a large ancient wooden door.

"Wow." Amelia gasps. "That's something."

"How'd you do that?" Stet asks.

"All I did was squeeze the sphere," she answers in disbelief, "That's all I did."

"Good to know."

They follow the Scuts' lead and walk down the torch lit staircase. As they step onto the landing before the door a hologram appears upon the circular metallic platform at their right, and declares in an ancient unknown language.

"spuwrho shgow rihshmuhrawshdrng shmuw rhoshduh woytuwroh shfharih shghorngshfuwrow shkuhwoytuw woh shduwruh tuwryu shkuh rawshduh rehshfowrow shfowrawsrng shbowwuhshmrngshbow ruhtuw waw shkuhruw shgowwow srng shkow rihshghorng shduhwoh shgah rng sfhawuhshbuh wyu shkuwrow shbuh reh tuwrho shfha rahshkuwwoytuw wohshduwruhtuw rheshkuh wowyho shnohreh"

Abruptly the small figure disappears as the large door shutters awake, cracking its aged seal in a plume of dust. They watch as it slowly yawns open before them revealing the stone passageway hidden behind it.

"Any idea what our little friend said?" Stet asks.

"Something about a beginning guardian's key." She shrugs. "I think."

"Good enough for me." Stet points his thugs through the open door and says to Amelia with a friendly tone, "Shall we?"

They walk through the open doorway together and as the door begins to close they notice a medallion sitting on a pedestal to their right. A stunning mural depicting a winged beast within a star rests upon the wall behind it. Amelia stares in awe at the colorful masterpiece whilst Stet looms at her back.

"It appears as if this creature is of some importance," Amelia states, studying the painting. "What does the star represent I wonder?" she asks aloud, while handing Stet the sphere and removing the medallion carefully from the pedestal. "This is amazing," she says awestruck, staring at the medallion within her hands.

"What is it?"

"A medallion of a female's face, who bears green gems for eyes. I don't know what she's supposed to represent though," she answers. Amelia ponders with excitement as questions flood her mind while watching the crackling flames of the torches that line the arched walkway, *What does the painting have to do with this medallion? How are they connected? Who did all of this?*

"Shall we continue?" Stet's voice interrupts her thoughts.

She looks at Stet and then to the ivory statue waiting at the end of the short corridor. After a moment, there is a flash of blue light as she stores the medallion into her inventory. They stroll side by side down the old moss-ridden stone walls. Stet's thugs stand within the large room in front of the effigy as they enter.

"Look at that," Amelia says with wide eyes.

"It is quite the sight," Stet comments.

"I wonder if the sphere in its hands is the same one we used to reveal the dungeon's entrance," she ponders aloud, studying the inscription at its base.

"Whatever you say my dear."

He meanders around the statue's base and joins the Scuts positioned before the three paths behind it. Amelia joins them and immediately notices a mysterious glyph above each one. She looks to her pad in haste hoping to decipher them. Vigorously she scrolls through her notes with a bewildered expression worn upon her face.

"I have no idea. There is nothing here," she exclaims in frustration.

Stet motions for two of his goons to travel down each of the halls. He watches beside Amelia with his remaining four thugs. Each Scut pair reaches the center of their respective corridor which activates the pathway traps, killing them all.

After a few moments of deliberation Stet says to the group, "Time to head back and regroup."

"Six of your guys were just killed!" she exclaims in confusion. "Regroup? What do you mean regroup?"

"Happens all the time. Now come along my dear," he says unfazed, walking away from the carnage. "Time to go."

"What?" she says exasperated, "Do you grow them or something?"

"Maybe. Now let's go," the Balgorex says forcefully.

Stet was not playing and Amelia knew it, time to get out while she still could. She couldn't afford to get into trouble, Tytus would kill her if he knew she was on Niushki alone. The group exits the dungeon and ascends its stone steps. As they reach its top, Amelia looks back over her shoulder and witnesses the entire stairwell fade away rapidly.

Back at the exo-crafts, Stet and his thugs prepare to depart, as he explains, "We're gonna head back and return when we know a bit more about this, ah, situation."

"I'm sure the Olensi could help, and together we could uncover its secrets," she suggests. "Maybe work as a team?"

"Sounds delightful," he says, as a goon strikes her over the head from behind, knocking her out with a rock. "How 'bout not, my dear."

⊜ 6

"Amelia... My dear," Stet says quietly, staring at her.

Amelia observes as one of his two goons take up position on the opposite side of the room's entryway. She hears a shot echo as the thug posts at its edge. The goon falls, blood streams from his forehead, he's dead, definitely dead. Her head pounds, her arms are heavy, and her wrists are sore, from the constant abrasion from the shackles above her head. Good times.

"I take it you've managed to retrieve the dungeon's secret?" Stet shouts over his shoulder to the killer loudly.

Amelia watches as the shooter appears within the doorway and guns down the last thug. The goon stands momentarily before collapsing onto the floor. Stet slightly smiles at her then turns to face the killer standing within the room's entrance.

With a final chuckle, Stet says, "You'll earn yourself a mark for this." The Balgorex's throat's then sliced spraying blood onto the wall.

She recognizes the fair skinned species of the killer immediately, it's the rare and endangered Akiko. They're a violent and primitive species, but intelligent, they should be protected. Of course, the Olensi haven't bothered with it. Why would they? It walks past as Stet falls to his knees holding his throat while gurgling blood. The Balgorex face-plants the floor while slightly twitching as the Akiko deactivates his weapon and studies the small room. He glances at her, then walks to the storage closet and attempts to open the locked door.

What is he looking for? She wonders.

She sits silently as the killer walks back over to Stet's body and rummages through its pockets. He comes away holding a key within his palm. The Akiko looks at her briefly then stands and strolls back to the door unlocking it. Amelia listens as he searches through the items inside.

Maybe he's not as dangerous as he looks. He just slit Stet's throat and killed a lot of guys in cold blood, but he could, um release me, right? Yea probably not. He's already covered in blood, might as well just add mine.

He emerges from the closet and smiles at an item within his hands as a child would with a new-found toy. He slightly tilts his head back and forth while staring at it, grinning happily.

He's a child. Or at least... What is happening? Amelia wonders in shock. Then asks him bewildered, "All this, for that?"

"Yes indeed. For the most part," he answers, admiring the energy cell.

"You gonna kill me too?" she questions saucily.

"I am still deciding."

His words are direct with a hint of sarcasm, but strong and confident. Definitely not a child. He strolls over and crouches in front of her grinning widely. His menacing gaze locks upon hers as he holds out his hand and presents a glowing orb. Amelia stares at it within his palm as he questions her.

"What do you know of this?"

She knew little of the orb and even less of the Akiko crouched before her. His inquisitive yellow eyes are just as frightening as the grin he wears upon his face.

He would have killed me already if that was his intention, she rationalizes. "May I ask your name?"

"You may, I am Jadecan. What do you know of this?"

"I know nothing of that orb," she says honestly.

"What did you do to end up like this?" he asks, referring to her chains.

"Nothing," she answers and sighs, as Jadecan tilts his head threateningly. "Fine." Then tells him the story of how she met Stet and the dungeon they discovered together.

♀ Within Twilight

⊖ 7

Jadecan stares at Amelia for a few moments. It was a pretty decent story and believable, sounds like something Stet would have done. Frankly, the Akiko would have probably done the same had he been in the Balgorex's position.

"You woke up here?" he asks.

"Yes," she answers, "He was hoping to use me as a translator, among other things."

"How was that?"

"Not well." She laughs.

Amelia looks away in terror and squeezes her eyes shut as Jadecan swiftly cuts the chains of the shackles above her head. The Akiko's bone blade marks the stone wall as it slices through the rusted chains. A small chain dangles from each of the irons still bound to her turquoise wrists. She slowly turns while staring at her freed hands. Her heart races as she shakes fearfully sitting in front of him.

"Th... th-thank you," she stutters, as he gets up and walks away. "I'm alive... I'm alive."

She sits in shock with her hands still held out in front of her for a few moments, then frantically removes the irons before getting up and moving quickly after him. Amelia steps around Stet's body and then over the one beside it carefully as she enters into the hallway outside the room. Jadecan watches as she shutters at the pool of blood the bodies lie in. He continues down the hall, maneuvering through the couple of corpses residing within.

"Hey!" she calls, quickly moving down the hall toward him.

"Yes," he says calmly.

"So," she says, catching up to him as he turns the sharp corner. "What's the energy cell for?"

Amelia stops, noticing the body lying in the archway ahead of her as he walks through into the well lit room behind it. The short corridor leading to the arch was less than half the width of the hallway she had just left. He chuckles amused at her hesitation, it wasn't going to be easy for her to get around the dead Reogki.

"My friend," he answers, smiling over his shoulder. "The one she has is broken."

"Must be quite the friend," she says to herself, sidestepping along the wall past the corpse.

"You know without these bodies you would still be locked up down here," he states, walking up the stairs to the enclosed bar with a laugh. "Stet was once a friend of mine as well. We were actually somewhat close. Would you believe we used to work together?" The Akiko then adds in an angry tone, "I did not like 'em to begin with."

Jadecan emerges from the staircase in between the two halves of the shelving unit and heads for the open doorway on the room's side. He leaves the enclosed bar and advances for the complex's exit while Amelia quickly ascends the stairs after him. He makes his way for the violet room's exit and watches as she strolls along the stone counter of the bar. She stops and retrieves something from off the counter before continuing after him. Most likely an item the Balgorex or his goons had lifted from her, it's of little or no importance to the Akiko. In other words, he could likely care less.

The complex's door opens, and he steps out of Stet's Place onto the white dust of Niushki with Amelia close behind. Baby sits upon the landing pad directly ahead, her black body illuminated by the purple light of the complex's rotating sign. Jadecan marches in the saucer's direction as Amelia abruptly stops at his back. He peers over his shoulder and notices her frantically looking about the terrain as smoke rises from his destroyed exo-craft near Baby.

She calls, as a gust of wind blows through the landscape. "Jadecan? What is that?"

"That," he says, setting his eyes upon the destroyed vehicle. "That Amelia, was a hover-craft."

"What happened to it?"

"Looks to have been destroyed," he answers, as it begins to rain and Baby's ramp extends out toward him.

She eyes Jadecan standing in front of the ship, and yells, "Why didn't you kill me?"

Jadecan thinks for a few moments, then turns to face her. The rain picks up drenching the Cerulean's jet black hair as her beautiful lilac eyes stare back at him.

"I did not feel like it."

"Are you gonna feel like it later?" she asks.

"An interesting question, of which I say no, have a good life," he says, turning back toward the ship.

"Mind if I tag along?" she calls causing him to turn back and face her. "Look, I'm not even supposed to be here. I can't call anybody and the terminal is forever away. Please, I promise I won't be a problem."

"You already are." He ponders for a few moments, and states, "Sure, why not."

She moves toward his observant gaze and walks up the ramp, stopping briefly at his side. "Thank you, again," she says, and continues past him onto the ship.

He surveys the dome complex whilst thunder rumbles, and as it fades he turns away from the drowning dust, joining her onboard. The ramp retracts as he sits in the smooth black chair next to Amelia. Baby's interactive console projects out before them as the entire deck of the ship comes alive with a dark blue light. He places his hand upon the interface and as he does, the saucer begins to gradually take off.

"What's your friend's name? The one who needs the power cell," Amelia asks, while the ship launches.

"Baby," Jadecan answers, as the saucer flies away from Stet's Place.

"That's an interesting name," she says, her lilac eyes glancing about the interior of the craft.

"I agree," Baby says.

"That's curious. Does the interface commonly talk without being directed?" Amelia asks.

"Usually," Jadecan answers.

"Oh," Amelia asks Baby surprised, "And who are you?"

"I am Baby. And who might you be?"

"This is Baby?" Amelia asks Jadecan.

"Yes," Jadecan nods, his hand still on the blue interface.

"A flying saucer is quite the friend." Intrigued at the concept, she answers Baby, "I'm Amelia, it is nice to meet you."

"She was a prisoner of Stet's," he explains.

"You released her?" Baby asks, sounding somewhat surprised.

"I did."

"Well, this was unexpected. She seems nice," Baby says.

"Thank you, you do as well." Amelia giggles and asks, "Where are we heading?"

"Nowhere." Jadecan pauses, and asks Baby in a irritated tone, "What happened to you?"

"A Balgorex starship's tractor-beam, nothing to be concerned about. I am fine," Baby answers. "We currently have no specific destination in mind, Amelia."

"So, is your energy cell the one that's broken?" Amelia asks, as the Akiko scoffs at the answer to his question.

"Yes," Baby answers.

"I've replaced one or two before," Amelia states. "If you'd like I could help."

"We would appreciate that. Thank you," Baby says.

"No problem," Amelia says, with a genuine smile. "Would you mind dropping me at the terminal afterwards?" she asks Jadecan.

"If you can fix Baby's energy cell, we will take you to your terminal," Jadecan says.

⊖ 8

Baby lands on the bare surface of the moon outside a small gloomy stone complex. The words one on top the other read, Along the Way, in white lights within a square sign sitting on the building's rectangular roof. The sign's dim glow struggles to reach the soaked dusty terrain while the rain slowly vanishes. A few windows evenly spaced apart sit on either side of its single door entrance.

"Where are we?" Amelia asks.

"Along the Way," Jadecan says grinning. "A place we can safely rest."

He removes his hand from the interface and the ship powers down as the blue glow inside the deck fades into blackness. Amelia sits in the darkness momentarily as Jadecan leaves the ship bearing for the bright center entrance of the structure. His yellow eyes lock upon the entryway as the wind howls and Amelia sets foot on the damp landscape behind him. He pulls open the glass door and is greeted by the motel's Drakon owner Skall, who stands behind its front desk.

"Welcome cousin," Skall greets.

On each of the lobby's cream-colored walls hangs an impressive painting depicting different scenes of Niushki's terrain. Jadecan approaches the marbled front desk ahead of him. The yellow lights lining the beige ceiling above him soak into the black carpet beneath his feet. On both sides of the white desk lies a small hall leading off to the motel's few mundane guest rooms. Skall's small and watchful white eyes are attentive within his dark green reptilian face as Jadecan approaches. His slender yet powerful physique is reminiscent of the Akikos. Although the Drakons may lack the Akikos infamous blades, they make up for it with a lethal brawny tail.

"Room for one?" Skall asks, "Perhaps a shower to remove the blood. I suspect that it is not yours."

"Room for two," Jadecan answers, as Amelia walks inside.

"I see," Skall says, eyeing the Cerulean. "And for how many cycles are we staying?"

"One," Jadecan answers, with Amelia now standing at his side.

"Good. And how are we paying?" Skall asks.

"Units," Jadecan answers, placing a few gold coins onto the counter.

"Room for two, one cycle... 10 units," Skall says, retrieving the coins from off the counter. He holds out his open scaly hand in front of the Akiko, and states, "Room 7." A key materializes within his light green palm in a flash of blue light. "Enjoy your stay."

Jadecan takes the key and progresses to the right walkway with Amelia close at hand. They pass by two of the four doors along the hall's right wall and arrive at Room 7. Jadecan unlocks and opens it while Amelia studies the mural covering the corridors entire left wall in front of the guest rooms.

"What does this represent?" she asks, looking back at him.

Jadecan looks at the simple Scut underground tunnel-like complex painted upon the wall whilst remembering the skirmishes he used to regularly have with them. A line of figures representing Reogki stand on the surface of the hive as they massacre the Scuts inside.

"What once was," he answers, gesturing her inside the open door. "Let's get some rest."

⊖ 9

Jadecan awakens from a dream, well, more of a nightmare. He has them often. The Akiko lies staring up at the pale ceiling of the motel room. He gets up sitting on the edge of the small raggedy bed facing the room's only window. The Akiko stares outside at the constant twilight present on the moon's surface radiating from the planet on its horizon. He steps to the large single pane window and glances back, noticing Amelia's side of the bed is empty. He would raise an eyebrow if he had one, wondering where she could have gone, as she's entirely absent from the room. Looking back out the window before him at Baby's black circular body he takes note of the saucer's blue light glowing through its viewport, and then heads for the room's exit.

Jadecan leaves the room and casually strolls down the hall to the lobby, as Skall asks, "How was the stay?"

"Well," he answers. "Did you happen to see my companion?"

"Why yes," Skall answers. "She passed by here not too long ago."

"It has been a pleasure," he nods respectfully, while placing the room's key on the counter.

"Pleasure is mine." Skall smiles and says as the Akiko turns to leave, "I have come across a rumor that may be of interest to you."

"Continue," Jadecan says, turning back to the Drakon.

"It is my understanding, the nearby Kiwiwa have a Reogki problem," Skall says. "At Yano's village near the Great Opening."

"Thank you." Jadecan turns away from the counter.

"You are always welcome here," Skall states, as Jadecan makes his way for the exit, yet again.

Jadecan's shadow slowly disappears off the front desk into the black carpet, as he strides beneath the lobby's yellow lights heading for the motel's glass door. He walks through stepping out onto the damp dust and paces for Baby as Amelia starts to descend the lengthening ramp. Niushki's breath howls drying the terrain as she looks out at him.

"I've replaced the energy cell," Amelia says, stepping off the ramp. "Your ship's quite knowledgeable. If I didn't know any better, I'd say it's sentient."

"She is to me," Jadecan says, standing in front of Amelia.

"According to her, you should be able to connect your holo-system, somehow," she says, following him up the ramp. "I've never heard of such a thing, but whatever, what do I know."

"Hello," he says, stepping into the blue light of the deck.

"Good to see you," Baby says.

"How are you feeling?" he asks, as they sit in the black seats in front of her interaction console.

"More like myself," Baby exclaims happily, "Thanks to Amelia, the majority of my systems are back online."

"It was nothing." Amelia blushes.

"That may be so, but we thank you." The Akiko nods gratefully in her direction.

"I am now able to access my Inner-Thought. Allowing remote communication of paired technologies," Baby says. "If you would like you may integrate this into the autonomic technology you refer to as a holo-system. This will establish a connection between us," she explains, as a small black box materializes on top of her blue interface.

"Interesting," Jadecan remarks, picking up the black box and without hesitation scans it into his inventory.

"Okay, wow... that looks very much like a data block," Amelia says, "Or what the Olensi would call a Binox."

Hello Jadecan. We are now successfully paired, Baby speaks as if she is a thought within his head.

"Is everything okay?" Amelia asks, after a few moments of silence.

"Yes," Jadecan answers, grinning and staring into her lilac eyes. "All is well."

He places his hand on the blue console initiating the saucer to take off. Baby lifts and hovers for a moment before gliding away from the motel.

"What is it, you do?" Amelia asks.

"I do?" Jadecan asks, his mind obviously elsewhere.

"Well I mean..." she says, trying to make small talk. "What are you going to do after dropping me off?"

"Survive."

She sets her gaze to the planet behind the mountains on the horizon, and asks, "Do you have plans after the terminal?"

"I do."

"Care to share?" Amelia probes.

"There is a Reogki problem." He looks over at her briefly. "I am to deal with it."

"Oh, is this something you often do?"

"Yes."

"What is the problem with the Reogki?" she asks.

"They do not belong here. They kill and steal land."

"That's terrible! How long has this been going on?"

"Too long," he answers in a sullen tone. "They have been a problem for quite some time. Lately they have been harassing the peaceful Kiwiwa, as their Runuoscha I will not stand for it. The Kiwiwa saved my life, I will do all I can to rid them of the Reogki plague."

"Really?"

"Indeed."

"Wow, that's amazing. The saving your life part, anyway." She asks after a bit of silence, "So I take it, you can understand and communicate with them?"

"For the most part."

"Are you going to see them before you deal with the Reogki?"

"Yes."

"You mind taking me with you and dropping me after?" she asks, eager to join him. "I have always wanted to talk with the Kiwiwa, but could never understand anything they said for the life of me. They're apparently one of the oldest, if not the oldest species on Niushki. I would really appreciate it."

"That was not part of the agreement."

"Oh, okay... I understand, I was just asking." She sighs.

I believe this to be the "bound one" the tome spoke of. It would be wise to allow her to join you. She could be of help, Baby states. Then says out loud, "It is my opinion you have her join you."

"I promise I won't get in the way," Amelia pleads, her vibrant eyes staring at him.

He glances at her briefly then stares out at the silhouettes of sitadoom flying in the vastness before him, and after a few moments says sharply, "Fine."

♀ Blue Light

⊖ 10

Baby settles near a small Kiwiwa village. A large fire burns in its center as shadows dance on the walls of the Kiwiwa's small stone huts. A herd of their six-legged stout mounts, juguke, roam about freely dragging their bellies while foraging the dust for what little flora it produces. A few sitadoom circle overhead with their arrow tip tails streaming behind them as they effortlessly ride the subtle winds.

"How will you help them?" Amelia asks, as the ship's blue light fades.

"By killing the Reogki," Jadecan bluntly answers.

"I suppose that should've been obvious," she says, nodding at the notion. "That sounds effective."

He gets up leaving the ship and notices she's deep in thought, staring as if lost within the mountains on the black skyline. She watches as a line of torch-bearing Kiwiwas march in their direction, whilst Jadecan steps off the ramp onto the white terrain. The Kiwiwa Ruogji Yano approaches, trudging through the dust with the help of his large Kiwi Staff, the symbol of a Kiwiwa Elder. His two right arms swing in stride as he lumbers with his left ones gripping the staff. Yano's pale skinny body stands disproportionate to the pure black eyes and large oval head now looking up at Jadecan.

"Caspa Runuoscha," Yano greets.

"Caspa Ruogji," Jadecan says bowing, as Amelia arrives beside him. "Deogma Amelia, Ruogji," he gestures to Amelia.

"Geoth, geoth," Yano declares, turning toward the village.

Baby's ramp retracts as they follow behind Yano and the rest of the Kiwiwa to the small village. "This is nice. How often do you visit the Kiwiwa?" Amelia asks, walking at Jadecan's side.

"Often enough."

"Oh, okay," she says, gesturing to Yano walking in front of them. "How long have you known your friend there?"

"Yano?" Jadecan says, "Quite some time. I have known many of the Kiwiwa Ruogji for many cycles."

"Kiwiwa Ruogji?" she asks.

"The Kiwiwa leaders are known as Ruogji," Jadecan explains, watching a couple juguke graze as they pass alongside them.

They arrive in the village whose grey huts form a circular perimeter around the fire. The powerful blaze animates as a strong breeze flows through. Jadecan and Amelia join the Kiwiwa about the campfire, placing themselves upon the ring of rocks. They gaze into the fire's brilliant orange flames whilst basking in its radiating heat. The presence of the blaze sets the atmosphere, it calms the mood while soothing the aura. The large fire is a staple of all Kiwiwa villages and is easily one of the most recognizable sights on the moon's landscape.

"What do you want with the Kiwiwa?" Jadecan asks, his white skin glowing in the fire's amber light.

"To be honest," she says, "I am hoping they know something about the Watchers."

"I see. I believe what you refer to as Watchers are what the Kiwiwa call Vikerumu." He looks over at Yano sitting next to him.

"Vikerumu," Yano exclaims.

"Vikerumu?" Amelia whispers to Jadecan sitting next to her.

"Indeed."

"Caspa," Yano declares, standing with the help of his Kiwi Staff.

Jadecan glances over at Amelia as Yano begins to boast about the Akiko, and how their creator delivered him to the Kiwiwa. The Cerulean's face glows, she's as happy as can be. The Akiko turns his gaze to the fire as they listen to the Ruogji speak.

"Niguunta onji yuchefe, sifewata onji vayaha viunta. Geshuwionta onji reze. Kafe fechuan Reogki shechuobmi lata zeor. Yaanze lata osfeazath. Kafeha kepayafe lituke sion olke shuketutaki. Kafeha ochga olke kafe sushuwi Caspa. Kafe ninobukeha Vikerumu ostaowfegekeva eth. Kafe reninobukeha Caspa odul kafe Kiwiwa pa Runuoscha, favathimuof lata ziohva. Nipaha Vikerumu vikeru onteta daem. Ostaowfegeke daem deonni kafe fechuan Reogki. Ostafuod Caspa. Kafe vapachunoonta onji reze. Nipaha le tanosi eth onji kafe fechuan Reogki."

"Ostafuod Caspa," the Kiwiwa and Jadecan say in unison.

"Ostafuod Caspa?" Amelia asks, "What is that? To be honest I understood absolutely none of that."

"It means praise Caspa."

"And who's Caspa?"

"Caspa is the creator of the Kiwiwa people and protector of these lands. The Vikerumu are her guardians," Jadecan answers, "I am their Runuoscha. Their Champion. They believe Caspa delivered me to the Kiwiwa to rid them of the evil Reogki."

"Really?" Her alluring eyes enticed by his reply. "Here." She retrieves a pad of sorts from her holo-system and brings up an image of a Watcher upon it. "Ask him if the Vikerumu looks like this," she says, handing Jadecan the device.

"Vikerumu?" Jadecan asks Yano, gesturing to the picture.

"Vikerumu." Yano nods in agreement.

Jadecan gives the device back to the Cerulean as a stone bowl's handed to Yano, who then takes a sip of its liquid concoction. After which, the Ruogji passes it to the Akiko who also drinks of its potent elixir before handing it to Amelia.

"What is this?" she asks.

"Rumu Litafethi. It is a part of their ritual. To gain entry into Caspa's divine dwelling, you must drink of the sacred mixture," Jadecan says.

She slowly inhales the strong dark red liquid before partaking of the alcohol hesitantly, then quickly passes it to the Kiwiwa next to her. "Goodness. Wow." She exhales, covering her mouth in shock. "That's intense."

"You okay?" he asks, somewhat concerned.

"Never better." She giggles, appearing to be already slightly intoxicated. "How are you?"

"The same," he answers, unaffected and peering into the dancing flames of the fire.

⊜ 11

Jadecan wakes up on top of a woven rope bed inside one of the Kiwiwa stone huts with Amelia sleeping quietly rolled over next to him. The Cerulean had blacked out relatively quickly from the Rumu Litafethi, it was something the Akiko wasn't expecting. He gets up and heads to its small entrance then glances at her briefly before leaving through the tan juguke hide covering the doorway. Best option was to have her bunk with him, for the safety of herself as well as the Kiwiwa.

With the planet staring back at him from the horizon, he paces for Yano's dwelling as a draft carries the fuming thick black smoke of the fire. He passes through the sitting rocks while the smell of burning wood lingers in the air. A few juguke lie resting outside Yano's place as he strolls past them for the entryway.

He pulls aside the juguke hide resting within the hut's doorway and sees Yano standing before a stone altar. The slightly bowed Ruogji chants in front of a white bust which sits upon a table with candles burning around it. He stops, becoming aware of the Akiko's presence.

"Caspa Ruogji," Jadecan greets, stepping through the doorway.

"Caspa Runuoscha," Yano says, looking over at him.

"Reogki?" Jadecan asks, "Where are the Reogki?"

"Kafeha the imlimike kafe vanireze getawimu. Oltaka onji kafe Great Opening. She pa chuanzedofe ochgaki gu Floating Rock. Kawi sa halata simihikialcha Runuoscha."

"Floating Rock it is then." He bows then looks up and says, "I will be leaving the Cerulean here. I will be back for her, my friend. Caspa Ruogji."

Yano nods, saying, "Caspa Runuoscha." He bows as Jadecan leaves.

The juguke raise their heads taking notice as the Akiko stands in front of the huts entrance. Amelia watches standing in front of their hut as Jadecan walks toward her from across the ring of sitting stones.

"What was in that mixture?" she asks, as he approaches. "In the elixir we drank."

"I am not sure," he answers. "I have been told Vikerumu is the main ingredient."

"I would've liked some kind warning about its effects beforehand," she says.

"That is nice, I will consider it. If there is a next time."

"Okay..." she says uneasy to the grinning Akiko. "So they drink their creator's guardian's blood? Is that... is that right? That doesn't sound right."

"No, that is correct."

"Weird... but okay," she says. "The Vikerumu's blood is apparently euphoric in one way or another. Interesting."

"Sure."

"Do you... hmm...." She hesitates. "Do you have to grin... like that? All the time? It is very.... It's uncomfortable. It makes me uncomfortable, it is quite frightening."

"Yes," he answers. "I do."

"Okay... So now what?" she asks. "Are you going to deal with the Reogki?"

"Yes," he says, walking away from her.

"I guess I'm staying here then," she says somewhat unsure.

"Yep, try not to get killed," he comments over his shoulder.

"Fine, I will consider it." She laughs. "If anything it gives me the opportunity to hang out with the Kiwiwa, it's why I came along anyway." She asks as he ambles away, "Where are you going?"

"Floating Rock," he answers over his shoulder.

"Sounds nice," she says, standing in front of the hut. "Have fun."

You are going to leave her here? Baby questions.

"I am," he says, trekking toward the ship resting outside the village. "She will be safe here."

Do you trust her here? Alone with the Kiwiwa?

"She is no threat," he says, as the saucer's ramp begins to extend out in front of him. "She will also not be in my way here."

This is true. Are we going to Floating Rock? Baby asks.

"Yes," he answers, strolling up the ramp into her command deck. "I am to deal with the Reogki. It is my duty as the Runuoscha."

⊜ 12

Baby lands near the edge of a crater, this part of the Niushki is riddled with many of them, most of which are rather small. Well, small in comparison to the much less frequent larger ones. Jadecan strolls through the pale colored wasteland leaving Baby behind him on the craters edge. The blue glow of the Reogki outpost lies just ahead of the approaching Akiko.

Scans show Floating Rock's compound to be sparsely populated. Of insignificant threat. Surprising. Also to note, some of these craters do appear to be fresh. Relatively speaking. May have something to do with the low population, Baby says.

"It is possible," Jadecan says. "Will make killing them that much easier."

I suppose. Why is Amelia interested in these Watchers? Baby asks.

"I do not know," he answers, "I did not ask, it is of no importance. It does not matter."

Why would it not matter?

"When you think about it. Nothing truly matters."

If that is so, then why help the Kiwiwa? Why slaughter the Reogki? There are some things that do, to an extent, matter. In my opinion.

Jadecan saunters in silence whilst sitadooms fly overhead and a subtle breeze blows as usual. He watches the white dust swirl into the grey stones as he treks ever closer to the large metal structure which makes up the complex.

"I do not know," he answers. "There is a part of myself that wants it to matter, but yet, I know it does not. No matter how many Kiwiwa I save... no matter how many Reogki I kill... it will not matter in the end. It is strange however, I do agree there are some things that do matter."

How do you know it will not matter?

"I am unsure, I just do."

In the end? Are you referring to death?

"Yes," he answers.

Well, I believe it matters. If it was not for you, we would not be having this conversation. That matters to me. If it was not for you, Amelia would still be chained up. Most likely to be never found. She would have probably died. That matters to her. You have made a difference. Sh'lyn believes you to be important as well. If you did not indeed matter, he would not have gifted you his glyph.

"I get the point," he says. "I appreciate what it is you are trying to do."

Jadecan steps off the dust onto a wide walkway to the side of a large metallic plateau in front of the outpost. Small blue lights line the curving path which connects to the well lit platform. He walks onto its smooth silver surface and advances to the outpost's central entryway. Its second storey overhangs significantly above him. This is not at all what he expected.

"I do not think this to be Reogki," he says, standing before its large single door staring at the pillars who seemingly hold up the outpost's second level.

I agree. There appears to be three individual life forms within the complex. I believe this to be a research facility. Residents are likely to be scientists, probably harmless. They do not seem to have noticed you.

"Three?"

Yes, Baby answers.

He studies the entryway's door which besides being about double the height, appears to be similar to the one on Stet's Place. Just to the left of the entrance is a large square frame housing an impressively sized bright green screen. He's seen this type of tech once before, it's a hand scanner. A camera appears, coming out of the wall above the door and points down upon him.

"Hello. I am Dr. Cassandra. Whom am I speaking to?"

"Jadecan," he answers.

"Hello Jadecan, pleasure to make your acquaintance. Is there something I can help you with?"

"I am looking for some Reogki. I am told they are here."

"Reogki?" Cassandra says unsure. "Oh, there aren't any Reogki here, not that I am aware of anyway. We are from Solarius, we're the research and development division of Oteniko."

"Oteniko?" Jadecan questions to himself. "You are not Reogki?"

"I don't believe so, if I understand the terminology correctly. May I ask why you are looking for these Reogki?"

"For reasons," he answers.

"I see," she says slowly. "I believe I understand. Well, I don't think we are Reogki, or at the very least, not the ones you are searching for."

Disgruntled, he turns away from the doorway as the blue lights of the outpost flood the moon's dust around it. He watches as sitadooms fly across the planet sitting on the skyline.

Turning back quickly, he spats, "What is it you do here?" He intensely glares up at the camera.

"I'm not at liberty to say," she answers. "I am sorry, it is classified."

"Fine," he utters, then turns away and heads for the corner of the outpost. "You are not Reogki. That much is certain."

A small railed walkway lines the side of the silver compound. He strolls toward the back of the outpost below the overhang which carries on, wrapping around the entire square complex.

There appears to be no other settlements nearby. Leaving one to wonder, where are the Reogki? Baby says.

"I think these are the Reogki," Jadecan says, walking out onto the outpost's back deck confounded. "Interesting, I have never heard of this Oteniko."

The crater's rim sits underneath the complex and extends further for quite some distance, showcasing a large boulder hovering at its center, known as Floating Rock. He leisurely walks along the barrier admiring the magnificent scene. The walkway's railing continues fencing along the balcony's edge, running around to the front of the compound.

What are you going to tell the Kiwiwa?

"I will tell them the Reogki are no longer here," he answers.

And what of the Oteniko outpost?

"To stay away. To keep their distance, even though they are not Reogki," he answers, stopping at the corner of the balcony in front of the walkway.

Jadecan looks upon Floating Rock again for a few moments, then treads back to Baby. He walks, the wind howls as he does, his thoughts wandering from Amelia to Stet as Baby's words echo in his head, *You have made a difference*. The saucer's ramp extends out to the approaching Akiko. He halts before her, looking back at the outpost and the Floating Rock behind it.

Are we heading back? Or are you having second thoughts?

"Yes," he answers. "We are leaving. There is nothing here."

He advances, disappearing into the ship. Baby's interaction console forms in front of the Akiko who sits staring out at the hovering rock now barely visible within the crater behind the outpost. A storm of dust rages beneath Baby as she lifts off and spins away slowly flying back toward the Kiwiwa village.

⊖ 13

Jadecan steps off Baby's dark ramp onto the white dust. A few juguke roam alertly beside the saucer whilst observing the Akiko and approaching Kiwiwa. A few Kiwiwa sit upon the sitting rocks as black smoke rises from the large fire at the village's center. Amelia stands in front of the small stone hut with her arms crossed watching from some distance.

"Caspa Runuoscha," Yano greets, gesturing to Jadecan with his Kiwi Staff.

"Caspa Ruogji," Jadecan says, with a slight bow.

"Geoth. Baonshe eth om kafe vachehikisu taonmeva," Yano declares, heading for the village.

Jadecan follows the Kiwiwa and heads for Amelia as he enters the village. She stands unmoved, her eyes peering at him with her arms still crossed. Her black hair flows over top her smooth dark horns as Niushki's breath rolls through.

The swirling dust is as pale as the approaching Akiko's skin and as he nears, she asks, "How'd it go? You deal with the Reogki?"

"No," he answers, the bitterness too obvious.

"No?" she says surprised. "It's going to be okay. It will be fine." She tries to comfort him.

"They are not Reogki," he explains. "They are Oteniko."

"Oteniko?" she asks puzzled. "As in the tech enterprise Oteniko?"

"I do not know," he answers unsure, but clearly done with the conversation.

"What are they doing here?" she questions herself, whilst relaxing a bit as Jadecan leaves to join the Kiwiwa seated upon the sitting rocks. "Wait, wait! Are they still there? They're still there right? You didn't kill them did you?" she asks, hastily walking after him.

"I left them as they were," he answers, casually strolling for the sitting rock next to Yano. "For now."

The fire rages as a few large sitadooms soar overhead. Pieces of juguke rotate on a spit, roasting within the flames. Jadecan's white skin glows in its orange light as he sits next to Yano. Vyn looms on the horizon as Niushki's wind gently blows animating the fire. Yano looks over at Jadecan whilst gripping the Kiwi Staff with one of his left hands as Amelia seats herself beside the Akiko.

"Runuoscha, kafe sushuwi Caspa thifeul thicheda hala om halata balataimha wu kafe Floating Rock, Runuoscha. Kafe Vikerumu vikeruoj onteta hala or lezeosoj hala nipayafe kafe Reogki ol nithu. No vaosonyafe thicheda kafe

Niguunta or jusuhosi kamife geoth wu osguva. Jionta kafe vapayafe onji kafe Kiwiwa osfeazath no daazfe kafe Runuoscha pagegeonnizisalesi dasa keguya. Kafe Reogki ol nithu?"

The Ruogji questions him, it's a simple enough question. He simply wants to know if the Reogki have been dealt with. It's only the Akiko's job as the Runuoscha. Well, Jadecan answers no, and attempts to explain why. He hopes Yano will understand and tells him the best he can about the odd predicament they find themselves in.

"Kafe Reogki ol nithu. Yafefeos paviha," Jadecan says visibly in thought, gesturing in the direction of the Oteniko outpost, "Kiwiwa ol na imlu linosu datuke, ol Reogki, Oteniko. Yafefeos paviha. Kafe Reogki ol nithu."

"Oteniko. Kafe linosu pesheha datuke sa Oteniko? Olke Reogki? Yafefeos paviha deonni Oteniko?" Yano asks. "Sa Oteniko rezeha wu Kiwiwa?"

"Rezeha?" Jadecan asks, unsure of the words meaning. "Kiwiwa yafefeos paviha Oteniko."

"Runuoscha nipayami Oteniko ol nithu. Zenoyafe le visi kafe Reogki," Yano proclaims.

"Runuoscha nipayami Oteniko ol nithu?" Jadecan asks Yano, gesturing toward the outpost.

"What is he saying?" Amelia says quietly to Jadecan.

"I believe they would like me to kill Oteniko," he answers, staring at Yano, who gestures with his Kiwi Staff in the direction of the outpost. "I am telling them to keep away. I do not believe they accept that as a solution."

"Well, you're not going to do that. There are other means. Violence is not always the answer," Amelia states.

"Oteniko ol nithu," Yano declares.

"Try telling that to them," Jadecan says, sternly to Amelia.

"Oteniko are my friends," she says emotionally. "The Olensi and Oteniko have been allies for a while. How about you take me to them, and I promise we can figure something out. You do not need to kill them. Okay? Can you please… just give me a chance. I can talk to them."

"That is not how I do things."

"Well, that is kind of obvious," she says.

"Fine." He laughs softly. "Why not, I will take you to speak with them."

"Thank you," she says.

"Whatever," Jadecan mumbles under his breath.

"What does ol nithu mean?" she asks. "They've used that term quite a bit."

"In short 'to get rid of'," he answers.

"Oh, so Oteniko ol nithu means, 'to get rid of Oteniko'?"

"Sure," he says.

"Ossheosthe the juguke," Yano demands. "Ossheosthe the juguke."

A couple of Kiwiwa head for the roasting juguke. They cut it into slices with sharp stone knives and begin to pass them around the sitting stones on small stone plates.

"What is that?" Amelia asks, as Jadecan is handed a portion. "Is that food? I am starving, please tell me that is food. I haven't eaten much of anything in days," she says exhausted.

"Roasted Juguke," Jadecan answers, biting into the tender meat with his sharp dagger-like teeth. "It is indeed food. Really good food."

Amelia's given a slice while he speaks, she sits staring at the sizzling meat momentarily, then takes a small bite. "Mmm, is good." She nods happily impressed. "I had something while you were off doing what it is you do. I'm not sure what it was but, it wasn't this." She smiles, taking a bite.

"Hala zenoyafe kafe taonguunsi juguke?" Yano gestures to Amelia who looks to Jadecan for translation.

"He is asking if you like the juguke," he says.

"I do! Yes!" She nods to Yano.

"Hami," Jadecan says to Yano. "Pefe zenoyafe."

"Pefe zenoyafe," Yano exclaims, as all the Kiwiwa erupt in cheer.

"Pefe zenoyafe," Amelia says laughing.

♀ Amber Glow

⊖ 14

Jadecan wakes up next to Amelia inside their small stone hut. He briefly admires the light green-skinned Cerulean as she sleeps quietly beside him before getting up and heading for the hut's entry. The Akiko pulls aside the juguke hide covering the doorway and peeks outside as she speaks.

"Hey," she calls softly.

"Sleep well?" he asks, glancing at her.

"Yes, did you?"

"Time to get up," he says, after a short pause.

"Fine," she remarks.

Jadecan leaves and stares at the planet as he strides for Yano seated within the sitting rocks. A group of young Kiwiwa surround him as he tells a story. Jadecan sits among the young ones and listens to Yano's tale.

"Omgefe pa sushufeki fehaoj senifa zewasi she Kiwiwa chuanzedofe, pefe wuzesi duontaogva onji lizeop vayaha or osgamuku hezeze onji zenobuke. Kiwiwa jusuhosi leta pega wu kapi, pefe vafusi ol. Reogki oshoy wu chuanzedofe ketutaki shewu yuchefe sizu or jionzejathi halakisu Kiwiwa ruansi shewu leta datuke. Ilonwiof shewu ruansi ohta, le wuzesi leta zipaha thicheda hezeze onji zenobuke. Reogki rufahosi heme wuonya hezeze onji zenobuke or iloj. Reogki onzesi or hishusi, vafusi le nizu shudu, yufeki paviyafe hezeze onji zenobuke chufasalesi. Vashegefe kafeki Kiwiwa jufeki getutaodsi thicheda Reogki tuulan hezeze onji zenobuke shuketutakiva."

Yano finishes the story and is immediately bombarded with questions from the young Kiwiwa. Jadecan sits smiling as they excitedly talk over one another loudly. After a few moments of constant questions and bickering from the young ones, Yano speaks as Amelia arrives.

"Olthi ruansishuki, thife lote suopdu. Yumufe nifaimtava?"

"Ruogji!" the young Kiwiwas whine in unison.

"Ol, ol," Yano says. "Na zipaha. Emosontakefake niwiuntava yibeethva thicheda Runuoscha."

"What did I miss?" Amelia asks Jadecan, while Yano talks to the young ones.

"A lady lived in a Kiwiwa village," Jadecan explains. "One day a Reogki came and stole something from the lady, then fled the village. He got tired and slept. When he awoke, what he had stolen vanished. Ever since then, the Kiwiwa have been cursed with the Reogki until the stolen item returns."

"Interesting," she says, then gasps adorably as the young Kiwiwas get up and leave. "They're so darn cute!"

"Indeed," he says, with a small smile. "They are."

"What did the Reogki take from the lady?"

"I do not know." He shrugs. "Something important."

"Runuoscha," Yano says, as the last young Kiwiwa leaves. "Kiwiwa sutawifeku. Kafaya jionta reze hala sion. Nipaha

Vikerumu jionzejathi ostaowfegeke. Oteniko ol nithu. Runuoscha."

"There it is again, Ol nithu. You gonna tell him we are not gonna Oteniko ol nithu?" she asks, with a concerned tone.

"No, I am not." Jadecan chuckles. "Caspa Ruogji," he says to Yano in respect.

"Caspa Runuoscha," Yano says, as Jadecan rises and leaves.

"Okay," Amelia says, following him. "You aren't going to do it though, right? Oteniko ol nithu? You're not going to, right?"

"If I can help it, I will not," he answers without pause.

"Okay… I mean, I suppose that works," she says. "I'm sure this is all just one big misunderstanding. Everything will be fine, I'm sure of it."

"We shall see."

⊖ 15

Amelia stands in front of the Oteniko outpost's large door. Vyn sits on the black skyline as Jadecan watches behind her. She glances back at the crossed armed Akiko as the blue lights of the compound glow upon his white skin. The large bones protruding out from his elbows are fearsome, quite an unnerving sight to be had. She shudders while the wind sweeps and the complex's camera emerges from above the large door.

"Hello," Cassandra greets in a somewhat surprised tone.

"Hi, I'm Amelia," she says, looking up at the camera waving. "And this here is Jadecan."

"I am Dr. Cassandra, it's a pleasure. I have already met your friend there, he had stopped by here briefly, around a day or so ago."

"Yes, he did," Amelia says. "When he told me of an Oteniko outpost nearby, I just had to see it for myself. I don't think I've ever seen Oteniko anywhere else besides Solarius, of course. Well, I don't think I've actually ever seen an Oteniko outpost, now that I think of it."

"You're Cerulean, correct?" Cassandra asks.

"Ah, yes," Amelia says, "I am."

"What brings you out here?" Cassandra asks.

"Well, it's kind of a long story."

"I suppose it would be," the doctor says. "Is Jadecan a friend of yours or...."

"Yes." Amelia laughs. "He is. He can be a bit um." She glances at the Akiko behind her and then turns back to the camera after some of a pause. "Yea, he's ah, he's him."

"Well, this is all very unexpected," Cassandra says.

"Yea, tell me about it," she animatedly says.

"Please, come and join us inside."

"Thank you," Amelia says, as the door slides open.

The bright white light from inside the outpost floods onto the platform through the entryway. Amelia's shadow stretches toward Jadecan as she turns to him smiling, appearing rather proud of herself. He chuckles quietly, then follows her inside. They stand just within the outpost as the door seals behind them.

A decent sized silver room is present before them. A large blue screen accompanied by a few consoles sit on the wall to their right, as a realistic image of Niushki rotates within it.

Green and blue lights blink on and off as if in a pattern on the kiosks before it. Cassandra stands in front of Amelia and Jadecan next to a rectangular table in the center of the room.

She is rather tall, easily a couple heads taller than Jadecan. Her lavender skin is nearly the same color as Amelia's eyes, just a bit lighter. Another of the same species sits with a weapon resting upon its leg at the table behind her. Cassandra's small green eyes are inviting yet perilous. Her white hair hangs just above her shoulders, her tone friendly and forthcoming.

"It's not often we get visitors." She smiles.

"I imagine not," Amelia says.

"Please, come have a seat," the doctor says, gesturing toward the table. "This is Meshel," she says, referring to the other one behind her.

Amelia introduces Jadecan and herself again, while placing themselves at the table beside one another. A teleporter sits behind Cassandra and Meshel who sit across from them. A blue liquid ripples filling the teleporter's interior whose smooth oval steel frame is about as large as the outpost's entrance.

"So how are things, how are the Ceruleans?" Cassandra asks.

"Good," Amelia answers. "Same as usual. How 'bout Oteniko? I see they have you all the way out here."

"Yeah." Cassandra laughs. "They're good, they have us cataloging. Mainly undiscovered species and so on, well, unnamed I should say. But overall, not bad." She looks over at Meshel. "I mean, we have made some new discoveries, breakthroughs in research and such. Most of the time it's places such as this though, a lot of moons. Are you here with the Olensi or did you come by yourself?"

"I'm here by myself, but I'm also with the Olensi, it's complicated," Amelia says.

"That's usually the case," the doctor says, looking over at Meshel. "Yea, anyways, what are you doing out here?"

"Same as you, for the most part." Amelia smiles. "At the moment I'm here doing my own research, with the Olensi's permission. Well, mostly with Captain Tytus's permission."

"Ah, how is Captain Tytus?" Cassandra asks, as another of her species walks out of the teleporter carrying a tray of plates of food behind her.

"Good," Amelia answers. "How many of you are here?"

"Oh… sorry. Just the three of us," Cassandra says. "This is Lex, our amazing Chef. If it wasn't for him, we would starve out here." She smiles and thanks Lex as he places a plate of food before her. "I do all the sciency stuff and Meshel here," she says, placing her hand on Meshel's shoulder. "He makes sure we don't get killed doing it." She watches as Lex places a plate before Meshel, Amelia, and Jadecan, then asks, "You said you've been to Solarius? Do you go there often?"

"As often as I can," Amelia says, as Lex returns through the teleporter. "I have a friend who lives there. Actually, her dad is the current leader of Oteniko. Um, Tarkano."

"That's right, I had forgotten he had a child. A daughter if I remember correctly," Cassandra says, looking to Amelia for confirmation.

"Yep, Lenora," Amelia says, delicately placing a cubed piece of meat into her mouth. "Wow, this is good, it sorta reminds me of juguke," she says, looking over at Jadecan, who nods in agreement.

"That is seared setani," Cassandra says proudly. "Not easy to come by, but every so often, we get lucky. How did you and Lenora meet? Was it through business with Oteniko? The Ceruleans don't commonly stop in the neighborhood of Solarius."

"We met through my dad. Tarkano and he were good friends. He died though so..." Amelia says remorsefully. "So, seared setani, huh?"

Jadecan notices the sadness in her tone. She looks at him and smiles. He had always suspected there was more to her beautiful smile, hidden away behind those bright lilac eyes of hers.

"Seared setani," he says. "I like it."

"I'm sorry," Cassandra says sincerely to Amelia, and then pauses for a moment realizing the sensitivity of the topic. "The Akiko are native to Niushki, yes?" she asks Jadecan.

"Indeed," he answers.

"That's actually somewhat related to why we are here," Amelia says, glancing over at Jadecan.

"How so?" Cassandra asks.

"Well the Kiwiwa have expressed concern about your presence here, with you being so close to their village and all," Amelia explains.

"Ah, I believe Jadecan said he was searching for some Reogki when he had stopped by previously. I am guessing the two are related?"

"Yea, they think you are Reogki," Amelia answers, then points to Jadecan. "And sent him here to make you leave."

"I see," Cassandra says.

"Yea, with that being said I'm sure if you were to show them you mean them no harm, that you're not a threat and not Reogki, they'd be fine with you here. Like a peace offering or something, I dunno. I'm sure this is something Meshel has done a few times."

"I have, it is something we could do." Meshel says to Cassandra, "It's a good idea, we would most likely benefit from it as well."

"Okay, do you think they'd be open to such a suggestion?" Cassandra asks Jadecan.

"If done for the right reasons, I believe it to be possible," he answers.

"That's good enough for me," Cassandra says. "Let's give it a go."

⊖ 16

Jadecan stands on the back deck of the outpost with Meshel, who like Cassandra, towers a couple heads or so taller than the Akiko. Meshel's small green eyes and lavender skin are qualities not commonly found on the moon. Amelia had said they were of the species Yonalitu, and quite frankly, they all look the same to him. They admire Floating Rock hovering in the distance within the crater, as sitadooms fly across the dark star-filled sky and the planet stares from the horizon.

"I'm sure we can work something out." Meshel says after a brief silence, "Quite the sight, huh? We don't know why or how it floats, it just does."

"The Kiwiwa say Floating Rock is where the Reogki who stole from the lady rested." Jadecan speaks, leaning on the metal rail. "What he stole vanished there. Underneath the rock. When the stolen item returns, the rock will no longer float. Falling to the crater below. That is how the Kiwiwa will know the curse of the Reogki is no more."

"What do you think?" Meshel asks. "You believe that?"

"It is just a floating rock," Jadecan answers. "No more. No less."

"Well, a floating rock is certainly something." Meshel chuckles.

"Indeed."

"I'm gonna see what the girls are up to," Meshel says. "Would you care to join me?"

Jadecan leans on the fence momentarily viewing the scene, then turns away and follows Meshel around the compound. They stand on the large silver platform in front of the building as Meshel places his hand upon the green screen next to the outpost's entry.

"After you," Meshel says, as the door slides open.

"Jadecan," Amelia says, as he steps inside. She picks up the medallion off the table in front of her. "Cassandra says this green-eyed female is most likely a representation of the Kiwiwas' Caspa. Pretty interesting, huh?"

Jadecan sits next to her as Meshel places himself next to Cassandra. Lex walks out of the teleporter carrying a tray, upon which sit four steaming mugs.

"I was telling her of how we met and why the Kiwiwas call you Runuoscha," Amelia says, as Lex places a mug before each of them. "She says she has never heard of any glowing ball of light, but does know of Caspa and the Watchers."

"What do you know of Caspa?" Jadecan asks Cassandra.

"I know the Kiwiwa believe her to be a great deity," Cassandra answers, as Lex disappears through the teleporter behind her. "I know she originates here with the Kiwiwa, and although she is seldom found in other places, for the most part she is unique to Niushki. I also know that the Watchers, or the Vikerumus, are said to be her messengers. All in all, she's a powerful celestial being, of sorts. That is pretty much the extent of what I know."

"Interesting," Jadecan says.

"Yes, quite," Cassandra says. "Do you believe in her existence?"

"No," Jadecan answers. "I do not."

"Well, that answers that question then." The doctor laughs. "I would like to thank you, Jadecan, for rescuing Amelia. It very well may not have been what you intended to do, but be it as it may, you did. And I, we, are grateful, and better for it."

"You are welcome." He nods.

"I hear you retrieved a glowing orb, or a ball of light, from the dungeon?" she asks. "Is that correct?"

A flash of blue light erupts from his palm as the glowing orb materializes within his hand. He rolls the large glass-like ball across the table to Cassandra, who catches it within her large hands. She spins it on top of the table before her, studying it as its bright light illuminates her round lavender face.

"It seems solid and heavy," she says. "I am not sure why it is glowing, or what could be causing it. As for what it is, without further research and examination, I do not know. If you would like I could study it, privately of course, and see what all I can find. I am intrigued, and would like very much to conduct some of my own research, if you would allow it," she says hopeful. "I can not promise anything, but I will definitely give it my undivided attention."

Another flash of light erupts from Jadecan's palm as he retrieves the key. He rolls it to Meshel who retrieves it from the table and holds it out within his palm for Cassandra to see. The silver inscribed sphere is a quarter of the size of the glowing orb and appears insignificant in comparison within Meshel's giant open palm.

"That is the key," Jadecan says. "I am assuming they are related."

"It is probable, where is this dungeon? Would you mind taking us there?" Cassandra asks.

"If you can indeed come to an agreement with the Kiwiwa, I will take you to the dungeon's location," Jadecan answers.

"Sounds good to me," Cassandra says.

"And you may conduct your research on both the orb and the key," Jadecan says. "As it is anyway, I have no use for them."

"You might as well take the medallion too," Amelia says, sliding it to Cassandra.

"Thank you again, this is most fascinating. We will be careful," Cassandra assures them. "They will be safe with us. You have my word."

"How do we go about the Kiwiwa?" Meshel asks, placing the key on the table in front of him. "They trust you, what would you have us do? What would they be most comfortable with?"

"I will take Cassandra to meet with the Kiwiwa's Ruogji, Yano," Jadecan answers. "No one else will come, they would be most comfortable with that."

♀ Black Cloak

⊖ 17

Yano and a few Kiwiwa can be seen outside of Baby's viewport heading toward her, as the village's fire burns as usual behind them. The planet watches from the skyline as juguke graze the barren dust. Jadecan and Cassandra prepare to leave the ship while Baby speaks.

"Good luck, Cassandra."

"Thank you, Baby," Cassandra says, as the blue light of the deck coats her lavender skin. "I appreciate that."

Jadecan exits the ship with Cassandra close behind. Yano waits at the foot of the saucer's black ramp watching as they descend.

Yano raises his Kiwi Staff as they step onto the dust before him. "Caspa Runuoscha."

"Caspa Ruogji. Deogma Cassandra." Jadecan gestures to Cassandra standing next to him.

"Geoth, geoth," Yano says after a few moments, walking back to the village.

"What is deogma?" Cassandra asks, as they follow the Kiwiwa.

"Someone who is a friend," Jadecan answers.

"Ah, I see," she says.

Jadecan enters the village while Cassandra falls behind him admiring the Kiwiwa's stone huts. Yano saunters with the help of his Kiwi Staff in the direction of the sitting rocks as juguke roasts above the open flames center.

"He is their leader?" Cassandra asks, watching Yano slowly amble along.

"He is," Jadecan answers. "He is among the oldest and most respected of the Kiwiwa clans."

Jadecan takes a seat on the rock next to Yano, as Cassandra places herself on the rock next to him. The juguke spins slowly in the fire before them. A few young Kiwiwa stand close to the orange blaze as Yano speaks loudly to the young ones.

"Wuon gejaod wu gejaod. Heme paviha niha ruansishuki."

They retreat a few feet from the fire and sit. The Kiwiwas' young are usually not present during visits from outsiders. Jadecan senses something special is about to happen. Yano stands with the help of the Kiwi Staff and advances a few steps forward. The entire clan goes silent as the Ruogji looks around at the Kiwiwa seated upon the sitting rocks. After a few moments, he speaks in a proud voice while periodically glancing over at the Akiko.

"Niha jifezejathi Kiwiwa. Kafe Reogki tapachudofe lata zeorva yaanze lata osfeazath. Kafeki Runuoscha paososohta. Reogki ol nithu. Runuoscha ostaowfegekeva or zewava thicheda Kiwiwa. Lova ostuke Kiwiwa chitadu. Simimuteva tachefe onji Kiwiwa. Zipagefe nuomsu eth. Jinuanha. Kiwiwava Runuoscha ol nithu. Kiwiwa Runuoscha. Niha jifezejathi Kiwiwa, yuwi vapaha hala?"

"Runuoscha. Runuoscha. Runuoscha," the Kiwiwas chant, their voices powerful.

"Runuoscha," Yano says, turning and gesturing to Jadecan with his Kiwi Staff.

Jadecan stands and steps to Yano. Understanding the importance and significance of the moment, he kneels before the Ruogji respectfully. He stares at the white dust swirling at his knee as the chanting Kiwiwa quiet. A Kiwiwa kneels at Yano's side holding a stone box within their outstretched hands. Another holds an iron rod and places the spade shaped end of it into the fire.

"Runuoscha," Yano declares, opening the box. "Thiohta kamife thicheda daomonta. Pa sunoal deonni kafe Ruogji onji reze Kiwiwa gezefava." He removes a green gem attached to a gold necklace from the box. "Reze yuon odfe Runuoscha. Tumamuduor kafe emosontakefagefe onji kafe sushufeki dutha. Ostafuod Caspa!"

"Ostafuod Caspa!" Jadecan and the Kiwiwa proclaim in unison.

A couple of Kiwiwa retrieve the necklace from Yano, bowing in the process, and then place it around Jadecan's neck. The fire rages behind Yano as the wind sweeps. They back away from Jadecan as the iron rod's removed from the blaze and handed to the Ruogji, who gestures for Jadecan to stand with his Kiwi Staff.

"Duor Runuoscha," Yano says. "Thicheda kasa niluya tuosom halata vayashe hala thianze jugeoth omfe thicheda kafe Kiwiwa." Jadecan rises.

Yano brands Jadecan's left breast with the Kiwiwa symbol, a spade. The same as the three large tattoos running up his back. He stands still, his face stern, as Yano holds the glowing red end of the rod against his chest.

After a few moments he removes it, and declares, “Kiwiwas Runuoscha ol nithu. Kiwiwa Runuoscha!”

The Kiwiwa cheer loudly, their voices mighty and proud as Jadecan bows before Yano. “Athke eth ohke,” the Ruogji says, lifting his Kiwi Staff proudly. “Athke eth gefeathlitawife. Ostafuod Caspa!”

“Ostafuod Caspa!” Jadecan and the Kiwiwa proclaim in unison.

The Akiko returns smiling alongside Yano to his sitting rock, and says to Cassandra while taking his seat next to her, “Now we eat.”

“Sounds good,” she says, nodding happily. “That was amazing. Oh my goodness, that was an experience. Congratulations.”

“Indeed,” he says, as stone plates of juguke are passed around the sitting rocks. “Thank you.”

They begin to eat, and as they do Jadecan tells Yano of the events that took place at the Oteniko outpost. How he talked with Cassandra, and why he has brought her here to the village to meet with the Ruogji. After some conversation between the two of them, they come to an agreement and smile at one another happily.

Jadecan turns to Cassandra. “Give Yano the medallion.”

Cassandra retrieves the medallion from her holo-system and holds it out in front of Jadecan, for Yano. The Ruogji takes it from her open hand and his small black eyes light up as he stares in awe at the image of Caspa engraved upon it.

"A gift," Jadecan says, gesturing to the medallion. "From Oteniko in the spirit of friendship."

"Kiwiwa pagegefeoske kasa sunoal," Yano says after a few moments. "Deogma Oteniko? Cassandra? Thife nizu sitashi kafe Rumu Litafethi. Ostafuod Caspa!"

"Ostafuod Caspa!" they all exclaim.

"Yano accepts your gift," Jadecan says. "You must now drink of the Rumu Litafethi with them. Then you will be deogma."

"What is Rumu Litafethi?" Cassandra asks, as the stone bowl containing the liquid concoction's handed to Yano.

"It is a part of their ritual," he answers, as the Ruogji hands him the bowl. "A mixture of different things. I believe Amelia said it had euphoric properties." He takes a sip and hands it to her, saying in a more serious tone, "You must drink it."

"Okay, well then, here goes nothing," she says, taking a sip.

⊜ 18

"The next thing I remember, we were waking up next to each other," Cassandra explains, sitting at the table in the Oteniko outpost. "Yano was in his hut. It seemed like the entire clan was already up. The young were playing. The entire experience was extraordinary. I thoroughly enjoyed it. I highly recommend."

"Good," Meshel says, with a slight laugh, sitting next to her. "So it was a success."

"Indeed," Jadecan says, sitting next to Amelia across from Meshel.

"Did it hurt?" Amelia asks Jadecan, gesturing to the Kiwiwa's brand on his chest.

"No. It did not."

"You mean a lot to them. I get it, I understand why." After a brief pause Amelia smiles, and says, "So, what now? What's next?"

"We will take them to the Reogki outpost," Jadecan answers. "Where the ball of light was found. As promised."

"In the meantime, let us drink some tea," Cassandra says, smiling. "I feel I may need to purge my system of that um, interesting elixir."

"Yeah, it is certainly that." Amelia laughs.

"Amelia, out of curiosity," Meshel asks, following a few moments of laughter. "Have the Olensi discovered anything of interest in regard to Vyn?"

"Most of it is classified," she answers. "I, myself, don't know much about that. I know it's still restricted and that our satellites still orbit the planet. Otherwise, I mean, I know what you know."

"What is it you know?" Jadecan asks the table.

"Oh, I'm sorry" Amelia says, realizing Jadecan more than likely knew nothing of the matter. "So, a very long time ago, like when we were only capable of star gazing long time ago." She laughs. "There was an advanced species living on the planet. They would stop by Cerulea every now and again, but one day they just disappeared." She shrugs.

"So the story goes," Meshel says, as Lex appears out of the teleporter and places a steaming mug of tea down in front of each of them. "Sorry, go on," he apologizes to Amelia.

"No worries," she says. "When the Ceruleans became a space faring civilization," she explains to Jadecan. "They formed the Olensi and soon after, they stopped by and discovered the planet to be void of fauna, for the most part." She thanks Lex as he places a mug before her.

"That, is the crazy part," Cassandra says. "Flora covered the planet, and still does. Perfect conditions, yet barely any fauna at all to speak of. I'm sorry, I get really exited when it comes to subjects like this. It's your story, please continue."

"Thank you," Amelia says playfully, taking a sip of her tea. "Come to find out, a biological weapon was used at some point. At first, we thought they used it on themselves, but that appears to not be the case."

"So, for the most part, that has been established?" Cassandra asks, as Lex disappears through the teleporter behind her. "They didn't destroy themselves?"

"I believe so," Amelia says. "I'm not sure, but I think that's the direction they're leaning."

"Interesting," Cassandra says, sipping her tea.

"So, that's the legend of Vyn," Amelia says to Jadecan, who nods in appreciation. "There probably is more. That's just what I know."

"If they'd allow others to visit, they'd probably know a lot more," Cassandra says. "Just saying."

"Oteniko would've done the same," Meshel says to Cassandra. "The Olensi just got there first."

"Whatever," Cassandra says with an attitude. "One, Oteniko couldn't have done what the Olensi have done, even if they had gotten there first. And two, even if that is the case, I still think they're jerks. No offense, Amelia."

"None taken," Amelia says, sipping her tea. "I feel the same, a lot of the time."

"So Jadecan," Cassandra says after a brief silence. "Ever since our trip to the Kiwiwa, I've been trying to make sense of something."

"Make sense of what?" he asks.

"I don't want to sound like, like, well, I was wondering where Baby came from. I don't think that you, it's just that, she is, she is rather unique," she says.

"She is," he agrees.

"I don't believe I have seen another like her," Cassandra says. "Not that there isn't I mean, the universe is a vast place, and anything is possible. I just haven't come across anything quite like her."

"What do you think she is?" Amelia asks Cassandra. "I've been wondering that same thing myself."

"She appears to be bio-mechanical, a living technology. She appears ordinary enough, I suppose, but her A.I., highly advanced," Cassandra answers. "How did you two meet?" she asks Jadecan. "If you don't mind me asking."

"I found her," he says after a long pause. "Or maybe she found me. It was a long time ago. We were both in a bad place. That is all."

"Okay, I understand. You don't have to talk about it if you don't want to," Cassandra says.

"I wish not to."

- ⊜ 18 -

"Understood. So, what about this Reogki outpost? Does it have a history or anything?" the doctor says, changing the topic.

"Besides being old, not that I am aware of," Jadecan answers.

"Hmm, I see. How do you want to go about this?" Cassandra asks Meshel.

"I will accompany him there, make sure it's safe and then report back," he answers. "I believe that to be the safest way to go about it."

"I agree. Will that work for you?" she asks Jadecan.

"It will indeed."

⊜ 19

Baby sits in the background before a sheer cliff as Jadecan, Amelia, and Meshel walk toward the Reogki outpost. Meshel notices a flock of sitadooms around what appears to be a body, outside the compound's entrance. He investigates with his holo-weapon poised at the ready.

"There appears to be something over there," he says, pointing to the body with his weapon while looking over at Jadecan.

Jadecan watches as Meshel cautiously treads in its direction. The Yonalitu's weapon points ahead of him, sweeping the area as he goes. The subtle wind blows as Jadecan and Amelia leisurely follow behind him. The large dragon-like sitadooms attempt to defend the corpse, but retreat to the skies as Meshel fires his weapon into the air.

"Well, seems our friend here has seen better times," Meshel says, upon reaching the partially scavenged headless corpse.

Jadecan arrives at the scene next to Amelia who gags, and agrees, "Yea, I'd say so."

"Was the body here when either of you arrived previously?" Meshel asks them.

"It could've been," Amelia answers. "I really don't know."

The Akiko shrugs after looking at the Cerulean, and says, "Appears they were Reogki, they were most likely killed. They do not belong here."

"Seems a bit extreme, but okay," Meshel says. "Question is how long ago it happened. It's hard to gauge thanks to the sitadoom. From what I can tell though, the area seems clear. Is this what you would've done to us if we had been Reogki?" he asks Jadecan.

"Indeed," he answers, then after a quick glance at the corpse, the Akiko turns away and heads for the decrepit outpost with Amelia close behind. "You coming?" he calls over his shoulder to Meshel, who takes one last look at the corpse before following.

Amelia and Jadecan stand before the broken door peering inside as Meshel studies the worn stone walls of the outpost. "It appears to be quite old," Meshel says after a brief silence. "Cassandra would probably be able to accurately age it."

The Cerulean sighs thinking back to the events that transpired after leaving the dungeon. Her lilac eyes stare up at the cliff remembering what Stet had said about the Watcher, as her black hair gently sways in the wind.

"You think they're related?" she asks no one specifically, while staring up at the cliff.

"Who?" Meshel asks.

"The Watcher and this Reogki outpost. Stet had told me there was a Watcher up there," she says, pointing at the cliff top above the compound to their right. "It was apparently watching... if he is to be believed, anyway. He could've just been making it up."

"He could've been, or he was being truthful. Suppose we may never know," Meshel says.

"We will find your Watcher," Jadecan assures her.

She smiles nodding at him as they walk through into the empty and desolate dust covered room. The eerie silence within is deafening in contrast to the howling wind of the moon's dark terrain.

"Okay, this seems nice," Meshel says jokingly, deactivating his weapon.

Jadecan's weapon materializes within his hand as Meshel retrieves the key from his holo-system. He looks over at Jadecan and Amelia, then lightly squeezes the silver sphere.

"Hmm," he ponders, staring at the small sphere, before squeezing it in his large hand again. "Doesn't seem to be working. Not sure if I'm doing it right. All you have to do is squeeze it, correct?"

"Yes." Jadecan holds his hand out to Meshel. "May I?"

"Sure, can't see the harm in trying. It worked for you before, well it worked for the both of you actually... why not," he says, handing him the key.

The Akiko begins to slightly squeeze it, then scowls after a few moments in disappointment when nothing happens.

Releasing his grip, he hands it to Amelia. She in turn tries unsuccessfully as well, then gives it back to Jadecan, who passes it along to Meshel.

"So, now what?" Amelia asks, as the three of them stand, staring into the dismal room. "This was disappointing."

"I'm not sure," Meshel says, returning the sphere to his inventory. "We could head back. I'm sure Cassandra would love to scour this, um, outpost and surrounding area."

"Probably. I'm sorry. I don't know why it suddenly decided not to be working. I was really hoping...." She sighs. "It doesn't matter now."

"I'm sure there is still a good bit here," Meshel says, as Jadecan's holo-weapon dematerializes from his hand. "No need to apologize, it's fine."

Amelia sighs again as they walk out of the outpost back toward Baby. She stops midway behind Jadecan and peers up at the top of the cliff face. The wind sweeps while the Akiko stands at the foot of the saucer's ramp awaiting her. Meshel ascends into the ship as she begins to stroll once again. Jadecan watches, scanning the terrain as she approaches. She passes by him, shrugging with a slight smile. He surveys the moon's surface one last time before joining them onboard. The ramp retracts, then spinning gradually up, Baby lifts to fly off toward the Oteniko outpost.

The same mysterious entity who watched as Jadecan sped away aboard the exo-craft for Stet's Place, now watches as Baby flies away. The tall black cloaked figure, worshiped and revered by the Kiwiwa as the Vikerumu, is known to others as the Watcher.

♀ Part Two: The Stranger

"You are under the unfortunate impression that just because you run away you have no courage; you're confusing courage with wisdom." - L. Frank Baum, *The Wonderful Wizard of Oz*.

♀ Golden Rule

⊖ 1

Baby flies over the white landscape of Niushki away from the Reogki outpost, in the direction of the Oteniko complex. The sound of silence, for a long while, plagued the saucer's command deck, but undoubtedly, it was always meant to be broken. The echoes of laughter now resonate, as Amelia tells Meshel about the Kiwiwa, and how they wanted their Runuoscha to deal with Oteniko.

"He was like Oteniko ol nithu, Oteniko ol nithu, and I was like, how 'bout not." Amelia laughs, retelling the events of the Kiwiwa to Meshel. "We are not going to Oteniko ol nithu."

"Cassandra tells me they mean well," Meshel says, smiling seated behind them.

"They do," Jadecan says, with his hand on Baby's blue interaction console.

"She has a good heart, my friend." Meshel puts his hand on Jadecan's shoulder. "No harm will come to them. I assure you."

"There appears to be two small vessels approaching rapidly," Baby says, as a 3D image of an unknown ship is displayed within her viewpoint.

"Those appear to be Olensi Interceptors," Meshel comments.

"They are," Amelia confirms, looking over at Jadecan. "Well, this is great."

"We are being hailed," Baby says. "I suggest we open up communication channels."

"Fine," Jadecan says.

"Unknown vessel this is Olket 7 of the Olensi starship Cortnei," the Olensi interceptor calls. "Unknown vessel, please respond."

"I am here," Jadecan responds.

"Unknown vessel, we have detected a Cerulean citizen on board your starship," Olket 7 says. "Unregistered ship, alter your course to follow us. You are to be escorted to the Cortnei. Confirm directive."

"The Cortnei? Wonderful, that's Tytus's ship, and I'm obviously the Cerulean they're talking about. Well, this is going to be fun," Amelia says, she looks over and nods at Jadecan. "You don't really have a choice, just confirm you understand and follow them."

"Fine," he mutters and responds to the interceptor. "I understand the directive."

"Everything will be fine," Amelia comforts. "They're friends, there's nothing to worry about."

"We shall see."

Baby follows Olket 7's blue thrusters into space, as the other interceptor trails behind her closely. Her large saucer shaped black body is easily four times their size. As she leaves the moon's atmosphere, three large silver starships come into view.

"The cruiser right there, that's Tytus's ship," Amelia says, pointing at the center cruiser. "That's the Cortnei."

- ⊜ 1 -

The planet Vyn looms behind the cruisers, dwarfing everything in sight. Jadecan's yellow eyes lock on the planet in awe, as they approach the glowing blue force-field of the Cortnei's docking bay.

"Any idea how long this is going to take?" Meshel asks.

"I really don't know." She shrugs looking back at him.

"I don't like being away for extended amounts of time," Meshel says.

"I understand." Amelia nods. "This shouldn't take too long."

"What is going to happen? What are they going to do with us?" Jadecan asks.

"They are most likely going to I.D. the both of you, and register Baby," Amelia answers. "That's probably the extent of what they are going to do with you two. As for me, well... I dunno. Now, when Baby's registered, you will most likely have to pay a fee, but that's it." She pauses momentarily, then says, "I would suggest though, that she doesn't speak, like... at all. I don't think it'll be a problem, but just to avoid any possible issues, okay?"

"Okay," Jadecan says. "You hear that, Baby?"

"I did," Baby answers. "I am to not speak, I understand."

"Alright, that's good." Amelia sighs.

"What is wrong?" the Akiko asks.

"Nothing," she answers. "Nothing you need to concern yourself with."

"As you wish," Jadecan says.

"We are being hailed," Baby says, opening the channel.

"We will be landing within the Cortnei's docking bay shortly," the Olensi interceptor states. "Upon crossing the barrier, please proceed to station A6."

"Understood," Jadecan says, closing the channel. "I like it."

"You like what?" Amelia asks.

"Space," he answers beaming.

"Wait... have you not been to space?"

"I have not."

"My energy cell had not been functioning properly for quite some time," Baby explains. "Without it, space travel for organic lifeforms would be extremely dangerous. Death would be a likely outcome."

"To be honest, I had never really thought about it," Amelia says.

"Makes sense," Meshel says, shrugging. "No energy cell, no shields."

Baby gradually crosses the Cortnei's blue field entering into it's impressive circular bay. The bay's silver reflective walls and bright lights mirror within Baby's glass-like body. An hourglass shaped structure stretches from the floor's center to its ceiling, the Surveillance Tower. A large slanted viewport completely wraps around the tower's upper half's midsection, as several bays line the dock's walls encircling it. Baby hovers above station A6 for a moment, then steadily descends onto the busy platform. Olket 7 parks in the station in front of the saucer, while the other interceptor sets down behind it.

"Let me do the talking," Amelia says to Jadecan, who nods in agreement.

"This should be fun," Meshel says sarcastically, as Baby lands and begins powering down.

"Indeed," Jadecan says, watching as a group of four Olensi approach Baby.

Following Amelia's lead, the three of them walk down Baby's ramp to the waiting formal Olensi uniforms at its foot. Numerous interceptors can be seen throughout the bay, as Olensi roam about its large area. An officer steps forward, his gold collar and cuffs setting him apart from the others.

"Ma'am," he says, greeting Amelia.

"Commander Resean, so good to see you," Amelia says.

"We are here to escort you and your companions to the Captain, he is expecting you," Resean says. "This way please."

"Of course." Amelia smiles.

⊜ 2

They arrive at the Captain's quarters and are directed inside by Commander Resean, as its small single gold door slides open. Walking past Resean and his guards, the three of them enter into the cone-shaped bright room. The Captain sits behind his desk in front of a massive curved window, through which the star rich black expanse of space can be seen. A blue holographic screen projects out of the desk's center before him.

His large bronze horns extend from his forehead and spiral back alongside his square golden face. His magnificent long light brown hair flows over his broad shoulders, as his amber eyes glare at them standing before him. It's obvious, he's not exactly what you would call, happy.

"Thank you, Commander," Tytus says to Resean.

"Captain." Resean nods respectfully before leaving.

"Amelia," the Captain says in a powerful tone.

"Captain," she says cautiously, as the door slides shut behind her.

"And you are?" the Captain asks Meshel.

"I am Meshel, of the R&D Division of Oteniko, Captain." Meshel gestures to Jadecan. "And this here, is Jadecan, of Niushki."

"An Akiko?"

"Yes, Captain," Meshel says. "I, like you, was rather surprised."

"I bet you were," Tytus says, looking at Jadecan. "Well, I am Captain Tytus, now... upon my arrival, I initiated a scan of both the planet and its moon, as is protocol. Shortly after the initial sweep, I was informed of a Cerulean signal, and after a brief investigation, found it to be yours, as I suspected." He stares at Amelia. "If I remember correctly, you were here to meet with an individual by the name of Stet Stal, would that be accurate?"

"Yes," she answers.

"And it was to gather intel in regard to some of your own research, correct?"

"That is correct," she answers cautiously.

"Because of your contact's close relation to the Balgorex Jahrei, who has claimed this section of the moon," Tytus states, "You were to take with you a full detail, yes?"

Amelia nods in agreement. "Yea."

"Where is that detail?"

After a short silence, she answers, "I did not take one."

"Why?"

"I've never needed one before," she says.

"That may be true," Tytus says, "But that was not what we agreed upon."

"I know..." Amelia says.

"You do realize how dangerous the Balgorex are?" the Captain asks. "They could have killed you, or at the very least sold you into slavery. Your actions were reckless and irresponsible. I am disappointed, I expected more from you." After a brief pause, he asks Meshel, "I take it you're here cataloging?"

"Yes, and with respect sir," Meshel states. "I do need to get back to my assignment as soon as possible."

"I'll do my best to keep this brief," Tytus says.

"Thank you, Captain."

"Jadecan, would you like to register your starship while you are here?" the Captain asks. "If you would like to leave here with it, you will."

"Seems as though I do not really have a choice then," he says.

"I suppose not," the Captain says.

"Looks like I will be registering it," Jadecan states.

"Good, I will see to it that your stay is brief. The officers outside will escort you to a set of quarters. I will send someone over with a Binox, and once the required procedures are carried out, you may leave. That will be all."

"Thank you, Captain," Meshel says.

"Amelia, if you would please, remain here," Tytus says, as Meshel turns for the room's exit.

Jadecan stands looking over at Amelia while Meshel gestures for him to leave the room. "I'll be fine," she assures him, timidly smiling.

"As you wish," he utters, then advances for Meshel standing at the room's entrance.

Jadecan steps out into the brightly lit silver hall and glances back as the door slides shut, leaving Amelia alone with the Captain. A gold strip runs along the bottom of the corridor's walls, as white lights from the ceiling is reflected in the polished black floor beneath their feet. Commander Resean along with another Olensi officer is stationed on either side of Tytus's gold door. The Akiko and Yonalitu stand between them.

"This way." Resean gestures down the hall.

⊖ 3

Jadecan and Meshel sit at a rectangular table across from one another within the guest quarters. A large purple and gold emblem is engraved into the table's center. Two small beds dressed in violet sheets are positioned near the room's side wall. Meshel sits in front of Jadecan who faces the room's entry. All in all, it's not too bad of a room.

"An interesting symbol," Jadecan says, staring at the emblem on the metal tabletop.

"It is. That is the Olensi Emblem. It's quite old," Meshel says.

"What does it represent?"

"Well, a few different things. I believe the color gold represents stature and honor, while the color purple is for peace and progression. Cassandra would tell you gold is representative of conquest and power, while purple is for mendacity and arrogance," Meshel says, with a small laugh. "The curved V, the purple part of the emblem, is representative of, well... the Cerulean's horns. It's sorta what makes them... them. The smaller golden arrow shape within it is specific to the Olensi, as in the Cerulean's power structure. That symbol will change depending on where in their society you see it, whereas the V is universal."

"Interesting, does Oteniko have a symbol?" Jadecan asks.

"Yes, nothing as complex as this, it's a large O with a ship flying around it. How 'bout you? Do the Akiko have one?"

"Yes, it is a yellow banner," Jadecan answers.

"That's simple."

"What do you think Amelia and Tytus are talking about?" Jadecan asks.

"Honestly, it seems as if she disobeyed an order, or at the very least, did not stay true to their agreed upon arrangement."

"Will there be repercussions?"

"There most likely will be consequences," Meshel answers. "As to how steep, I do not know. I imagine they won't be that terrible, considering she isn't Olensi. I'm sure she'll be fine."

"That could be so, it is likely."

Meshel says, as a loud tone's heard throughout the room, "Appears we have company." He turns toward the entrance, and asks loudly, "Yes? Who is it?"

Resean's voice echoes within the room. "This is Commander Resean, by order of Captain Tytus I have with me Officer Henak, who holds within his possession the necessary formalities and procedures required for Jadecan's vessel registration. In accordance with Cerulean regulation they must be completed before his departure from the Cortnei. We are here to deliver them to Jadecan. Will you accept?"

"Well," Meshel says to the Akiko. "Go accept. I'll help you complete the process, it's not all that difficult."

Jadecan stands and leaves the table, walking across the black carpet toward the entrance, passing in front of the beds. He presses a small round button about halfway up on the door's side, opening the entry and revealing Commander Resean. The Commander moves to the side and Officer Henak steps forward before Jadecan. Standing about the same height as the Akiko, the Cerulean's light brown horns are small, and point slightly upward from his forehead.

"Jadecan, I presume?"

"Indeed."

"If you would," Henak says, holding out a blue pad in front of him. "Please place your hand on the scanner, confirming you have received the delivery."

Jadecan places his hand upon the device and a blue light begins to scan a few times. Shortly thereafter, it dissipates, as the screen turns a bright shade of green.

"Thank you, you may remove your hand now," Henak states.

"Oh... okay," Jadecan says, removing his hand.

A black box materializes on top of the green screen where the Akiko's hand once was. "Please, retrieve the Binox."

Jadecan picks up the black box, then nods at the officers and closes the door. Meshel sits at the table watching the Akiko as he strolls back over from the entrance.

"Ah," Meshel says, as Jadecan sits down. "The Binox, nice."

"What is a Binox?" Jadecan asks, handing it to Meshel.

"It's Oteniko tech." Meshel places it on the table and somehow activates its small blue holographic display. "Some call it a data block, some a black box, but it's officially known as a Binox. So, Jadecan, first pick up the box." The Akiko picks up the box and holds it within his palm, as Meshel instructs. "Now, you will see on its display, a question. All you have to do is think of the answer, and the Binox will do the rest. It's as easy as that. Go ahead, give it a try."

Jadecan reads and answers the questions within the Binox's projection screen.

What is the name of the vessel to be registered? Baby. Who is the owner of Baby? Jadecan Xtyct. Homeworld of Jadecan Xtyct? Niushki.

The black box's blue screen disappears and shortly after the Akiko looks up at Meshel, who asks, "All good?"

"Yes, now what?" he asks, as the Binox splits, becoming two pieces in his palm.

"Now, you scan one piece into your holo-tech, and the other into Baby. That's it, you're done."

The connection established between our systems also allows for data transfer, Baby states. *You may store my piece within your autonomic technology. After which, I will retrieve it, completing the registration process.*

"Interesting." He scans both halves into his holo-system.

♀ Silver Spoon

⊖ 4

The Akiko and Yonalitu have been chatting for quite some time, still seated at the small table. They talked about the Akiko for a bit, before revisiting the topic of the Olensi, and the Ceruleans. After which, Meshel told him of the tech-savvy Oteniko, and how he ended up with Dr. Cassandra. It was just starting to get somewhat interesting, when the loud tone interrupts, playing once again throughout the room.

"Yes? Who is it?" Meshel asks, pausing mid-conversation.

"Amelia."

"I'll be over momentarily," Meshel says, getting up and walking over to the door.

Jadecan watches as he opens the door and Amelia enters. She smiles at Meshel as he stands to one side gesturing her in. The door slides shut as she sets her light purple eyes upon Jadecan sitting at the table ahead of her.

"Please," Meshel says, gesturing to the chair he had been sitting in. "Have a seat."

"Thank you," Amelia says graciously. "I appreciate it."

"No problem," he says, sitting on the edge of the bed nearest the silver table. "So, how goes it?"

"Not terrible," she answers.

"What happened?" Jadecan asks, leaning slightly forward, his yellow eyes peering into her turquoise face. "After we left?"

"After you left," she says with a small laugh. "He mainly just explained how disappointed he was. Besides that... I told him of Cassandra and the artifacts. He said he would very much like to meet Cassandra, and of course see the artifacts, as was expected. At which point, I told him they actually belonged to you." Amelia gestures to Jadecan. "So, you may or may not have your own little meeting with him at some point, before you leave, I don't know. That was pretty much the extent of the lecture." After a short pause, she asks, "How 'bout you two? What have you guys been up to?"

"Well," Meshel answers, "The only major activity we invested ourselves in was his registration, which was fun. We got to play with a Binox, always a good time."

"Awesome," she says, looking at Jadecan. "That wasn't so bad, was it?"

"I suppose not." Jadecan shrugs.

"How much did they charge you?" she asks.

"Well, I don't think it cost him anything." Meshel laughs.

"And it was free?" She raises her eyebrows smiling. "Wow... I mean, Tytus did express how thankful he was, but free? Free is a big thing around here."

"He could've assumed he had no units," Meshel suggests.

"True," she says.

"So, what's the plan? How much longer is this going to take?" Meshel asks after a few moments.

"I have no idea. If I were to guess, not too much longer." Amelia smiles.

"Are you to suffer any repercussions?" the Akiko asks.

"No," Amelia answers. "Not this time, thankfully."

"Now who is it," Meshel says, as the room's tone plays again. "Yes?"

"I am sorry to bother you," Commander Resean says. "I bear gifts in the form of refreshments, courtesy of the Captain."

"That's progress, I suppose," Meshel says to Jadecan and Amelia, before heading for the room's entrance.

"What are you going to do?" Jadecan asks Amelia.

"Hopefully, continue my research," she answers, "But we shall see."

"What does your research consist of?" he asks, as Meshel thanks Resean.

"A few things, languages, different entities, one of which being the Watcher, um, artifacts and relics of course, like the ones you found. It's a bunch of different things. Some of them are related, some of 'em aren't." Amelia watches as Meshel places a bottle of red wine and three glasses onto the table.

"This is courtesy of the Captain," Meshel says, walking back to the edge of the bed and sitting. "He apologizes for any inconvenience he may have caused, and that we may leave when we are ready. He also added, we may stay for as long as we like, as well. Within reason, of course."

"There you go," Amelia says, looking over at Meshel. "You can leave whenever you so desire."

"Would you mind if I stay?" Jadecan asks Amelia.

"No, not at all, I'd like that," she answers, with a smile.

"Well," Meshel says, strolling back over and opening the bottle. "As much as I would love to stay, I can't. I hope you understand." He pours the glasses and after placing one before each of them, he raises a toast. "Here's to friends, good fortune, and long happy lives." They clink their glasses and drink. "And may we meet again in the near future," he says, as they place their glasses back on the table before themselves.

"Indeed," Jadecan says, "It is decent, but it is no Rumu Litafethi."

"Ain't that the truth." Amelia laughs.

"I'll have to try that." Meshel smiles. "Maybe next time."

"Be safe," Amelia says, standing and embracing Meshel. "Tell Cassandra thank you for everything, and we'll meet up the next time I'm on Solarius."

"Will do," Meshel says, as she releases her hold of him.

"My friend." Jadecan bows slightly after standing. "Travel well."

"Here." Meshel retrieves an item from his holo-system. "A little trinket to remember us by, in case we don't see each other again. I really have enjoyed our time together," he says, handing him a small circular badge. "Till we meet again."

Jadecan watches as Amelia escorts Meshel to the door. They embrace one last time before he advances through the entrance, and disappears around the corner. The door closes as Amelia walks back to the table, while Jadecan studies the blue Oteniko Emblem on the silver badge's face.

"That would mean a lot to someone like Meshel. Treat it like you would that gem around your neck," Amelia says, gesturing to Jadecan's gold Kiwiwa necklace. "It's a symbol of great honor, of loyalty, and a symbol of pride. Keep it safe."

"I will," he says, storing it within his holo-system.

"Well, I'm gonna get cleaned up. You should do the same."

"Will do."

"Afterwards, I guess I should show you around, considering you'll be sticking around for a little longer," she says. "I was planning on stopping by L&M anyway, you're welcome to tag along if you'd like."

⊖ 5

The two of them, both having showered and cleaned up, hastily leave the guest room. The Cerulean wastes no time at all, and with purpose, paces for the L&M Deck, whilst explaining the Olensi starships to the Akiko walking at her side.

"I don't know a lot about these cruisers," Amelia says. "They are really big starships. Most everything anyone needs is on their own deck. So, a quick layout, by no means extensive. We are on deck two, also known as Low Deck, guest and crew quarters, for the most part. Directly above us is where we are heading, the L&M Deck. It's where I spend the majority of my time when I'm on these vessels, mainly labs and medical bays, hence the name. Above L&M, as you know, is the Command Deck, the one Tytus is on. It consists primarily of the crew responsible for flying and commanding the ship. Beneath us, well, is everyone else, the Below Deck."

Numbered rooms line the white walls on either side of them. There are no windows, and although the hall itself was of decent enough size, Jadecan couldn't help but feel trapped. Let's just say, he's not too fond of small spaces. Bright lights run down the center of the curving corridor's ceiling, blurring into one another. The hall's grey floor, unlike the Command Deck's black one, is non-reflective, and appears to be a patchwork of metal plates. They pass by a couple of officers as they spill out of the hall into a large busy circular area. Seven other corridors, like the one they had just left, can be seen on the curved wall behind them. In the area's center sits eight glass tube elevators in the form of a diamond shape.

"With that...." Amelia stops in front of a glass elevator and looks over at Jadecan beside her. "Are you okay?" she asks the restless Akiko.

"I am fine," he answers, as if offended by the question.

She stares worriedly at him for a few moments, then faces the opening doors, and says, "Well, I really don't wanna be here that long." She steps inside the elevator with Jadecan. "I am not a fan."

"Same," he says.

"Good." She smiles as the elevator closes and begins ascending. "Well then before we leave, let's see if we can't find ourselves something to do."

"What do you have in mind?"

"Gonna see a friend," she says. "She's a part of the reason I ended up on Niushki. We have a common interest in some topics, one of which just so happened to be the Watcher, so I thought she may have something for us."

"Who is this friend?" he asks, as they come to a stop.

"Dr. Santer," she answers, stepping out onto the shiny white floor, as Jadecan peers around at the eight halls before him. "Each corridor is a loop of sorts," she says, noticing him staring at the halls. "It's literally impossible to get lost in here." She laughs. "You may not know where you're going but, at least you won't get lost."

"Intriguing," he says, watching as a few Olensi walk into one of the corridors. "They look like the ones below us."

"Indeed." She giggles, while walking around the tubes and gesturing for Jadecan to follow. "Come on."

He follows Amelia around the elevators. In front of them sits a very wide rectangular short pathway, leading to a long counter. Seven representatives stand behind it, each with a blue holo-screen in front of them. They approach the counter as security officers on either side of the corridor watch with their holo-weapons at the ready. An extremely solid silver door is present on either side of the counter. Amelia stops before the center individual, he looks through the projected screen at her for a few moments, then speaks.

"Yes? How may I help you?"

"I was hoping to see Dr. Santer," she answers. "Is she available?"

"Do you have an appointment?"

"No," she answers, as the representative eyes Jadecan cautiously.

"May I inquire what business you have with Dr. Santer?"

"Yes, of course," she says. "I am returning from an expedition she had assigned to me, with the information she had requested."

"Your name?"

"Amelia Venae," she answers, presenting her identification.

"Ah, I see, welcome Ms. Venae," he states. "I hope your trip was productive."

"It was ah…." She pauses. "Interesting to say the least."

"Very good ma'am," he says. "And your companion's name?"

"Jadecan," she answers.

"One moment," he says, while interacting with the blue projection. "Dr. Santer," the representative greets, as she appears on screen.

"Yes?" the doctor asks.

"Amelia Venae is here to see you, along with an individual by the name of Jadecan," he relays.

"Good, good," Santer says. "Please send them in, thank you."

"Very well," he confirms, as Dr. Santer disappears. "Do you require an escort?" he asks Amelia.

"I do not."

"Very well, you may proceed through the door on your left," he says, gesturing to the entry as it opens.

"Thank you," Amelia says, heading for the entry with Jadecan at her side.

The silver door closes as Jadecan walks slightly behind Amelia, who continues around a curved ninety-degree corner. They amble out of the short corridor into a decently sized black square room. A few purple couches line the walls on either side of them. Positioned in the room's center is an enclosed oval-shaped onyx counter. It's reminiscent of the one at Stet's Place, except instead of iron bars around a worn stone top, a continuous glass window wraps around a smooth metal one. A silver entryway very similar to the one now at their backs, presents itself on the wall to their right. Four Olensi sit within the oval enclosure, staring as they enter.

"Dr. Santer is on her way," one of them states through a speaker system. "Please make yourself comfortable."

Jadecan and Amelia seat themselves onto one of the couches. He sits beside her, feeling its soft fabric, as they wait for Dr. Santer. He looks over at Amelia, who stares back at him with her lavender eyes, smiling. The entrance slides open revealing Dr. Santer who strolls into the black room toward them. Her turquoise skin and dark horns are a lot like Amelia's, her eye's however have more of a teal color.

"Amelia," Santer greets. "So nice to see you again."

"The feeling is mutual," she says, as the two of them hug momentarily.

"And you must be Jadecan," Santer says, with a curious look upon her face. "It's a pleasure."

"Same," Jadecan says, with a slight bow.

"Well," Santer states, happily looking at Amelia. "Let's head to my office, where we can speak privately."

⊖ 6

Dr. Santer sits across from Amelia and Jadecan on the other side of her L-shaped black desk. A small blue display is projected from its corner to her right as another sits within the desk surface between them. Jadecan ponders quietly, studying the many holo-images sitting on the white walls, while Amelia explains the events that transpired on Niushki.

"After Meshel left we decided to come here," she says, looking over at Jadecan. "Well, I decided to come here, I asked if he'd like to tag along, and well, here he is."

"An Akiko," Santer exclaims. "I'm sorry, I am still both thrilled and curious about your presence. I am honored to have you here, within my office." She animates excitedly, talking to Jadecan. "How old are you? If you don't mind my asking."

"I am 3,244," Jadecan answers.

"What?" Amelia says, looking over at him extremely surprised.

"Is that in Niushki time?" Santer asks, her hands clasped together on top of the desk.

"Yes," Jadecan answers.

"I don't understand," Amelia says, scratching her head. "What does that mean?"

"Well," Santer explains, "Niushki revolves around its planet every 9 or so Cerulean days. So, every 9 Cerulean days is one full year on Niushki. Whereas Vyn, the planet it revolves around, takes roughly 357 days to revolve around its sun. Making its year 357 days."

"Okay," Amelia says, "So, how old is he in our years? Cerulean years?"

"Cerulea's year is 365 days," Santer explains. "Jadecan is 3,244, correct?" she directs to Jadecan, who nods in agreement. "Then he would be roughly 80, in Cerulean years."

"So," Amelia asks, raising her eyebrows. "He is over 50 years older than me?"

"I suppose," Santer says. "I take it you're in your 20's?"

"26," Amelia answers.

"Then yes, he is," Dr. Santer confirms. "He is 54 years older than you."

"How long do Akiko's normally live?" Amelia asks, looking over at Jadecan.

"I can live up to 16,000," Jadecan states.

"Normally," Santer answers, "350 to 400 years."

"How long do you normally live?" Jadecan asks Dr. Santer and Amelia.

"If we're lucky," Santer answers, "We can live upwards of 150, but usually it's closer to 120. So, around 5,000 in your years."

"Well," Amelia says, with a small laugh and smiling at Jadecan. "This was interesting, and very unexpected."

"Indeed," Jadecan says.

"Anyway." Amelia looks across the table at Dr. Santer. "Long story short, I didn't find out much in regard to the Watcher, outside of its local name Vikerumu. Other than that, there's the dungeon, which is inaccessible currently for whatever reason, and then there are the artifacts that Cassandra currently has, that's pretty much about it." After a brief pause she says, "I would like to go back, maybe spend more time with the Kiwiwa, I dunno, it's something. I would very much like to just get back to work. I really don't wanna hang around here for too much longer."

"I understand, I will see what I can come up with," Santer says.

"I would appreciate it, thank you." Amelia nods.

"No problem. On a side note, I have heard of this Cassandra you speak of," Santer says. "If I understand correctly, she's usually very forthcoming when it comes to subjects of that caliber. She is quite knowledgeable, I'm not too concerned about the relics being with her, they're in good hands. Is the dungeon you speak of where you found the artifacts?"

"Well," Amelia answers. "The large sphere, that Jadecan recovered, is from the dungeon. The key however, the small silver one with the inscriptions, Stet actually already had."

"I see," Santer says. "Did he happen to mention where he may have found it?"

"He did, he claimed a Scut had found it inside the old outpost. The one we found the dungeon in," Amelia answers.

"Very interesting stuff," Dr. Santer says. "Okay, well, I'm going to need some time to think about all of this, it's quite a bit to take in. In the meantime, I will see what work I have that the two of you could possibly do. I will warn you however, I believe the bulk of it is on the planet. With that being said, I'm sure we could work something out."

"Thank you again, doctor." Amelia smiles.

"Not a problem." Santer says, as they stand and prepare to leave. "Jadecan, I am going to do my best to help your species. I know the Akiko have suffered greatly in this last century. I had feared you were no longer with us, I'm happy to see that's not the case. Anything I can do to help, you let me know."

"Thank you, doctor," he says.

"Most of us here, were born with a silver spoon already in our mouths. The majority of us don't know what it's like to struggle, to have to fight to survive. I know you may feel very alone, but I assure you, you're not. If you need anything please let me know, and I promise you, I will do everything in my power to see that it comes into fruition."

Jadecan nods in appreciation. "I will keep it in mind," he says, and heads out of the office with Amelia.

♀ Clear View

⊖ 7

Jadecan awakens within the dimly lit guest room on the bed nearest the entrance. He sits on its edge for a few moments before heading over to the table. He looks over at Amelia briefly, who sleeps soundly on the other bed. After sitting at the table, he retrieves the token Meshel had given him from his inventory. He fiddles with it, recalling the sequence of events which led him here.

"Hey," Amelia calls quietly, lying on her side staring at him. "What ya doin'?"

"Nothing," he says, returning the token to his holo-system. "Just with thought."

"What ya thinking about?"

"A few different things."

"Like what?"

He stares at her for a moment. "It has been a while since I have seen another of my kind. I fear I may be the last. Baby once told me, a long time ago, 'Time is a funny thing,' she said, 'A moment may last forever, yet that forever, may last but for a moment.' I did not understand at the time." He chuckles. "I believe I do now."

"I'm glad you do." She laughs. "I have no idea what that means. I'm pretty sure I know what it's supposed to mean, but...." She trails off, then says, "I'm sorry, Jadecan."

"It is not your fault." He smiles. "You need not apologize."

A faint beep-like sound resonates from the small nightstand next to Amelia. She reaches over and retrieves her pad resting on top of it. After visibly reading for several moments, she looks up at Jadecan smiling happily.

"Dr. Santer," she says, "Has found something we could do, if we so desired. Now, it's not a traditional job, it's definitely something I can say I haven't done before."

"What is it?"

"By definition," she says, sorta questioning herself. "A delivery, I suppose, or more accurately, an escort. I'm not sure."

"What would we be delivering, or escorting?"

"A creature." She sits up and rereads the message on the pad. "We'd be returning it to its natural habitat on Vyn, I believe that's pretty much the extent."

"Interesting."

"Indeed." She Giggles. "If we're interested we are to report to Dr. Santer, and complete the required application process. And after that is done, we send it to Command to sign off on. Once approved, we retrieve the package, which is a creature in this case, and then start the mission. Seems simple enough, what do ya think?"

"I say we accept," he says.

"Okay." And after a brief interaction with the device, she announces, "And there we go. We have accepted the mission. We are to report to Dr. Santer within a day to confirm."

"When do we leave?"

"The longest part of this entire process is almost always getting the mission approved by Command," she explains, leaving the bed and walking over to him wearing a small black nightgown. "So, once it's signed off on, we will leave. Until then, we can get to know the little guy we'll be escorting." She sits across from him and places the handheld pad on the table in front of him.

A few images of a pink haired creature populate the pad's screen. Above the pictures is the creature's species name and number, cheiket sp. 143. Its face, tiny feet, and extremely long whip-like tail, appear to be a very deep black. Whereas its large ears, slender short haired body, and fluff at the end of its tail, are a bright pink.

"How big are they?" he asks, looking up at her.

"Excluding its tail, which is like three times its body size, it's about the size of my datapad. So, rather small," she answers. "I think it's cute, in a hideous kinda way. On a side note, it's also apparently predatory, and on occasion may bite. Oh, it's also a male."

"On occasion, I may bite as well," he says, as if defending the cheiket.

"I have no doubt," she says, with a smile and small laugh.

"When may we see him?"

"Whenever we want, I guess. We could go now and confirm with Dr. Santer if you'd like."

"Okay." He slides the device across the table to her. "Shall we?"

⊜ 8

"Now, I will warn you," Dr. Santer says to Amelia and Jadecan, who sit across from her within her office. "1-4-3 has quite the attitude, to say it lightly. As such, you are under no circumstances to release it from its containment cube. When you arrive at 1-4-3's release point, you are to place the cube down and return to your vessel. Once inside the vessel, you may then and only then release 1-4-3 from its confinement. Is all that clear?"

"Yes," Amelia answers, as Jadecan nods.

"Good, 1-4-3 is en route to my office, so you may see it, as you have requested. In the meantime, there are a few other details to be discussed."

"Okay," Amelia says, as Jadecan listens.

"You don't talk much do you?" Santer asks Jadecan.

"I speak when the need arises," he answers.

"Well," Santer says, smiling. "I wish the majority of the individuals inside this department were more like you." Amelia slightly laughs at the comment as Dr. Santer continues, "So, I take it you both will be taking on this assignment?"

"Yes," Amelia answers.

"And how will you be getting to the release point?" Santer asks. "By way of an Olensi transport or your own vessel?"

"We will be taking Jadecan's ship," Amelia answers, looking over at him. "Right?"

"Yes," he answers.

"The starship Baby, correct?" Santer asks, after a quick search.

"That's correct," Amelia says.

A knock echoes upon the door behind Jadecan and Amelia. "Yes, please come in," the doctor answers.

The door slides open, and two research assistants enter carrying a small clear box housing 1-4-3. They place the containment cube onto the desk while handing Dr. Santer a black remote. They then leave the same way they entered, all without a word spoken. Jadecan peers through the energy fused walls of the box into the black face of 1-4-3. Its large white eyes stare back as it lies on the silver floor of the cube.

"So," Santer says, "This is 1-4-3, also known as a cheiket. He's usually pretty docile, more often than not you'll find him doing what he is doing now. Lying about, very calmly. It's not until you encroach on his space, or go to touch him, that he becomes quite aggressive. He will bite, but the dangerous part is not so much his bite, as it is his retractable claws." She explains, looking at 1-4-3, "They are long, and extremely sharp, he could easily claim an eye with them. He is certainly capable of inflicting enough damage that ultimately could result in one's death. He's surprisingly relaxed though, if left alone of course."

"Well, I think he's adorable," Amelia says, as she watches Jadecan stare at 1-4-3 happily.

"He is." Santer smiles. "He's our adorable little killing machine." She pauses, and then says, "We've had him for quite a while now. I think it's about time he goes back home."

"I like him," Jadecan says, still staring at the creature.

"Now." Santer presents the remote to Amelia and Jadecan. "This is the remote for the containment cube. All you have to do is hold the button on the top of the remote, and then type in 1-4-3. Once that is done, the clear walls of the silver container will fade away, allowing 1-4-3 to just walk out. After which, you're done, assignment complete. You don't even need to retrieve the containment cube, you can just come straight back."

"Sounds good. How long do you think it'll be before we can leave?" Amelia asks.

"I don't think it'll be too terribly long, considering the nature of the assignment," the doctor answers. "It's pretty straight forward, and although there are risks involved, they're minimal. Only major part they may take some time considering is Jadecan's involvement. Between you and me though, they have been somewhat more lax when it comes to some restrictions. Given his recent interaction with the captain, it is my belief that he'll be just fine, but we'll see. Either way, I don't imagine us having to wait too long to get an answer."

"Why do you refer to him as 1-4-3?" Jadecan asks Dr. Santer.

"He's the 143rd species we've brought back from the planet to study," she explains. "We try not to give any of them 'pet names' to hopefully forgo any attachments to the specimens. Inevitably though, you will become somewhat attached to all of them, in some way. It's nearly impossible not to, but we know that eventually they will be returned to their natural habitats. I admit, sometimes it's hard, on occasion we'll get emotional seeing them go, but it's a part of the job. When all is said and done, it's what's best for the specimen."

"I imagine it would be hard." Amelia looks at 1-4-3 and smiles. "But all that matters is what's best." She asks Dr. Santer, "I take it you'll be in touch?"

"Yes," Santer answers. "As soon as I know anything, you'll be among the first to know."

⊖ 9

"I've been to Vyn once," Amelia says to Jadecan, as they step out of the elevator onto the busy Low Deck. "And while I was there, I stayed mainly inside the outpost." She stands in front of the glass tubes for a moment, before excitedly gesturing for Jadecan to follow. "Oh. Come on, you have got to see this view." Jadecan walks beside her as they stroll around the elevators. "And now that you've got something of a sample, what do you think of the Olensi?"

"They do not seem unusual," he answers. "Why do you not like them?"

"It's not that I don't like them. I like them just fine. I just don't agree with some of the things they do."

"I see."

They walk into the wide corridor in front of the elevators. A solid wall runs down the hall's right side, while an open small room sits about midway up its left. A very familiar circular metallic platform can be seen in the room's center. He glares as they walk by heading for the junction at the corridor's end.

"What is that?" he asks, narrowing his eyes.

"That is where you can pick up a bounty," she answers. "It's more for Hunters than us, although you may fit the bill."

"What are Hunters?"

"Well, if you need something done, and are willing to pay a small fortune for it, then a Hunter is who you're looking for. The bounties usually consist of a lot of nefarious activities though, like assassinations and so forth. It's a part of the Olensi that I don't completely agree with."

"I did not take them as ones to dwell in such things."

"Everyone does, it's complicated." She looks over at him, and after a slight pause, asks, "Would you be interested in something like that?"

"I would."

"I thought as much," she says, smiling. "Maybe you'll get a chance at some point, who knows."

"It is possible."

"Maybe before you do that, you could come with me to Solarius."

"To see your friend?" he asks, as they turn left into the silver T-shaped junction.

"Yes, to see my friend," she answers, as they enter the glass hall connected to the junction.

An Olensi cruiser can be seen in between the Cortnei and Vyn as they walk the transparent hallway. Jadecan notices a few red lights periodically blinking as he looks out at the planet.

"What are the red lights?" he asks, staring out at Vyn.

"Satellites. There's quite a few of them," she answers. "Unless you've got an Olensi clearance code, I'd suggest not heading toward the planet. They are quite deadly."

"Cassandra was serious when she said no one could visit," he states.

"Ah yea, she was." Amelia gestures toward the grey cruiser before them. "And that is the Kadu, the Cortnei's sister ship."

"Interesting, they look very similar."

"They do." She laughs. "They are identical in almost every way. They each have their unique characteristics, but for the most part, they are exactly the same. Almost all Olensi starships of the same class are pretty similar." She pauses briefly, then asks, "Quite the view, huh?"

"It is." Jadecan smiles.

"I thought you might appreciate it. What do ya think of Vyn?"

"I find it... different," he answers. "It has always been there, my entire life, watching from the horizon, but somehow, it is not the same, from out here. It is so much more vibrant than I had imagined."

"It is definitely that." She glances over at him. "It's definitely that."

"Dr. Santer took 1-4-3 from Vyn?"

"I doubt she did, but someone did, yes," Amelia answers. "I'm sure he'll be happy to be back home. It's not very often I get to do an assignment like this. It's kind of exciting, it feels good, you know?"

"How long do you think we will have to wait?" he asks.

"Well, she did make a good point, of you not being a Cerulean and all. They've never allowed outsiders onto the planet before, so I dunno. Hopefully not long."

"Why the restrictions?"

"I honestly don't know," she answers. "But maybe Dr. Santer's right, and it's not as big a deal as it used to be."

♀ Vibrant Sky

⊖ 10

Jadecan awakens from a dream to the sound of Amelia's voice. "Hey," she says quietly, as he comes to. "You okay?"

"I am fine," he answers, sitting up and glancing around the dimly lit quarters, as she sits on the bed's edge. "What is it?" he asks in a somewhat angry tone.

"You appeared to be having a nightmare," she says softly. "I was just… I just wanted to make sure you were okay."

"I am fine," he repeats. "As I have said."

"Okay." She walks away toward the table. "You don't want to talk about it, that's fine, I understand."

"There is nothing to talk about," he says, getting up and sitting at the foot of the bed while she takes a seat at the table.

"So." She changes the topic and retrieves her datapad. "We've got an update."

"Good," he says, rubbing his temples. "Are we set to leave? Has the assignment been approved?"

"It has, and we are set to leave," she answers, "As long as we agree to the terms and conditions."

"I thought we already had," he says, walking over and sitting in front of her.

"We did to Dr. Santer's," she says, looking up from the device into his yellow eyes. "It looks as if Captain Tytus is busy elsewhere, he's apparently tied up in a meeting with the Fleet Commander. So, Commander Resean has approved our assignment in the Captain's absence, as is his job as Tytus' second. As one would expect, he wrote up his own terms and conditions. I doubt he wants to end up on the wrong side of the Captain. So, this is merely his way of making sure that doesn't happen. I don't blame him, and honestly, they're reasonable."

"What are they?"

"First," she explains, "we are to go by the book, no exceptions. So that means, once we arrive on Vyn, we check in as is protocol at the nearest post. We go straight from there to the release point, we complete the assignment, then head back with no delay. Other terms include, confirmation of starship Baby, and really just reconfirming all of Santer's terms and conditions. Then Dr. Santer is to sign, confirming she has read and understands these as well. Looks like that is it."

"Reasonable."

"Yes, very," she agrees. "Okay, so we have just accepted everything and sent it to Dr. Santer to do the same." After a brief pause, she asks, "Are you sure you're okay?"

"I am fine," he answers. "It was but a dream."

"Do you have them often?" She places the pad down onto the tabletop.

"I suppose. It is of no importance."

"Fine, if you ever want to talk about it, I'm here," Amelia says to Jadecan, who nods in appreciation, as she looks upon the green gem around his neck. "It looks good on you. It really does." She smiles. "Thank you, for everything. I don't think I've ever actually thanked you for saving me."

"You have, in any case, it was nothing," he says. "I thank you as well."

"For what?" she asks. "I haven't really done much of anything."

"You have been here. You have yet to leave."

"No, I haven't and don't plan to, why? Why would me not...." She trails off, then asks, "Have others left you before?"

"I have gotten used to being alone," he says after a moment. "I live a dangerous life, and am a dangerous individual. There are not many that would stick around as you have."

"Well, I am not leaving," she reassures him playfully. "And you don't seem that bad. You can be a bit difficult, but that's understandable."

He smiles. "You are indeed special."

"Thank you, I guess." She giggles.

Amelia looks down at the datapad sitting on top of the table. A beep-like tone plays while she reaches for it. Jadecan watches with his hands clasped in front of him as she interacts with its blue screen. She looks up at him with a smile and slightly nods while picking up the pad.

"Everything is good. Dr. Santer has signed the agreement, and we are to pick up 1-4-3 when we are ready. That was easy."

"And rather quick," he adds.

"I'm not complaining," she says, with a small laugh. "And we have just received our clearance code, which is good for three Vyn days. So, the sooner we get going the better. I am gonna let Santer know we will be on our way shortly to retrieve 1-4-3. Anything we need to do before we leave?"

"I do not believe so," he answers.

"I didn't think so, just checking." She puts away the device in a flash of blue light and stands. "Alright, let's go get our little cute package and get ourselves out of this hellhole," she says, smiling happily.

⊜ 11

Retrieving the creature took some time, but it wasn't too bad. The entire process was pretty straight forward, nothing too overly complicated. A cut and dry simplistic hand off, pretty much. A welcomed oddity, it's rare for things to run so smooth.

Jadecan holds 1-4-3's containment cube at his side as their elevator descends from the L&M Deck. He raises the box up and looks into the large white eyes of the black faced creature. 1-4-3 trills at the peering Akiko as Amelia giggles at his side.

"Soon buddy," he says quietly, with a slight smile. "Soon."

The glass door of the elevator opens, revealing the Below Deck. Jadecan follows Amelia out onto the grey metal floor. The bright deck's corridors greet them as they leisurely walk around the tubes. They begin down the level's main hall, same as they've done on the other decks of the cruiser. Amelia glances over at Jadecan as they stroll down the short corridor for the Cortnei's docking bay.

"It's gonna be nice not being here, even if it's only for a couple of days," she says. "I'm already thinking about what to do when we get back. Maybe we could take a brief break and travel to Solarius, maybe we could see Lenora. What do you think? What would you like to do after this?"

"I had said on Niushki we would find your Watcher," he answers. "I say we continue searching for the Vikerumu."

"We could." Amelia shrugs. "I suppose while we're doing that we could stop by the Oteniko outpost, and possibly see Cassandra and Meshel. They might not have left yet."

"Indeed," he says, as they leave the silver corridor and enter into the large circular bay.

The bay's lights reflect off Baby's glass-like body sitting in front of the Surveillance Tower directly ahead of them. Jadecan glances up at the slanted viewport of the tower as they walk by Olket 7 still resting on the pad beside Baby.

"Why help me search for the Vikerumu?" Amelia asks, walking up Baby's ramp into the ship. "Is it just because you said you would?"

"It is important to you," he says, sitting next to her as Baby's interior blue lights activate. "And yes, I said I would, so I intend to do that." He places 1-4-3's containment cube onto his lap.

"Well, isn't that nice of you," she says, inputting the clearance code and release point coordinates into the ship's blue interaction console. "We should be fine now Baby, you are more than welcome to speak. Are you able to read the coordinates?"

"Yes," Baby answers. "Appears our first task is to check in at the Olensi outpost O-56. Are we to head there now?"

"Yes," Amelia answers, looking over at Jadecan, who watches as 1-4-3 sleeps.

"Jadecan?" Baby questions, looking for his approval.

"Do as she says," he says, glancing up from 1-4-3 at the hourglass shaped Surveillance Tower. "Would you like to give it a go?" he asks Amelia, gesturing to the projected console.

"Sure," Amelia answers back excitedly. "Okay," she says to herself, placing her hand upon the blue screen. "Here we go."

Baby takes off and slowly glides for the hangar's blue barrier. Amelia watches the ship's reflection travel along the bay's silver walls while Jadecan admires the pink haired cheiket sleeping peacefully. It gradually opens its large white eyes and stares back at him. After a few moments, the creature lets out a large yawn and slowly closes them once again, as the saucer crosses the force-field into space.

"You said you have been to the planet?" he asks, looking up from the cube at the large world in front of them.

"Yes," Amelia answers, her hand still resting on Baby's console. "I enjoyed it. It's definitely one of the prettiest places I've been to."

"We will be entering the atmosphere of the planet shortly," Baby says, as Amelia focuses on the console.

"Anything of interest?" Jadecan asks, checking on 1-4-3.

"I have not detected anything of concern," Baby answers. "We are currently being scanned by a few of the Olensi satellites." Jadecan watches the blinking red lights of the satellites in the distance. "Stand by." And after a few moments, she says, "We have been cleared and will be entering the planet's atmosphere soon."

"Very nice." Jadecan smiles.

The ship flies through Vyn's atmosphere and emerges above the Olensi outpost O-56. She effortlessly dives for the silver compound over top of the planet's rolling green hills, as Jadecan stares out in awe at the vibrant landscape and bright blue sky.

"What do you think?" Amelia asks.

"It is nice," he answers, looking over at her.

"We are being hailed by O-56," Baby says.

"Starship Baby," O-56 states. "This is the Olensi outpost O-56, please respond."

"This is Baby," Jadecan responds.

"We're on assignment from Captain Tytus," Amelia says after a brief pause. "We are requesting landing clearance."

"Clearance granted," O-56 says. "Please proceed to the main hangar bay. Confirm."

"Main hangar bay confirmed," Amelia states, while Jadecan views the nearing square outpost. "Thank you."

"It is quite a nice place," Jadecan comments, admiring the planet.

"It is," Amelia says, as Baby comes to a gradual stop, hovering above the complex.

Amelia smiles at Jadecan as the saucer descends into the small open circular hangar in the center of the metallic outpost. The ship touches down gently onto the concrete floor of the structure, as Amelia and Jadecan prepare to disembark. They advance off Baby's black ramp toward the three Olensi waiting for them.

"Welcome to O-56," the middle small horned officer greets.

"How are you doing?" Jadecan says to the resting 1-4-3, as he follows behind Amelia.

"The cheiket, specimen number 1-4-3?" the middle officer questions, gesturing to the containment cube at Jadecan's side, clearly intrigued by the pale skinned Akiko.

"Yes," Amelia answers, presenting their assignment's I.D. number.

"Everything looks good," the officer says, scanning the I.D. with his data-pad. "Checks out. Now to see 1-4-3. May I?" he asks, looking at Jadecan.

"Yes, of course," Amelia answers, looking over at Jadecan, who then lifts the cube up to the officer's eye level.

"1-4-3 is present," the officer states, staring into the black face of the pink haired creature. "Everything checks out," he says, scrolling through the pad's blue screen. "You are good to go."

"Thank you," Amelia says, while Jadecan smiles at the cheiket, then lowers the cube back down to his side as the two head back to Baby.

"That is it?" Jadecan asks, looking up at the blue sky above the saucer.

"Yep," she answers, boarding the ship. "Now off to the release point."

They saunter into the blue light of the ship's deck, seating themselves into it's black chairs. Jadecan places the containment cube back onto his lap, as he rests his hand upon the console before him. Baby smoothly takes off and hovers momentarily above the outpost. Her black body gleaming in the sunlight as she slowly glides away.

⊖ 12

Baby flies over one of the planet's many massive rainforests toward a large mountain range. Its peaks disappear into the dense cloud cover as the sun sets behind her. A tall waterfall cascading off the summit's side soon becomes visible, as Jadecan looks out at the treetops beneath them. The Akiko and cheiket watch each other as Baby gradually slows, landing in a clearing next to a river below the falls.

"We have arrived," Baby says, making contact with the soft grass filled landscape.

"Where exactly is the release point?" Amelia asks, admiring the beautiful scene.

"It appears the release point is directly behind the waterfall," Baby answers, the blue lights within her deck dimming slightly. "Initial scans of the immediate area show nothing of significance."

"Good," Jadecan states, as the last bit of sunlight fades away from the environment. "It is about that time buddy," he says, looking at 1-4-3 lying on the silver floor of the cube in his lap.

"I'd rather wait till the sun returns," Amelia states.

"How long will that take?" he asks.

"Not sure," she answers, retrieving her datapad. "Around ten to twelve hours, I don't remember exactly."

"Given our clearance codes 63 hour lifespan, one full day would be 21 hours," Baby says. "Making the planet's day and night cycle around ten and a half hours, respectively."

"Interesting," Jadecan says, staring up at the glowing white moon in the night sky. "I take it that is Niushki?"

"Yes," Baby answers.

"Seems so small from here," he says.

"Yea, it does," Amelia agrees, and then looks down at her pad for a few moments. "Sunrise should be around eight hours from now, if this is accurate."

"50 hours remain before the code expires, at daybreak we would roughly have 42 hours left," Baby says. "It would be wise to complete the assignment, and return to the Cortnei well before the code's expiration."

"I agree." Jadecan looks over at Amelia.

"Probably for the best," Amelia says, as Jadecan gets up and places the containment cube on the seat behind him. "Wait, what are you doing?"

"I will return," he answers, heading to the rear of the saucer as the blue tinted black floor opens, revealing the ship's extending ramp. "I am going to step outside."

"Really? You don't say." Amelia shakes her head, rising from her seat. "I'll join you."

"No, how 'bout not," he says, looking back over his shoulder. "It would be safer if you remain here."

"Okay, whatever." Amelia slowly sits back down. "If you say so."

"Keep an eye on our friend," he states, walking off the ship.

The sound of the waterfall fills the moonlit landscape as he sets foot onto the soft light green terrain. The ship's ramp retracts while he stands motionless in front of it, taking in the alien environment. He stares out in wonder at the dense forest before him, its green foliage the likes of which he has never seen. A beige sandbank sits to his right, ahead of the slow flowing waterway. He looks up at the pale moon above the crest of the cascade for a few moments, then strolls for the riverside.

He stops at the dark blue water's edge peering across the channel at the thick growth along its opposite shoreline. Baby sits behind him in a small clearing outlined by the treeline of the forest. He listens to the sound of the waterfall crash into the river's end while methodically studying his surroundings. After a brief few moments, he glances over and casually heads for the mist filled base of the falls.

How is everything? Baby asks.

"Everything is fine," Jadecan answers, traveling along the sandy bank of the waterway. "I will be back shortly."

He comes upon a solid stone outcrop to the side of the cascade. The Akiko steps onto the ledge of the rocky shelf and follows it to a large cave entrance hidden behind the falls. The waterfall roars as he looms within the dark cave's entryway. His holo-weapon forms inside his hand as he steps into the large open cavern before him. Jadecan eyes several large rock formations scattered throughout the large cave, while admiring the glowing violet colored moss attached to its walls. The weapon fades away from his grip, as he stares out at the empty grove in the cavern's center. Well, this was less interesting than he had hoped.

"How is 1-4-3?" he asks Baby.

He seems well. As well as one could be, confined within a small cube.

After some deliberation, he begins to trek back off the rock ledge along the soft sandbank. Upon returning to the riverside, he gazes at the moon's reflection in the calm water and heads for the saucer. Baby's ramp extends out toward Jadecan while he views the lay of the surrounding land. He stops briefly before venturing back onto the ship and glances up at the bright Niushki within the star rich black sky.

How was it? Baby asks, as he strolls into the dimly lit deck of the ship.

"It was fine," he answers, looking over at the blanketed Amelia who quietly sleeps on the dark floor.

She was watching you for a while. Suppose the events of the day finally caught up to her, Baby says, as Jadecan sits in the black seat Amelia had been sitting in.

"It is likely," he quietly says, watching as 1-4-3 sleeps within the confinement on the chair next to him.

You should get some rest. Day break is in roughly four hours.

"Yea." He sighs. "I will, in a bit."

♀ Stunning Grove

⊖ 13

Jadecan awakens still seated in front of Baby's viewport. The bright day shines in through the window as he eyes a few puffy clouds moving across the blue sky. He looks over at the sleeping 1-4-3 while Amelia still slumbers silently behind him.

"Hey buddy," he says quietly to the cheiket, whose white eyes light up as Jadecan speaks. "How did you sleep?"

"Daybreak was about three hours ago," Baby states. "There is around eight to nine hours of daylight left. You should get moving as soon as possible."

"Understood." He gets up and gently shakes Amelia, waking her.

"Yes?" She sits up and looks about the ship. "I… I must've fallen asleep," she says, as he crouches at her side.

"Seems so," he says smiling, amused by her statement. "Get yourself together. It is about time we release 1-4-3, okay?"

"Yea." She nods, while he stands and advances to the rear of the ship. "Yea, yea I'm getting up."

He walks down the ramp back out into the lush environment. It's much greener now in comparison to several hours ago during the dead of night. Jadecan shields his yellow eyes while looking up at the bright light of the sun. Its warm rays beam down upon him enveloping his entire body in a magnificent heat. The constant sound of the waterfall echoes throughout the terrain as he peers at its crest over top the forest. This is indeed an immaculate place.

"Hey," Amelia says, stepping onto the grass behind him. "Here, take him," she says, as he looks back at her walking toward him carrying 1-4-3's confinement. "It's beautiful, I love it." Jadecan takes the containment cube from her and smiles at the creature.

"Hey buddy," he softly says to the cheiket, as Amelia strolls for the riverside.

His tiny pink haired buddy squeaks playfully as the Cerulean's black hair gleams under the strong sunlight. He lowers the cube to his side and follows her onto the sandy bank of the waterway. She stands adoring the scene as the water's calm blue surface ripples peacefully while the cascade roars violently at the river's end.

"Look at that," she says, pointing up to the sky. "I wonder what they are."

"I am sure Dr. Santer would know," Jadecan says, looking up at the multi-winged creatures gliding by lazily far above them. "Come on." He walks away in the direction of the waterfall.

"I love the sound of water," she says, walking closely behind him along the river's edge.

37 hours remain till code expiration, Baby tells Jadecan, as they step onto the grey stone shelf at the falls side.

"Here we are," he quietly says to 1-4-3, as he strides for the large cavern's alcove.

"Wow," Amelia says in a shocked tone, as the falls roar at their backs. "This is quite the place."

Jadecan advances into the grotto, for the small collection of dark green trees at its center. He slightly descends the rocky shelves to the swampy terrain of the cavern floor, then heads for the grove. The cheiket trills softly as he arrives and places its containment cube down onto the soft wet ground.

Taking note of the few dark passageways leading away from the grove, he glances back at Amelia. “It is quite nice.”

“Yes, it’s very pretty,” Amelia agrees, strolling through the marsh. “Is this the place?” she asks, arriving at his side as the sound of the waterfall resonates within the cavern.

“I believe so,” he answers.

We are at the correct location, Baby states.

“I suppose this is it,” he says softly to the creature, crouching at its side. “Goodbye my friend.”

“Okay,” Amelia says, as Jadecan stands facing her. “Guess now we return to Baby?”

“Yes,” he answers, ambling away from the cheiket for the cavern’s entrance.

“I bet he’s happy to be home,” she says, trailing behind him.

“Yea.” He looks back at 1-4-3 while Amelia walks toward him. “I am going to miss you,” he softly says, then ventures out of the cave.

The crashing sound of the waterfall thunders prominently, as they stroll along the sandy bank toward Baby. Vyn’s bright blue sky and intense sunlight bear down upon them, as they saunter into the grass filled clearing the ship rests within. Amelia passes by Jadecan continuing up the saucer’s ramp as he stops at its base and surveys the area briefly, before joining her on board.

"It is for the best," Baby says, aware of how Jadecan felt about the creature. "It will be happier within its natural habitat."

"Yea," Jadecan agrees somewhat sadly, then smiles while sitting beside Amelia. "Shall we?"

"Yes," Amelia answers, retrieving the small remote and holding it out before him. "Would you like to do it?"

"I would." He gently takes the remote from her hand, and says after a few moments of staring at the device, "Live well my friend." He holds down the top button and inputs the numbers 1-4-3 onto its number pad, releasing the creature from the containment cube.

⊜ 14

"Where do you live on Niushki?" Amelia asks, breaking the long silence that's been within the ship ever since they left the clearing. "Do you stay at places like Along The Way? Or do you have like, a home?"

"Baby is my home," he answers, his hand upon Baby's blue interface.

"That makes sense," she says.

"Where is your home?" he asks, peering out at the Olensi facility O-56 ahead of them.

"On Cerulea. The Olensi had given it to my father as a gift. When he died it passed down to my mom and me. It's a beautiful place, I loved it. I spent most of my younger years and then some with them there. Everything was great till...."

She pauses momentarily. "When he passed my ah, my mom she, well, I haven't been back in quite some time."

"I am sorry. Those must have been difficult times."

"Yea," she says, with a small smile. "Thank you."

"We do not have to talk. I am happy to just sit here with you."

"Please forgive my interruption," Baby says after a brief silence. "We are being hailed by O-56."

"Starship Baby, this is O-56, please confirm mission sp. number."

"Sp. number is 1-4-3," Amelia confirms. "All is well, are we okay to land?" she asks, as they fly for the outpost's main hangar.

"Starship Baby landing clearance granted," O-56 states. "Please proceed to the main hangar bay."

"Thank you," she says, closing the channel. "You know Baby, I forget you're here sometimes."

"It is fine," Baby says. "I understand."

Jadecan looks over at Amelia's smiling turquoise face as the ship prepares to land. The saucer hovers briefly above the circular bay, then gradually begins to descend, it's black body spinning slowly while it does.

"You don't have to come," Amelia says, as Baby makes contact with the concrete floor. "You can stay here," she adds, standing. "This shouldn't take long."

"As you wish," he says, removing his hand from the ship's interaction console.

Jadecan watches Amelia walk to the back of the ship as its blue interior lights dim. She advances down the ramp, disappearing from sight as she enters the outpost's silver docking bay. He observes as she walks toward the same three Olensi Officers they had met during their first visit to the compound.

"What are you thinking?" Baby asks.

"I worry about 1-4-3," he answers. "What if the containment did not open as designed?"

"It is doubtful," Baby says. "But I suppose it is theoretically possible, however unlikely."

"It is possible, though."

"It is an understandable concern. We currently have 34 hours before code expiration. We could revisit the release point briefly, alleviating some of your concern," Baby suggests.

"Sounds good. Let us do that," he says, watching Amelia interact with the officers.

"You seem happier while in the presence of Amelia," Baby comments. "Would you mind if she were to stay with us?"

"I would not," he answers. "I would prefer if she did."

"I suggest you explore the possibility with her," Baby suggests. "I am almost certain if given the option, she would choose to stay."

"I will extend the offer." He nods. "Once we are back aboard the Cortnei."

"Very well," she says, as Amelia ventures back to the ship.

Jadecan sighs sitting back in the black seat, while reaching for the green gem resting on his chest below his collarbone. He loosely holds the stone as Baby's interface appears and Amelia walks onto the deck. The Akiko releases the jewel and places his hand upon the glowing console whilst the Cerulean seats herself.

"Are we set to return?" he asks.

"We are," Amelia answers. "All is well."

"I would like to return to the release point," he says, staring out at the few Olensi busily moving about the bay.

"Why?" she asks.

"To see that the containment cube did indeed open," he answers.

"You're worried 1-4-3 could still be locked inside the box." Amelia smiles. "Sure, if it makes you feel better, I don't see why not. How much time do we have?"

"We have roughly 34 hours," Baby answers.

"That's a good bit of time," Amelia says. "The Cortnei is expecting us though. I suggest we be quick, okay? We're supposed to head straight back, but I'm down."

"I will not be long," he assures her, at the very moment Baby lifts off the concrete floor.

"You kinda can't be." She laughs, giving him a look.

⊖ 15

Baby sits in the clearing behind Jadecan and Amelia, who walk away from her toward the river's edge. They stroll along the sandbank for the bellowing waterfall as dusk begins to set on the planet.

There is approximately three hours of daylight remaining, Baby says to Jadecan, as he and Amelia step onto the stone shelf beside the falls.

Upon reaching the cavern entrance, Jadecan notices a strange looking individual crouching next to the open containment cube inside the grove. The cascade roars behind him as Amelia arrives at his side. She almost immediately lets out a short gasp covering her mouth and staring at the mysterious character with wide eyes. Jadecan casually advances down the rocky shelves onto the marshy terrain of the grotto as Amelia stands in shock behind him.

"Why hello," Jadecan says calmly, while approaching the character who stands abruptly facing him.

"Um... ah oh-hello there," he stutters, as Jadecan stares up into his small brown circular face atop his long muscular neck.

"How is it going?" Jadecan asks, glancing down at the empty containment cube between them as Amelia strolls up alongside him.

"You're a Flunari," Amelia comments, looking up into his large sky blue eyes. "What are you doing here?"

"Well, I... I was." The Flunari stumbles over his words as he speaks, "Cond... conducti... ah yes, conducting some um..."

"What is your name?" Jadecan asks, grinning.

"Oh ah... my name?" the Flunari asks, gesturing to himself.

"I suppose I could be referring to the Flunari behind you," Jadecan says, somewhat annoyed.

The Flunari stutters, looking behind him, "Th-there's... there's... there's not ah." He turns back to Jadecan. "There isn't anyone behind me, good sir."

"I am aware," Jadecan says in a very serious tone.

"My name... is Sophis," Sophis says. "I am a... Sophis."

"I've heard that name before." Amelia looks over at Jadecan, and ponders out loud to herself, "Where have I heard that name?"

"Pleasure to meet you, Sophis." Jadecan slightly bows with his yellow eyes glaring at the Flunari. "I am Jadecan, may I ask what business you might be… how did you put it again," he says, straightening his stance more so than usual. "What business you might be conducting, good sir. Yes, that is it. I believe that was the term you so elegantly used."

"I was, ah… I am," Sophis explains, "Collecting some of… well sir, I was… I was collecting some of this… this moss, you see here… glowing around us."

"Why? For whom?" Amelia asks, then retracts the question almost immediately. "Actually never mind. May I see your clearance I.D.?"

"My… my clearance I.D.?" Sophis asks, obviously uneasy.

"I don't think he's supposed to be here," Amelia says to Jadecan.

"No no, ah… yes um." Sophis searches about himself. "I have it here… I have it here somewhere… It's ah…" he says, as the Akiko looks over at Amelia.

Jadecan reaches for his chest almost instantly as Amelia crumbles unconscious at his side. He removes a dart-like object with a scowl and studies it briefly, then angrily peers across at Sophis. The Flunari stands both afraid and surprised, shakily pointing a small holo-weapon at him.

Jadecan lunges at Sophis who holds out his hands in defense before him. The Akiko quickly slices off the hand and forearm of the Flunari that once held the weapon whilst activating his own in the process. Blood drips off Jadecan's bone blade onto the swampy terrain as Sophis falls to the ground in front of him crying out in anguish.

"I suspected I would end up killing you," Jadecan states, during the act of pointing his holo-weapon at Sophis' small head.

The Akiko looks back over his shoulder at the Cerulean lying on the wet ground behind him. He glances at Sophis' arm resting beside him, and almost as soon as his head turns, the Flunari abruptly disappears out the corner of his eye. He glares at the ground and deactivates his weapon, then turns back to check on Amelia. Jadecan walks over and kneels beside her, then removes the dart lodged in her breast. After looking her over, he gently picks her up and slowly treks back out of the grove.

Is everything okay? Baby asks, as he leaves the cave while the cascade roars.

"Amelia is unconscious, otherwise everything is fine," he answers. "I am currently carrying her. We are on our way back to you."

He continues around the stone shelf stepping down onto the sandbank, whilst cautiously looking about the terrain and carefully carrying Amelia within his arms. The sun sets while he strolls onto the grassy field Baby sits within. Her dark ramp's already extended as her blue light glows upon it, awaiting him. Jadecan walks up into the ship and gradually lays Amelia down where she had slept during their first night here.

"It would appear we have a stowaway," Baby says, in the act of him sitting onto one of her black chairs.

He looks over as 1-4-3 jumps onto the seat next to him and Baby's interface appears below his outstretched waiting palm. It quickly wraps its long tail around itself, curling up into a small pink ball, content, and purring the whole time. Jadecan watches it struggle to keep its eyes open before it appears to finally drift off to sleep.

"Hey buddy." He quietly chuckles while the ship launches and flies for the darkening sky of the planet.

♀ Burgundy Judge

⊜ 16

A couple of Flunari brothers known as Sophis and Idyn walk casually through the bustling metropolis of Orphan City. The city's multistory buildings of varying sizes line either side of a wide metallic roadway, the Orphan Highway. Hover-crafts speed by as they stroll along the slightly elevated walkway at the roadside. Their small brown turtle-like faces sit atop their extremely long muscular necks, as their tiny bodies maneuver through the variety of species walking around them.

"What do you think she wants?" Sophis asks, pacing beside Idyn.

"The Fitura?" Idyn looks over at Sophis briefly. "Most likely what your friend Lucius was telling me."

"Lucius?" Sophis asks.

"Yes," Idyn answers, peering around the large city's gorgeous silver landscape. "He says, unless we can find another source for the reactors 'Violet Fuel', we will most likely be forced to make some difficult decisions in the near future. Considering our current method of obtaining it, I tend to believe him."

"He is most likely correct," Sophis says.

"Yea, he's rarely wrong," Idyn states, smiling. "Something you two have in common. With that being said, it's the only source of energy this city's little bioreactor will accept. So, we don't really have a choice, we got to do what we got to do." Sophis nods in agreement. "If only the reactor was less picky, it would make things much, much easier."

"It would," Sophis agrees. "It is strange that, whomever may have built this city, chose a bioreactor as its primary energy source to begin with. With so many other viable options, why a bioreactor? It's quite intriguing."

"Sure, intriguing," Idyn says, rolling his large light blue eyes. "I do believe you had suggested that this 'whomever' was some ancient culture from Vyn. They either weren't aware of those other options, or took it upon themselves to be difficult."

"Why yes, all of that may indeed be true." Sophis laughs admiring the bright lights of the city. "Considering the moss grows only on Vyn, it does make it plausible the city's architects came from the planet. No matter what, whoever it was, was obviously quite advanced for their time. This is quite the achievement."

"It's a moon, Sophis," Idyn states somewhat sarcastically, gesturing to the surrounding scene. "They simply cut a huge hole out of it and stuck a city inside."

"I suppose that's true," Sophis says, looking up at the dark rocky ceiling of the artificially carved out cavern far above them.

"Well, in any case, here we are." Idyn chuckles. "Feeding a reactor to sustain the city we live in." He laughs as they advance toward a silver structure alongside the expressway. "When I thought about the future, this isn't how I imagined it. Close, but not quite."

Sophis smiles as they take a seat on one of the two cherry colored leather-like couches at the roadside pickup station, S37. A glass pane stretches out at an angle above from the solid red wall at their backs somewhat enclosing the pair of sofas. They set their gaze in front of them at the passing hover-crafts briefly, as a bus-like hover vehicle pulls up at the pickup's curbside.

The white oval-shaped craft stops and extends a small ramp from beneath the doors at its center. The brothers board the long glass topped transit, taking a seat next to each other within one of the many bleached comfortable chairs. The fully automated bus retracts its ramp while closing its doors, then returns to the fast-paced Orphan Highway.

"I hate taking these things," Idyn comments, inputting their destination into the blue holographic screen projecting from the back of the seat in front of him.

"As many times as we have taken this trip." Sophis glances over at Idyn. "One would think you'd be used to this by now."

"Thank you, Sophis," Idyn says, with a slight smile, focusing on the display before him. "I appreciate that," he says, as the projection disappears. "And there we go, off to the Speran."

Sophis watches quietly as the city passes by outside the window he sits next to. Idyn always sits next to the narrow aisle of the transit, allowing Sophis to have the window seat. It was custom for Flunari offspring to go their separate ways after leaving their naris, or parents. To not do so, went directly against their culture and was often met with the young being disowned and abandoned. Idyn knew however, Sophis wouldn't have survived long on his own, and took it upon his shoulders to look over him. The price you may ask? They were outcast, and Idyn was publicly shunned nearly everywhere he went on their homeworld, Malorad.

"How is that project you've been working on for the Fitura?" Idyn asks. "Any new developments?"

"Yes," Sophis answers excitedly, removing his gaze from the viewpoint and turning to Idyn. "I believe I have solved the problem. I will know for sure once I acquire a subject and test it. Would you care to volunteer?"

"I would love to." Idyn smiles.

Sophis' mind worked quite a bit differently than most others of his species, well, most others of any species. It's that fact for the most part, which led to Idyn making the decision to look after him, against their naris' wishes. It didn't take long for him to realize how Sophis' intellect, although amazing, was not going to protect him from the brawn commonly found among the Flunari. Malorad is an eat or be eaten type of world and Sophis, well, he was going to be eaten.

Soon after his fateful decision, Idyn began searching for a residence outside of Malorad. He met Mr. Nix after a while on Solarius, a nice enough character, who introduced him to Natasha, who just so happened to be from a little place known as Orphan City. And the rest? Well, let's just say, it worked out.

"Once you fix the issue and complete her project," Idyn says. "Maybe you could continue working on Mezrich for me?"

"I have been," Sophis says. "A bit here and there. He's actually quite complex. I will complete him though, I promise."

"I know you will," Idyn says confidently, "I have no doubt."

"Do you believe the Fitura will appreciate the device?" Sophis asks, as the transit comes to a stop.

"I do," Idyn answers, as a few passengers exit and afterwards the craft returns to the expressway. "I believe it's going to be very useful. There are just way too many obvious advantages to having it. A cloaking device that allows you to be anyone you want?" He shakes his head grinning. "I'm sure she's going to be quite impressed, I know I am."

"Almost anyone." Sophis smiles. "There are limits, although not many."

"Sure." Idyn chuckles, as the craft slows heading for the S1 pickup station along the roadside.

Sophis looks out at the tall blue windowed Speran as the bus comes to a halt. A heavily guarded pale stone wall surrounds the white triangular complex, and the green pasture it sits within. The many colorful blooms of the different alien plants and streams flowing around them, make it one of Orphan City's most beautiful sights to behold. The city's elected leader, the Fitura, calls this place home. That figure, for over a year now, has been a Yonalitu by the name of Natasha.

"Should I tell her about it?" Sophis asks, looking over at Idyn.

"No," Idyn says, stepping out into the aisle. "Once it's complete sure, but only then though." He gestures Sophis in front of himself. "After you."

Sophis does as his brother instructs, and steps out into the aisle before him. They step out of the hover-craft and stand on the stone sidewalk staring over the white wall at the Speran in the distance. It's the only location in the entire city built almost completely out of stone. Similar to most of the city's structures, it was constructed using a seemingly-aware self-repairing metal and glass. It's an ancient technology, even the city's brightest minds have yet to successfully replicate it. Sophis has tinkered with the concept, but even he is unable to fully comprehend it.

"I wonder what it must be like to live here?" Idyn ponders out loud.

"I bet it's amazing," Sophis says.

"It kind of has to be."

The bus returns onto the roadway, as Sophis follows Idyn, who walks alongside the wall for the secured entrance of the compound. The center of the boundary slopes inward leading to the Speran's only entrance, a solid bus-wide silver rectangular blast door. A couple of cameras sit on either side of the large door, one of them pans the area in front of the busy expressway while the other points toward the complex's entrance.

A few of the Speran's Militia peer down from atop the wall as the Flunaris approach. More often than not, you will find they are the red skinned Grogans of Enyigo. Their black armor and matching helmets hide their appearance. It is common with the majority of the complex's guards.

As the brothers reach the gateway, a white hologram appears within it, declaring, "State your business."

"Idyn and Sophis Wonax," Idyn states, while they each present a spinning yellow holo-identification within their open palms. "Here as requested by the Fitura."

The hologram dissipates as the large entrance splits into thirds and slowly opens. Sophis stares up at the Speran Soldiers before continuing with Idyn through the doorway. They begin their long trek toward the Speran on the cobblestone pathway through the beautiful environment, as the entrance closes behind them.

⊜ 17

The Wonax brothers step off the cobblestone path onto the short stone staircase before a large plaza in front of the Speran. They continue across the white concrete of the courtyard, admiring the huge fountain and pond at its center as they stroll around its base. Idyn waves to the two Speran Militia standing at the complex's entrance while Sophis watches the colorful fish within the clear pond. He looks up from the aquatic lifeforms swimming lazily about, then trails behind his brother for the Speran's entrance.

As usual, the Grogan Untako was on duty. He lives within the complex and rarely wears a helmet. It's not like it's mandatory or anything, just sorta rare to see among the Speran soldiers. Idyn told Sophis the Flunari and Grogans were not known to get along, upon noticing the abundance of them when they first arrived into the city. It quickly became clear however, this was not the case here. Probably for the best, considering the majority of the Orphan Militia is Grogan.

"The Wonax brothers," Untako exclaims as they approach, the Grogan's triangular dark blue face grinning.

"Yep," Idyn says, smiling back. "Guilty as charged. How have you been, Tak?"

"I'm well," Untako answers. "Yourself?"

"Good, actually," Idyn says, as the other helmeted Speran Guard approaches. "Quite good."

"You know the drill," the soldier states, as Idyn and Sophis stand before them with their arms raised. "All molecular technologies on or within your holo-system will be deactivated once inside the Speran. This is your last chance to retrieve anything you may need while within the complex," he explains, holding a Binox and viewing its projected screen, as it scans each of them in a wave of blue light. "Clear," the soldier declares to Untako, after the scan completes and the blue screen of the black box disappears.

"Business as usual?" Untako asks, while advancing toward the Speran's single door entrance.

"I believe so," Idyn says, strolling behind him as Sophis follows closely.

Untako places his hand on the green pad at the door's side, opening it. Sophis rarely spoke during these times. He isn't much of a social individual, shying away from most interactions if he can get away with it. His brother on the other hand is definitely the opposite, quite talkative, popular, and confident. All of them are traits Sophis lacks.

"Idyn, Sophis," Untako says, slightly bowing to the pair.

"Untako," Idyn says, while he and Sophis slightly bow back and then pass through the open door of the Speran.

The entrance closes behind them as they walk onto the complex's main glass-like reflective white floor. A large beautiful clear chandelier sits above them as they head for the Speran's check-in counter. Sophis peers back at the courtyard behind them as they advance forward.

The walls of the Speran were different from most others. On the outside of the compound they were solid white, but on the inside they were completely clear, appearing to be made of glass. The Speran's walls also seem to be unbreakable, in fact as far as they were concerned, they're indestructible, just like most of the ancient city. The whole city to this very day, seems to be aware, it took a while to get used to that fact alone. Even now, as he stares through them at the fountain, he can't help but feel, they are watching. The entire city is watching.

Sophis and Idyn approach the single representative known as Valex, standing behind a white counter. Being a Ventriku, a peaceful species from the waterlogged moon of Ortikil, which orbits the planet Zandrashi, he is unique in many ways. He's quite special, quite special indeed. He's of the only known waterborne species, who also happens to bear one of the longest lifespans in the universe. Having both gills and lungs, the Ventriku are not bound to the water in any way. They could decide to live their entire lives terrestrially, as Valex has. Most however, prefer the aquatic lifestyle.

"Valex," Idyn greets, looking into his dark violet face.

"Sir." Valex nods, as the tendrils hanging from the corner of his mouth sway with the motion. "Good to see you again."

"You as well," Idyn say, as Valex's orange eyes search through the blue screen projecting from the countertop before him. "We have been summoned by the Fitura."

"It does appear to be so," Valex says, interacting with the projection. "The lift is now available, sir. Hope all goes well."

"Thank you," Idyn says, as he and Sophis nod and advance for the open elevator to the left of the check-in. "Oh, you may find this interesting. Nix had said a few days ago, while we were at the Gabbin," he tells Sophis, as they step inside the bright silver interior of the elevator. "That the Fitura had granted Stet that locator, he requested." Sophis gives his brother a somewhat surprised look, as the door slides shut and the lift ascends. "Yea, said he was the one who delivered it."

"That is interesting." Sophis pauses, and adds, "Also unwise, did he give a reason, as to why?"

"No." Idyn chuckles. "And I didn't ask, it was a quick comment. We were drinkin', talkin' to Gynn, you know how we can get. Didn't really think about it 'till much later."

The elevator slows and comes to a stop. It slides open revealing Natasha's secretary Shea, a Yonalitu, sitting behind her beautiful opal desk directly before the elevator. It probably made the Fitura's job easier having a secretary of the same species as herself. She is clearly awaiting their arrival, with her bright green eyes staring down upon them as they walk out onto the level's blue carpeted floor. To their right, past Shea's post, sits several potted plants continuing down the Speran's clear outer wall, while on their left, is a short white corridor leading to Natasha's office.

"The Fitura has been expecting you," she states, traveling around the counter.

"We are aware," Idyn says somewhat sarcastically, his circular light brown face looking up at her and smiling. "You look great. How have you been?"

"If you would," she says, while walking to the Fitura's office, implying they follow.

The Wonax brothers trail behind the lavender-skinned white-haired Shea as she escorts them to Natasha's office. The Yonalitu of Halovom weren't the tallest in the city, but they certainly were close. They, like the Flunari, are very similar in appearance to one another, making it sometimes difficult for other species to differentiate between individuals. Idyn has a thing for Shea and Sophis does not fully understand why. It logically makes no sense, but this is the case with his brother, a lot of the time.

"You have any plans later?" Idyn asks, as they stop before the Fitura's office.

"I do," she answers, obviously not interested as its door slides open.

"Thank you, Shea," Natasha says, sitting behind her black desk within the large clear walls of her office. "Please, come in." She gestures to the brothers while Shea nods and heads back down the short corridor to her post. "Well, I hope your trip here was good," she says, as they walk onto the shiny dark floor, admiring the gorgeous view of the city over top the green trees outside.

"It was, Ms. Fitura," Idyn says, sitting with Sophis in the maroon chairs across from her.

"I'm happy to hear that," she says, scrolling through one of the white screens built into the surface of the large boomerang shaped desk. "Now, the reason for why you are here. So, not too long ago, I'm sure you have heard." She looks across at Idyn. "I had granted Stet the locator he had been requesting. In return, he was to get together a set of codes, enough to last us quite a while. Which he did, allowing us to bypass his place on Niushki and head straight to Vyn."

"That's good," Idyn comments.

"Agreed," Natasha says. "Only issue is, between then and now, the Olensi have apparently upgraded their satellites, and in doing so, have changed the pass codes. Rendering the ones Stet had issued us, useless." Sophis and Idyn look at each other as she explains, knowing what is to come. "He has agreed to replace the codes, with a new set."

"As he should," Idyn states.

"He has the new set," she says, "And is currently waiting for you two to retrieve them."

"When do we leave?" Idyn asks.

"As soon as you can," she answers, as a long silver cylindrical object materializes above the screen in front of her. "Here is your locator," she states, gesturing to the device floating above her desk between them.

"Short and sweet," Idyn says, taking the locator and standing.

"Remember, he is not to be trusted," she reminds them, as they slightly bow respectfully before her.

"Yes, of course, Ms. Fitura," Idyn says, before leaving the office with Sophis.

⊖ 18

Idyn's small teal-bodied starship, the Scyther, descends onto a landing pad near a dome stone structure. The bay's white lights come alive tracing its square outline, welcoming the compact ship's descent. Above the complex hovers a violet sign reading, Stet's Place.

"This should be fun." Idyn smiles at Sophis as the Scyther settles onto the bay.

"I suppose so," Sophis says, glancing up at the slowly rotating sign.

The brothers saunter out of the small side door of the triangular ship. They step down onto the silver platform and venture out into the white dust of the moon. Mountains fill the dark landscape as large sitadoom fly overhead within the endless star filled sky. A howling wind rolls through, as they head for the dull colored building.

The structure's sliding door opens as they near, revealing the violet saturated room behind it. Wooden tables populate the open room as the compound's entrance slides shut behind them. The few ant-like Scuts sitting about the area acknowledge the brothers entrance. Stet, the head honcho of the place, watches from within a barred bar from across the room. Sophis follows as Idyn advances through the tables over to the circular counter the Balgorex stands behind.

Besides Gynn, the Balgorex residing in Orphan City, the four eyed thick bodied species was definitely not to be trusted. They are infamous throughout all corners of the known universe. Their only upside, as far as Sophis was concerned, is they are from the planet Tresindom. The planet itself is normal enough, but it's binary star system, not so much. Idyn peers up into Stet's four eyes through the metal bars separating them.

"How's it goin'?"

"Not too bad," Stet answers. "How 'bout yourself?"

"Pretty good," Idyn says. "Well as usual, we are here by request of the Fitura."

"Straight to business, I like it," Stet says, while Sophis admires the dark wooden shelving unit behind him. "Well, you ready?" Stet asks, placing his hand face up on the stone countertop.

"I am," Idyn says, positioning his small brown hand beside Stet's bulky tannish one.

Sophis watches beside Idyn as they activate their molecular inventories. Stet retrieves the pass codes, then transfers them over to Idyn with a single swipe. The entire process takes a mere moment, and is over almost as soon as it begins.

"Thank you." Idyn nods at Stet while they deactivate their holo-systems.

"Pleasure doing business with you," Stet says, with a tip of his hat. "Come back anytime."

Sophis and Idyn slightly bow, then stroll back to the entrance of the complex. Their dark skin appears burgundy under the violet light of the place. Sophis' light blue eyes peer around the room while the Scuts watch the brothers' every move. Idyn subtly stretches his long neck, extending his small face through the open door of Stet's Place, before walking back out onto the white dust of Niushki. Sophis looks back at Stet one last time, before waddling through after his brother.

"That wasn't so hard," Idyn says, casually heading for the Scyther as Sophis follows.

"That was surprisingly easy," Sophis states. "I will say that, although he may appear to be rather suspicious, he actually has been quite helpful. I may have only dealt with him a couple of times, but overall he doesn't seem too terrible."

"Yea, well, don't let him fool you, Sophis," Idyn says, looking over his shoulder while boarding the ship. "It's the nice ones you should be worried about." He steps onto the vessel with Sophis close behind. "You know for being so smart, you are a terrible judge of character."

"Thank you," Sophis says sarcastically, as they sit next to each other before the ship's tinted viewport.

"We'll work on it." Idyn lightly punches Sophis' shoulder as the Scyther's interior white lights activate. "Fitura," he says loudly, as the vessel launches.

"Were you successful in the retrieval?" Natasha asks, appearing as a blue hologram within the front window of the ship.

"Everything went smoothly," Idyn answers, as the Scyther leaves the moon's atmosphere. "We're en-route with the package, we'll be arriving shortly," he adds, while Sophis inserts the locator into the center console.

"Very well," she says, then fades away as the ship jumps into hyperspace.

⊜ 19

Sophis emerges from a dark stone passageway into a large cavern, he's been here many times. The city's bioreactor's violet fuel can be found growing on the walls of this specific cave as a luminescent moss. Idyn found it strange and doubted such an advanced species would base the entire livelihood of the Orphan City on it, considering how rare the moss is. It has been found only on Vyn and absolutely nowhere else, and it's not for a lack of searching. So his doubt, was warranted, but nonetheless, they apparently did.

A small grove sits in the grotto's center surrounded by many rock formations, while the waterfall at the cave's mouth bellows. Sophis has always enjoyed this place, he finds it quite relaxing and rather beautiful. He notices a shimmer out of the corner of his blue eyes, strange, there seems to be something lying upon the wet ground of the grove. The Flunari makes his way down the rock platform onto the swampy terrain, and waddles for it.

As he nears the collection of small trees, it becomes apparent it's a cube of sorts. He continues strolling into the green marsh, and crouches at the side of the box, as the cascade roars. He recognizes the tech, it's definitely Oteniko. It appears to be a containment cube, a common device mostly used by its R&D Division. Idyn would agree, if he were here, but he's not.

"Why hello," a hauntingly somewhat sarcastic voice says.

Startled, he rises quickly. "Um... ah oh-hello there." His heart drops upon making eye contact with the voice's owner. *It's an Akiko, this can't be good*, he thinks to himself.

Its small yellow eyes glare while it grins menacingly. The violent Akiko's large fearsome bone extrusions are even more frightening now seeing them for himself.

What is it doing here, how did it get here? He asks himself, as a Cerulean paces quickly toward the Akiko from behind. *This is definitely strange. Is she with the Akiko? That would be an odd relationship.*

"How is it going?" the Akiko asks, glancing down at the empty containment cube between them as the female Cerulean strolls up alongside it.

"You're a Flunari," she comments, her violet eyes stunningly gorgeous. "What are you doing here?"

"Well, I... I was." Sophis stumbles over his words, "Cond... conducti... ah yes, conducting some um...." He's unsure of what to say, the Flunari hasn't been in this type of situation before.

"What is your name?" the Akiko asks, clearly hostile.

"Oh ah... my name?" Sophis says, gesturing to himself terrified.

"I suppose I could be referring to the Flunari behind you," the Akiko answers threateningly, almost appearing to have said it jokingly.

He looks behind him, just to be sure. "Th-there's... there's... there's not ah." He turns back to the Akiko, and says, "There isn't anyone behind me, good sir."

"I am aware," the Akiko says, in a very serious tone.

"My name... is Sophis. I am a... Sophis."

"I've heard that name before," the Cerulean says, looking over at the Akiko. "Where have I heard that name?"

The Cerulean did seem familiar, had they met before? Whatever the case, it had become apparent however, she and the Akiko did have some sort of relationship.

She speaks to it as if... no, that can't be right. None of this makes sense, he debates with himself.

"Pleasure to meet you, Sophis." The Akiko slightly bows without taking his sight off Sophis. "I am Jadecan, may I ask what business you might be... how did you put it again," he says, straightening his stance almost as if it was mocking the Flunari. "What business you might be conducting, good sir. Yes, that is it. I believe that was the term you so elegantly used."

"I was, ah... I am," Sophis says, rather put back by the Akiko's vocabulary, which is to him, quite impressive. "Collecting some of... well sir, I was... I was collecting some of this... this moss, you see here... glowing around us."

"Why? For whom?" the Cerulean asks, then retracts the question almost immediately. "Actually never mind. May I see your clearance I.D.?"

"My... my clearance I.D.?" Sophis asks, clearly out of options, he's going to have to do something.

"I don't think he's supposed to be here," the Cerulean says to the Akiko beside her.

"No no, ah... yes um," Sophis says, searching about himself. "I have it here... I have it here somewhere... It's ah...."

As the Akiko glances over at the Cerulean, the Flunari activates his trusty S-I holo-weapon. A unique creation of his own which fires his own special projectiles. Sophis, unlike most others in this everyone-for-themselves type of universe, is not a killer. The Akiko before him though, surely was. As such, he spent a good bit of time and resources creating different things, the Orphan Class S-I Tranquilizers are one of those things. It's named after his brother and himself, the Sophis-Idyn Darts, or in short, the S-I Darts.

He quickly fires a single dart at both the Cerulean and the Akiko, striking them each in the chest. The Cerulean immediately crumbles, the Akiko at her side however, barely even flinches. It glares angrily at Sophis, whilst pulling the tranq from its chest. The Flunari stands shaking in front of the Akiko, his weapon still poised and pointing as it grins before him. Without warning, it spins, and Sophis instinctively places his hands out in front of him in defense of the Akiko.

Sophis screams in anguish as he falls to the wet ground, his right hand and forearm that once held the holo-weapon no longer a part of his body. The arm has been cut off by the violent Akiko with a single slice, it now lies in the mud just to the side of the attacker. The Flunari looks up from the flat of his back into its cold yellow eyes while whimpering afraid and suffering.

"I suspected I would end up killing you," the Akiko states, while activating its own holo-weapon and pointing it at his head.

He is going to die here, right here in the marsh... then miraculously the Akiko glances away from him once again, checking on the unconscious Cerulean behind him. It must really care or, well, how could the Akiko have known what Sophis was about to do. The Flunari retrieves a small device from his holo-system, a short range teleporter, another unique invention of his. He presses the red button in its center and instantly teleports to the top of the waterfall.

Sophis lies upon the lush green grass beside the river in front of what was once his brother's ship, the Scyther. He glances at his missing hand and forearm, then cries painfully as he stares up at Niushki, sitting in Vyn's waning blue sky. The cascade roars whilst Sophis slowly stands and heads for the small teal bodied starship resting behind him. A ramp folds out from beneath an opening door on the vessel's side.

Idyn loved this ship. Sophis collapses, and sobs at the thought.

"I m... m-miss you," he weeps, lying on the silver floor of the compact vessel. "I'm s...s-sorry, I'm so-sorry."

♀ Part Three: The Wanderer

"For even the greatest of horrors irony is seldom absent." - H.P. Lovecraft.

♀ White Star

⊖ 1

Jadecan stands before Captain Tytus who sits behind his desk, in front of his quarter's large curved window. They talked for a while, and although the captain's not pleased with the sequence of events that happened on the planet, he was willing to set it aside, giving the Akiko the benefit of the doubt. Jadecan stares at Tytus through the blue projection above the tabletop, as the stars twinkle in the blackness behind him.

"After returning to the Olensi Compound O-56." Tytus reads from the blue screen before him, his large curled horns shining in the bright light of the room. "You both returned to the release point, to confirm that the creature, cheiket sp. 1-4-3, was released successfully. Is that correct?"

"Yes," Jadecan answers. "That is correct."

"Upon returning to the release point, and confirming the successful release of cheiket sp. 1-4-3, you became aware of the Flunari, later identified as Sophis. Is that also correct?" Tytus asks, taking his amber eyes off the screen to look at Jadecan.

"Yes, it is."

Tytus stares at Jadecan for a few moments and then returns to the screen. "You then approach Sophis and proceed to interrogate. After a brief interaction, in an attempt to escape, he fires, from an unidentified holo-weapon, two Orphan Class S-I Tranquilizers, striking both Amelia and yourself. Resulting in the sedation of Amelia, with yourself being unaffected." He looks up from the projection. "Is that right?"

"It is."

"That's a strong sedative, impressive." Jadecan nods in response. "You then attacked Sophis, cutting off his right hand and forearm in the process. He then disappears right before your eyes," Tytus says, looking up from the screen. "He disappears right before your eyes, is that right?"

"Yes."

"Interesting, that's new," Tytus comments. "You proceed to check on Amelia, and carry her back, unconscious, to your starship. After which, you return here. Is all that correct?"

"Yes."

"Hmm." Tytus sighs sitting back in his chair and crossing his arms, staring at Jadecan.

"Where is Amelia now?" Jadecan asks, after a few moments of silence.

"She is currently under the care of her doctor," Tytus answers.

"Doctor who?"

"Dr. Leeus."

Jadecan nods. "I see. How is she?"

"She is awake and recovering, as we speak," Tytus answers. "She is fine, my boy."

"May I see her?"

"After we are done here." Tytus clasps his large hands on his desk. "Had you and Sophis met before?"

"No."

"Have you had any type of communication or interaction with Sophis, directly or indirectly, at anytime before or after the events that took place on Vyn?"

"No, not that I am aware of."

The captain pauses for a moment, then asks, "It is my understanding that you knew the individual known as Stet Stal, is that true?"

"I did," Jadecan answers. "What does he have to do with this?"

"Is it true you killed him?"

"It is."

"What was your relationship with Mr. Stal?" Tytus asks.

"Complicated. I fail to see what he has to do with this."

"What exactly did Mr. Stal do on Niushki?" the captain asks.

"I am not sure, mainly buying and selling items of interest," he answers. "What does it matter?"

"It matters, because it's believed that he could have been supplying the Orphan with clearance codes. And if that is indeed accurate, it would explain how Sophis has been bypassing our satellites."

Jadecan stares inquisitively at Tytus. "Orphan? What is the Orphan?"

"The Orphan City, my boy," the captain answers. "Have you not heard of the Orphan?"

"I have not."

Captain Tytus sits quietly, his long light hair flowing over his broad shoulders while his golden face stares at Jadecan, obviously deep in thought. "Dr. Santer tells me, you are nearly a century old. In all that time, you have not once heard of the Orphan?"

"I have not."

"Well, the Orphan is an orphaned moon, do you know what that is?"

"No."

"In a nutshell, it's a moon that has escaped the bonds of its planetary neighbors. It's not unique in that regard, there are many orphaned moons, my boy. This one specifically, however, happens to also have had a city built inside it, known as Orphan City. It's the only one of its kind that we know of. It is a known fact, that Sophis comes from there."

"Why not go there and ask them?" Jadecan asks.

The captain chuckles. "We would if we could. You see, unlike the planet, or your moon Niushki, an orphaned moon's not easily found. They are speeding through the cosmos at extraordinary speeds, making them extremely difficult to locate, but not impossible."

"How does Sophis find this orphaned moon? If he is indeed from this Orphan City, like you say."

"It's rumored," Tytus answers. "That they have created a device that allows the user to locate and travel to it. This device, if our intel is correct, is known as a locator. It's assumed that your friend Stet may have, within his collection, one such device."

"I know nothing of this locator," Jadecan states. "I also want nothing to do with it."

"Fair enough." The captain smiles. "I suppose we are done here then. You are free to go."

"Where can I find Amelia?"

"She is on the L&M Deck. I'll have Commander Resean escort you to her room."

"Thank you," he says.

Jadecan turns to leave and as he does, Tytus says, "I appreciate everything that you've done for her, Jadecan. You have saved her life twice now. That's a debt I don't think I could ever repay." The captain pauses briefly. "I will not forget it."

⊜ 2

Commander Resean and Jadecan sit upon one of the purple velvet couches in the black room of the L&M deck waiting for Dr. Leeus. The sofa they sit upon is the same one Amelia and he had sat on while they waited for Dr. Santer. He stares over at the room's silver entryway briefly, before setting his eyes on the Olensi inside the enclosure at the room's center.

Moments later, the entrance slides open, revealing a Cerulean wearing a long white coat. He's the tallest and skinniest Cerulean Jadecan has seen thus far, not as tall as a Yonalitu, like Meshel, but tall nonetheless. He strolls out of the entryway toward them, his robotic left leg is much quieter than one would have suspected as he walks across the shiny black floor.

"Commander Resean, Jadecan," the Cerulean greets. "I am Dr. Leeus."

Jadecan bows slightly, looking into his dull colored eyes. "Hello doctor," he says, noticing the doctor's broken left horn. "How are you?"

"I am well," Leeus answers. "Thank you for asking. I hope you are, too."

"I am."

"Good, good." The doctor looks at Resean, and says, "Commander, I'll take it from here, thank you."

"Very well." Resean nods, and says to Jadecan before leaving, "I hope all goes well."

The doctor and Jadecan watch as the commander leaves through the short black walled corridor disappearing around its sharp corner. "This way, Jadecan," Leeus says, heading for the silver door. "Please, follow me."

"How is she?" Jadecan asks, walking slightly behind the tall light skinned Cerulean.

"She is fine," Leeus answers, sauntering through the doorway. "There appears to be no ill side effects. She will remain here for a couple more days however, it's in her best interest."

Jadecan follows Leeus down the bright hall toward two Olensi seated behind a white counter. They look up briefly, as the pair enter the tiny room at the corridor's mouth. Amelia and he walked this same route with Dr. Santer, but instead of traveling down the short hallway on the room's left wall, they trek down the one across from it. Dr. Leeus approaches the silver door at its end and hovers his wrist over the green pad at its side, opening it.

"Welcome to the Medical Wing," Leeus states, strolling through the open door whilst Jadecan trails close behind.

They walk out onto the grey floor of the bay, alongside the wing's administrative counter. Many Ceruleans, all presumably doctors in long white coats, busily walk about the large room, their voices resonating within its pale walls. Numbered rooms line the wall on their right side as they continue past the silver counter. Jadecan follows as the doctor makes for the hallway ahead of them.

"She is in bay 22," the doctor says over his shoulder, as they casually pass by the rooms now running on either side of them.

Jadecan takes a mental note of the numbers on his right, which are as follows: *12, 14, 16, 18, 20, 22.*

"Here we are," Leeus states, knocking on the bay's door. "Amelia, it's Dr. Leeus. I am here with your friend, Jadecan, may we come in?"

"Yes, of course," she answers from inside.

Dr. Leeus enters the room with Jadecan. "How are you feeling, my dear?" he asks Amelia, walking up to her bedside.

"I feel fine, doctor." She smiles. "Best I've felt in a while."

"I'm glad to hear it," Leeus says. "Your test results came back great, you're in good health. As expected however, traces of the S-I sedative are still present within your system. With that being said, it should be completely gone within a few hours. So, it's nothing to be alarmed about."

"That's good," Amelia says.

"Agreed. Okay, any questions before I leave you two?"

"No," Amelia says. "Thank you, doctor."

"You're very welcome." Leeus nods, then says to Jadecan, "I have taken the liberty of checking you in myself. When you're done, please check out at the administrative counter."

"As you wish."

"Thank you." The doctor bows, and says to Amelia before leaving, "I'll be back later to check on you. Okay, I'll leave you two to catch up."

"How are you?" Jadecan asks, as Leeus leaves.

"Good," she answers. "I actually feel great. How are you? I hear the sedative had absolutely no effect on you."

"It did not," he says, standing at her bedside. "The captain as well, was intrigued by that."

"He would be." She laughs. "What does he think about all this?"

"I am not sure," he answers. "He was not happy but appeared to take it well. He also seemed more interested in Stet's connection to some Orphan City, than he was in Sophis. Was rather strange. Besides asking if I had met Sophis before the incident, he was not a big part of our conversation."

"Did he tell you Sophis is from Orphan City?"

"He did."

"I suppose he explained what the Orphan is?" she asks, he nods confirming. "Did he mention what Stet had to do with this?"

"Indeed. Something to do with a device known as a locator."

"Oh, really?" She raises an eyebrow. "Well, I guess it makes sense. It has been suggested that he may have been in cahoots with the Orphan."

"Really?" he asks surprised.

"Yea, I know, right? I mean honestly, I didn't think the Orphan would realistically associate with someone like Stet. But if desperate enough, for whatever reason, I guess they could have. I suppose they had no other options? I dunno." She shrugs.

"What does it matter?"

"Well, it matters." Amelia lets out a small laugh. "The Olensi have been trying to unravel that mystery for quite some time."

"Interesting."

"It is that," she agrees. "From what I understand of Sophis though, he's actually pretty gentle, considering he's a Flunari and all, outside of him, of course, shooting us both." She laughs amused. "Although, I mean, gentle or not, it doesn't resolve him of knowingly trespassing on classified Olensi territory, on numerous occasions. I mean, this isn't his first time. The punishment, if caught, could be quite severe. Like, they may kill him, severe."

"I see, but who is Sophis?"

"Hmm." She sighs. "I'm not entirely sure, he's a lot like me in some ways. I had forgotten that I had actually met him on Solarius, many years ago." She explains, "I remember he was very intelligent, a bit odd, but smart nonetheless. At the time, I had just recently met Lenora, who was going through a rough breakup with...." She ponders for a few moments. "I think his name was Six, or something like that. He actually worked at Oteniko, alongside her father, which is how they had apparently met."

"The same Oteniko as this?" he asks, retrieving the Oteniko Badge Meshel had given him.

"Yep, the same place," she answers. "But anyway, what was I saying again? Oh yea, right.... So, this Six character was good friends with Sophis' brother, so naturally we knew of each other. But it's not like we were close or anything, you know? That's pretty much the extent of my relationship with him."

"I see."

"Anyways," she says, with a smile. "What are you going to do? Considering I'm kind of stuck here, not able to do much of anything, at all."

"I am not certain," he answers. "I may return to the Kiwiwa, see how Yano is doing. May even stop by the Oteniko outpost."

"Are you going to come back? Will I see you again?" she asks.

"I will return in a couple cycles. Maybe I will go with you to see Lenora. There is a good chance I will go, if you would like."

"I would like that." She smiles. "I would like that a lot."

⊖ 3

Baby settles onto the white dust of Niushki outside of Ruogji Yano's Kiwiwa village. The cool aroma of the moon rides the subtle winds, welcoming Jadecan, as he steps onto the desolate terrain. Yano stands in front of a few Kiwiwa, awaiting him. The thick smoke of the village's fire bellows in the distance, as the shadows of its flames dance upon the surrounding stone huts.

The pink short haired 1-4-3 rests upon Jadecan's shoulder purring quietly, its long black tail wrapped around his neck. The Olensi had decided to let the Akiko keep the creature, as thanks for his saving of Amelia. A nice gesture, one he much appreciated.

"Caspa Runuoscha," Yano greets, as a herd of juguke roam about dragging their bellies whilst foraging around the ship.

"Caspa Ruogji," Jadecan says, with a slight bow.

The Akiko follows Yano and his fellow Kiwiwa family toward the village, while a few large sitadoom circle overhead. As they stroll closer he notices a familiar stranger, a Drakon, seated among the Kiwiwa on the sitting rocks in the community's center. The red flames of the fire glow upon its dark green reptilian skin as Vyn stares from the horizon.

"Geoth," Yano says, gesturing in the direction of the sitting rocks with his Kiwi Staff as they enter the village. "Kafeha leshu wu odfe kafe, Runuoscha."

"I see," he says, venturing for the sitting rocks alongside Yano and gently petting the small head of the cheiket. "Hey buddy, what do you think of Niushki?"

"Why hello, Jade," the Drakon greets, her small white eyes watching as they approach. "It is good to see you."

"Good to see you as well, Sycora," Jadecan says, sitting on the stone beside her, as Yano places himself on the one next to him. "It has been a long time. How have you been?"

"Still here." She smiles. "I see you haven't changed a bit. Who's your friend?" she asks, referring to the creature lying on his shoulder.

After a few moments, he answers, while looking at 1-4-3, "I think I may call him Buddy. I am not sure." He boops the cheiket, and asks it, "What do you think?"

"I think it's a great name," Sycora says, looking at the pink haired creature. "Hey there, Buddy."

"Why are you here?" he asks, loosening Buddy's tail still wrapped around his neck.

"Searching for you," she answers, staring into Buddy's black face, whose large eyes stare back curiously. "He's a cute one. Where did you find him?"

"It is a long story," he says, returning his gaze to the fire before him. "Why have you been searching for me?"

"Well, as it happens, I may have heard a bit of gossip, involving you."

"Yea, like what?"

"Well, rumor has it, you're responsible for killing Stet. Would that be true?"

"It is," he answers, watching as the Kiwiwa converse with each other around the fire. "What of it?"

"What of it?" She laughs. "Well, for one, Jahrei isn't very happy about it."

"He most likely is not."

"He definitely is not." She smiles. "He has put a Death Mark upon you, and is willing to pay a good many units for your head."

"Is that so, how many?"

"Enough." She nods with wide eyes.

"Are you here to collect?"

"I was offered the opportunity," she says, laughing softly. "I didn't turn it down, I suppose I'm still deciding. We'll see. You know, besides being one of the most successful Balgorexes on Niushki, Stet was also respected by many, including Jahrei. No one is happy about this." She pauses, shaking her head. "They run this place, they have for as long as I can remember. It wasn't smart, Jade, there's a lot of characters that could really use those units. The Balgorex aren't ones to be trifled with, and yet, here we are."

"I appreciate you telling me," he says, as Yano is handed a stone bowl of Rumu Litafethi.

"It's not just Jahrei either. They're offering anyone, and I mean anyone, the opportunity. It's hard living, life here isn't easy you know."

Jadecan pats Buddy on the head. "It is not so bad," he says, while Yano sips the elixir and passes it to him. "It could be worse."

Sycora laughs softly, as he offers her the liquid mixture. "It is not so bad? It could be worse?" she says, clearly amused by the statement, while taking the bowl from him. "They aren't going to just kill you," she explains, smiling and sipping the concoction, then passes it to the Kiwiwa beside her. "They rarely ever do that. They are going to kill you, and then go after everyone close to you, but I guess you're right. Yea, it could be worse."

"Runuoscha," Yano asks, while a couple of Kiwiwa prepare a spit of juguke to roast across the flames. "Thianze hala dupaha or ohke thicheda eth?"

Niushki's wind gently blows as the Akiko stares at Vyn looming on the horizon. "Hami, Ruogji."

"Honestly, I've missed you. There was a time we were close," Sycora says, looking up at the moon's dark star filled sky. "I remember we used to stare up at them, watching them. We used to give them names. Those were good times." She smiles. "I miss them."

"I do as well," he says, lost in the dancing fire. "I do still think about them."

"I am sorry," she says, also looking into the orange flames. "I really am."

"I am too."

The pair sit in silence for many moments, as the flames crackle before them. Jadecan glances at the few sitadoom circling overhead remembering all too well the times Sycora and he had once shared, so long ago. Niushki's wind rolls through lifting the pale dust effortlessly as he exhales and closes his eyes, if for only a moment, in peace. He opens them quickly as Sycora swiftly swings a white holo-blade for his throat. Buddy hisses fiercely at the Drakon as Jadecan catches her hand.

"I do miss you," she says quietly.

"I know." He smiles holding her wrist.

The Kiwiwa look on silently as the two peer into each other's eyes. Jadecan grins widely before swiftly killing her with a single swipe of his bone blade. He watches as the starlight fades from her face and lets go of her hand. She slowly falls, leaning onto his shoulder lifeless.

♀ Crimson Mist

⊖ 4

Jadecan walks away from Baby who rests on the white dust behind him. The pink cheiket lies on his shoulder with its long black tail tightly wrapped around his neck as he heads for the gloomy stone complex of Along The Way. He glances up at the dim white lights of its square sign while he strolls for the entrance. Thunder rumbles on the horizon threatening Niushki's clear black sky while sitadoom stare down from atop the structure. He pulls open the glass door and enters, stepping onto the black carpet inside.

"Welcome cousin," Skall greets, his small watchful white eyes attentive within his dark green reptilian face.

"Hello cousin," Jadecan says, walking through the cream-colored lobby for the marbled front desk the Drakon stands behind.

"Room for one?"

"No, I will not be staying. I have come seeking your help."

"I see." Skall eyes the pink cheiket on Jadecan's shoulder. "How may I be of service?"

"What do you know of Jahrei?"

"What is it you wish to know?" Skall asks. "He is a Balgorex. He is also much more formidable than Stet. I believe they were close, like brothers. It is my understanding you killed Stet, is that correct?"

"Indeed," he answers without pause, "I did."

"I suppose you are here because Jahrei has put one of his infamous Death Marks upon you?"

"I am," Jadecan answers, retrieving a small slice of roasted juguke and feeding it to Buddy. "I am hoping you can help in some way to get rid of it."

"A Death Mark is difficult to remedy," Skall states. "It is possible, be it extremely difficult, but definitely possible."

"I understand."

Skall says after a few moments of silence, "Sycora had passed through here not too long ago, searching for you. She asked about your whereabouts. I of course, did not divulge such information. May I inquire if she found you?"

"You may," he answers. "She did."

"Was she after the Death Mark?"

"She was."

"Hmm, I see." Skall smiles after a few moments. "There may be a way to remove this mark, I must warn you though, it will not be easy."

"So you have said."

"You must first find the Coin Dealer," Skall says. "They will remove what has been placed upon you, but at a cost."

"Where can I find this so-called 'Coin Dealer'?"

"Within the Great Opening." Skall holds out his open scaly hand in front of Jadecan, and says, "You will need this." He smiles as a large gold coin materializes within his light green palm.

"What am I to do with this?" he asks, taking it from Skall's hand slowly.

"It is your payment," Skall answers. "They will accept nothing else. When they ask what it is you are doing there, reveal to them the gold coin."

"That is it?" he asks, studying the ancient looking dull coin.

"Yes." Skall nods, his white eyes gleaming in the lobby's yellow light.

The Akiko stares at it for a few moments intrigued at the concept. Both sides of the coin appear to be the same, each bearing the image of an oil lamp. He looks up at Skall as he stores it into his holo-system with a flash of blue light.

Jadecan slightly bows. "Thank you, cousin." He adds, grinning widely before turning away from the marble counter, "I will not forget this."

His shadow slowly disappears into the black carpet as he strides beneath the lobby's amber lights. "You are always welcome here," Skall states in a somber tone, as Jadecan arrives at the glass entrance.

He looks back at the dark green Drakon for a moment, then nods and pushes open the door, walking out into the pale dust. He paces for Baby underneath the star lit black sky as the planet looks on from the horizon. The once looming storm has passed, for now.

I do not trust him, Baby states.

"I do not either," he says, strolling up her dark ramp. "It is of no concern."

I believe he intends you harm. It is concerning.

"I understand your concern, but you need not worry. However, you are most likely correct," he says, stepping into the blue light of her deck while petting Buddy still perched on his shoulder. "Sycora was his sister, I expected nothing less. I would have done the same."

I disagree, you would have killed him.

"This is true."

What is it you intend to do?

"I intend to find this Coin Dealer, he speaks of," Jadecan answers, as Baby's interaction console appears below his outstretched palm.

"You surely are kidding," Baby says. "You can not be serious."

"I am serious."

Baby slowly rises, almost disappearing into the moon's black sky. The stars glimmer in her reflective dark body as sitadoom watch from atop the structure now below her. She hovers momentarily before speeding off in an instant for the Great Opening, leaving the dimly lit complex of Along The Way behind her.

⊖ 5

Baby lands beside a massive rock wall inside one of the moon's large craters. Her deck's blue light slightly dims, as Jadecan peers out at the large cave entrance carved into the daunting barrier before them, the Great Opening. He looks over into the black face of Buddy lying across his shoulder while loosening the cheiket's tail still wrapped around his neck.

"How about you stay here," he says, placing the pink furball on the seat next to him.

He watches as it yawns and curls up into the chair purring gently. Buddy's large white eyes struggle to stay open, before finally closing and drifting off to sleep. Jadecan walks out of the saucer and stands in the dark terrain of the crater as the saucer's ramp retracts.

Have you heard of this Coin Dealer before now? Baby asks.

"I have not," he answers, advancing toward the grand opening. "We shall see if they even exist."

Niushki's breath howls whilst sitadoom fly overhead. Their large webbed wings and long arrow-tipped tails streaming behind them as they glide on the moon's subtle winds. He stands before the Great Opening, then looks back at the ship briefly before venturing into the dark unknown beyond. The twilight of the surface slowly dissipates as the cave's entrance gradually becomes smaller with every step he takes deeper into the tunnel.

After a while of wandering through the eerily silent passageway, a crossroads begins to take shape ahead of him. Violet lights glow along the rough rock walls in the distance while the sound of dripping water echoes from ahead. He approaches the break in the tunnel and realizes the lights on its walls radiate from a moss growing upon them. The luminous flora reminds him of the growth within the grove he had met Sophis in, on Vyn. Could this be the same moss?

"Hmm," he utters, coming to a halt before the split.

A crumbling stone bridge across a giant chasm on his left, a continuous descent deeper into darkness on his right, not much of a choice. He strolls over to the wide broken cobblestone walkway and peers down from its edge into the endless void below. Across from him on the other side of the haunting depth waited nothing. Nothing, but the endless slate barrier of the chasm's walls, stretching for as far as the eye can see. The bridge appears to have led nowhere, broken or not.

"Interesting," he whispers.

A white hologram of the same small hooded individual from the dungeons entrance appears beside him. He recognizes it immediately.

"smuhruwshnohrng sgohrngshduh rehshguhwuhshduh wyu shkohrng shbuh woy tuw wohshfah rng shmharho shbuh wohtuw rowshmrngshduh woytuwwow shfhawuhtuw ruw shgow ruh tuwroh shfharow shfowrawtuw rho shkuhwyushkoh wih"

"Sure, why not."

He retrieves the large dull coin Skall had given him and reveals it to the hologram. The hologram abruptly disappears as a clear holographic bridge presents itself before him, completing the broken cobblestone walkway and connecting the two sides of the chasm. A torch blazes at the mouth of a narrow arched stone corridor now awaiting him on the other side, seemingly appearing out of nowhere. After a few moments he walks across, and upon reaching the crackling flames of the torch, he observes the bridge fading away behind him.

He ventures into the small grey hall for yet another blaze which has been placed before its sharp angled corner. The torch fire's shadow dances upon the stone block walls while illuminating them with its warm orange light. The Akiko traverses past the corner for the final torch and stone steps at the passageway's end. A large marble chamber presents itself as he stands peering up at its white ceiling from the foot of the staircase. Four large beautifully decorated pillars quickly become visible as he strolls up the stairs into the bright torch lit square room.

He pauses upon entering into the large area and glares at a small black lamp atop a pedestal in the room's center before him. Cautiously he walks toward it, expecting the unexpected. He peers around the reflective walls of the room, remembering the beast and glowing orb as he strolls ever closer, unsure of what his next step could bring. The gold trimmed black vessel now sits within his reach. He stops and admires the ancient oil lamp's intricate design briefly before slowly attempting to retrieve it from the pedestal.

As his fingers touch the lamp's beautiful dark glass, a violet mist streams upwards erupting from its mouth. There above the lamp now floats an exotic white being, a Shaitan, whose waist continues into the purple mist flowing from the spout of the vessel. Chains dangle from its large crossed arms and waist as it stares down upon the Akiko.

"I am Zliyek of Sibasheki. Who dares awaken me?" the Shaitan bellows.

"I am Jadecan of Niushki," he says confidently. "I have awakened you."

"Why have you awakened me, Jadecan of Niushki?"

"I wish to remove the Death Mark put upon me by the Balgorex Jahrei."

"Present Jahrei with the Cerulean Hulikon's head, and the Death Mark will be removed," Zliyek states loudly. "You have three days. If not done, your life will be forfeit."

"I do not accept those terms," Jadecan says strongly.

"You live on a placid island of ignorance, in the midst of black seas," Zliyek states loudly. "You have three days," he adds, vanishing back into the lamp. "If not done, your life will be forfeit."

"I do not think so," Jadecan angrily says, attacking the black lamp. "We are far from done here."

He attacks the device with everything he's got, over and over, getting angrier with every unsuccessful attempt. After several attempts and desperately trying to remove it from the pedestal with all of his strength, he stands tired and hopping mad before it. Fuming, he screams in a towering rage. Breathing heavily, he turns away, clenching his teeth as he strolls back to the marble room's exit. He descends the stone stairs and reenters the narrow passageway.

Jadecan walks out of the hall's mouth and stops at the broken bridge's edge. He glares across the chasm to where he had shown the large gold coin to the hooded hologram. The torch flame burns behind him as he looms at the walkway's ledge, teeming with madness. The bridge had faded when he reached the narrow corridor, he now stands pondering how to cross the darkness before him. The moss glows upon the dark cave walls on the other side while the sound of dripping water echoes throughout the large cavern.

The white hologram reappears beside him, asking him the same question, yet again.

“smuhruwshnohrng sgohrngshduh rehshguhwuhshduh wyu shkohrng shbuh woy tuw wohshfah rng shmharho shbuh wohtuw rowshmrngshduh woytuwwow shfhawuhtuw ruw shgow ruh tuwroh shfharow shfowrawtuw rho shkuhwyushkoh wih”

Jadecan retrieves the dull coin, same as before, revealing it to the hologram. It abruptly disappears, and the coin disintegrates into dust as the holographic walkway presents itself once again. He saunters across, and as expected, the bridge and torch lit corridor fade away once he sets foot onto the cobblestone of the other side.

“Three days.” Zliyek’s voice echoes as a Vikerumu watches the Akiko venture back through the dark tunnel toward Baby. “You have three days.”

⊜ 6

The black saucer nears one of the brightly lit landing pads of a large two-storey light blue complex. The bay’s white lights come alive, tracing its square outline as she gently touches down upon it. Jadecan peers out of the ship at the large rectangular sign attached to the structure’s top half reading, the Gloom, in a strong crimson light. There are a couple of other starships parked upon the few bays encircling the multistory building, a rarity found almost nowhere else on the moon. Very few places on Niushki supported such a following, the Gloom was one such place. He stands preparing to disembark for the building as the pink cheiket situates itself upon his shoulder, wrapping its long black tail around his neck as usual.

Baby rests illuminated in the structure's bright red light as he treks for the black metallic door on the complex's smooth rounded corner. He was seldom anywhere near here due to his species' hostile reputation and known affiliation with the Balgorex. The Gloom's owner however, Ternaan the Grogan, knew many of the moon's residents, and if he was to find Hulikon, this Grogan was most likely his only way. Unless of course Hulikon wasn't on Niushki, and even if the Cerulean was, he would have to make it through the Gloom's notorious bionic Drakon bouncer first to find out.

"What brings you here, Akiko?" the bouncer asks the approaching Jadecan, while looming in front of the complex's door.

"I need to speak with Ternaan," he answers, staring up into the small red eyes of the mostly robotic Drakon.

"Regarding what?"

"I am searching for a Cerulean. I am hoping your boss can point me in his direction."

"Be quick, Akiko," the Drakon states, not moving.

"Thank you." Jadecan grins and walks around the large mechanical Drakon through the structure's entrance.

Jadecan stands inside the heavily crowded scarlet strip club as the complex's door slides shut behind him. Electronic music plays as three half-naked Cerulean females dance atop platforms within the dazzling DJ lights of the open room. He glances at the long black bar and tables behind them, then makes for one of the staircases situated on either side of the joint. He peers about deafened by the loud obnoxious music and strolls around the crowd. Upon reaching the steps he advances up to the balcony overlooking the dancers below. The Akiko stares at the two Grogan guards positioned on either side of Ternaan's red door whilst climbing the carpeted steps. Their triangular dark blue faces watch as he walks onto the blood-red carpet of the balcony and heads their way.

"What do you want?" the Grogan guard nearest him questions.

"I have come to speak with Ternaan," he answers, standing before the cherry colored Grogans. "I am Jadecan."

"And I am Sadae," the Grogan says sarcastically, and laughs. "Are we supposed to know who you are?"

"I have come to speak with Ternaan," he repeats sneering. "Now, go tell him I am here."

The two guards stop laughing, and the three of them stand leering and quiet. "Wait here," Sadae says, eyeing the pink cheiket resting on Jadecan's shoulder, then looks over at the other guard while shaking his head and entering Ternaan's den.

The Akiko and the remaining Grogan glare at each other in silence, as they await Sadae's return. He stares into the Grogans small black eyes as the crimson light of the Gloom melds into its red skin. After a long few moments the door to Ternaan opens, and outcomes Sadae.

"Please," Sadae says, with a fake smile, standing outside the entryway. "Step inside."

"Jadecan," Ternaan exclaims, standing behind his small luxurious scarlet desk. "Please sit." He gestures to a couple of comfortable black chairs before him. "To what do I owe the pleasure?"

"I am searching for someone," Jadecan answers, as they seat themselves. "A Cerulean by the name of Hulikon, have you heard of him?"

"First," Ternaan declares, his eyes wide and admiring Buddy. "What is that?"

"That is Buddy," he answers, glancing at the cheiket. "Have you heard of him?"

"Hulikon?" Ternaan asks, still fixated on the creature.

"Yes."

"I may have heard of him. Why are you looking for him?"

"I have my reasons."

"I see," Ternaan states. "I guess you don't really need to know where he is then."

"I require his head," Jadecan says, grinning.

"You mean like, his actual head?"

"Indeed."

"That's interesting," Ternaan states. "Hmm, I suppose I could tell you where this Hulikon character is, as long as you do something for me in return. You know, I scratch your back, and you scratch my back. That type of thing."

"What is it you want?" Jadecan asks.

"Nothing too complicated," Ternaan answers, retrieving a large silver syringe-like technological object from his holo-system. "You know what this is?"

"No, should I?"

"Well, probably not," Ternaan answers, admiring the metallic cylinder. "It's experimental Oteniko tech. A sort of extraction device, I suppose you wouldn't know what it is."

"What do you want me to do with it?"

"I want you to take it and insert it into this Hulikon," Ternaan explains. "It doesn't matter where you stick 'em, stick 'em in the eye for all I care. Wherever you end up stickin' 'em though, keep it there till this turns green," he says, showing Jadecan a red light on the back of the object. "Now, the catch. Unfortunately, he must be alive during the process, the entire process. Once this light turns green however, by all means, cut his head off. Think you can manage that?"

"Yes."

"Then we have an agreement?" Ternaan leans toward the Akiko. "I'll tell you where you can find Hulikon, and you'll keep him alive long enough to complete the process. Afterwards return to me, deal?"

"We have an agreement."

"Great," Ternaan says, handing Jadecan the object. "Do I need to explain how we've never had this conversation?"

"You do not," Jadecan says, looking at the device briefly before storing it within his holo-system. "I understand."

Ternaan says, after a few moments, "Excellent. You can find him at the Broken Horn, in Drakon Rock."

"Thank you."

"It's been a pleasure doing business with you, Jadecan."

"The pleasure is mine, Ternaan," the Akiko states, rising from the black chair and after a slight bow advances to the den's entrance, as Buddy repositions himself on his shoulder.

"Maybe we could do this again sometime," Ternaan says, as Jadecan reaches the entryway.

"We shall see."

Ternaan smiles, with a small chuckle. "Happy hunting, Jadecan."

♀ Blood Lake

⊖ 7

Jadecan looms, staring at the small colony of Drakon Rock as Baby rests a good way behind him. Yellowish bright lights surround the fog-filled town glowing in the distance. He stands glaring at the single dusty road running through its center. The moon's wind sweeps whilst he strides through the pale dust and a few sitadoom watch from overhead. The Akiko has been here once before, many, many years ago, a lot has changed since then.

He approaches the colony's large stone archway and stops briefly before it. He admires the stylish words of Drakon Rock glowing in a blurry white light hovering inside the top of the arch. Jadecan continues into the dense mist as an eerie stillness falls upon the town. He casually strolls down the wide road in between its stone multistory buildings. Several decrepit exo-crafts float upon a large concrete slab at his right, while a few Reogki look on from the balcony of the duplex on his left. Moving past the narrow alleyways which separate the town's lantern lit buildings, he makes for the complex of Broken Horn.

A couple of Drakons wander by through the haze gawking as he steps onto the long wooden porch of the saloon-like building. The music of a piano resonates from inside while a lone Cerulean leans on one of the tavern's stone pillars drunk and rambling underneath its overhang. The small horned Cerulean is skinny as a twig, Jadecan doubts he's the one he's looking for.

"Do you know a Cerulean by the name of Hulikon?"

"Can't say I do," the Cerulean stutters, wasted and unsteadily walking toward him. "Actually I think, hmm, maybe… maybe, is he the one in there?" He burps gesturing to the Broken Horn then stumbles into Jadecan, while saying, "Maybe I dunno, hey, hey, I just wanna drink, you know? Think ah, think you can get me a drink?"

Jadecan forcefully pushes the drunk off him onto the wooden deck and towers silently as the pale Cerulean rolls around laughing in front of him. Niushki's breath rolls through whilst he inhales, taking in the cool moon aroma, then swiftly stomps the drunk's face in, knocking him out. He observes the unconscious Cerulean briefly, before venturing through the paneled batwing doors of Broken Horn.

He stands inside and scans the small dimly lit pub as the few Ceruleans seated at its worn wooden tables eye him cautiously. The brown Drakon barkeep gazes from behind the faded amber bar while pouring a couple of shots for a Cerulean sitting at the counter. The Akiko peers around the tattered yellow walls taking note of the four other Ceruleans at the tables as well as the one Drakon positioned at the piano on the taproom's side wall.

"Is there a Hulikon here?" he bellows.

"Who wants to know?" the Cerulean at the bar asks, throwing back a shot.

"I do," he answers. "Are you Hulikon?"

"Yea, Mr. I Do," the tan spiral horned Cerulean answers, getting out of the bar stool and facing him. "I might be, what do you want?" Holo-weapons form within their hands as the music abruptly stops. "Did Jahrei send you?"

"Are you, or are you not, Hulikon?"

"I am."

Shortly after a brief staredown, the two raise their weapons and begin firing on one another. Hulikon soon finds himself slowly sitting upon the stone ground. He's been struck three times in the chest and watches as Jadecan exchanges rounds with the other Ceruleans within the tavern. After a few moments, a veil of silence follows the quick firefight.

Jadecan looks over at the Drakon before the piano, who quickly places himself onto the bench in front of it and begins to play. The bartender raises his hands as Jadecan meanders casually for the dying Hulikon leaning against the bar. Blood flows from the two wounds upon the Akiko's chest who now crouches at the fading Cerulean's side.

"Do you know who I am?" Hulikon asks in a raspy voice, with blood streaming out the corner of his mouth.

"You are dead," he answers, as Hulikon attempts to stab him with a holo-blade.

Jadecan easily catches his hand and effortlessly crushes it within his grip. Hulikon screams, cursing in agonizing pain whilst Jadecan retrieves the extraction device. The Akiko grins, then rams its long needle into the Cerulean's neck and begins watching the blinking red light on its end.

"Hold still," he says to the shivering Hulikon, and after the light turns a solid green he removes it. "That was not so hard, now was it?"

"They will hunt you," Hulikon says, as Jadecan activates his own holo-blade.

"I will be waiting." He takes hold of one of Hulikon's large horns and begins to slice off the still conscious Cerulean's head.

He stands gripping one of the horns of the decapitated head and turns to the Drakon. The bartender's white eyes stare as Jadecan grins widely, bleeding profusely from his wounds. The pianist plays, the notes of the music are soothing yet dark, a haunting melody, the likes of which all the current audience enjoys.

"Would you care for a drink?" the barkeep asks, pouring a shot before Jadecan.

"Thank you," the Akiko says, taking the shot. "My apologies." He gently places the small glass down and drops a few gold coins onto the bar. "I hope it makes up for the mess."

"You are welcome here anytime, cousin," the Drakon states, as Jadecan ambles for the batwing doors of Broken Horn.

⊜ 8

The town of Drakon Rock glows through the dense fog behind Jadecan, who saunters toward the black saucer sitting on the horizon. The planet watches as many small rodent-like creatures follow the trail of blood left by the decapitated Cerulean head hanging at his side. He glances up at the dark sky as the white dust swirls below his feet from a sudden gentle breeze. The smell of death lingers in the cool air.

A large copper Balgorex starship slowly appears in the distance beyond Baby, and before long, it becomes evident it intends to land near her. The rust covered vessel gradually comes to a stop and as the Akiko approaches, it descends sending the ground beneath it fleeting away. Its rear vertical wing-like structures pierce the hard moon surface, while a row of spike-like appendages extend from its bulbous head, digging into the terrain.

Baby rests dwarfed in front of the giant pirate ship. Jadecan advances past her into its shadow. He watches as a group of the ship's crew lowers by way of an elevator from the rear of the vessel. The platform contacts the ground, and Jadecan notices it to be none other than the big bodied Balgorex, Jahrei. The large gangster walks out a few yards and stops, awaiting the oncoming Jadecan, as his Scuts drag out a hooded individual from behind him. They throw the bound character down in front of Jahrei execution style, forcing them onto their knees facing the Akiko.

"Jadecan," Jahrei greets, his four eyes locked upon him.

"Jahrei." He bows slightly after stopping a few feet from the prisoner and presents Hulikon's head. "Recognize him?"

"Indeed," Jahrei answers, eyeing the decapitated Cerulean's head. "Good ol' Hulikon, woulda dealt with 'em myself if it weren't for the Olensi. The prick's been making my life difficult for a long time now. They ain't gonna take too kindly to you taking out one of they boys." He adds, as Jadecan tosses the head onto the ground before him, "I am impressed, I had assumed you'd show up at my fortress lookin' to cut off my own head, not present me with one of my enemies. You woulda failed of course." He chuckles. "Interestin', hell, I will accept ya offer and remove the Death Mark under one condition."

"What condition?"

"Trial by combat," Jahrei answers, gesturing for his Scuts to remove the hood from the prisoner. "Winner walks away with they life." The Scuts reveal Ternaan to be the prisoner kneeling in front of the Akiko. "No weapons, a good ol' fashioned fight to the death. Whaddya say?"

"It isn't a fair fight," Ternaan shouts, as the Scuts cut away the rope binding his hands. "He lives for this, this is what he does. I don't stand a chance. Jadecan you have to tell them, this isn't a fair fight," he pleads.

"They know," he answers, striding for Ternaan who stands quickly in response as Jahrei and his goons back away.

"Wait, wait," Ternaan shrieks in terror, as Jadecan spins embedding his elbow's blade into Ternaan's side. "Uhh, ah," he groans in agony, staring into Jadecan's yellow eyes. The Grogan peers down at the Akiko's bone lodged in his side, and screams, "Wait!" Jadecan yanks his bone out of Ternaan, dropping him to his knees. "Please," Ternaan begs, trembling as blood flows out of his mouth. "Please… wait." He gurgles, spitting blood onto the white dust, and as he attempts to reach out, Jadecan spins again, separating his head from his body.

Sitadoom circle overhead as the Grogan's headless body tumbles over. "Consider the Death Mark removed," Jahrei states. "And as our ol' friend Ternaan would say." He laughs sinisterly. "It's been a pleasure doin' business with ya."

Jadecan bows as Jahrei and his goons trek back toward the large vessel. Vyn looks on from Niushki's horizon while the Akiko walks beneath its dark sky to the black saucer resting upon its white dust. Baby's ramp extends, revealing the blue light of her command deck as well as Buddy posing at its top eagerly awaiting him.

⊖ 9

The pink haired Buddy sits on Jadecan's shoulder as he walks off the ship and stands staring at the dark treeline before him. The planet looms behind the mountains in the distance while a fog shrouds the forest and blankets the terrain. The Curtain before the Mountains of Despair is what the blackened woodland he now stands face to face with has been dubbed. He's been here a handful of times over the decades, and in an odd way, the obscurity of the grove has him feeling more at peace than the open clear environment of the moon. The hidden entrance into the Akikos' sanctum, the Refuge of Otok, dwells near the peak's summit whilst strange creatures scurry within the mist of the growth around its base.

He advances into the black woods to cleanse in the weeping waters of the sacred red lake of Sh'lyn, the Lord of the Akiko. The bloodstained leaves shrill through the howling wind of Niushki as he prowls within the musty smells of the thicket beneath their trees' canopy. The Akiko trudges deeper into the bramble. The saucer behind him is no longer visible as yellow eyes appear to glow through the haze within the darkness watching. Following a long trek in silence, he stops briefly before meandering out of the brush and wandering out onto the wretched wine colored dust, encircling the murky lagoon.

The cheiket tremors in fear at the peril of the threatening environment. Jadecan continues across the chilling bank for the ominous quiet waters of the red lake. The dreary shoreline's solemn nature soothes his aura as Buddy jumps off his shoulder onto the dismal dust in fright whilst he steps into the louring liquid. He glances back at his shivering friend in an attempt to comfort him, and then slowly wades further into the curdled blood shallows. Standing in the marsh's center with the shoreline obscured through the ghostly still fog, he gradually kneels and begins to meditate. The haunting dark surface of the lake breaks around his waist as he sits within a deep trance amidst the eerie silence.

After a long while Baby calls forth, summoning his attention, *Jadecan.*

"Yes?" he asks quietly.

A few Ceruleans have arrived by exo-craft. They bear lanterns and appear to be on the hunt. I believe them to be of Drakon Rock.

"Have they made their way into the woodland?"

They seemed hesitant at first, but yes. They have all ventured inside.

The Akiko rises from the red lake and begins to amble toward the excited cheiket dancing on the shoreline. Before long the screams of the Ceruleans pierce the darkness, their cries of terror conjuring up the grin he now wears across his cold face. Buddy runs up Jadecan's leg and returns to his place upon the Akiko's shoulder as he treks for the dark growth beyond the edge of the lagoon's festering dusty bank. Jadecan knew all too well the effect the bleeding grove had on the uninitiated. He silently chuckles as the afflicted become quiet, and wonders, did they perish before the horrors of the forest or kill each other after succumbing to its insanity?

Thunder rumbles as he walks into the brush while the cheiket's tail firmly wraps around his neck. The smell of death lingers within the damp fog while the taste of blood flows onto his dark tongue. He trudges on for quite some time through the lush foliage before walking out into the broad ring of bleak wildwood surrounding the peaks. The Ceruleans who once yelled in agony now lie scattered throughout the dismal trees dead. Some shot to death, while others have been savagely dismembered. They had, like so many before them, succumb to the madness of the forest.

"Please," a waning voice begs, "Please, kill me."

Jadecan peers over in the sound's direction and discovers a bloodied Cerulean, leaning against one of the sombre trunks barely holding on to life. The Cerulean's arms lie at his side, torn away from his body, while one of his legs sits severed in front of him. His eyes long for death, pleading with the Akiko to end his suffering. The perilous leaves of the dire woods rustle as Niushki's breath howls through its vile mask of decay.

Jadecan looms, and whispers in the darkness, "No."

The withering Cerulean cries as the Akiko strides back toward Baby away from the mass slaughter. Fire streaks across the moon's black sky illuminating the terrain in a reddish yellow glow as he steps out of the gloom ridden woodland. In all of his eighty years he has never seen a phenomenon such as this, and marvels at the sight. The saucer's blue light appears within the fog in front of him as he stands absorbed in the display happening above.

The tiny Buddy cowers in fright upon his shoulder, whilst Baby's voice beckons, *It is the sign for you to seek the Tome of the Old Ones.*

⊜ 10

The black saucer lands within the Mountains of Despair before the three winged ebony statues who guard the otherworldly entrance into the ancient sanctuary of Otok. Jadecan stares out at the large crown topped onyx columns which surround the giant skull faced sculptures in front of Baby. He looks over at the cheiket resting on the dark seat next to him and smiles admiring his little pink-haired friend. After a few moments, he pets its head gently while stating for it to stay, then rises slowly and walks to depart the ship.

The sitting effigies watch as he strolls down the saucer's ramp and steps out onto the darkened surface of the Despair Mountains. Thick cloud-like remnants of the fire which flowed across the moon's sky slowly dissipate and reveal the stars hiding behind them. He studies the scene and advances for the great monument. The Akiko approaches the lead sculpture and stops briefly glancing about the terrain. The trio of statues form a large triangular shape within the impressive ring of pillars encircling them. A spherical pale dust-filled crater sits among them in the triune's center. Vyn looks on as he saunters past the effigy and makes his way toward the white dust behind it.

Sitadooms soar overhead as he ambles into the powder and kneels within its heart. He etches into the dust the Lord of the Akiko's glyph, and as he does, the crowned heads of the obelisks ignite whilst Niushki's winds come alive, animating their blue flames. A phantom-like being appears before the kneeling Jadecan outside the dust. The Faceless One, or so it's come to be known, wears a yellow mask and a shapeless robe of some heavy black fabric. The entity extends out its dark skeleton hand, and as the Akiko stands taking it, they are both instantly transported to the sanctum.

The white dust at his feet transforms, becoming the starless obsidian floor of the Refuge of Otok. A large lightless pyramid slowly rotates floating above a small pedestal while the Faceless One beckons at his side. A halo of candle lit lanterns orbit the podium as two snake-like statues on either side of it look down upon the black book resting upon it, the fabled Tome of the Old Ones. The masked phantom shadows Jadecan as the Akiko moves for the dark book. He strolls into the ring of fire and stands before the pedestal as the Faceless One watches. The Akiko glares into the malign eyes of the foreboding face embedded into the book's cover.

The Akiko had come here for generations after being shepherded by the Faceless One, in seeking the Old One's wisdom and guidance. The Old One of the Refuge of Otok, Sh'lyn, would then choose one of the Akikos to become his vessel to walk amongst the clans. In doing so, he would share his vast knowledge and intellect. This went on for centuries until the Old One's disappearance, following a dire warning.

"Death will come by way of stars, upon the wings of wind. In the time of the Elder, only the faceless shall remain."

The Tome of the Old Ones appeared shortly after their disappearance without explanation. Exactly when and why it came into existence is unknown, and its purpose a mystery. Although the Faceless One is without a voice, the book itself speaks in riddles and claims to be of the boundless Ol-Vaj. It declares itself to be omniscient as to know and see all of spacetime all at once. It promises infinite knowledge and power to the Key's Master, the title given to the one who after completing the thirteen challenges hidden within it, receives its mysterious key.

"They who sign my pages in their own blood will be given a new secret name and one of thirteen trials. Complete them all to restore the key to the Elders' Vault, the prison of the Old One, Azaros, the One Above All. Praise the Key's Master, for all the knowledge and power in the universe will be theirs."

"J'dkyn." The dark tome speaks. "The first of thirteen has come to pass. Present thy glyph to receive the second."

Jadecan conjures up the self-appointed Mark of J'dkyn, a spade, above the pedestal in between the book and the rotating pyramid above it. The bright yellow flaming shape forms by mere thought as if by magic. Within the confines of the Refuge of Otok he possesses a power like none other. A blessing bestowed onto him by the Great Ol-Vaj upon his inking of blood on the pages of the Tome of the Old Ones, all those years ago. The Akiko slightly bows as the book opens and writes out in bloodied ink the second trial.

"You must locate the wanderer. You will find within, an outcast, the mournful brother, he will be your guide. Soon after, a dreaded one will emerge, who's green eyes are so bright, that the Elder's will lose sight. Only after their righteous mission, will you return."

The tome shuts abruptly, vanishing as the Mark of J'dkyn fades and as the lantern's candles go out, the rotating pyramid comes to a stop. Utter silence emerges throughout the obsidian sanctum as he turns away from the now empty pedestal. The Faceless One extends out its hand as it had done before, and upon taking it, the Akiko reappears alone, once again, standing inside the white dust on top of the Mountains of Despair.

♀ Emerald Box

⊖ 11

Jadecan wakes up and stares at the pale ceiling of one of Along the Way's motel rooms with Buddy curled up sleeping on his chest. He pets the cheiket's head gently, waking it, then gets out of the worn bed and strolls over to the window, while it migrates to his shoulder. The twilight bleeds from the surface illuminating the dark carpet before it, as he looks out at the black saucer resting on the white dust.

"Any progress on the wanderer?" he asks, as sitadoom fly across the horizon.

I have come up with only one wanderer thus far, Baby answers.

"Who?"

You. You fit both the wanderer and the outcast. For reasons unknown however, I do not believe you to be the one the Tome of the Old Ones speak of. As for the dreaded one, the cause of the Elder's loss of sight, and their righteous mission, I am at a loss. I am sorry Jadecan, this may take some time.

"I understand," he says, turning away from the window and walking to the room's door. "I will be out shortly."

He steps out into the cream-colored hall and heads for Skall who stands behind the motel's marbled front desk. The Akiko stops briefly and admires the mural of the Scut complex painted on the corridor's wall. Amelia had questioned him about it the time they had roomed here together. He remembers it well and smiles at the memory. After a moment, he turns away from the painting and continues toward Skall as Buddy purrs perched on his shoulder happily. The Akiko strolls over and stands before the watchful white eyes of the Drakon.

"I hope your stay went well," Skall says.

"It did," Jadecan answers. "Thank you."

"I have given your wanderer dilemma some thought." Skall smiles at Buddy.

"I assume you have an answer of sorts," Jadecan states, placing the room's key on the counter. "I am intrigued."

"I am as well, cousin," Skall says. "I believe this wanderer to be one of two things."

"Interesting."

"It is either an unknown individual, not too different from yourself. Or, I believe it to be, more than likely, a location, known as the Wanderer."

"Wanderer, you say? I have not heard of this Wanderer location," Jadecan says, with wide eyes. "Where can I find this place?"

"It is known by another name," Skall says. "You may also know it as the Orphan. It is a moon, supposedly. I myself have only heard of it. I can not even guarantee its existence. With that being said however, I do believe it to exist."

"I see. I suppose you do not know where or how to find this moon?"

"I do not," Skall answers. "I do apologize."

"There is no need." The Akiko nods. "I appreciate your help, as always."

"You are always welcome here, cousin."

"Thank you." Jadecan bows and saunters for the exit.

He ambles for the glass entrance of the motel whilst glancing at the impressive paintings hanging upon the walls on either side of him. Skall's eyes follow as Jadecan treads out of the entryway and ventures into the dark terrain of Niushki. Vyn glares from behind the distant mountains upon the saucer and the Akiko advancing toward it.

"What are your thoughts?" he asks Baby, while petting the cheiket.

On the wanderer being the Orphan?

"Yes," he answers, as her ramp extends out awaiting him.

I believe it to be likely. It does seem plausible. I suppose our next course of action would be finding the locator Captain Tytus spoke of. If we are indeed going with the wanderer being this said Orphan. I do agree it is the best candidate thus far, would you agree?

"I do," he answers, strolling into the saucer's blue light.

Very well. Do you have any idea where we are to go from here?

"If Stet did indeed possess this locator." Jadecan sits before Baby's interaction console as Buddy migrates to the seat next to him. "I do not believe it to still be at his place. I recommend we search out whoever may have raided his place since. They will have it."

Indeed, I believe the thought to be correct. How do you intend to find them?

"There is a shop near Stet's Place, they would have most likely stopped by there," he answers, launching the saucer. "The owner owes me his life. I say we give him the option to relieve the debt."

⊖ 12

A tiny run down L-shaped white stone repair shop presents itself before an advancing Jadecan. A greenish light shines from a sign attached to the complex's main building which reads, Taj's Fix. The pale dust swirls from the gentle winds as he makes for the garage's main entrance with Buddy poised on his shoulder. A few juguke roam near Baby who gleams in the twilight parked behind him.

A few Nudruk who are busy working on an exo-craft take notice of the Akiko as he passes by. Their widely spaced small black eyes watch cautiously as the building's emerald light coats their pink tinted skin. Jadecan walks through the doorless entryway and is greeted almost instantly by the repair shop's owner, a Nudruk by the name of Taj. He stands behind a wooden raggedy front desk as a dim yellowish light illuminates the messy small room. Jadecan had saved this particular Nudruk many, many years ago and still vividly remembers it.

It was a dark gloomy cycle, he had stopped by for a basic repair on an exo-craft he had lifted from some Reogki. Good times. Their blood was still warm and fresh, he could smell it as he strolled toward the shop. The cool moon air was clean as ever, the subtle breeze perfect, and there it was staring him in the face. The scene of scenes, a normality of life on the moon. A couple of armed Ceruleans and three Nudruks on their knees bound before them, execution style. He killed them all, every one of them, well everyone but Taj. Yea, good times. It was perfect.

"Jadecan," Taj welcomes, it's obvious he's uncomfortable, and a bit concerned.

"Taj." Jadecan bows slightly. "How is business?"

"Oh, very good. Very good," Taj answers, taking notice of the cheiket. "Are you here to collect? I do have some units, it's not much, but I do have some–"

"Are you aware of Stet's death?"

"Ah, yes," Taj says, taken aback. "I didn't like 'em anyway. He wasn't good fa business. Why… why do you ask?"

"Has anyone stopped through since? I am looking for those that may have raided Stet's Place, shortly after his death."

"I, I don't know…" Taj stutters.

"I will make you a deal. You hand me a copy of your database between then and now, and we will be even."

"So," Taj says, "As in no more debt? All is well?"

"Yes, you no longer owe me, I no longer collect. You keep your units. No debt. What do you say?"

"You're not going to kill me, right?" Taj asks, obviously still a tad bit concerned. "I mean, I'll still give you what you want, if you are. I was just, I was just wondering."

"You may keep your life. For now."

"Okay, that's fair I suppose." Taj retrieves a small memory card from a drawer within the desk and hands it over to Jadecan. "Here ya go."

"Thank you," Jadecan says to Taj, as he takes the device from him and scans it into his inventory.

"You are welcome," Taj says shakily. "Also, because we're friends. We're... we're friends, right?"

"Sure."

"Ah, that's good. So anyway, a few Olensi had passed through here recently," Taj states. "They were looking for you."

"Really. Why? What did they want?"

"They say there is a reward out for your capture, and wondered if you had been around. I of course, said no, and that I hadn't... wasn't aware of who you were."

"Did they say why?"

"Ah yes, for murder," Taj answers, somewhat casually.

"I see. Thank you, Taj." Jadecan bows slightly chuckling, and adds before exiting the area, "It has been nice catching up. I must, however, take my leave. I appreciate your help. Have a nice life, my friend."

Taj shouts after a few long moments to the Akiko, who is now on his way back toward the black saucer sitting in the distance, "Anytime, my friend!"

Sitadoom glide across the planet on the horizon as the large juguke foraging around Baby observe the approaching Jadecan. The working Nudruks outside eye the Akiko whilst he strides away from the complex of Taj's Fix.

This Olensi bounty could become problematic. I do not believe it is going to be as easy to lift as a Balgorex's Death Mark.

"Indeed, it will not."

I assume it is for the beheading of Hulikon. Seems his threats have merit.

"Indeed," he states, ambling up the ramp into the saucer as Buddy jumps from his shoulder onto the dark floor inside. "Seems to be the case."

Do you think Amelia could be of help?

"I do not," he answers, sitting before her viewpoint as the cheiket curls up in the seat beside him. "I do not believe it would be wise to involve her."

"Agreed," Baby says. "Would you like me to search through Taj's data card for any possible matches? As to hopefully confirm the identity of the Stet's Place raiders?"

"Yes." He retrieves the device from his holo-system and places it on top of Baby's interaction console. "If you would."

"I could have easily just retrieved it from your system myself," Baby remarks. "As I did with the Binox."

"True." Jadecan chuckles. "I had forgotten, old habits die hard I suppose. My apologies."

"It is fine, I understand. I have also noticed a difference in your demeanor, since your recovery of the glowing orb," Baby says, whilst the card disappears from the console. "Are you feeling alright?"

"I am," he answers, sitting back in the chair and grinning at the sleeping pink haired cheiket. "I appreciate your concern. I assure you, I am fine."

⊜ 13

The stars look on as the Akiko walks beneath the black sky. Sitadoom fly overhead as a light rain begins to fall while he advances toward an impressive dark wooden wall. A couple of lightly armored Reogki stand guard at the boundary's large gated entrance. They have definitely noticed him, which is well, for he wasn't hiding. He strolls casually for the entryway and stands calmly before them, grinning widely. They stare with their weapons poised at the ready, their light green faces as pale as the dust at their feet. A couple of red banners bearing the Balgorex emblem of a dual ringed planet ripple in the wind atop the wall as torches blaze on either side of the entrance.

Jadecan looms, admiring the grand barrier and reminiscing about old times. He used to come here quite a bit while in the employment of Stet, as well as a few times after their separation. They were, in a word, what one may call friends, to an extent of course. They would hang out, drink, get into fights, you know, the usual things. Good 'ol Candenn, or 208 as some outsiders would call it, it's not too bad a place, considering. Stet and he had initially met here, the town's actually quite decent, for a settlement on Niushki anyway.

"What do you want?" one of the guards bellow, after somehow finding the courage to speak. "We don't want any trouble."

"I am here to speak with a friend," he answers, bowing. "Nothing more."

The two guards look at one another, then back at Jadecan. "Really?"

"Yes."

"You are here just to see a friend?" the Reogki asks a bit surprised, as the rain begins to fall harder.

"Indeed."

"Huh," the guard mutters, with a small smile. "It's been a long time Akiko. I heard.... Well, we heard about Stet. Heard Jahrei had put a Death Mark on ya fa a bit. Must've done somethin' spectacular though." The guard chuckles. "As you are known to do."

"Indeed."

"We aren't lookin' for any trouble, my friend," the Reogki states.

"No trouble will come of me."

"Good, then welcome back to Candenn."

"Thank you," he says, as the wooden gateway creaks open revealing the busy town behind it.

The Reogki guards watch as he ambles through the entryway into the colony. Jadecan looks back over his shoulder as the bulky gate closes, and he continues down the main muddying road of Candenn. Reogki parade about, and besides a few curious stares, they pay him no mind as he makes his way through the crowd. Seems as if a lot can happen in a decade or two. It was not all that long ago they would have gone stiff at the mere thought of an Akiko. It appears as though the times are a changing, as one would say.

Open shops present themselves alongside the town's main strip, appearing to be like a bustling metropolis of sorts. Its marketplace has definitely grown since last he was here. He observes as merchants advertise their goods to the passing townsfolk. You can find just about anything in a place like this. Food? Check. Clothing? Check. Weapons? Check. The necessities are all there, and of course, if you are looking for something a bit more unorthodox, you can find that as well. Good 'ol Candenn, yea it's not too bad a place considering.

The Akiko drifts out of the crowd and disappears in between a couple of shops into the residential maze of varying stone buildings beyond. He heads for the farthest parts of the colony, the cheapside, the decrepit shacks lining the back of Candenn's outer wall. Jadecan trudges through the pale drenched ground as thunder rumbles and the black sky vanishes behind a gloom-ridden grey cloud cover. The smell of wet dust fills the narrow walkway as the sound of rain pummeling the metal roofs of the complexes echo throughout the congested torch-lit colony. The Akiko strolls through the town's alley-like passageways and takes note of a Reogki standing outside one of the smaller shanties up ahead. He ponders briefly, then heads for the outsider, hoping to be pointed in his friend O'an's direction.

O'an, like he, had worked for Stet many, many years ago. In fact, O'an was there when he joined the Balgorex's ranks, and he was still there when the Akiko left. The goon was usual enough, but over time it became clear he was a bit more than your regular throw away. Most of the common fodder was just that, common fodder. They would survive a run, if lucky maybe two, but to end up here? In Candenn, retired? No, that didn't happen. For you see, O'an is a Scut, and Scuts well, didn't make it to retirement. Unless of course, your name is O'an. Rumor had it the Scut was here, and if indeed the case, Jadecan knew he'd be on the cheapside. Where else would an old Scut, be housed?

He stops some distance away from the Reogki, recognizing the look of worry worn upon his face. "I am looking for a Scut, nothing more," he shouts through the roaring rain.

"There," the outsider yells back, gesturing toward an abode not far from where he stood, before disappearing into the hut.

The Akiko treads for the shack as the constant rain lets up ever so slightly. A torch dances in the howling wind outside the hut's rusted reddish door. He stands momentarily, then knocks twice, while thunder quietly rumbles overhead. The sound of a lock undone, is followed by the slight opening of the metal entrance. A large yellow eye belonging to a Scut peers through the crack at Jadecan. Its two antennae feel about the metal entry while it speaks in a sequence of clicks. It's the typical language of the bug-like species.

"Yes?"

"I am looking for one known as O'an," Jadecan states. "Do you know of him?"

"I may, who want to know?"

"An old friend," he answers.

"Jade? Is that you?"

"Indeed, O'an," he says, bowing.

"It is good to see you," O'an says, opening the door. "Come on inside out the storm. It is not much, but more than most of us have."

"Thank you," Jadecan says walking inside and closing the heavy hatch behind him.

"Why this side of town?" O'an asks, while taking a seat at a wooden table in the middle of the tiny area. "Looking for something?"

A decent fire rages at a nook in the corner of the square room below a brick chimney while a bunk of hay rests on its opposite side behind O'an. A quaint little place, not bad for a

Scut. The Akiko strides across the hard concrete floor and sits at the table across from O'an. The hearthside illuminates everything with an orangish glow as the two talk over the crackling of the fireplace and the raging storm outside the Scut's worn home.

"Indeed," Jadecan answers. "I have come across a few names. Wondering if you may have heard of them."

"What are the names?"

"Ostrin, Creks, and Gaarli. I am thinking one, if not all, may have raided Stet's Place. I am searching for a specific item, and believe one of them may have it."

"Ah." O'an smiles. "Gaarli met a gruesome end at the hands of some Reogki. I do not think however, he has ever been to Stet's Place. What is it you are lookin' for?"

"A device known as a locator."

"I see. I know of this locator and where you will find it."

"You do not say."

"Why yes, I do say." O'an laughs. "I was there when Stet was given it. It was around the time he built his safehouse."

"Interesting. What happened to it?"

"I have it here with me. He showed up here in disguise, and gave it to me to hold onto. I suppose he thought the best way to keep it hidden was to give it to the one no one would suspect."

"An intelligent move." Jadecan chuckles. "Smart, he was not wrong. I would never have suspected you. Suppose luck would have it, I show up here."

O'an gets up and retrieves a long dark wooden box from within the bed of hay. "I have kept it here ever since, and wondered what may become of it." He returns to the table and places it before Jadecan. "I suppose with Stet dead, he has no use for it and will not be coming back for it. I must apologize in advance though, I believe it to be no longer functioning."

"What makes you say that?" the Akiko asks, opening the box and removing the long silver cylinder inside. "It is surprisingly rather light."

"It is," the Scut agrees. "It once had a thin ring of light on either end of it. That light has gradually disappeared over time, and as you can see, it is now completely gone."

"Interesting," he says, studying the device.

"Who knows, it may function just fine, and the light was just a light," O'an says, as Jadecan scans the locator into his inventory. "Why were you searching for it? Do you know what purpose it serves?"

"I believe it is meant to locate a place known as The Orphan," he answers. "I am to find something there."

"Well," O'an says, with a small chuckle. "That is interesting. I hope you find what it is you are looking for, my friend."

"I as well," the Akiko says. "I as well."

♀ Prismatic Wildwood

⊖ 14

Jadecan stands at the foot of Baby's ramp in front of the Curtain before the Mountains of Despair, and as it retracts behind him, he ventures forth in search of the Mistress of Quietus secluded within. Glowing yellow eyes watch as the Akiko trudges through the thick undergrowth. A dense mist lingers in the moist still air while haunting sounds echo throughout the grove's sparsely spaced trees.

He strolls through the dark woodland in search of the fabled dwelling of the mysterious witch, a small hut said to have large dark scaly legs which constantly moves about the fog-filled forest. The elusive mistress is known to aid those who unwittingly seek her out. However, those unfortunate enough to be deemed unworthy of her help will never again leave the Curtain before the Mountains of Despair. Baby has confirmed the device does not function as O'an had suggested, but also added that it is probably nearly impossible to recharge. She states it had once been alive, which is odd. And that its lifespan is well, rather short. Jadecan comes in hopes the mistress can do the impossible and breathe life once more into the Orphan's locator.

After some time of wandering amidst the lush thicket, an eerie voice whispers, as a chilling breeze crawls from behind him, "Jadecan."

He turns slowly, nothing, nothing but the darkness and ghastly silence that's always been there. A large tree begins to gradually move, which comes alive and creeps out of the shadows before him. It's an ancient guardian known as the Athpeha, whose charcoal armor-like skin appears to be made entirely of bark. A pair of large antlers flow out of the keeper's forehead above where one would have had eyes. It, though, has no face whatsoever to speak of. The Athpeha's long rough arms rest at its side as it steps closer, its huge trunk-like legs easily the size of the undaunted Akiko themselves.

"Jadecan," the voice grimly repeats, clearly coming from the mouthless keeper.

"The Mistress of Quietus," he says with confidence.

The ambience surrounding him subtly changes ever so slightly as the sound of footsteps trudging through the brush echo from behind him. He looks over his shoulder, taking his eyes off the Athpeha but for a moment. Nothing, nothing but the crimson leaves of the woods rustling in the gentle wind. The Akiko returns his focus to where the keeper stood. It's vanished, nowhere to be seen, and a giant tree now resides where the guardian once was. Everything becomes still, and an uneasy calmness spreads as Jadecan feels a strange presence looming at his back.

"Jadecan," a scandalous yet innocent sounding female voice beckons.

"Mistress," he greets, facing the young and beautiful fiery haired maiden.

He bows gazing into her vibrant green eyes as the mistress' infamous tiny wooden hut sits atop its two scaly sitadoom-like legs behind her. A ring of flaming skulls levitate while slowly orbiting the talon-tipped three-toed feet of the cabin. The Akiko's only heard stories of the Mistress of Quietus, but in all the tales, beauty's not used to define her. In fact, she's always portrayed to be the opposite, a disfigured grotesque elderly hag accompanied by death itself. This stunning dame was not at all what he expected, but nonetheless, he welcomed it.

"You hope I can bring life to that which has none." She giggles.

Jadecan looks a bit confused and slightly tilts his head. "I do."

"You wonder how it is that I know," she says, with a smile, clearly amused. "I am aware of a great many things."

"So I have heard," he says cautiously.

"Your friend Skall is correct. The Orphan is indeed what you are looking for," she says in an oddly sinister way. "Question is, how badly do you want to find it?"

"Depends." He shrugs.

The mistress laughs quietly. "Sh'lyn speaks highly of you, it's actually quite adorable. I'll make you a deal, Akiko. Retrieve for me an ancient jewel known as The Sight's Gem and I will rekindle your locator's lifeforce. You must be quick however, for death's followed closely by decay."

"Another quest," he states. "I suppose I should not be surprised. You need something just like everyone else, you are no different." She scoffs at the remark, as he asks, "Where can I find this gemstone?"

"So eager." She smiles and answers, "You will find it inside the Diamond Chamber within the Great Temple of Eye. As a bonus, bring me it's caretaker's heart, and I'll give you, as a gift, a token of my gratitude."

"I have not heard of this place."

The flaming skulls stop and as the small hut sits into the blood-soaked brush behind her, they slowly float over to the mistress. "Step through the gate, and you will find yourself just outside the shrine." She holds out her hand to Jadecan, and as a clear white quartz skull appears inside her palm, she says, "Place this onto the altar inside the temple's grand chamber to summon the shrine's caretaker. Complete its trials to become worthy of the gemstone."

As she speaks, the skulls form an oval beside her, and whilst the mistress walks back to her hut, a shimmering portal appears between them. The ghostly blue flames of the skulls sway in the breath of Niushki as the Akiko glares into the otherworldly gateway. A large moonlit blue stone ziggurat, who's completely engulfed in a flourishing jungle-like wildwood, looks back at him. He watches as the Mistress of Quietus disappears into her wooden cabin, before heading for the pyramid and vanishing through the threshold.

⊜ 15

Jadecan emerges from the gateway and sets foot onto a grassy clearing in front of the temple. The mirror-like portal flickers at his back as he strolls for the shrine beneath a star littered night sky. Strange chirping sounds resonate throughout the green woodland while a red moon watches from overhead. A large inscribed sphere sits on a pedestal atop the flight of stone steps before the ziggurat's torch-lit entrance.

The Akiko makes his way through the grassland toward the pyramid as a soft breeze blows through the trees of the lush forest around him. He cautiously strides, stopping at the foot of the steep stone steps and studies the dark terrain before continuing up the long staircase. After some time of climbing the worn cracked steps, he finally reaches the plateau at their top and takes note of the statues kneeling on either side of the dull spherical monument.

The stone orb's covered in an extraordinary amount of glyphs, they're alien but familiar. The writing is extremely reminiscent of the ones written into the key Stet had given him. The monument itself could very well be a giant replica. He admires the scene briefly before sauntering around the globe for the pyramid's entryway. He stands in front of the entrance of the ziggurat and looks down at the corridor's sandstone steps ahead of him, before venturing for the glowing doorway below.

A grand chamber greets him through the opening at the stairs' end. A brightly lit solid block table rests within its center, surrounded by many intricately designed columns. He slowly approaches the stone altar while glancing around the darkened corners and outer walls of the square room. A torch blazes on each of the pillars facing the small stone slab. The Akiko looms while retrieving the mistress' crystal skull from his inventory. Jadecan places it gently onto the table's surface and backs away. After a few moments, it shoots up and floats above the altar for a brief period before completely disappearing.

Complete blackness now surrounds him, somehow he's standing somewhere else entirely, as if teleported without his knowing. He glares about the darkness expecting to see the red eyes of a winged beast, but instead is greeted by an iridescent being. It steps out of the shadows, towering in front of him. It's extremely tall and has no recognizable face. The prismatic character holds out its large chromatic closed hands toward the Akiko as if presenting him with the simple choice of, pick a hand.

He stands in a mesmerized trance for quite some time. How long exactly? He may never know. The Akiko jolts awake and realizes the psychedelic effect its appearance has had on him. Lost in wonder about how long he's been out, he quickly points at its left effulgent fist.

A rippling black water surrounds the confused and now utterly alone Akiko, stretching into the emptiness as far as the eye can see. He peers squinting through the twilight at the intense white overcast forming above him. Standing but for a moment, he begins to wade through the extremely shallow liquid as a huge pyramid rapidly rises out of the depths ahead of him. It stops as a bright beam of light shines from the sky, illuminating a small shrine at the very top of the ziggurat.

Dark featureless entities begin to rise up out of the water all around him. They loom, shimmering as if made of the fluid themselves. Without warning, they swiftly race for him, screaming in a tone so deafening, it nearly brings the Akiko to his knees. He spins violently, slicing all those near. The apparitions turn into water and crash back down into the liquid as he bolts for the pyramid's staircase leading up to the temple. He runs through the shallows cutting down everything standing in his way. Upon nearing the complex, the Akiko impressively leaps and lands onto the sandstone steps.

The apparitions pursue madly as he climbs like nobody's business. With astonishing speed, the swarm quickly cuts into the Akiko's lead, and as he nears the ziggurat's top, a giant wave of black liquid flows down. He lowers his shoulder and continues for the shrine. He pauses just before the impact and braces for the inevitable. It hits, and he immediately feels as if someone has taken hold of him and attempts to pull him backwards. Jadecan fights the unyielding urge to fall and miraculously in a feat of mere strength, he begins to slowly trudge forward.

The wave completely engulfs the Akiko and relentlessly pulls him in the opposite direction. He tires more and more with each grueling step he takes. Finally, he reaches the small stone temple and extends out his hand for the levitating crystal skull within. His legs have become numb and in coming to the realization that he may not actually make it, he roars furiously. In a last ditch effort, using all of what is left of his remaining strength, he agonizingly pushes forward. Stretching as far as he physically can, he screams and as his fingertips barely touch the skull, he loses consciousness.

⊜ 16

The Akiko awakens sitting on the hard floor of a small stone cell. His hands lie at his side, each are bound in their own rusted shackles and chained to the worn wall. A torch blazes ahead of him across from the room's open iron door. It's quiet, unnaturally quiet. It's obvious this is but another trial. He sits calm, his senses on edge as he ponders his next move carefully.

"Baby," he whispers, peering down at his shackled hands and as moments turn into minutes, there is no response, none whatsoever.

A curiously odd voice echoes from outside the room, "Baby? Hmm, who is this Baby?"

Giving no reply, Jadecan sits in silence trying to imagine what its owner may look like. It seems well, in a normal enough way, considering the given circumstances. Strange however, almost appeared as if, well, he's not entirely sure. He'll cross that bridge when he comes to it. Besides, when all is said and done, it really doesn't matter who they are.

There must be some sort of barrier preventing his signal from reaching Baby though and that is a problem, but ultimately, not surprising. He glares once again at his bound hands, then slightly tugs, testing the chain's authenticity. They're true, but do offer a few feet of slack, enough to stand and quite possibly even move about.

After apparently hearing the chains rattle, the voice beckons once more, "Ah, you must be wondering where the key is? I know where you may find thy key." It then exclaims in a slightly higher excited tone, "If one were to withhold in wait for that perfect moment, you would say and agree that that one was indeed?" The Akiko ponders confused at the apparent riddle. "Oh come on," the voice says, irritated after a few moments. "That's an easy one. If one were to withhold in wait for that perfect moment, you would say and agree that that one was indeed, doing what?"

Jadecan peers around the room, then stands and walks forward. Almost immediately the chains become taut. Well, there's indeed enough slack to stand, but that's about it. He glances behind him and notices a golden shimmer upon the dull stone, a key. The Akiko kneels, picking it up off the floor and inserts it into one of the shackles, it's the one. He was sitting on it. He unlocks the other and looms free of his chains, turning his attention to the cell's open entrance.

I was sitting on it? He thinks to himself. *Is that the answer?*

Jadecan strolls for the doorway and upon stepping outside it, he stands for a moment in front of the crackling flame before the cell. He looks about the short stone block corridor, to his right a solid wall and at his left a wooden door. Without any other apparent option, he meanders for the wooden entryway. The riddler has to be through there. As he approaches, the Akiko notices a face sitting within the wooden door. After a brief contemplation, he glares upon the face and attempts to pull the entry open. The face's eyes open and stare. It smiles gleefully as Jadecan rivals its ominous gaze.

"You found it," the face speaks, almost whispering. "It took you a bit of time, but here you are."

This is clearly the riddler. "Who are you?" he asks bitterly.

"Oh, the hostility." The face chuckles slowly, and answers in a low tone, "I am Wooden Face."

The Akiko growls in response. "Wooden Face. Pleasure to meet you, I am Jadecan."

"Oh, I know who you are," Wooden Face states. "Do you know why you are here?"

"There is one torch in this corridor," he says clearly annoyed, his yellow eyes threatening. "I will burn you to the stone."

"I believe you," the face says unconcerned. "I can save you the effort however, that will not work."

A short pause followed by a reluctant sigh. "I am here to retrieve the Sight's Gem for the Mistress of Quietus."

"The Mistress of Quietus." It scoffs. "What did she promise you in return? Unlimited power? The answers to all your questions? Whatever it was, I can guarantee you, she will not meet her end of the bargain, Akiko."

"She will," he states in a dark tone. "I will guarantee it."

The Wooden Face laughs hauntingly. "Oh, you will try my friend. You will try. Tell me, what is it you are here for? Why do this for the Mistress?"

"I need her to bring life back to a device," he answers.

"She will do no such thing," it says as if insulted. "What she has sent you to do is impossible. The Sight's Gem is not a physical object, it cannot be retrieved nor removed."

"We will see."

"It matters not," Wooden Face answers, with a bellowing laugh. "Solve my riddle and the Sight's Gem will be yours."

Moments pass, after which he asks, "What is your riddle?"

"What is binding that enthralls, awaiting us all, and leads all unhindered, that can't be changed or altered?"

"I am not sure?"

"Allow me to rephrase, Akiko. What binding enthralls and awaits us all, leading all unhindered, but cannot be altered?"

"Death," he answers unsure.

"Try again," Wooden Face states. "You are close."

After some time, he guesses, "Time."

"Last try, Akiko." It repeats slowly, "What is binding that enthralls, awaiting us all, and leads all unhindered, that can't be changed or altered?"

A long pause, followed by his answer, "Fate."

"I'm impressed," Wooden Face says. "Very well done. That is correct."

The wooden door creaks open and after a few moments, Jadecan walks through. A glimmering golden room shimmers in front of him. At its center, a levitating large black obelisk awaits as the door closes behind him. Its shiny reflective body spins slowly as he walks across the gold floor and stands before the dark lustrous pillar. The object comes to a stop as the Faceless One appears at his side. The yellow masked phantom looks down upon Jadecan and gestures toward the obelisk, speaking for the first time to the Akiko.

"The One Above All," the Faceless One states, its voice as ghostly as its appearance.

"J'dkyn." The cenotaph speaks in a harrowing tone. "I am Ol-Vaj, the Great Azaros, the One Above All. I see Lord Sh'lyn has chosen the Key's Master wisely."

"He has," Jadecan says confidently, kneeling. "I do not fail."

"This we know. We know well," Ol-Vaj states. "You have found one of my orbs, you must find the other twelve. Only then can we restore the Akiko to their rightful place at the Old Ones side."

"The glowing orb?" Jadecan asks.

"Yes," the Great Azaros confirms. "Together, they form the key to the Elder's Vault, my prison."

"I have given the orb to Cassandra of Oteniko," the Akiko says worryingly.

"Fear not. The orbs will seek out one another, and once fully restored, will seek out the Key's Master. Only the Key's Master can release me from the vault."

"I will find them all," Jadecan states.

"Avoid the Elder at all costs," the One Above All says.

"Who is this Elder?"

"Your fates, are intertwined," Ol-Vaj answers. "I will not say any more than that, but know J'dkyn, you are destined to meet."

"What of the Orphan's locator?"

"The Mistress of Quietus will revive it. She will have no choice," the Great Azaros answers, as Jadecan finds himself back within the grand chamber of the ziggurat.

The Akiko stands before the Mistress' crystal skull, which now sits upon the stone altar facing him. He retrieves the skull from the solid block table and scans it into his holo-system. The torches of the intricately designed columns dance as he walks past them, heading back to the Mistress' portal.

♀ Bleeding Dream

⊖ 17

The black wood's bloodstained leaves shrill through the howling wind of Niushki as the Akiko emerges from the portal. The musty smells of the thicket beneath the canopy welcome him as the Mistress of Quietus scowls before him. Yellow eyes glow within the fog watching, as the portal dissipates and the skulls return to the cabin behind her.

He bows as the red haired maiden speaks. "Azaros isn't going to save you, Akiko."

"So be it." He growls, retrieving the locator and tossing it to her. "Do as you are told."

"Did Azaros tell you?" She smiles, catching the locator. "No, I suppose he wouldn't." A thin ring of white light glows near both ends of the device. "Why would the Great Azaros tell you, an Akiko, anything." She tosses the locator back to Jadecan.

"Thank you." He nods with a slight bow peering into her green eyes grinning. "The Sight's Gem. A beautiful jewel. Shame, you will never see it."

"You will fail, Akiko," she states. "You will die violently and alone. A fitting end to your kind. There is nothing you can do to stop it."

The smell of death lingers within the damp mist as the sound of thunder rumbles in the distance. He turns away from the Mistress, ignoring her words and venturing back toward his black saucer, resting outside the Curtain before the Mountains of Despair. The Akiko trudges through the crimson thicket as the witch vanishes and the rain begins to fall.

Jadecan? Baby calls.

"Yes," he answers, wandering the foliage.

The Gloom's bionic Drakon is here. I believe he is awaiting you, she says, as he steps into the wildwood the Ceruleans had gone mad in.

"Delightful." He smiles nearing the edge of the treeline.

Jadecan can now see past the blackened forest's edge and peers up at the giant Vyn looming on the horizon of Niushki's dark landscape. He steps out of the woods onto the white dust and continues ahead, disappearing into the blanket of dense smog as thunder growls overhead. After some time, the fog begins to thin and the saucer starts to take shape, revealing the robotic Drakon now advancing in his direction.

"Akiko," the red eyed Drakon greets hostilely, stopping a few paces from Jadecan.

"What do you want?" he asks surly through the crashing rain.

"The Mistress wants the Sight's Gem," the Drakon answers in a combative tone, walking to the grinning Akiko. "And you, she wants dead."

Jadecan walks to meet the oncoming Drakon. The pair pick up speed as they near one another. In an attempt to strike the reptilian, the Akiko spins jumping at him, and as the bone bounces off the lizard's metal side, the Drakon grasps him firmly by the neck. Jadecan grips the reptilian's silver metallic arm whilst being held up and suspended in the air.

After a few moments the Drakon pulls Jadecan to just a pace or so away from his snake-like face, stating in a ruthless tone, “You are nothing.” He forcefully throws him back toward the forest’s shrouded edge.

The Akiko hits the muddied ground hard, but gets up almost as quickly as he makes contact and roars at the approaching bionic lizard. With his head angled down, and his yellow eyes fixated on the target, Jadecan pivots to his side, hunching ever so slightly, ready for the reptilian’s onslaught. The Drakon’s robust tail lashes out for the Akiko, who crouches below its massive weight. Jadecan feels a rush of air almost as strong as Niushki’s winds pass overtop of him, as the reptilian’s burly tail misses. The Akiko instinctively slices as the tail sweeps back over him, cutting it away from the Drakon, who screams in agonizing pain. The hefty tail hits the wet ground with a thud, bloodying the white landscape at their feet.

Jadecan screams, turning as fast as he can in a furious rage and cuts through the reptilian’s metal, embedding his right bone deep into the lizard’s side. The Akiko struggles to remove the blade to no avail, and then looks up at the Drakon who’s louring as it stares back growling angrily. The reptilian pounds down hard onto Jadecan’s shoulder, cracking the Akiko’s bone lodged in its side, and as thunder rumbles, Jadecan cries out in pain. The lizard continues to hammer Jadecan’s shoulder violently, cracking the bone a little more with each foray, before finally snapping the blade and sending the Akiko dazed to the blood-soaked ground.

The rain pours as the Drakon stumbles, falling to its knees beside Jadecan while gripping the Akiko's bone still stuck in its bleeding side. The barely conscious Jadecan looks over at the fatally wounded reptilian kneeling beside him, before standing himself up slowly. The Akiko sways drunkenly in front of the Drakon, then steadies, and with one precise swing, decapitates the reptilian. Jadecan limps a few paces past the falling body of the lizard before collapsing motionless.

⊜ 18

Jadecan stands, surrounded by a huge group of screaming Reogki outside one of their colonies. His blades cut the dust as Niushki's wind howls, animating the torches resting within the outsiders cold hands. The dark moon sky looms overhead as the stars watch. The Akiko's been in this situation before, it's a common scene, this however didn't look good.

He glares into their flush faces, whilst they scream angrily threatening him, "Murderer! Monster!"

Last time he was in this position he wasn't alone, but he left that way bloodied and beaten, he remembers it well. He fought alongside the last of his tribe, they should've fought harder, suppose it doesn't matter now. They were slaughtered by the Reogki, no different from the ones surrounding him now, they're all the same. Vyn looks on from the horizon, whilst a few common sitadoom soar before it. It's been a long time since he's seen another Akiko, he very well could be the last, it's likely he is.

"Kill the Akiko!" they shout violently. "Kill the Akiko! Death to the Akiko!"

They meant it, they always did. The large crowd fumes, it was only a matter of time, before finally, they boil and overflow. A Reogki lunges from the crowd with a blade held above their head threatening to bring it down upon the Akiko. Jadecan spins quickly dodging the attempt, while slicing through the Reogki's waist, cutting him cleanly in half. Blood sprays covering all but those directly at his back. The crowd roars and rushes the lone grinning Akiko at its heart. He's comfortable, and although outnumbered ten to one, he'll take these odds any cycle.

Jadecan twirls like a top as the first of the swarm reaches him, instantly killing the lucky ones while easily dismembering and fatally gutting the rest. Parts of Reogki fly as blood speckles his pale skin, the smell of death lingers as they surge again. He slices over and over, cutting them down without mercy. Running was never an option and besides, they deserve this.

An odd sensation ripples through his body, he peers down to see a sharp point sticking out of his shoulder, just below his chin. He's been stabbed through the back. Blood streams down the blade's dull worn edge and as the Reogki responsible pulls it out, the Akiko spins furiously, embedding his bone blade into the Reogki's skull. You can hear the crack of the skull as the blade splits it like a coconut, stabbing into the brain. Jadecan stands foaming at the mouth and glaring at the Reogki, as it sways confused before him. He fiercely roars removing the bone, sending chunks of the Reogki's brain matter flying through the dark terrain.

The Akiko forcefully pushes the stunned Reogki to the ground in a blind rage and without warning, another sharp sensation floods his body. He's been stabbed through the back again, and this time straight through the chest. Dark blood flows from his mouth and streams off his chin, converting the white dust at his feet into a red lake. He smiles, it's not so bad, there are worse ways to go.

The Akiko feels a hand upon his back and after a moment, he's aggressively pushed off the blade. He falls to the ground barely conscious dying in a pool of his own blood. Weapons fire, followed by screams of agony, as Jadecan rolls over onto the flat of his back. He lies listening and smiling as a scaly reptilian hand gently rests upon his blood-soaked chest. He looks up to see a green Drakon kneeling at his side.

"Hey, you're going to be alright," the reptilian says softly.

The low bellowing voice of Stet echoes from behind her, "How is he, Sycora?"

"He's alive, but barely," she answers, as the Balgorex arrives.

"You gonna get up, Akiko?" Stet asks, his four brown eyes locked upon Jadecan. "Or are you content with dying there?" He puts his large tan hand on Sycora's shoulder and gestures for her to move. "What are you my friend?" the Balgorex asks, as Sycora rises and Stet replaces her crouching at Jadecan's side. "Are you weak, or are you strong?" Stet pauses, looking about the dim landscape. "The weak don't last long here, but you know that. Don't ya?" The menacing Balgorex states in a powerful tone, whilst standing and walking away, "Get up Akiko, I don't have all day."

Jadecan rolls over and slowly rises from the red dust, covered in blood. He looms hunched over and barely able to stand, yet somehow he walks forward, his vision a blur. The Akiko makes out the large silhouette of the Balgorex just ahead, he's surrounded by many smaller figures, most likely Scuts. Sycora stands at Jadecan's side, watching as the Akiko gradually treks in their direction with his hand covering the stab wound on his chest.

Jadecan falls to a knee and as Sycora rushes to his side, Stet's voice bellows again, "Do not help him. If he is to survive he must do this himself."

The Akiko stares at the ground as the Balgorex's voice echoes in his head. *What's it going to be Akiko? Are you going to get up, or are you going to die here?*

⊖ 19

The rain pours, drowning the dust as the Akiko opens his eyes but a crack. He lies face down, watching the drops impact the muddy ground. The sound of thunder cracks as he begins to rise like the dead from a grave.

Jadecan, Baby's voice calls with concern.

"I am here." He coughs, wiping the blood seeping from his mouth.

Are you alright?

"All is well," he answers, staring up at the pitch black rumbling sky.

He looks over his shoulder at the headless Drakon body behind him, then sighs at the sight of his bone in its side. The

Akiko looks down at his broken elbow's blade as grief washes over him, he'll have to deal with it somehow. Thunder growls as he strolls for the Drakon's body. He crouches beside it, and pauses momentarily, before taking hold of his broken bone and forcefully ripping it out of the reptilian. Jadecan stares longingly at it, then stores it into his holo-system.

The dark treeline of the woodland is barely visible through the thick fog, as he glances at the reptilian's head lying within a bloody puddle to the side of the Drakon's body. After a few moments he chuckles, and makes his way back to the black saucer awaiting him. The ship's blue light bleeds through the dense haze as he saunters up its dark ramp into the command deck, silent as always. The saucer's console forms whilst he places himself in the black seat before it.

"I am sorry," Baby states, as the pink haired cheiket jumps onto the Akiko's shoulder from off the seat next to him.

"It is fine," he says, petting his little pal and smiling. "I am happy to see you. Did you miss me?"

"He's mainly been sleeping," Baby says. "I believe he's been napping in that seat the whole time you have been gone. I do not think he has moved, not even once."

"I suppose that is to be expected." He laughs.

"I suppose so," Baby agrees. "Where to now? I have taken the liberty of retrieving the locator from you. It is functioning."

"Good," he states, placing his hand onto the console. "Let us go and look about this Orphan."

"Is there anything you would like to do before we leave?" Baby asks.

"No," he answers, launching the ship. "I think I am done with Niushki for now. Think a change of scenery would do me good."

"It could do no harm," Baby says, as the saucer glides for the stormy sky of the moon. "Also while you were out, I scanned for the Olensi vessels that were at one point, in orbit of the moon. I was concerned, due to Taj's remark of the bounty put upon you."

"I had forgotten," he says, somewhat embarrassed. "I apologize. It had slipped my mind. I suppose this means we cannot leave Niushki."

"Actually, on the contrary," Baby states. "My scans came up empty. I was worried however, that my scanning range may not have been sufficient to detect them. This, if indeed true, has since been rectified with our approach toward the atmosphere. They have at some point left from orbit."

"Interesting."

"Indeed." And as they leave the atmosphere, she says in a baffled tone, "There appears to be significant debris within the moon's orbit. Almost...." She pauses briefly. "I believe there to have been a battle of some magnitude, resulting in the destruction of a vessel, if not multiple. It is difficult to tell, but I am almost certain that a battle of some sort did take place."

"Are there any vessels in the area?" Jadecan asks. "Is there anything, at all?"

"No. The planet's, as well as Niushki's orbits, are both void of anything consequential. There are no signs of any vessels, we are alone," Baby answers. "It would be wise to leave. There is nothing you can do here."

"We should stick around and investigate."

"I would rather not," Baby states. "I do not care where we go. However, I am not keen on staying out here. If you are still wanting to go to the Orphan, there is no better time than now."

"Fine." He sighs. "How do we go about this locator?"

"You will notice on the projection before you, a cylindrical image," Baby explains. "It's a representation of the device, press it to initiate the activation process. Afterwards, input your code by voice into the onscreen prompt."

"I do not have a code," he states rather confused, staring at the prompt.

"You do now. It is 1-4-3. You may change it at any time."

"1-4-3," he says slowly. "Now what?"

"Simply state, activate," Baby answers.

"Understood." He states loudly, "Activate."

Space begins to warp around the saucer in a mind-bending kind of way. Jadecan stares out in wonder at the spectacle as time appears to stop briefly. In the blink of an eye, the black saucer and the Akiko are pulled inside at an unnerving pace, vanishing into the emptiness.

♀ Part Four: The Survivor

"I think we're all mentally ill. Those of us outside the asylums only hide it a little better." – Stephen King.

♀ Cold Address

⊖ 1

A dark frozen moon floats in the vacuum of space as the black saucer emerges out of nothing and heads for it. Emptiness, no planets, no nearby stars, just the lone lifeless moon before the approaching starship Baby. Jadecan stares out at the icy rock, his small yellow eyes glaring whilst the pink cheiket purrs on his shoulder.

"Is that the Orphan?" he asks, still bleeding from his wounds from his fight with the Drakon.

"It appears to be so," Baby answers. "We are in route to a cavity within the moon, I believe this to most likely be the Orphan City."

"Interesting," he says, looking over at his broken bone blade and grimacing in pain.

The ship shakes, and Baby states, "Seems we have been grabbed by a tractor-beam of sorts. We have been scanned and are being hailed."

"This is Roland of the Orphan City," the hailer says. "Please identify yourself. I repeat this is Roland of Orphan City, incoming starship please identify yourself."

After a few moments, the Akiko answers, "I am Jadecan of Niushki."

"Jadecan of Niushki," Roland says, "You have entered into Orphan space, we have no choice but to pull you in. Security will greet you upon your landing."

"This will be interesting," Baby states, as Jadecan closes the channel.

"Indeed."

As Baby nears the Orphan, many circular tunnel-like blue force-field entrances gradually become visible. They are very similar to the Cortnei's docking bay's single field. A large rock tunnel lined with red lights can be seen through the force-field the ship is heading for. Jadecan looks on as green lights start to pulsate around the entrance's circumference while the black saucer passes through. Baby emerges onto the other side and as she does, the red lights of the tunnel change, becoming green.

A giant cavern filled with dozens of large silver platforms hover within thin air and presents itself before the approaching saucer. All of them are populated with a lot of different types of crafts, although mainly starships rest upon them. It's evident these are the Orphan City's landing pads, and they are impressive. Jadecan stares in awe as they slowly glide into the expansive cave-like bay. It, and the dozens of clear horizontal tubes running along its walls, slightly curve away from view in the distance. Extremely fast moving capsules move along the cavern within the tubes all around them. They seem to serve as a form of transportation traveling to and from the many suspended platforms. Surprisingly, they aren't much bigger than the Cortnei's elevators, although a lot sleeker in design.

"Wow," he says quietly. "This is impressive."

"It is," Baby agrees. "Very impressive indeed."

The saucer nears one of the massive platforms and begins to gradually land upon it. A group of six black armored and armed individuals wait on the landing pad as the ship touches down before them. They approach the vessel cautiously. Jadecan watches the group as they near with their holo-weapons ready, it's apparent they mean business.

"Seems this is my stop," he says sarcastically, while gently petting Buddy who's still perched on his shoulder purring.

I will be here, Baby states, as the Akiko gets up and removes the pink cheiket from his shoulder.

"Where else would you be?" He places his little friend onto the black seat he was just sitting in. "No one in, no one out. I will return."

As you wish, Baby confirms, as Jadecan walks to the back of the ship.

The Akiko strolls down the saucer's dark ramp and grins at the six armed individuals awaiting him. Blood flows from his wounds and as he steps out onto the silver platform, Baby's ramp retracts quickly from behind him. He glares around at the other starships parked along the edge of the large rectangular area as the guards stand in front of him within its lengthy center walkway in between them.

He glances at his broken blade briefly, then says, "Why hello."

"Jadecan, I presume?" the supposed leader of the group asks.

"Indeed."

"You don't look so hot," the leader states, as the other five soldiers stand on either side of him, their weapons locked on the Akiko.

"I am fine."

"Is there anything in your ship that we should be aware of?"

"There is a pet of sorts onboard," the Akiko answers. "A creature, known as a cheiket. It is very dear to me, I would appreciate you leave it be."

"I see, we'll leave it be, no worries," the black armored character says approaching Jadecan. "Now, if you would please, hold your hands out before you."

Jadecan does as he says, and the guard binds his wrists together with some sort of blue holo-cuffs. He is now apparently a prisoner of the Orphan. They are organized and seemingly formidable, unlike any Scut or Reogki he has faced before. The leader of the group removes his black helmet and stares, his small eyes glaring unafraid, a Grogan. His blue triangular face and red skin are like the rest of his species, unique and vibrant. The crest on the Grogan's head however is a bit different, it's relatively large, distractingly so.

"I am Corporal Ry," the Grogan leader says. "If you would, this way." Jadecan nods and obliges, as Ry continues, "You must forgive the greeting, I hope you understand. Characters don't just show up here unannounced. You do know where you are, right?"

"I do," he answers, whilst they meander toward one of the many small square platforms at the landing bay's end. "This is the Orphan. Correct?"

"It is indeed," Ry says casually. "That's definitely a start. What brings you to our little frozen rock? You runnin' from somethin'?"

"In a way," he answers, glancing at his broken bone briefly.

"Yea," the Corporal says, as they begin to board the small platform. "Most that end up here are." He yells out to the group once all are aboard, "Let's go."

"Yes, Corporal." An officer salutes.

The tiny platform detaches from the main bay and as it does a blue protective sphere forms around it. "Off we go," Ry says, while Jadecan admires the impressive view.

Jadecan peers around at the many floating platforms, each one abundant with starships, there are hundreds of them. Yet not a single vessel has launched since his arrival, in fact the entire bay seems to be void of anyone, besides the apparent black armored guards scattered about the platforms.

"Where is everyone?" he asks the Grogan Corporal.

"Oh." Ry chuckles, understanding the Akiko's confusion. "No one really leaves the Orphan once they're here. How did you find us? Did you arrive by locator?"

"Indeed."

"Really? How'd you come by a locator?"

"An old friend," Jadecan answers.

The platform nears a railed catwalk running alongside the cavern's wall, adjacent to one of the clear horizontal tubes. A few guards stand within an opening in the walkway's railway awaiting them. As the platform docks with the catwalk, Jadecan studies the large white elliptical capsule inside the tube, it's much larger than he had previously expected.

"An old friend, huh?" The Corporal chuckles dryly.

"Indeed," he says, as the group departs the platform.

"After you." Ry gestures the bound Akiko onto the catwalk before him.

Jadecan steps in front of the Grogan and follows the other guards out onto the walkway. He continues to trail behind them to the capsule as the Corporal and one other guard follow at his rear. The white capsule's clearly a transportation device, a shuttle of sorts, and a large one at that. It seems to get bigger and bigger the closer he gets. Many windows run down the side of it, through which the Akiko can see several rows of seats within. They stroll for the small flight of stairs leading up to the capsule's open double door entrance and as the guards in front of him board the elliptical craft, he glances back at the Corporal who directs him onboard.

Jadecan walks up the steps into the capsule and stands inside its brightly lit interior as the Grogans begin to seat themselves before him. The transport's beige seating booths appear to be meant for no more than two decent sized individuals and the guards fit that bill nicely. The Akiko though, not so much, he's a tad bit smaller than a Grogan. An empty booth right up front presents itself to Jadecan, most likely intentionally done, makes sense.

"Take a seat, my friend," Ry says, standing at the Akiko's side. "You don't want to be standing when this thing launches."

The doors close behind the Corporal as Jadecan nods and seats himself in the open booth. Ry places himself next to the Akiko, and not long after the shuttle begins to slowly move.

"An old friend, huh," the Corporal says again, while quickly glancing over at Jadecan and chuckling.

"Indeed," Jadecan says, and as the word leaves his mouth the transport significantly picks up speed.

⊖ 2

Jadecan turns away from the constant passing solid silver wall outside the window and smiles at the Grogan Corporal seated beside him. The entire ride thus far has been rather silent, besides the occasional statement made here and there by the Grogan at his side. It's been quiet, real quiet. He's stopped bleeding, and the pain is almost non-existent now, so that's a plus. The fast healing and high tolerance of pain are just a couple of the many benefits of being an Akiko.

The shuttle gradually slows as he returns to the passing solid barrier outside the capsule's window. Almost immediately the barrier disappears and a large sleek walled station replaces it. Although rather large, the area itself is sparsely populated and with nothing but more armed guards at that.

Jadecan sets his eyes upon the shuttle's reflection in the station's brightly lit bluish-grey walls, as Ry states, "Well, here we are, the Shuttle Station."

Two guards stand a few paces away from the shuttle's double doors outside the capsule as it comes to a halt. The

Corporal stands and gestures Jadecan out of the booth before him as the Akiko stares at the guards waiting outside. He smiles at the Grogan, then leaves the booth and makes his way to the capsule's now open exit. The Corporal and his team follow behind as Jadecan steps off the Shuttle onto the smooth waxy floor of the station.

He stops before the guards standing outside the shuttle's double doors and looks around the mostly empty station as Ry stands at his side. The Corporal's five squad members walk around them as the shuttle's doors close at their backs and slowly departs. Jadecan notices a strange hard-bodied character waddling through the station in the foreground behind the guards. It carries within its hands a broom, or something very much like one, and seems to be cleaning as it goes, definitely a custodian of sorts.

"Ah," Ry states, smiling and noticing Jadecan's interest in the character. "That's a Gekkon," he explains. "They maintain a lot of the stations throughout the city. They're a strange bunch, but who isn't." He laughs. "Anyway, shall we?"

"Indeed."

"If you would please," the Corporal says, "Follow me."

"As you wish."

The Grogan walks ahead of Jadecan in between the guards after his team. The Corporal's squad has halted before a hall along the station's back wall, awaiting Ry and himself to join them. The Akiko watches the Gekkon wander about the brightly lit station as he trails behind the Corporal. The two station guards follow behind him with their weapons held tightly within their hands.

The Gekkon's scaly greenish skin looks quite tough, and most likely is, considering the large dark-colored shell upon its back. It moves at a decent pace, venturing from one waste bin to another about the area. It's obvious however, speed's not a strong suit of theirs, instead it seems as if defense is the species main strength.

Jadecan returns his focus to Ry who strides through the middle of his team standing at the mouth of the hall. He follows the Corporal's lead and does the same. The guards in turn form up in the rear and march into the hallway after them. A large silver blast door sits directly ahead of the group, sealing the corridor after a few dozen paces. Corporal Ry stops in front of the only door along the hall, and as the entryway slides open, he glances over at Jadecan, before advancing inside. After a slight hesitation, the Akiko continues after the Grogan Corporal with the rest of the guards close behind.

He enters into a black room lit with a red light, a vast contrast from the shiny bright blue walls of the station outside. A subtle thud echoes as the door slides shut at his back. His yellow eyes lock onto the dark plum-colored door ahead of him, as Corporal Ry stands to its side before a large window. The Grogan stares through the glass pane into the blue light of the medical room within. Jadecan quickly peers at the guards poised on either side of him, then joins Ry at the viewport. He looms beside the Corporal whilst eyeing a slender walking machine within.

The brightly lit room appears to be your typical medical room, nothing too unusual. It sports a single patient bed as well as several monitors and a good bit of counter space, for obvious reasons. The slender walking machine roams about, likely acting as the medical professional, it seems normal enough. A very sleekly designed bipedal artificial intelligence for sure, but normal nonetheless.

Jadecan glares at the scene for a few moments. "Would this be the medical wing?"

"It would indeed," Ry answers.

"I see," he states, as the Corporal knocks on the window.

The robot turns its attention to the viewpoint, almost as if it didn't know they were there. Jadecan watches as the droid interacts with one of the many monitors around itself and after a few moments, the door to the room opens. He looks over his broken bone and bound hands, then at the Corporal standing at his side.

"Go on," Ry says, as the Akiko returns his focus to the medical bay before him. "We'll be out here. Only the patients are permitted to enter. That would be you."

"As you wish." The Akiko casually passes behind Ry for the open entry.

He stops momentarily at the entrance and stares at the silver robot, who stares back. It's small circular head and glowing golden eyes are similar in size to Jadecan's. Besides being a few heads taller than himself standing at about the height of a Yonalitu, like Meshel, it and the Akiko are built similar in body structure. He steps through the entrance, and as the door slides shut behind him, the robot gestures toward the white bed at it's side.

"If you would please, have a seat," the droid says, its voice sounds quite normal and female. "I am an M-S 32, a medical specialist droid. You may call me Lisa."

"I am an Akiko. You may call me Jadecan," he says, placing himself on the edge of the bed.

"It is good to meet you, Jadecan," Lisa states, as she places herself into a metal chair beside him. "This looks recent," she comments, looking over his broken bone.

"It is fine."

"May I inquire how it happened?" the droid questions, while retrieving a small white scanning device from off a table next to the bed.

"It broke during a battle," he answers, after a short pause of recollection.

"I am sorry," Lisa says, as Jadecan stares off into the space before him. "It is repairable, that's some good news I suppose." She scans him with the white tool. "I am sorry though, it is never easy losing a piece of oneself."

"Thank you." He nods.

She stares at the instrument briefly, then states, "Well, you're clean of any foreign pathogens, that's also some good news. Now, to do a little blood work. We're almost done, you'll be out of here soon."

Jadecan watches as she returns the device to the table and retrieves from it a stretchy rubber band of sorts. She ties it around his forearm, then taps his arm a few times before taking a tiny cloth from off the same table.

"How is that?" Lisa asks, referring to the elastic band she had just wrapped around his forearm.

"What is this?"

"That's a tourniquet," she answers. "Is it too tight?"

"No."

"Excellent," she says, wiping down the part of his forearm below the tourniquet with the cloth.

"What are you doing?" he asks curiously.

"I am preparing to draw some of your blood," she answers, disposing of the cloth into a metal waste bin next to the table. "It's a simple procedure, nothing to worry about." She retrieves a small needle from off the table. "You've got good veins, should be easy. Now you're going to feel a slight pinching sensation." She slowly slides the needle into his arm. "Okay, good," she says, as blood fills into a small tube connected to the needle. "And there we are," she states, releasing the tourniquet whilst removing the needle and applying gentle pressure to the puncture with a gauze. "That wasn't so hard, right?"

"It was not," he answers, as she covers the puncture with a small bandage.

"You've been a delight, Jadecan," she says, getting up and walking to the counter behind her.

"Is that it? Am I to leave?"

"It is indeed," Lisa answers. "You are free to go."

"Thank you," Jadecan says standing, and after a few moments of hesitation, makes his way for the bay's exit.

⊖ 3

The bound Akiko is being escorted away from the medical bay by Ry and his squad to an interrogation room located in a completely different part of the station. They file out of the corridor away from the bay back into the main station. The same Gekkon still waddles about as the group marches through the area for a flight of stairs ahead of them. The Akiko glimpses the Gekkon briefly as they walk, before focusing his attention on his and the guards' reflection within the station's sleek glass-like walls.

It's quiet as they stroll up the somewhat steep set of stairs. Jadecan watches Ry and the two guards before him as they lazily pace up the steps. His reflection's as clear in their black armor as it is in the blue walls at his side. It seems as if the walls of the station, as well as its floor, and the armor of the guards, are made of the same glass-like substance. It definitely looked to be so, but appearances are sometimes, if not too often, deceiving. An almost immediate sharp turn greets them at the top of the steep staircase.

They turn the bend and continue down the shiny walls of the hexagon shaped corridor of equally spaced apart closed entryways. They line the hallway on their right, and after passing by a few, the Corporal stops once again before an entrance. The single silver door slides open and as it does, he stands to the side whilst gesturing the Akiko inside.

"It's been fun," Ry states, as Jadecan passes in front of him behind a pair of guards who entered the room before him.

Jadecan nods and follows after the two guards, as the remaining three trail behind him. The room is almost an exact copy of the Medical Bay, glass pane and all. Only difference is, instead of being dark and lit with a red light, this one is silver and lit with a cool blue one. He once again ventures over to the large rectangular viewport and peers into the room beyond.

Only a decent sized metal table and a couple of greyish chairs can be seen within the white walled room. It appears to be rather clean and other than the table and chairs it's completely void of anything else. Jadecan hears the sound of a door sliding open and turns toward it. One of the guards is facing him next to the now open entryway leading into the empty room.

"If you would," the guard says, gesturing him inside.

"As you wish." He strolls over and walks in front of the guard entering the room.

The door slides shut abruptly behind him. He stands momentarily glancing about the empty room, then casually makes his way for the chair on the opposite side of the table, facing the entryway. The Akiko sits himself in the metal chair whilst placing his bound hands on the hard tabletop before him. Jadecan studies the holographic handcuffs around his wrists for a brief moment, before bringing his attention to the viewpoint in front of him. His reflection stares back, it's apparently one-sided, of course it is.

After some time, the entry slides open revealing a species Jadecan has never seen before. It's dressed in a modest mahogany trench coat and carries within a scaled hand a notebook. It stands in the doorway and stares at him with its dark small eyes. A black fedora rests upon its head and as the brown rough skinned character walks over, the door shuts at its back. It seats itself in the grey chair directly across from the Akiko while taking off the hat and placing it onto the table.

"I suppose we should begin with salutations," the individual states, looking at Jadecan and placing the notebook down onto the silver tabletop before him. "I'm Mr. Nix, who are you?"

"Jadecan."

"Well, Jadecan," Nix says, whilst lighting a cigarette and retrieving a small ashtray from out of his coat. "This is how this is going to go. I am going to ask you a series of questions, and you are going to answer those questions to the best of your ability. Do you understand?"

"I understand," Jadecan answers, as Mr. Nix sets the ashtray down before himself.

"Great." Nix puffs the cigarette and opens the notebook. "Where would you be coming from?"

"Niushki."

"Ah yes, Niushki, nice place. I've been there a few times throughout the years," Nix says, exhaling a bit of smoke. "How's Niushki?"

"It is fine."

"What did you do on Niushki?"

"What do you mean?"

"What is your profession? Or do you not have one?"

"I do not have one," Jadecan answers.

"The M-S 32 says you are an Akiko," Nix explains, ashing the cigarette. "Apparently you're a rare species. Is that so?"

"So I have heard."

"How did you come into possession of Stet's locator?"

"An old friend."

"So I've heard," Nix states, taking a drag. "Who is this old friend?"

"O'an."

"O'an? How did O'an end up with Stet's locator?"

"Stet gave it to him."

"Stet gave it to him?" Nix asks.

"Yes."

"Why did Stet give O'an the locator?"

"To hold on to."

"Why?"

"Stet did not believe anyone would suspect O'an of having the device," Jadecan answers. "That is why."

"Why would no one suspect O'an of having it?"

"Because he is a Scut."

"So why did Stet allow O'an to give you his locator?" After some time of silence and a bit of smoking, Nix adds, "He didn't allow it, did he? How do you know the Scut? How do you know O'an?"

"We worked for Stet."

"Worked? So you don't anymore? I suspect O'an doesn't either, is that correct?"

"It is."

"I suppose O'an just handed over the locator?"

"He did."

"Is Stet aware that you have his locator?"

"He is not."

"Stet will find out and when he does, he will kill O'an," Nix states confidently. "You do know that?"

"He will not find out."

"What makes you so sure?"

"He is dead."

"Really?" Nix exclaims. "Hmm, interesting. Stet is dead? How? How did he die?"

"I killed him."

There is a brief pause as Nix stares across the table at the Akiko. Jadecan glares back as Mr. Nix puts out the cigarette in the ashtray and leans back in his chair whilst folding his arms across his chest.

"You killed Stet?" Nix asks, after a few moments.

"Yes."

"Why?"

"He attempted to have me killed," Jadecan answers. "He left me no choice."

Silence again falls over the small room as the two stare at each other. "How did you get Stet's locator to function?"

"The Mistress of Quietus. She got it to function again."

"The Mistress of Quietus?"

"Yes."

"Blake," Nix calls loudly, not taking his eyes off the Akiko.

A voice answers from Nix's wrist, "Yes, Mr. Nix?"

"Who, or what, is the Mistress of Quietus?"

The voice answers without pause, "The Mistress of Quietus is a supernatural being who appears as one of two things to those who seek her out. A fiery haired maiden to those who are worthy of her help, or as a hideous monstrosity to those who are not. The Mistress of Quietus dwells deep in the Akiko's Curtain before the Mountains of Despair, on the moon of Niushki. She is said to live in a hut within the forest, which is usually described as standing on Drakon-like legs that are ringed with levitating skulls. The Mistress of Quietus who is commonly associated with the Athpeha, the ancient guardian of the forest, is also said to have a strong connection to the sacred red lake found within the forest, known as

Blood Lake. The Mistress of Quietus, because of this, is also commonly associated with Sh'lyn, the Lord of the Akiko. The Mistress of Quietus appears as either a donor or villain, or may be altogether ambiguous."

"Interesting," Nix states. "So a witch. Let me get this straight, you kill Stet, then you go to O'an's to retrieve Stet's locator. You then take said locator to this Mistress of Quietus, who somehow magically gets it to work again, is that right?"

After a few moments, Jadecan nods. "Yes."

"Okay." Mr. Nix leans forward and clasps his hands on top of the table in front of him. "That's quite the story, I'll give you that. How did you know Stet had the locator?"

"It was rumored he had some sort of device. I did not know what kind of device, however."

"I see," Nix states, writing in the notebook. "Have you ever heard of an individual by the name of Sophis?"

"I have."

"Have you met this, Sophis?"

"Yes."

"Where did you meet him?"

"On Vyn," Jadecan answers.

"Where on Vyn?"

"I am not certain," Jadecan answers. "A cavern of sorts."

"Under what circumstances did you two meet?"

"I do not understand."

Nix rephrases the question. "Why were you at the cavern?"

"I was completing a job for the Olensi."

"I see," Nix states. "Is that something you often do?"

"It is not. It was the first and last job I will do for them."

"What was the job?"

"Releasing a creature they had taken from Vyn back into its natural habitat on the planet."

"Were you successful?"

"Indeed."

"Okay. I suppose after releasing the creature you run into Sophis?"

"Yes."

"Did you know who he was when you initially saw him?"

"No."

"What happened during your encounter with Sophis on Vyn?"

"We talked for a short while, and then he attacked me."

"Why did he attack you?"

"I am not sure," Jadecan answers. "I do not believe he was supposed to be there. I think that is why. I do not know for sure, however."

"Did you retaliate?"

"Yes."

"Was it just the two of you? Yourself and Sophis?" Nix asks. "Or were there others at the scene as well?"

"There was another."

"Who?"

"A Cerulean by the name of Amelia."

"Why was Amelia there?"

"She accompanied me during the job."

"She was helping you with the job?"

"Yes." Jadecan nods.

"What happened after you retaliated? Did you kill Sophis?"

"He somehow disappeared before I could."

"But you did intend to kill him?"

"Yes, at the time."

"At the time?" Nix asks. "If given another opportunity, would you kill Sophis?"

"I have no reason to at the moment."

"I see." And after a few moments, he lights another cigarette, and states, "I think I get the general idea. Why did you come to the Orphan?"

"I was left with no other option. I have nowhere else to go."

"I believe you," Nix says, nodding his head whilst closing the notebook and taking a drag. "I'm told there is a cheiket on your ship, is that true?"

"It is."

"Well, it is to stay there, for the time being." Nix ashes the cigarette. "Does it have enough food and water for a few days? If not, we will supply it."

"It does."

"Good."

He stares at Jadecan for a moment or two then retrieves his notebook and hat from off the silver table. The Akiko watches as Mr. Nix puts the fedora on and then disappears through the entryway without saying a word. The door slides shut, leaving him alone to ponder on what all had just happened. He glances down at his bound hands atop the table in front him, then stares at the smoking ashtray. After a couple of minutes, the door opens revealing the black armored Corporal standing outside the entrance.

♀ Crystal Cell

⊖ 4

Jadecan sits on the edge of a mattress inside a small square holding cell. He's already been here for a few hours, and it's unknown how long it'll be before he's released. Apparently, he'll be here till they decide what to do with him. At least they removed the handcuffs, there is that.

A clean undressed bed and toilet are all that accompany him inside the bare walls of the brightly lit holding cell. He stares at the white wall ahead of him, then to the shimmering blue edged clear holo-barrier at his right. It seems significantly darker outside the room, making him feel somewhat as if he is on display. Suppose he very well could be, he would make quite the display.

After what felt like an eternity, the sound of a door sliding open and closed can be heard from down the corridor just out of view from the holding cell. Footsteps echo throughout the hall getting closer with each passing second. Before long, a mechanical armed Flunari cautiously strolls into view and looks in at Jadecan around the cell's barrier's center. Jadecan slowly stands and casually walks over to the long-necked Flunari, knowing exactly who the brown skinned tiny bodied individual is. The Akiko stops before the Flunari and stares up into its sky blue eyes through the barrier separating them.

"Sophis." Jadecan grins. "I see you are doing well."

"Why yes," Sophis says nervously. "I'm... I'm doing fine."

"What are you doing here?"

"I heard an Akiko was... being held here," Sophis stutters. "Said his name was... Jadecan. I had to... to see you for my... myself."

"Here I am."

"Yes.... Here you are indeed." There is a silence as the two eye each other. "Why are the Olensi after you?"

"Apparently they are not fond of me killing them."

"I suppose... they would not be."

"Yea, I suppose so," Jadecan agrees.

"Is it true you um, you killed Stet?"

"It is." After a brief silence, Jadecan asks, "What does it matter?"

"Stet was... important," Sophis states. "Nix seems to think he... he got what he deserved. I think it's... unfortunate. I'm sure you did... you did what you had to do."

"How was he important?"

"He helped us with... our reactor."

"Sounds fun."

A couple of moments pass, followed by Sophis stating, "Yea, I'm sure we could... find another to help with it."

"How did he help with the reactor?"

"He helped us, um, get the fuel for it."

"The fuel? I suppose this fuel is special?"

"Yes, it is indeed," Sophis answers. "A moss... a luminescent moss that... that is quite difficult to find."

"Is that why you were inside the cavern? You were collecting the moss?"

"Yes."

"A luminescent moss? As in, it glows?"

"Yes. As in, it glows. Bio-luminescence is… is quite rare in flora, so… yes. It's quite difficult to find."

"I did find the sight of it rather intriguing," Jadecan tells Sophis. "I have since seen a glowing moss on Niushki. I cannot say if it is the same moss, however."

"Really?" Sophis' blue eyes light up. "It likely would be… as I've said, it's quite rare."

"Why do you not grow it here?"

"We have tried, but for one reason or another… we cannot seem to um… to get the necessary requirements right for its survival," Sophis explains. "We are still… still working on it."

"I bet you are."

"Would you be able to… show me where it is on Niushki?"

"I suppose," Jadecan answers. "Will I be released if I do?"

"It is a possibility."

"If so, I suppose I could show you where it is."

"I will… will talk with Mr. Nix about it. How is the Cerulean that was with you in the um, cavern?"

"She is fine."

"That is good. I am sorry, for shooting yourself and… and your friend. I did not mean you or your friend, any harm."

"I see that," Jadecan states. "She has referred to you as a gentle soul. I tend to believe her."

"I believe I… I remember her… from Solarius."

"She has said that about you as well."

"I'm glad she is okay."

"I am too. She also stressed that you likely would be killed by the Olensi, if they were to ever get a hold of you. She hoped that would not come to pass," Jadecan explains. "She seemed somewhat fond of the few memories she had of you." After a few moments, he adds, "I am not your enemy, but I can be. I would much rather be an ally to you and this Orphan City."

"I am going to see... see what I can do, to help you with your um, situation."

"I would appreciate that."

"You must understand however..." Sophis states, "That even if you were to... to be released, it is unlikely... you would be permitted to... to leave."

"I understand."

"Very well. I will see what I can do. Is there anything I can do for... for you in the meantime?"

"No, I do not believe so."

"It is good to see you, Jadecan. It's been nice talking with you," Sophis says, then walks back toward where he came from just out of view of the cell.

⊖ 5

The Akiko and Flunari are seated inside a large oval shaped Olensi hovering transport moving at an impressive speed. Jadecan glances at the robotic right arm of Sophis sitting next to him whilst vividly remembering their encounter on Vyn. He remembers well the shock and fear worn on Sophis' small face as he savagely cut off the Flunari's arm. At the time it felt as if it was the right thing to do, now he wasn't so sure. Odd how things change.

He returns to the window and watches as many other types of hover-crafts zip by on the wide metallic roadway all around them. This is as Sophis calls it, the Orphan Highway. They left the Shuttle Station a while ago and are now in the heart of the bustling metropolis of Orphan City.

It took some time, but Sophis was able to negotiate his release, somehow. As for the details of the release, well, he is to consider guiding a team to the moss on Niushki. As for the Flunari, you could say he got the short end of the stick. Jadecan is to be Sophis' responsibility and any trouble caused by him will fall squarely onto the Flunari's shoulders. As to where he'll be staying in Orphan City, well, he'll be living with Sophis, of course. Yea, you could say he got the short end of the stick.

"This is our... our stop," Sophis states, as the fully automated bus-like hover-craft stops and extends a small ramp from the doors on its side.

Sophis smiles as he speaks. Jadecan smiles back, he now somewhat understands Amelia's fondness of the odd Flunari who is Sophis. He's strange, this is true, but likable and for the most part, harmless. Jadecan in fact believed Sophis would have difficulty harming even a fly, much less one such as himself.

The pair leaves the bleached booth and makes their way for the transport's open doors. Sophis leads and Jadecan follows as they depart the transport down its white narrow ramp. They step out onto the very sleek and shiny roadside walkway in front of a couple of cherry-colored couches. A large meadow of vibrant green grass stretches far and wide behind the sofas as the highway rages behind them.

"Interesting," Jadecan says, as the bus' ramp retracts from behind them and the transport returns to the fast-paced Orphan Highway.

"This is a pickup station," Sophis states referring to the cherry sofas, as a Grogan walks on either side of a Nudruk in between Sophis and Jadecan and the pair of couches. "Pickup station S37 to be exact. You wait here if you wish to catch... to catch a bus."

"Really?"

"Yes. My place is not far from here," Sophis says, strolling away from the Pickup Station. "This way."

The duo walk side by side without a word said for quite some time. Various types of species walk by frequently as they make their way down the silver footpath. Some Jadecan recognized like the Grogans and Nudruks, but others he did not. Jadecan admires the beautiful brightly lit city as a constant flow of hover-crafts fly by next to them.

"Thank you, Sophis," he says, breaking the long silence.

"You are welcome." Sophis smiles looking down at the Akiko with his large light blue eyes, and says, "I'm glad everything worked out."

"I am as well." And after a few moments, he remarks on Sophis' mechanical arm, "The arm looks good."

"You think so?"

"I do."

"I did it myself," Sophis exclaims. "Oddly enough... I enjoyed it. Not the loss of the arm, of course. But the creation and the... the installment of this one, I did enjoy indeed."

Jadecan chuckles. "You enjoy doing that sort of thing?"

"Yes, I'm what you could... could call a tinkerer."

"A tinkerer?"

"Why yes," Sophis answers. "I find en... enjoyment in fixing what is... what is broken or... improving on what is already... already working to make it... it better."

"Interesting."

"I could... help you with your... your broken bone," Sophis says, gesturing to Jadecan's broken elbow blade. "It may take some ah time, but I think I could... could do it if... if you'd like."

"I would appreciate that," Jadecan answers. "Thank you again, Sophis."

"You are welcome."

The pasture on their left abruptly ends as they walk on by, leaving it behind them as the smooth silver buildings of Orphan City take over. The vehicles drastically slow as they venture deeper into the metropolis. Jadecan watches as the once fast-paced highway turns into a congested mess beside him as the pair walk alongside it. Before long, the walkway becomes just as congested, if not more so.

"This is it." Sophis stutters a couple dozen paces later, "This is where... where I... I live... the... the Greenview Apartments."

Sophis strolls for the multi-door front entrance of the apartment complex as Jadecan stares up the side of it. It's quite tall and has a slight greenish tint mixed into its silver coloring, giving it a unique appearance amongst the numerous others lining the sidewalk with it. The Akiko follows the Flunari's lead through the motion censored entryway onto the main floor of the building.

Jadecan stops inside after a few paces and admires the room before him. Giant glass chandeliers line the ceiling as Sophis continues on ahead. From the elaborate design of the red carpet at his feet to the stylish tawny walls of the complex, this is truly a masterpiece. Sophis stops in front of one of the four gold colored elevators which run up the right side wall of the open room. He presses a button to the side of it as Jadecan makes his way to him.

"I am ah, a couple of floors up," Sophis says to the approaching Jadecan. "It's a nice place. One of the... the nicest."

"I can see that."

There is a ding followed by the elevator opening. The Akiko follows the Flunari inside the ornamental small box elevator. It's reflective gold walls and ruby colored carpet are just as elegant as the main hall of the Greenview Apartments. The doors of the lift close as the pair turn to face them.

"Floor three," Sophis says aloud.

The elevator smoothly ascends and stops following another ding soon thereafter. Sophis looks over at Jadecan and smiles as the doors of the lift slide open. Sophis and Jadecan casually meander out of the gold box onto the vermilion carpeted floor outside it, while a character of the same species as Nix walks by them boarding it.

"What is that?" Jadecan asks, referring to the character as the lift's doors close.

"What is... what is what?"

"I have not seen that species before. It is of the same species as Mr. Nix."

"Oh." Sophis laughs. "That is a Minorak."

"Interesting."

"Ah yes, they're an... an interesting species," Sophis states, strolling down the corridor.

A lantern-like light extends from beside each entryway on either side of the surprisingly wide hallway. Sophis stops at the second door on their left and retrieves a keycard from his holo-system. The Flunari inserts the card into a slot underneath the lantern, then turns the round copper knob of the door and pushes it open.

"Here we are, home sweet home," Sophis says, removing the card from the slot. "Well, come on in."

Jadecan follows Sophis through the entrance. The Flunari closes the door after the Akiko walks inside. Jadecan is almost instantly greeted by a levitating droid.

The legless robot's round head tilts slightly as it studies the Akiko. Its small grey eyes look to be nothing more than a pair of bolts, with its torso being merely a small simply made body with two robotic arms. A blue glow is barely visible below the hovering droid's torso, and as it floats before Jadecan a slight humming sound can be heard.

"Oh, don't mind Mezrich," Sophis says, walking past Jadecan and the floating machine into the room. "He's a... nevermind, come, come. Let me show you... show you where you'll be staying."

Mezrich trails Sophis who walks across the maroon colored carpet of the apartment toward the back of a burgundy sofa. The square room is clean and rather empty as an unlatched door leading to what appears to be a bedroom, most likely Sophis', is present on its left wall. A closed entry sits across from the open entrance whilst the restroom at

Jadecan's left side stares at him. A gold and white fan spins on the ceiling directly above the couch as Sophis strolls around the sofa and faces the Akiko.

"You will be here," Sophis says, looking across at Jadecan and gesturing toward the couch in front of him. "It's ah, not much but...." He shrugs.

"It is fine," Jadecan states, still standing before the entryway having yet to move. "Thank you."

Sophis nods and gestures after a moment to the open door on his right, and says, "That is um, my room and ah that is my... my workshop." He points toward the closed door on his left, then gestures around him, and adds, "And this... this is the um, the main room. This is where... where you will be staying. And that is... the restroom." He points to the open door down from his room, then glances at the droid hovering at the side of the sofa. "And you've... you've met Mezrich there."

"Did you construct Mezrich?"

"Yes, he was ah... he was to be my... my brothers." Sophis pauses before facepalming, and stating, "Oh, I am going to be late... oh my, late, late, late." He walks around the sofa and advances to the apartment's entryway toward Jadecan who still hasn't moved. "Make yourself at um, home... I will return."

Sophis hastily exits the apartment, leaving the Akiko alone with the hovering robot. The two awkwardly stare at each other in silence as the sound of the gradually spinning fan and humming of the droid, seemingly become louder with each passing second. Hurried footsteps approach and stop outside the apartment's entrance. Sophis' voice mumbles incoherently as the door clicks and swings open behind the Akiko.

"I ah... hmm..." Sophis says. "If you would please... come.... Come with me."

"As you wish," Jadecan states, looking over his shoulder at the round blue eyes of Sophis, then quickly glances at Mezrich as he turns away from the robot and leaves the apartment.

He shuts the apartment door and strolls down the hall for Sophis who makes his way toward the elevator entry. "I'm not to um, leave... well, you're just... just going to join me at... at lunch today."

"Where is lunch?" Jadecan asks, as the pair arrive at the lift.

"I am not sure... just yet," Sophis answers. "I will be stopping by my... my work first."

"Work?"

"Yes, I ah... I work at um The Crystal," Sophis answers, as the elevator dings and its doors slide open. "It's a... a tech company. It specializes in mostly... well, I specialize in... in bio... biotechnology," he says, strolling into the lift alongside Jadecan. "It's where I spend most of... most of my time. If I am not here, I am there."

"Sounds nice."

"It does," Sophis agrees, as the elevator doors close and begins to descend.

⊖ 6

Sophis and Jadecan step off a shuttle before a pickup station in front of The Crystal's large circular complex. The ramp of the hovering bus retracts from behind them and pulls away as they advance past the station for the reflective silver building. They walk side by side on the metallic walkway whilst Jadecan admires the immaculate glass-like buildings of the Orphan City all around him.

"Who built the city?"

"No one is entirely... entirely sure," Sophis answers, walking up the few steps before The Crystals entrance. "I believe the architects... are... were... were from Vyn."

"If you say so."

"I do say so," Sophis states, as the pair walk onto the wooden landing in front of The Crystal. "It's thought that... that since well, it was once thought... thought that the moss or... the Violet Fuel as it is referred to... could only be found on the planet so, logically it ah... makes since the original species that con... constructed the city would... would also be from there considering...."

"Do not hurt yourself, my friend."

"What?"

"Nothing, Sophis. Nevermind."

The solid shiny doors of the complex slide open as the two approach. Sophis walks through with Jadecan close at hand and continues for the circular front desk directly ahead of them. A small rather adorable looking character smiles from behind the desk as it watches the duo stroll in its direction. Jadecan peers around the large lobby in both awe and confusion as he follows Sophis toward the smooth counter.

The walls of The Crystal are different now, much different now. They were solid on the outside, but now they are completely see through, appearing to be glass, as opposed to the sleek metallic silver they looked to be when he approached. They even seemed to be moving. If you stared at them for long enough, it almost looked like a slight ripple could be seen occasionally flowing through them, almost like they were made of some sort of liquid.

"Intriguing, you think?" Sophis asks, noticing the Akiko's wonderment.

"Indeed."

"It took me a good... good while to get used to it. The Crystal and the Speran are the only two... two locations within the city that... that have these kinds of two-way... two-way walls."

"They appear at times to be moving," Jadecan says. "It is almost as if they are made of liquid."

"The whole city is... is that way. You will feel at times... you are being watched."

"Being watched? By whom?"

"The city," Sophis answers, as they arrive at the front desk.

"Sophis, so good to see you," the tiny greyish skinned character from behind the desk exclaims happily, as they approach. "Is that an Akiko?" it questions, after gazing at Jadecan for a few moments.

"Yes," Sophis answers, gesturing toward Jadecan standing at his side. "This is Jadecan... Jadecan, this is Rew," he states, looking at Jadecan and gesturing to Rew standing behind the desk before them.

"Why hello, Rew."

"Hello, Jadecan," Rew says joyfully, his tiny bead-like black eyes staring as he smiles happily. "I have never met an Akiko, this is quite exciting. How are you? Is Sophis treating you well?"

"I suppose so," Jadecan answers, with a small chuckle, amused by Rew's excitement of meeting him. "And what are you? I have never met one such as yourself, as well."

"I am a Shellot," Rew answers. "I'm from a planet known as Galick. And you? Where are you from?"

"A moon known as Niushki."

After a moment's pause, Sophis asks Rew, "Is Lucius here?"

"Oh yes," Rew answers. "He is indeed."

"I figured as much," Sophis says. "We shall head that way, thank you. It is good to see you Rew."

"No, thank you." Rew smiles at Jadecan. "It's been a pleasure, my friend."

"It has," Jadecan says, as Sophis strolls past behind him.

"Come, come," Sophis states, walking away from the front desk. "This way."

Jadecan trails behind Sophis as he makes his way around the counter to an entryway a few paces away from where Rew stands. A large metallic frame housing a hand-sized green screen, not too much different from the one next to the entry of the Oteniko outpost on Niushki, sits to the right of the white door. Sophis places his chestnut-colored hand onto the screen and after a second, or two, the entrance slides open before them.

- ⊜ 6 -

The Flunari moseys through the door into the white narrow corridor with the Akiko close at hand. The entry shuts at their backs as they saunter down the short hall for yet another entrance that sits just a few paces in front of them. The corridor is possibly wide enough for the two of them to walk side by side, but if so, definitely not comfortably. Above the entryway ahead of them sits a small black box accompanied by a red light, it's likely a camera. Sophis casually waves above his head as the two near the corridor's end. And as he does, the door opens revealing a large lab of sorts.

The entry slides shut behind them as they enter the lab, and a voice proclaims, "I will be ready in just a moment."

Several tables and shelving units populate the open extremely white room. Microscopes as well as beakers sit upon the shelves and silver tables, they are a common sight along with other scientific equipment within the room. They stand in front of the colorless doorway for a few moments, before a Shellot pops its small head from around a corner a few paces away from them, and smiles.

"Hey, Sophis," the Shellot says. "I'll be done in just a moment."

"You are fine, Lucius," Sophis states, as Lucius retracts his head back behind the shelving unit. "I had feared I was… I was late."

"You are not late, in fact I am the one that is late," Lucius says. "I was supposed to be done with this analysis an hour ago, but at least it is done now."

The Shellot walks out into view and advances toward them, as Sophis says, "How was today?"

"Today was good," Lucius answers, basically standing in front of them.

"This is Jadecan." Sophis gestures to the Akiko at his side. "The plus one… I was telling you… you about."

Jadecan looks down at the tiny Shellot and nods. "It is good to meet you, Lucius."

"It is nice to meet you too, Jadecan. I have to ask, but why are you only wearing pants and no shirt?"

"I have never worn a shirt."

"We do have some amazing outfits that would fit you though. They would give you more protection while not limiting your mobility or flexibility in any way. Similar to the uniform I am wearing. We could schedule a time for you to get sized. What do you think?"

"No."

"That works. So where would you like to eat?" Lucius says, with a hungry smile.

Jadecan grins happily, he has thoroughly enjoyed this encounter. It's been a long time since he has genuinely felt delight after meeting an individual. If the circumstances of their initial encounter had been different, he most likely would have felt the same about Sophis. As it is however, Sophis has grown on him, and he is quite fond of the both of them.

"Well, I was thinking… we could do… do the Gabbin," Sophis answers, while glancing down at Jadecan. "They have more… options for us."

"Excellent," Lucius exclaims, as the three of them head out of the lab. "I have been wanting to try their new linchamo soup. I hear it is phenomenal."

♀ Albino Dish

⊖ 7

Lucius asks Jadecan, who sits in between himself and Sophis at the Gabbin's bar, "You are from where again?"

Jadecan glances over at Lucius as a Balgorex that's not too different from Stet works behind the counter before them. The Gabbin's a decent sized place and set up similarly to how Stet's Place was. It's a bit nicer however and doesn't sport the iron bars or Scuts Stet was so fond of. Also had a few more tables as well as a slightly larger floor space. It's rather crowded and busy and doesn't appear to be slowing down anytime soon. Jadecan watches as the cooks of the restaurant do what they do best directly behind the bar in front of them.

"Niushki," Jadecan answers, while watching the big bartender wander about.

"Niushki," Lucius states. "Isn't that...."

"Yes," Sophis answers, as Lucius looks over at him. "It is indeed."

The large Balgorex strolls over and stands in between the cooks. "Sophis... Lucius," he says, nodding at the both of them, then locks his four brown eyes upon Jadecan. "I see we have a newcomer. Who might this be?"

"This here is Jadecan," Sophis answers.

"Welcome Jadecan, I am Gynn. A pleasure to make your acquaintance, my boy." The Balgorex exclaims proudly, "I serve the finest cuisine and the most extraordinary top shelf in the whole of Orphan City. Ain't nowhere bestin' the Gabbin, you can't find a better dish, or drink for that matter, anywhere else. What shall it be? Maybe the linchamo, a favorite of mine. We now have a linchamo soup as well."

"Linchamo soup for me," Lucius exclaims.

"Then linchamo soup you shall have, my boy." Gynn looks over at Sophis. "What will you be having?"

"Linchamo soup for me as well," Sophis answers.

"Very good." The Balgorex asks Jadecan, "What about you, what will you be having?"

"I am not sure, what are my options?"

"The menu's quite vast lad." Gynn chuckles. "But for one such as you, maybe roasted juguke, or seared setani? Both are delicacies on Niushki."

"Roasted juguke," Jadecan answers. "I will have that."

"A great choice," Gynn exclaims. "The finest roasted juguke in the whole city, and what will you lads be having to drink?"

"Three Achord teas," Sophis answers.

"Very well." Gynn walks to the shelves behind him.

Gynn retrieves three mugs from the shelving unit in front of them as Lucius picks up where he had left off. "Niushki, I have not made it out to that system. The farthest I have gone is Halovom, the Yonalitu homeworld. Have you ever been there?"

"I have not," Jadecan answers, as Gynn places a steaming ceramic mug of Achord tea before each of them.

"I will be back shortly," Gynn states. "Enjoy."

"What is Achord tea?" Jadecan asks, as the Balgorex strolls away.

"Achord is a herb from Malorad, my homeworld," Sophis answers. "I have always… always felt better once having some… of the tea."

"I see," Jadecan says, taking a sip of the brew.

"I have researched some on Akikos, your species is an interesting one," Lucius states. "My species has a shared communal culture, but ours focuses more on the advancement of what you might call magic and science. Which I think is one of the reasons we make such good engineers, we can figure out how things work from multiple perspectives. Are there any mystical or magical type things on Niushki?"

Jadecan chuckles and smiles at Lucius. "I did find a glass orb of sorts. Suppose it is mystical or magical as you would say."

"Did it have any… any interesting properties?" Sophis asks.

"It glowed," Jadecan answers. "Otherwise, no."

"Fascinating, where is it now?" Lucius asks.

"It is with Dr. Cassandra of Oteniko. She wished to study it."

"Interesting," Sophis says, looking across Jadecan at Lucius.

"Oteniko… hmm. I wonder if it is related to the Olensi campaign," Lucius says aloud looking at Sophis. "They seem to be searching for different items of ancient origins. This orb seems like it would be of significance to them." He says to

Jadecan, "I heard somewhere in my travels, can't remember where right now, that there are a number of other glowing orbs scattered about the universe. Have you heard that as well?"

"I have heard something akin to that," Jadecan answers.

"I've heard that as well," Sophis agrees. "According to legend... if one were to... to collect them all, they themselves would be... ah... would become like a god, of sorts."

"Really?" Lucius asks. "Where did you hear that?"

"I believe... I believe Idyn had... had shared that with me," Sophis answers. "I do not know where he ah... where he had heard it from though. He hated using the term 'God' however, and opted instead to use the term 'System Lord', which for all intents and purposes is the... the same thing."

"Hmm... System Lord." Lucius contemplates to himself. "I have heard that term somewhere before, wish I could remember where." And after taking a sip of tea, he asks, "Anyways, I have always been intrigued by such topics. Where did you find this glowing orb?"

"Inside a hidden dungeon within an abandoned Reogki outpost." Jadecan grins glancing at the both of them seated on either side of him. "I had to use a special key to reveal the dungeon's secret entrance. Dr. Cassandra has that as well."

Gynn treks back to them impressively carrying three plates within his hands. "Two linchamo soups.... One for my friend Lucius, and one for my pal Sophis," He places the glass plates down before them and while placing one in front of Jadecan, he adds, "And the finest roasted juguke for our friend Jadecan." The Akiko begins to chow down almost as soon as the plate hit the counter.

Lucius and Sophis have been staring across the Akiko at one another for a bit of time now. They're both in awe of the Akiko's voracious appetite and are still trying to comprehend what he has just told them regarding the glowing orb and its key.

Gynn watches the pair stare at each other for a few moments, but eventually concern gets the best of him, and he asks, "Is everything okay?"

After a couple of moments, Sophis answers, "Yes… yes. Everything's fine. Thank you, Gynn."

"A secret key and a hidden entrance," Lucius says, as if talking to himself while Gynn ambles away. "Have you ever heard of the legend of Ol-Vaj? He is an Old One, sometimes referred to as the Great Azaros, or the One Above All."

"I have not."

"Legend states," Lucius tells, "That Ol-Vaj fought a centuries-long war with the Elder One, over who would rule the universe. The winner would reign supreme over all, and the loser, which was Azaros in this case, would be locked away until a chosen one releases him from his prison."

"Yes," Sophis states, consuming a bit of soup. "That is correct. I remember Idyn telling me this. Although, according to him, Azaros was destroyed as opposed to locked away and his ah… his essence was… was stored into twelve or thirteen orbs… I'm not positive as to the number of orbs… but, by collecting them all, however many that may be, you would ah… acquire Azaros' power. Making you a… a System Lord, if you will. I suppose you would… would become like an Old One, as Azaros is."

"Who is this Elder One?" Jadecan asks.

"It has always been referred to as the Elder One," Lucius states, drinking his tea. "I am not aware of any other name it really goes by."

"Is there only one Elder One?"

"Yes," Lucius answers. "There is a single Elder and Older One, and if the legend is to be believed, neither can exist without the other. Which is why I am confident that Azaros has been locked away, and not destroyed."

"That is, that is interesting," Jadecan states.

"Agreed," Sophis says, drinking some tea.

"How is everything?" Gynn asks, after strolling back over to the three of them. "I hope you are each satisfied with your chosen dish."

"I believe we are," Sophis says. "I am rather impressed with the linchamo soup, very good indeed."

"I agree," Lucius states. "I would definitely order it again, very delicious."

"And the roasted juguke?" Gynn asks Jadecan.

"It is good."

"Very nice," Gynn exclaims. "Can I get you boys anything else? Maybe more tea?"

"No... no, we are fine," Sophis answers. "Thank you, Gynn."

"Very well. I'll be back by in a bit, enjoy," Gynn says, walking along the bar away from them.

Lucius looks over at Sophis and after a few moments, says to Jadecan, "I hear you are staying with Sophis, he's definitely got a very nice place up at Greenview. What do you think of Orphan City so far? Are there any cities like this on Niushki?"

"There are not," Jadecan answers. "There is nothing like this on Niushki. This is quite an impressive place."

"It is," Lucius agrees. "There is nothing on Galick like this either, nor on Malorad, correct?"

"That is correct," Sophis says. "I believe Solarius has got similar cities. They are not ah… quite like the Orphan's but… they are similar."

"Agreed," Lucius states, consuming a bit of his soup. "They are impressive in their own way. Do you two have any plans for later?"

"After we… we leave here?" Sophis asks Lucius, who nods. "No, well… we'll most likely head back to my… my place. Get some… some rest and relax. It's been… it's been an experience. You? What are… are you doing after this?"

"I'll be heading back to the lab," Lucius answers. "I have a few hours left and there is always work to be done. I hear there's a card happening tomorrow though, we could go together if you would like."

"What is a card?" Jadecan asks.

"It is a fighting competition," Sophis answers. "There are usually three bouts, each ah… consisting of three… three rounds. With the last one being the ah… the main event. It's the most popular form of… of entertainment here in the city." He looks at Lucius, and asks, "Who is the main… main event?"

"If I remember correctly," Lucius says, "I believe it is Eryn, the Grogan Champion, against a Nudruk, surprisingly."

"Really? Who?" Sophis asks.

"To be honest, it's probably Tefan," Lucius answers.

"Wow, he's... he's come a long, long way." Sophis asks Jadecan, "Would that... that be of interest to you?"

"It would indeed," Jadecan answers, with a grin.

"Excellent, I will see you guys there then," Lucius exclaims. "Well, I have to head back to the office soon, but wanted to let you know that things are getting weird around the lab," he tells Sophis. "Lately there have been council officials roaming through the building in restricted sections. I do not know who gave them clearance, but was advised by my superiors to let them have full access. Everything just feels ominous lately, best keep attentive. If I find out anything else, I will let you know."

"That's relatively odd. We'll have to discuss that... in a bit more detail later." Sophis looks at Lucius who nods. "Are you leaving now?" Sophis asks.

"Yeah, I probably should," Lucius answers, getting off the bar stool. "The linchamo soup was amazing. We should do this again sometime."

"Indeed," Jadecan agrees, nodding to Lucius.

"Nice meeting you, Jadecan," Lucius states.

"Likewise," Jadecan says.

Lucius then looks at Sophis. "Would you mind if I stopped by in the morning?"

"Not at all," Sophis answers.

"Sweet," Lucius states. "I'll see y'all tomorrow, have a good one."

⊜ 8

The Akiko sits in the dark on the magenta sofa inside Sophis' apartment. He and the Flunari had been back for a few hours chatting about the events of the day. At some point they began talking about the events on Niushki and how he ended up in Orphan City. He told him of how he and Amelia met as well as the events at the Kiwiwa village. Jadecan recounts his meeting with Tytus and how he ended up in the cavern on Vyn. Sophis listened as Jadecan described the finding of Stet's locator, which eventually resulted in his broken bone.

It was a good talk, during which he showed Sophis the missing piece he had stored away in his holo-system. Sophis asked if he could use it to aid in his reconstruction of the broken bone. Jadecan obliged, giving it to him to hold onto. Not long after, the Flunari left for his workshop along with Mezrich, leaving him alone to rest. The sound of the fan spinning slowly above him is all that can be heard, as he quietly chats with Baby.

"Baby," he whispers.

Yes?

"How is Buddy?"

He is fine. He spends most of his time sleeping.

"Good," he states, with a small laugh, staring into the darkness before him. "How are you?"

I am well.

A few moments pass. "What is your opinion of this Orphan City thus far?"

Seems normal enough. However, I am unable to see what you have been witness to. With that, there are a couple of things that have interest to me, that pertain to this Orphan City.

"Intriguing, like what?"

First, was a conversation between yourself and Sophis, within The Crystal.

"Which one?"

His own voice along with Sophis' plays in his head as Baby replays one of their conversations. *They appear at times to be moving. It is almost as if they are made of liquid,* Jadecan states.

Sophis answers, *Indeed, the whole city is... is that way. You will feel at times... you are being watched.*

Being watched? By whom? Jadecan asks.

The city, Sophis answers.

Baby says, *This conversation between you and Sophis, has intrigued me the most. It is as if the city itself is alive, and if that is indeed the case, it is most likely very similar to one such as myself. If your words are indeed true, which I have always known them to be, and if this Sophis is to be believed as well, then at this very moment we are being watched by none other than the city itself.*

"Interesting," Jadecan remarks. "It was concerning."

Indeed. It is rather discomforting to say the least. I also found the talk between Lucius and Sophis, regarding Azaros and the glowing orbs intriguing as well.

"How so?"

I was under the assumption it was not common knowledge, yet that seems not to be the case. I find that somewhat interesting.

"I, like you, did not believe it to be a known fact," Jadecan says. "Is there anything else you found of interest?"

Besides the lack of knowledge or conversation pertaining to the Elder One, who for all intents and purposes is the presiding System Lord, no. With that being said, I believe it would be beneficial to keep an eye out for the outcast, the mournful brother the Tome of the Old Ones spoke of. He is to be our guide to the next orb, they are supposed to be here.

"Understood. What are your thoughts on Sophis?"

I am a fan of both himself and Lucius. It is unfortunate the circumstances under which you two met, and surprisingly, it does not seem to have negatively affected his view of you, like one would have thought. It would be unwise to trust him however, considering the amount of time you have known him. What are your own thoughts on the matter of Sophis?

"I am a fan," Jadecan answers. "I do appreciate both Lucius and himself. I also find our initial encounter unfortunate, it is strange, life is, quite strange indeed."

Life is indeed strange. Get some rest while you can, Jadecan. It's not often you are presented with the opportunity.

⊜ 9

The Akiko awakens as a knock echoes throughout the white walls of the apartment, someone is at the door, and it's probably Lucius. He rises like a corpse from a grave as Sophis quickly emerges from his room and bee-lines for the apartment's entry.

"I'm coming, I'm coming," Sophis states, heading for the door.

The humming sound of Mezrich resonates behind Jadecan, who stands slowly and turns to the entrance as Sophis unlocks and opens it, revealing the Shellot. The Akiko strolls around the burgundy sofa and looms to the rear of Mezrich who hovers a few paces from the back of Sophis. The tiny Lucius wanders inside and waves at Jadecan as the comparably giant Sophis closes the door behind him.

"Hey Jadecan, good seeing you," Lucius exclaims, walking across the carmine colored carpet toward him, while Sophis strides back to his room.

Jadecan nods. "Good to see you as well."

Lucius stares up at Mezrich as he approaches the floating robot. "And how are you Mez?" he asks, tapping his hand on the robot's body. "Hope things have been good with you."

"He is doing quite well," Sophis says, shutting the door to his bedroom and walking out toward the sofa. "Are we still on for... for the event later?"

"Of course, but we've got plenty of time if there is something you want to do," Lucius answers.

"Ah, well, before we... we get too carried away," Sophis says, continuing past Jadecan for his workshop. "I was working in the workshop last night and... and made our friend Jadecan here, something."

"Cool," Lucius states, as Sophis opens the door and disappears inside.

"It took some... doing," Sophis says from inside the room. "But I think that...." He meanders out of the workshop carrying what appears to be a large curved silver blade. "That

I have successfully constructed... your replacement," he says, presenting it to Jadecan.

With it now in front of him, he can clearly see what it is, and it is extraordinary. The Flunari had apparently spent the night recreating the missing piece of his broken bone, and it was done exceptionally well. Truly astounding.

"This is amazing," Jadecan says, smiling pleasantly surprised.

"Thank you," Sophis says pleased. "I used the piece you... you gave me to hold on to as a... a reference. I dare say... I believe it's almost an exact copy... of the original."

"Indeed."

Sophis inspects his creation, whilst saying to Jadecan, "We could... we could try to attach it... later, if you'd like."

"Sounds good to me," Jadecan answers.

"Very good." Sophis disappears back into his workshop. "We could attempt to install it after the event," he says from inside the room.

"As you wish," Jadecan states, as Sophis re-emerges from the workshop without the reconstructed blade.

"Is there anything you would like to do, Jadecan?" Sophis asks, while shutting the door.

"Not that I am aware of," Jadecan answers.

"You have... anything in mind?" the Flunari asks the Shellot.

"We could get something to eat," Lucius answers. "The Gabbin seemed to be a good pick for all of us last time."

"That works for myself," Jadecan says.

"Very well," Sophis states, strolling hurriedly past Jadecan for his room. "I have got to get a few items... I may be... a few moments."

Jadecan nods as Lucius chuckles, and says, "He always seems to be running around."

"Indeed," Jadecan answers, as Mezrich flies past in between him and Lucius for Sophis, whom at this point has disappeared into the bedroom.

After a few moments, Lucius asks, "What is the gem on your necklace, is it an emerald? It's a decently sized one."

"I do not know, I suppose it could be," Jadecan answers, while watching Mezrich come to a stop, hovering outside Sophis' slightly open door, almost as if the droid's prohibited from entering.

"Emeralds are the most common of the green stones. There are numerous others, but more often than not, it's an emerald," Lucius explains. "Where did you get it?"

"It was a gift."

"Ah well, it is very nice," Lucius says.

"A Ruogji of a Kiwiwa village had given it to me," Jadecan states, gently gripping the gemstone. "I treasure it."

"You have mentioned them before." Lucius nods. "They seem rather important."

"They are family."

Lucius smiles up at the Akiko standing a few paces from him, as Sophis says, "I apologize for... for keeping you waiting."

"No worries, Jadecan and I just talked a little while waiting," Lucius states.

"Is Mez not to enter your room?" Jadecan asks Sophis, as the Flunari strolls over to them with Mezrich close at hand.

"Oh no," Sophis answers, glancing over at the dull grey machine hovering at his side. "He very well may. I have found however, if I do not invite him in he… he will usually wait just outside the… the entry."

"That is, different," Jadecan states.

"Are we set… set to leave?" Sophis asks the both of them.

"I hope so," Lucius answers, "Because I don't know about you two, but I'm starving."

Jadecan lets out a small laugh. "I am with him," he says to Sophis, whilst gesturing toward Lucius.

⊜ 10

The three of them sit at one of the small square tables inside the Gabbin. Sophis and Lucius seat themselves across from one another as Jadecan sits between them facing the bar they had sat at the first time they were here. Gynn ambles back and forth behind the bar, same as he did yesterday. It doesn't appear as busy though, in fact, they are some of just a few of the individuals here at the moment. A tall salmon skinned Nudruk wanders from the bar toward them as Sophis and Lucius chat about work and Jadecan listens.

"We have known it was just a… a matter of time. It is finite, it is not… not a sustainable source of energy. We must f-find a different… method of powering the… the city," Sophis explains, referring to the moss from within the cavern on Vyn. "Even if this Great Opening Jadecan speaks of has... has a good bit, it would only last us... so long."

"True," Lucius states. "The council should have considered one of the alternative energy options I presented to them. If they had, we could have started construction on the project, and would have most likely been running off it by now. Ditching the bioreactor all together, but no, they had to be stubborn about it."

"How is everyone?" the Nudruk asks, arriving at the table. "I'm Jaymi, I'll be the one taking care of you. Is there anything I can get you to drink?"

"Achord tea, please," Sophis answers.

"And for you?" Jaymi asks Lucius. "What will you be having?"

"Achord tea as well," he answers.

She looks up at Jadecan sitting across from her. "The same," Jadecan states.

"Okay, I'll be right back with the Achord tea in just a moment," she says, then saunters away from the table back toward the bar.

"You had proposed the... the fusion reactor... as the best alternative at the time, I believe," Sophis says to Lucius, as Jaymi walks away.

"What exactly does this reactor do?" Jadecan asks.

"It runs our life support and shielding technology," Lucius answers.

"It keeps the city... separated from space, allowing us to live here... comfortably," Sophis adds. "The city's in sort of... well, its own tiny bubble. Without the reactor, the bubble... would pop, so to say."

"Yes." Lucius nods. "It supplies us an artificial atmosphere, considering the moon itself doesn't have one. Without the reactor the whole city would be unlivable and succumb to the vacuum of space."

"I see," Jadecan says.

"Having it all powered by a bioreactor would be fine," the small Lucius says, "If it weren't for the rare organic material that it requires."

"This is where the... the moss comes in," Sophis tells Jadecan, as Jaymi strolls back toward them carrying a tray of three mugs. "It's what we refer to as the... the Violet Fuel. It's what Stet had helped us acquire... and now with him dead... it has become, more of a problem than... than it already was."

Jaymi places a mug before each of them, and asks, "Have we decided on anything, or do we need more time?"

"I will have the ah... the leyli eggs with a side of... of Gabbin fries," Sophis answers, as Jaymi activates a device that appears to be linked to her holo-system.

"I'll have the mismah cakes and a side of Gabbin fries too," Lucius says, as she interacts with the blue screen projecting from her wrist.

"And you?" the waitress asks, her black eyes looking up from the screen at Jadecan.

"Raw setani," he answers.

"Would you like Gabbin fries on the side as well?" she asks.

"I would."

Jaymi punches in the order and deactivates the device. "Okay, I'll be back with your food in a bit."

"Raw setani?" Lucius asks Jadecan, as Jaymi ambles away.

"Sophis?" a female voice calls from behind Lucius, as Jadecan begins to say something in response.

The Akiko looks over and watches as an albino Drakon walks over toward them. She's close to the Akiko's height and build, be it a bit slenderer, which is surprising considering the Drakons are known for being on the thicker side. Her long thin tail flips back and forth as she strolls for the table. The Flunaris' light blue eyes light up as he stares at her marching to him.

"Kit?" Sophis exclaims, standing and embracing her in front of the high table before Jadecan. "Wow, it's been… it's been a long time. How have you… have you been?"

"Good," Kit answers, her light green eyes staring up at Sophis.

"Sorry." Sophis gestures to the table. "This is Jadecan."

"Hi Jadecan," she says, as he nods.

"And you… you already know Lucius," Sophis adds.

"Hey Kit," Lucius says, as Kit waves at him.

"Have you eaten yet?" Sophis asks her.

"I have not," she answers. "I just walked in."

"We have an… an available seat here at the table." Sophis gestures to the empty metal stool beside him and Kit, across from the pale Jadecan. "Would you'd like to… to join us?"

"I'd love to, thank you," Kit says, and as she seats herself, Sophis returns to the tall chair across from Lucius beside her. "An Akiko, in Orphan City. That's not something you see every day." Kit smiles at Jadecan across from her.

"I was not aware that the Drakons had found their way here." Jadecan grins in response.

"There's a couple of us here," she answers, her small round snake-like face grinning back. "Did you come from Niushki?"

"I did," he answers. "Did you?"

"Yep, I left that place the first chance I got. I am not a fan of the Balgorex, I can not stand them," she states, then quickly glances over her shoulder at the bar behind her. "I mean Gynn's okay, but otherwise no, not a fan. And since they pretty much own Niushki, there was absolutely no way, I was going to stay there."

"It is not that bad," Jadecan says, sipping his tea.

"Suppose it's... it is a matter of perspective," Sophis states. "Jadecan has... has only been here a few days."

"Oh," she says.

"Yeah, I enjoy hanging out with him," Lucius adds, looking over at the Akiko and smiling gleefully. "It's been fun, and interesting."

"I'm happy to hear it." She smiles in response as Jaymi arrives in between Lucius and herself with the food.

The waitress begins placing the plates down before the guys, whilst asking Kit, "Can I get you anything, my dear?"

"I'll have that," Kit answers, pointing to Lucius' plate.

"The mismah cakes with a side of Gabbin fries?" Jaymi asks.

"Yes," Kit says.

"And to drink? Will you also be having the Achord tea?"

"Might as well," Kit answers playfully.

Jaymi nods smiling, then questions the table, "Can I get you guys anything? Perhaps more tea?"

"No, I do not think so," Sophis answers. "Thank you."

"Okay, I'll be back in a few with your tea, dear," Jaymi says to Kit, before walking back toward the bar.

"Do you boys have any plans for today?" Kit asks, eyeing Jadecan as he chows down on the setani.

"We're going to… to the card later," Sophis answers, taking a bite of his leyli eggs.

"I was debating on going to that myself," she states.

"You should," Lucius says, drinking his brew. "It'll be a fantastic fight."

"Maybe I will," she says, with a flirtatious giggle. "I am going to stop by the Kurat briefly beforehand, you are welcome to join me if you'd like."

"The Kurat?" Jadecan asks, looking over at Sophis.

"Yes," Sophis answers. "It is a sort of… library and shrine, dedicated to the… the Goddess of Fertility, Vulena. It is one of the largest temples… here in the city."

"It's a rather unique architecture," Lucius adds. "Rumor has it that Vulena built the Kurat herself. However, most of the temples here were not on the Orphan originally."

Jaymi arrives with Kit's tea and places a mug down before her. "Here you are, my dear."

"Thank you." Kit smiles.

"You are very welcome. Your food will be just a few moments," Jaymi says to Kit. "And how are we doing?" the waitress asks the rest of the table.

"Good," Sophis says. "Quite good."

"Indeed," Jadecan adds.

"Awesome. Do we need a refill?" she asks Lucius, noticing his tea to be mostly gone.

"Hmm… yeah I could, thanks," Lucius answers.

"Okay, I'll be back in just a moment," Jaymi states.

"Who is this Vulena?" Jadecan asks Lucius, as the Nudruk leaves.

"She's one of the oldest deities, and the most prominent one here in the city," Lucius answers. "She's from the same pantheon as Azaros."

"One could argue," Sophis states, sipping his tea. "That her All-mother's word is as powerful as the… the Fitura's."

"It's possible, her followers are prevalent here," Lucius says, shaking his head. "Sadly, because of that, she has heavy influence."

"In any case," Kit states, picking up her mug. "I am heading that way and will meet you in the lyceum after."

"I would like to meet this Vulena," Jadecan says.

"You are welcome to tag along if you'd like," Kit says, drinking her brew. "The All-Mother's always there."

Jadecan nods, as Lucius looks across the tabletop at Sophis, and says, "Well, if that's the case then you can count me out. I will stop by the lab to complete a few last minute things, and meet you at the arena's entrance afterwards, if that's ok?"

"That's fine," Sophis answers. "We'll meet at the… the fight afterwards."

♀ Obsidian Scales

⊖ 11

Jadecan, Sophis and Kit walk off a shuttle before a black triangularly shaped building, the Kurat. The Akiko and Flunari follow close behind the white Drakon as she strolls across the metallic walkway for the stone cathedral ahead of them. The dark Kurat definitely stands out among the rest of the silver buildings of the Orphan City surrounding it. It's rather small in comparison and appears to have no windows to speak of, as well as a large V-like symbol centered about halfway up above its single entry.

"Have you met this All-Mother?" Jadecan asks Sophis, as they near the temple's entrance.

"Yes... I have been here once or twice," Sophis answers. "It has been a while since last I was here, however. The All-Mother... is a high priestess... of Vulena."

"And Vulena is this Goddess of Fertility?" Jadecan asks Sophis, while Kit opens the Kurat's heavy black door.

"Yes," Sophis answers.

"Vulena's said to have been a lover of Lord Sh'lyn," Kit says, looking over her shoulder whilst ambling inside.

"Well then, that is something," Jadecan says out loud to himself, as he and Sophis enter the Kurat behind Kit.

The large door slowly closes at their backs as they gradually stroll away from the Kurat's entrance. A giant obsidian statue stands majestically toward the front of the temple ahead of them while impressive rows of onyx bookshelves run down both walls of the long shrine beside them. A couple of large glass chandeliers hang from the ceiling above them, whilst small lanterns glow at the end of each bookcase. Jadecan eyes the black sculpture before him as he and Sophis follow closely behind Kit. The occasional individual can be seen within the isles going through the many thousands of books as the three of them walk down the Kurat's center.

"The All-Mother is in the chantry beneath us," Kit says, as they continue in the direction of the dark effigy. "She rarely leaves the Kurat, and spends most of her time in reverence of Vulena."

"You mentioned Vulena had been a lover of Sh'lyn. Do you know this to be true?" Jadecan asks Kit.

"According to the All-Mother, it is true," she answers. "And I am inclined to believe her."

"I see," Jadecan states.

"That however, does not make it fact," Sophis says.

"This is true," Kit says. "Believe what you will."

A large portrait about the size of Jadecan himself stares back from the statue's smooth pedestal as they near it. A very snake-like entity's imaged on the painting and strangely enough, appears to be moving. Jadecan narrows his small yellow cat-like eyes in response to the odd painting, and the closer he gets, the weirder the picture becomes. He stops before it and glares at the feminine life-like figure on the canvas.

The top half of the individual is clearly a female Drakon, with her bottom half being a serpent of sorts. She sits now barely moving, as the pencil shaded backdrop she rests upon sways violently behind her, as if undergoing some unseen significant storm. The Drakon gradually begins to turn its small head back and forth, then stares directly at Jadecan, while the dark portrait's background comes to a complete halt.

"What is this?" he asks, his gaze unmoving.

"That?" Kit asks, standing at his side. "That is Amada, the Constant Watcher."

"Very interesting," Jadecan states.

"It's an ancient relic," Sophis says. "Amada's said to be the Mother of All Monsters. Some argue that... that Vulena and Amada are the same. Just two different names for th-the... the same being, like Ol-Vaj and Azaros. So... you could be looking at a portrayal of Vulena herself or... something entirely different."

"You ready?" Kit asks, glancing over at Jadecan.

"Yes."

The Akiko follows as the Drakon walks around the large circular base of the effigy. Jadecan stops after a few paces upon realizing Sophis was no longer at his side. He looks back over his shoulder at the Flunari who has not moved a muscle. He still stands in front of the portrait, his light blue eyes looking at the Akiko, smiling.

"Are you not coming?" Jadecan asks.

"I am not permitted... to enter the sanctum," Sophis answers. "Only those following an entity of the Delga may... may venture below."

"Delga?"

"Yes, both Sh'lyn and Vulena are... are a part of the Delga," Sophis says. "They are of the same... same family you could say."

"You don't have to join me," Kit says. "You can stay up here with Sophis, if you want."

After a few moments of silence, Sophis says, "You should... should go. It's most likely in your... your best interest, besides, I'm not going anywhere. There is also... a good bit of reading material, I will be fine. Just ah, don't get into any... any trouble, okay?"

"I will not." Jadecan nods. "I will not be long, my friend."

He turns away from the Flunari and follows the Drakon's lead around the statue. Kit's tail flicks back and forth as she walks ahead of the Akiko for the staircase on the side of the sculpture. Jadecan trails closely, venturing down the curving steps behind her. Torches blaze along the stone block walls as the pair descend below.

He strolls off the stairs onto the gold floor of the Kurat's lower level while glancing up at the black ceiling. Kit has stopped and is looking back at him from the center of the small torch-lit room. Solid dark walls with no visible entries surround him as he strides in her direction. He opens his mouth to speak as he nears the pale Drakon and mysteriously is engulfed in complete darkness.

A ghostly blue fire lights after a few moments on the ground in front of him, illuminating himself and the area around it. It's very reminiscent of his encounter with the winged beast of the dungeon. He stands alone before the blaze, it seems he's no longer within the Kurat, hell it appears he's left the Orphan all together. A violet mist forms across from him and after a few moments Jadecan finds himself glaring into the face of Amada, looming on the other side of the blaze.

"Amada," he says, staring into the Drakon's unnaturally pure white eyes.

"I prefer Vulena," the serpent states.

"The Goddess of Fertility," he says.

"So, you're the high priest of Prince Fenric?" Vulena asks. "This chosen one I've heard so much about."

"Prince Fenric?"

"I believe you know him as Lord Sh'lyn," she answers. "You've already met a couple of our children."

"Your children?"

"Yes, my child," the Goddess answers. "We have quite a few children together."

"How many is quite a few?"

"Thousands."

The Akiko narrows his yellow eyes. "What of these thousands have I met?"

"The Sabosan of whom you've bested, and the Shaitan. It was a thrill to watch you complete Zliyek's task, I thoroughly enjoyed it, it was quite entertaining. None before you have managed to do so. Quite the accomplishment," she answers exuberantly.

"What do you want?" he asks carefully.

"Nothing," Vulena answers. "I merely wanted to see this great Champion of the One Above All for myself. I must say, Sh'lyn has chosen well, you do not disappoint."

"Jadecan... Jade." Kits voice echoes faintly, and the vision dissipates, as the albino Drakon stands before him staring rather concernedly. "You okay?"

"Yes, I am fine," he answers.

"Thought I lost you there for a moment." Kit lightly giggles, obviously still a bit concerned, then turns to face the wall behind her. "So... you ready?"

"Ready for what?" Jadecan asks.

She smiles as a simple crown-like symbol begins to etch itself into the stone wall before them. It glows a vivid violet for a few moments, illuminating the surrounding blocks, before promptly disappearing and being replaced by a brown wooden door. Jadecan watches as Kit strolls over and effortlessly opens the unadorned entry.

"The Refuge of Keleth," she says, gesturing inside. "When you are ready."

A lavish altar stares from the other side of the shimmering entrance at the end of a long orchid carpeted walkway. Endless rows of ebony pews run along either side of the pristine path as Jadecan peers at the extravagant cathedral awaiting him. Behind the altar stands a lady draped in a dark purple robe. The Akiko advances through the entry and heads for the altar before the albino Drakon who follows.

Jadecan arrives before the priestess and stands as Kit kneels at his side. "All-Mother," she says respectfully. "Standing before you is J'dkyn of Otok, the Key Master."

"You know me?" he asks, glancing down at Kit.

"We do, J'dkyn," the All-Mother answers. "Vulena has always been at your side, watching your every move. Loyal, brave, and true, you are quite auspicious. Do you know who it is you serve?"

"Not you," he answers slowly.

The Akiko turns away and strides back for the sanctum's luminous entry. He's had enough of this Kurat and its Vulena for now.

⊖ 12

Sophis, Kit and Jadecan wait for Lucius at a Pickup Station outside the arena's entrance. The Akiko watches as many hundreds of Orphaners cross a bridge over the busy highway for a dome-shaped coliseum on its other side. A sign very similar to the one at Stet's Place spins slowly above the large building which reads in a dark red light, Ashly.

"Have you been to one of these before?" Jadecan asks Kit.

"I have not," she answers, as a bus pulls up beside the stop.

The vehicle's doors open and out floods several individuals. "Lucius," Sophis says happily, as the small Shellot lumbers out of the craft. "So good to see you."

"You too." And after a moments pause, Lucius asks Jadecan, "So what did you think of the Kurat?"

"It was fine," he answers.

"Hmm... interesting," Lucius states. "Well as usual, I got busy finishing a project, so I'm a little bit late. Have y'all been waiting long?"

"Not at all," Sophis answers. "We should get... get going though, the card starts... relatively soon." The four of them head for the walkway along with a large group of other arena goers. "Do they have anything like this on Niushki?" Sophis asks, walking beside Jadecan whilst Lucius and Kit stroll slightly behind them.

"As in a card?" Jadecan asks.

"Yes."

"What is a card exactly?"

"It is a one on one fight," Sophis says.

"It was a bit more than that. Originally," Lucius explains, "What we refer to as a card, is actually derived from an ancient Grogan tradition called Donkosi. The name itself, in their language, means, all the power. It's an extremely violent sport, where two warriors fight one another to the death. It happened only once a year and was considered a great honor to be chosen to compete. Both contenders, were highly respected, regardless of the fight's outcome."

"Is that so," Jadecan states, sauntering onto the bridge.

"Yes, a grand celebration and funeral were held for the fallen warrior, both of which would be hosted by the victor. I've always found that part to be admirable," Lucius states. "Additionally the victor, who sometimes died from injuries themselves, would be revered as the greatest warrior of all, at least for that year. The spoils, as you might imagine, were quite lavish, and were shared among that Grogan's bloodline."

"I had forgotten about... some of that," Sophis says. "Very interesting stuff."

"In today's age however, Sophis is correct." Lucius states. "It is a one on one fight."

"That doesn't often happen." Sophis laughs, and says to Jadecan, "I do not believe there is... is a single death attributed to the... the cards as well. They are quite... quite safe."

"True, no one has died during the cards," Lucius states.

"That is disappointing," Jadecan says.

"I agree," Kit adds, with a small laugh.

"It's for entertainment now. Simply a one on one brawl to cultivate their skills. Nice thing is that other races can compete," Lucius states, as they walk off the bridge and head for the Ashly's entrance. "Lately though, people speculate the fights to be fixed."

"Really? What a shame," Jadecan says.

"Most everything's politically driven," Sophis says. "If it is indeed fixed, I'm sure politics are a big part of it."

"Agreed," Lucius says, as the group reaches the Ashly's large open entry.

They enter the coliseum behind many arena goers whilst hundreds of others file in after. Jadecan admires the gigantic dark walkway encircling the interior of the Ashly, as dozens upon dozens of stairwells descend from it toward the caged ring in front of him. It's dimly lit and extremely crowded, of all the places he's been to while here at Orphan City, this thus far is his favorite. There are no windows, no doors, it's a huge dome on solid steel stilts, it's entirely open and dark. A sort of twilight, and although different from Niushki's, it's similar enough to feel familiar.

"Who do you think is... is going to win the main event?" Sophis asks Lucius, as they wander for one of the stairwells.

"Who's the main card? I forget." Lucius laughs.

"The current champion, Eryn, is going up against... against Tefan," Sophis answers.

"I'll go with Eryn," Lucius states. "What do you think? Who do you have?"

"Although I am in belief that... that Eryn will emerge victorious," Sophis says. "I am rooting for Tefan. There has... has never been a Nudruk champion. I am... I am hopeful he'll be the first."

"Yeah, it would be good to see some other species win for once," Lucius states. "That being said, I don't think Tefan can do it."

"Is this mainly a Grogan sport?" Jadecan asks, walking down the stairs.

"It is," Sophis answers. "There aren't many other species that... that participate in these events."

"There was a Drakon that fought a while back," Kit says. "It was quite controversial, a big story at the time."

"That's right." Lucius chimes in. "There was once a Drakon who participated, and like Kit said, it was a big deal. If I remember correctly, he was also the only non-Grogan to ever become a champion."

"You are correct, the dreaded Phara. His scales were as black as space itself, unnaturally so," Sophis says. "I remember him well, Idyn had actually bet... bet against him and lost." He chuckles at the memory. "Good times."

"Wonder what happened to him," Lucius says. "It's like he just decided to leave the Orphan completely."

"It is rumored he went back home, to Niushki," Sophis states. "But I honestly do not know. I would like to believe that... that to be true. It would give it a sort of... sort of happy ending. It beats the alternative."

"What is the alternative?" Jadecan asks, standing to the side of an aisle.

"That he was killed," Kit answers, following Sophis and Lucius into the row.

"I vaguely remember now, gosh," Lucius exclaims. "That was quite a while back."

"Idyn and I, had actually only just arrived not too long before that," Sophis says, sitting in a seat beside Lucius. "It was an… an interesting time, to say the least."

"Did we know one another then?" Lucius asks, as Kit and Jadecan seat themselves next to Sophis.

"We did not," Sophis answers. "We became friends when I… I got the job at The Crystal. In fact, it was… it was Nix who introduced us to one another."

"Oh yeah, it was, wasn't it." Lucius laughs. "I remember the look on your face when you saw me, that was amazing."

"It was." Sophis smiles. "You know, it was rumored, that Nix was… was actually seeing Ashly… around that time."

"The Ashly?" Lucius asks in shock.

"Indeed," Sophis answers. "That Ashly."

"Ashly?" Jadecan asks, as if he's heard the name before.

"She's the founder of the card," Kit answers. "She was a big, big figure back in the day. Could have probably been a Fitura, if she had ever decided to run for the office."

"Was?" Jadecan asks. "Is she not anymore?"

"She died, a few years back," Kit says. "She was old, really old."

"Have you heard of her?" Lucius asks the Akiko.

"I might have," he answers. "A very, very long time ago."

⊜ 13

A light rain dampens the white dust of Niushki as Jadecan and a couple of Scuts head for a small stop known as the White Claw, on the outskirts of Stet's territory. A Kiwiwa village's blaze can be seen in the distance as Sitadoom glide over top the planet on the horizon. Their exo-crafts speed by at a rapid pace continuing onward toward the mission, and as a subtle wind blows the stone complex of the White Claw begins to take shape ahead.

The Akiko has been working for the Balgorex ever since their fateful encounter so long ago, outside that Reogki town. If it wasn't for Stet, he could very well be dead, a debt he intends to repay. As of late, he's been doing the Balgorex's dirty work, which unsurprisingly, consists of a lot of killings, among other nefarious activities. Occasionally however, he would unfortunately act as merely a runner, he isn't fond of the gig, but it's a part of the job. It doesn't matter where you live or what business you run, everyone pays a fee, and the Balgorex's runners are the ones who collect it.

He was sent out a few cycles ago in search of an individual Stet wants to be dealt with, as to why, it doesn't matter, it never does. As long as he's killing, he doesn't care. He's used the time wisely as always and has made a few stops along the way. In doing so, he has learned of his target's likely whereabouts, but not much else. The Akiko's sources are usually reliable. His methods of obtaining information is quite effective, and in most cases, fatal. It is tasks like this one he thoroughly enjoys and wished he got more often. His mission is simple: find and kill the black Drakon, by any means necessary.

Jadecan and the Scuts park their exo-crafts and leisurely walk for the complex's wooden door. The White Claw's an older place, it's seen a lot over the years. It's exchanged hands several times throughout the decades and has a bit of a reputation. It's not necessarily a bad one, but it's also not necessarily a good one either, whatever the case, it would not be a revelation to find the Drakon here. The Nudruk who runs it currently is a nice enough fellow, he's not the brightest, but he's still breathing, so there is that.

The Scuts pull open the small brown door as Jadecan surveys the grey building's terrain. He peers through the Claw's circular holo-windows whilst the two Scuts wander inside before him. He doesn't play well with others, preferring instead to be alone, but Stet of course suggested taking a couple of Scuts just in case, so he did. Normally he'd contest, but for whatever reason at the time, he didn't feel like it, so here he is, with a couple of Scuts. He hopes to not regret the decision. The Akiko saunters through the entry and stands momentarily as the door creaks shut at his back.

"Jadecan," the Nudruk bartender greets. "I wasn't aware you were going to be stopping by. May I get you a drink?"

The silverish pink skinned Nudruk stares intently from behind the bar, it's obvious the situation has him feeling rather uncomfortable. The Nudruks' name for one reason or another, escapes the Akiko. Odd, that commonly didn't happen. Jadecan looks over at the three individuals sitting at the bar and notices immediately the black Drakon, who pays him no mind. The Scuts stroll along the bar in front of him for the reptilian without pause, they tend to do that. The reptilian has now taken notice and understandably has a look of concern worn upon its dark face. The other two, the Cerulean and Nudruk who sit alongside the Drakon at the tabletop, mind their business, a smart move.

"Is there anything I can help you with?" the Nudruk barkeep Kem, whose name Jadecan has just remembered, asks.

"No," he answers, as the Scuts stand at the seated Drakon's back. "There is nothing you can help with."

The unnaturally darkened lizard slowly rises from his bar stool. "What do you want?" he asks demandingly. Then angrily adds after a few moments of silence, "Did Ashly, or that damn Minorak send you?"

"Neither," Jadecan answers, and as his weapon forms within his hand, he points it at the Drakon.

The wind of Niushki howls outside as the entire place goes still. Jadecan glares into the Drakon's small white eyes for a moment before firing two bullets into the reptilian's chest. He lowers his arm and watches as the Drakon falls to his knees in front of the Scuts. He could have easily shot the lizard in his head, skipping this entire sequence, but he rarely does. There's something about it, the whole process. Suppose, it's like a sort of entertainment. It's a hard life, why should death be any different?

The Drakon looks down at his bleeding chest for just a second, before setting his gaze upon the Akiko who fires a single shot into the black reptilian's skull. The lizard sways as blood begins to trickle down from between his eyes, before falling hard onto his face. The Scuts nudge the Drakon's lifeless body before heading back over to Jadecan, who still stands inside the White Claw's entrance.

He chuckles quietly to himself as the eerie silence looms evermore, and then fires two more times, killing the approaching Scuts. Kem looks on as the Akiko continues his killing spree. Jadecan pulls the trigger, killing both the Nudruk and Cerulean seated at the bar, before the insect's bodies even hit the Claw's stone floor. Jadecan stares into the small black eyes of the Nudruk barkeep, then grins and shoots him in the head, killing him instantly. The white energy weapon disappears dematerializing from his grip as Kem falls with a sounding thud.

♀ Mahogany Laser

⊖ 14

Jadecan sits upon a small metal stool within the Flunari's workshop. It's a small dark room with only one light source, which at the moment is being focused on the broken bone of the Akiko. Sophis rummages through the many items upon the cluttered tabletop before him as he sits at a desk beside Jadecan. Mezrich hovers at his side, watching while the long-necked Flunari mumbles to himself. After a moment or two, he picks up the silver blade he had created from off the table and turns to the Akiko.

"What did you... did you think of the fight?" Sophis asks. "I can't say I was... I was surprised with the end result." He compares the blade to the Akiko's unbroken one.

"It was... enjoyable," he answers.

"That's good," Sophis states. "Well, it's a bit larger." Sophis shakes his head and sighs, while looking at the blade.

"I am sure it is fine."

"Oh, it's nothing to be... to be concerned with." Sophis turns back to the desk with the contraption. "It's just a mistake that... that could have been... been easily avoided."

"We all make mistakes," he says to Sophis, who smiles. "I am sorry about the loss of your arm."

After a few moments, the Flunari says, "Thank you, I... I appreciate that."

"You had mentioned you had built Mezrich for your brother," Jadecan says, watching the dull droid hover behind Sophis. "Is your brother here, on the Orphan?"

"He is not," Sophis answers, fiddling with the blade. "He… he left a while back and… and never returned. I activated Mez sometime afterwards, he never… never got to…." His voice trails off and he sits for second. "I always said I would complete him, but… but always got sidetracked with… with some other project."

"Are you still working on Mezrich?"

"Yes," Sophis answers after a brief pause. "He is an ongoing project. The next upgrade I plan on… on doing with him is… installing a voice box. As you may have noticed he… he does not speak."

"Will that be difficult?"

"Installing a voice box? No, not really." Sophis positions the silver blade over top of Jadecan's broken bone. "It's just setting aside… some time to do it. Will not be difficult at all."

"If I can be of help, do not hesitate to let me know."

"Will do," Sophis says, then talks almost as if to himself while messing with the blade piece. "Okay, so… yea, that seems to fit… fit nicely. Now to… now to set it…." He looks about the table and calls to the robot. "I need that, bring me that." He gestures toward a device sitting on the far end of the desk, while asking Jadecan, "Where did your Cerulean friend, and you meet?"

"You are referring to Amelia?"

"Yes, yes I am."

"We actually met at Stet's place," he answers, as the Flunari retrieves a pair of goggles and puts them on. "It was unexpected."

"There's been a lot of that lately."

"Indeed." Jadecan chuckles.

"Very good," Sophis says to Mezrich, as the robot hands him the remote-like item. "I had met Stet a few times over the years, he… was a character." He points the remote at the base of the blade, and states to Jadecan, "If you would, don't move."

A red laser erupts from the device's end and as Sophis holds the blade piece in place, he moves the beam rather slowly along the contraption's bottom. Jadecan observes for several minutes as the Flunari intensely focuses on the laser. After quite some time, the red beam disappears and Sophis hands the item back to Mezrich. He removes the worn goggles and looks over his handy work.

"Hmm… seems good. How does it feel?"

"Feels fine." Jadecan answers.

Sophis slightly moves Jadecan's arm as he messes with the contraption. "Seems sturdy. What do you think? Would you like to get up… and move about for a bit? Just to be sure that… that you like it? Before we go about… go about making it permanent." Jadecan gets up and paces the small workshop, as Sophis asks, "How is the weight? Is it too heavy? Does it feel natural?"

The Akiko leaves the small room and begins slicing at the air while wandering around the apartment's sofa. "I am impressed." He admires the shiny blade. "Very well done, it feels rather natural. It is slightly heavier, but barely noticeable," he answers, sauntering back into the workshop and returning to the metal stool. "You are indeed, a tinkerer, my friend."

"Thank you, I'll take it." Sophis smiles happily. "Mez," he calls the droid again. "We are almost done," he states to Jadecan, as the robot hands him back the small remote.

"I have been wondering," Jadecan says, as Sophis rummages through the many items on the desk. "How did you disappear?"

The tinkerer picks up a tiny object and inserts it into the remote's backside. "From the cave?" he asks, glancing at his mechanical arm.

"Yes."

"I have... I have a small teleportation device," Sophis answers. "It's one of my many ah...." He looks at Mezrich hovering at his side. "It was one of the many projects that... that kept me from... doing things like his voice box."

"It is a handy device to have."

"Yes, yes it is," the Flunari says, then after a moment or so, he puts the goggles back on. "Are you ready? This may take some time."

"I am."

"Very good, here we go," Sophis says, activating the laser.

Jadecan watches as the laser's slowly guided along the blade's base while Mezrich hovers at the Flunari's side, seemingly doing the same. At about halfway through the procedure, Sophis turns off the laser and looks over what he's done thus far. After a few moments he begins to, once again, gradually guide the laser along the blade's bottom.

"I was hoping to have gotten... have gotten an update on your... your status by now," Sophis states, as he works. "If I don't have one by tomorrow, we'll be... we'll be most likely stopping by the station at some point."

"The Shuttle Station?"

"No, we'll be going to... to a different kind of station, the... the Adellic Station. It's a bit different, but similar."

"Sounds good," he says. "It would be nice to know what they plan on doing with me. I have considered, in depth, the topic of this Orphan team, and moss."

"And?"

"I am not comfortable with the idea."

"I understand," Sophis says, fixated on the beam. "Sadly though, I am not so sure you... you have a choice. I don't think the Fitura will... will accept that... that as an answer."

"There is always a choice."

"I'd like to... to believe that," the tinkerer states, smiling. "Is it true there's a... a cheiket on your ship?"

"It is."

"Very cool. They are a unique looking species. It is rare but, I would occasionally run across one... while on Vyn," Sophis says, concentrating on the laser. "When I did see one though, I would... I would make a point to stop what I was doing to watch 'em. They uh... they made it clear however, they wanted nothing... nothing at all to do with me. They didn't stay around long." The Flunari smiles. "It's been on your ship... this whole time?"

"Yes."

"It may be about time to... to check on it," Sophis says, his eyes glued to the laser beam as he slowly moves it along. "Probably be a good idea, to do that as well."

⊖ 15

Jadecan and Sophis step off a shuttle before a solid pale wall in front of a pickup station numbered, S2. The bus departs as they begin to stroll down the concrete sidewalk. A sign protrudes from out of the barrier ahead of them, with the word Adellic glowing in a yellow light. The Akiko looks across the busy highway and admires a large spear-shaped building on the other side. The complex is a good distance away and sits within its own valley, it sticks out like a sore thumb among the rest of the Orphan City surrounding it. Many black armored heavily equipped soldiers walk along the white stone wall encompassing it and the green landscape it resides in.

"That's the Speran," Sophis says, walking somewhat ahead of him.

"The Speran," he repeats to himself.

"It's where the Fitura lives."

"You have mentioned this Fitura a couple times," Jadecan says, setting his gaze upon Sophis. "What is this Fitura?"

"The Fitura is the leader of the city," Sophis answers. "They're elected and keep office for about... about ten years. At the moment it's Natasha, she's at the end of her term though."

"I see."

The two reach the station and continue through its motion activated doors, stepping inside. A long table and a couple of huge Gekkons await them as they stroll across the area's waxy white floor. It's a single level with a lone door off to the side of the desk, it's not too different from the Crystal's setup, minus the two-way walls and all. There's also a rather nice arrangement of black sofas around a polished coffee table on either side of the main entry. Jadecan follows Sophis, who strides for one of the Gekkons seated behind the reflective silver tabletop.

The large hard shelled species is more than double the width of the Akiko, and because of it, looks to be giant in comparison. It's definitely a reptilian of sorts and sports quite the beak, as well as a long well-kept grey beard. The Gekkon's small eyes watch the pair as they approach while Jadecan looks about the small room. There's not a single soul, besides themselves and the Gekkon's here at the moment.

"Hi," Sophis greets, nearing the desk with the Akiko.

The reptilian nods. "How may I be of help?" Its voice is calm, aged, and nonthreatening.

"We are here in hopes to see Mr. Nix," Sophis answers across the counter. "I'm eager to... to get an update, regarding a... a recent high profile traveler."

"The traveler's species and name?" the brown scaled old Gekkon asks, whilst messing with a screen within the table's surface before itself.

"Ah, an Akiko, whose name is Jadecan."

"And you are?"

"Sophis... Sophis Wonax."

"You are not scheduled for anything, Mr. Wonax," the turtle-like reptile states after a few moments. "And neither is Jadecan."

"No, no we are not," Sophis says. "I believe his ah… his face to face… is to be on his fifth day."

"That is correct." The Gekkon smiles at Jadecan, as if pleased to see him. "Appears you are two days early."

"I was supposed to receive an update the day of his… his departure, from holding," Sophis explains. "I never did, and have yet to receive any um… any update, none whatsoever."

"That is rather unusual." The reptilian points one of its large sharp clawed fingers at the Akiko. "Would this here be, said Jadecan?"

"Yes," the Flunari answers.

"And how are you?" the Gekkon asks Jadecan.

"I am well," he answers. "How are you?"

"I am good." The old reptile smiles, and asks Sophis, "How has he been these past couple of days?"

"He has been rather pleasant," Sophis answers.

"He has stayed with you this whole time, correct?"

"Yes."

"Without incident, I hope," the Gekkon states.

"Yes, I've had no problems."

"Good, I will make a note of it, and will send Nix your request."

"Thank you," Sophis says. "Will he receive it today?"

"Yes, I should have some sort of answer for you within the hour," the reptilian answers. "Is there anything I can do for you in the meantime?"

"No, I don't believe so, thank you again."

"You are quite welcome." The Gekkon asks, as a blue screen pops up before Sophis, "Is the information on file still accurate?"

"Yes, yes it is."

"Good, I'll give you a call, once I hear something."

"We will most likely be here," the Flunari says. "If it's not a problem."

"No, of course not," the old reptile says. "Please, by all means, have a seat."

"Thank you." Sophis turns away from the counter.

Jadecan trails Sophis who heads for one of the dark sofas and tables near the entry. As they near the sitting arrangement, a few data-pads can be seen scattered about upon the wooden tabletops. The Akiko and Flunari pick one up as they sit beside one another on the leathery couch. The lightweight-handheld device lights up as soon as it is lifted off the table.

Eryn wins by knockout. Jadecan reads. *One of the most eventful cards in Ashly's history ends with one of the greatest fighters further cementing his legacy. Aetom Eryn (Mr. One-Hit) shatters Ky (O' Boy) Tefan's enigma with a brutal second-round knockout ending the Nudruk challenger's undefeated run.*

He swipes left, and the article's replaced with a different one. The Akiko reads as he scrolls. *The Reaction, by Andell Arvey: For years the Orphan's Chief Financial Officer, Ian Py, has expressed concerns over the Fitura's use of the city's finances. In fact, it's no secret he's (Ian Py) been one of the current Fitura's hardest hitting critics, stating on several occasions that she (Avani Natasha) very well could be one of the "worst Fituras" the city has ever seen. From her handling of the energy crisis, to her controversial relationships, the Fitura's entire term has been, if we are to be honest, terrible. The Orphan has seen the largest influx of travelers, as well as a steep increase in crime, since Natasha has taken office. As the city's Chief Financial Officer puts it, "these last eight and a half years have been a literal nightmare, she (Avani Natasha) has just about bankrupted the city, and killed us all in the process. We (Orphan City) thank you, Ms. Fitura."*

"The Fitura is apparently not popular," Jadecan states, looking over at Sophis.

"No." Sophis laughs. "She surely is not. I've met her a... a few times, I don't know her too well, but she seems nice... from what I've seen. She allowed me to accompany my brother, when he was... was invited to stay here."

"She seems like an awful leader."

"Depends on the source, but yea, she's not... not widely liked," Sophis says. "She's not the best the city's had, but... she's definitely not the... not the worst. Not all of it is... is as bad as they would... would have you believe. It's all political, take everything with a... with a grain of salt."

"Mr. Wonax," the Gekkon calls.

"Yes," the Flunari answers.

"Mr. Nix will see you now," the old reptile states.

"Thank you," Sophis says. "That was quick."

⊖ 16

Jadecan sits in a small timber chair in front of Mr. Nix beside Sophis, the plush cushion beneath him squeaking if he so much as breathes. This certainly is not the most comfortable he has ever been, it's actually kind of a surprisingly small office, and rather dimly lit to boot. Not at all what the Akiko was expecting. He stares across the solid oak cluttered desk at the Minorak, who puffs on a cigarette as the city's bright lights bleed through the blinds of the large window behind him.

A black fedora rests upon Nix's head, and whilst he ashes the cigarette in a tiny ashtray before him, he leans onto the tabletop. Stacks of papers tower on both of its ends, it's almost as if the Minorak doesn't get out much. The Akiko and Flunari watch as Mr. Nix takes a flask out of his mahogany trench coat, he takes a swig, and then puts it back. Well then, this should be fun.

"So," Mr. Nix says, after taking in a deep breath and letting it out. "How are things?"

"Things are good," Sophis answers sort of nervously.

Nix takes a drag of the cigarette. "That's good, how are you?" he asks Jadecan.

"Well," he answers.

"The blade looks good." Mr. Nix gestures to the Flunari's handiwork attached to the Akiko's elbow. "I take it Sophis here, did that?"

"He did."

The Minorak nods his head and sits back. "How can I help you two?"

"I was wondering if any... anything has been figured out... regarding Jadecan here. I have... I have yet to receive any... any updates."

"I apologize, you should have received one by now," Mr. Nix says, "That's my fault." He pauses taking another drag and then ashes the cigarette. "But yes, there have been some developments."

"That's good, right?" the Flunari asks excitedly.

"Yes, yes it is," Nix states. "Okay so, I need to know how he's been these last couple of days. It will determine where we go from here. So, how has he been?"

"Good, actually," Sophis answers, looking over at Jadecan. "Very good. I've had… had no problems."

"None?"

"Yea, none. I haven't had a… had a single issue," Sophis answers. "He's actually been quite a… quite a delight. It's been… been rather enjoyable, honest… honestly."

"Okay, well if that's the case." Mr. Nix takes a drag. "The Fitura has requested that Jadecan take us to the moss' location on Niushki, sooner rather than later."

"How soon?" Sophis asks.

"I'm not certain." Nix ashes the cigarette. "He's going to have to see the Fitura for that."

"When is he to do that?"

"Not sure, I will let you know, as soon as I find out," the Minorak answers. "You will most likely accompany him, when he does." The Flunari nods, as Mr. Nix asks Jadecan, "So, what do you think of all this?"

"I am unsure what to think," the Akiko answers.

"Yea, me too," Nix agrees, taking a puff of the cigarette.

"So, are we… are we to just wait?" Sophis asks.

"It does appear that way," Nix states, taking another swig from the flask. "In the meantime," he says, putting it back into his trench coat and taking a puff of the cigarette. "You should take him by the Gabbin, it's a decent enough place."

"I… I already have," the tinkerer says, looking over at Jadecan, and then back to Nix. "We've been there a couple… a couple of times already."

"Oh, good, that's good." The Minorak ashes the cigarette.

"Would it be a problem if I were to stop by my ship?" Jadecan asks.

"To check on your cheiket, I assume," Mr. Nix says.

"Yes."

"No, no, not at all. Go ahead," Nix answers. "It has been cooped up in there for a few days, probably be best to see how it's doin'." He takes a drag and puts the cigarette out in the ashtray. "So, there you go, that's your update. Is there anything else you need?"

"No," the Flunari answers. "I… I don't… I don't believe so."

"I'll be in touch," Nix states, taking another swig of the flask.

Jadecan trails behind Sophis for the office's exit as Mr. Nix lights up another cigarette. They step out into the bright hall outside the dark room and quietly walk side by side for the door at the corridor's end. The entry opens as the two near, revealing the same couple of Gekkons poised behind the Adellic's front desk, who observe as they advance for the station's entrance.

"He does not seem well," Jadecan states to Sophis.

"He's fine… he's just…." The tinkerer pauses, and explains, "It's been hard these… these last few years. Mr. Nix was a close friend of… of my brother and… when he… when my brother disappeared, he didn't… he didn't take it well. None of us did. He misses him, we all do."

"I get it, I do," the Akiko says, as they leave the Adellic and make their way back to the pickup station. "I am sorry, Sophis."

"Thank you. It is difficult but, I… I make do."

♀ Lavender Visit

⊖ 17

Sophis, Jadecan, Corporal Ry, and a couple guards, step off a small hovering platform onto the massive floating terrace Baby rests on. The group walks toward the Akiko's black saucer parked near the back of the silver pad as Jadecan glances at the few other starships accompanying it. He grins at Sophis walking at his side as the Orphan soldiers follow closely at their backs.

Considering our current situation I do not believe it would be wise for me to be myself in the Flunari's presence, Baby states.

The Saucer's dark ramp extends revealing the faint blue light of its deck. "We'll wait outside," Ry says to Jadecan and Sophis, as they arrive at the ship.

The Akiko and Flunari stroll up into the ship as the guards await their return at the base of the ramp. Jadecan steps onto the dark floor and is instantly greeted by the little pink cheiket who squeaks joyfully whilst jumping onto his shoulder. Sophis watches, smiling as the Akiko walks toward the front of the saucer.

"It has been too long," Jadecan says to himself, while sitting in one of the black chairs and petting Buddy.

"It really loves you," Sophis states, placing himself in the seat beside the Akiko.

"Yea, I suppose so," he answers, looking into the cheiket's black face that's perched on his shoulder with its tail wrapped around his neck.

"What is your friend's name?" Sophis asks, referring to the cheiket.

"His name is Buddy." He retrieves a piece of setani meat and feeds it to the creature.

"It's a pleasure to meet you, Buddy," Sophis says to the cheiket, as it aggressively chews and swallows its meal.

He has mostly slept, Baby states, as Jadecan boops the creature's small nose.

"This is nice," the Flunari says, looking around. "It's quite cozy in here."

"Cozy," Jadecan repeats, with a small smile to himself. "It is. I feel the most relaxed, here, with Baby."

"Baby, is that the name of the ship?" Sophis asks.

"Yes."

"An interesting name, is that the one it came with, or did you name it yourself?"

"I am the one who gave her the name," the Akiko answers. "She is my everything."

"She's a... she's a lucky girl," Sophis says jokingly, but genuine. "You have a... have a great... great thing going here, Jadecan"

"Thank you." Jadecan feeds Buddy another piece of setani.

A chime resonates from the Flunari's tiny wrist and as he raises it up to his round face Mr. Nix appears as a blue hologram above it. "The Fitura would like to see you two in her office," the Minorak says.

“We’ll be on our way, shortly.” Sophis looks across at Jadecan as the image disappears. “That was... was kind of quick,” he states, lowering his arm.

I agree, this is all happening rather fast, Baby states.

“Why do you believe it to be so quick?” he asks Sophis.

“I... I truly don’t... don’t know.” A brief silence follows the Flunari’s answer. “I thought I was... was going to die... in that... that cave. I was... I was sure of it, but you....” Sophis lets out a small laugh.

“You would have,” the Akiko states. “If it was not for your tinkering, you would not be here right now.” He gently pets Buddy. “I am glad however, that you did not.”

“I am, too.” The Flunari chuckles quietly, and after a moment says, “Do you care for her? For Amelia?”

“I do, in a way.”

“I can’t help but... but feel like she is....” Sophis pauses briefly, and explains, “She is the reason I didn’t... I didn’t die that day. You looked so... so mad.” He laughs. “I was... you were terrifying, I was so scared... and then you....” The Flunari glances at his metal arm. “It was awful, just awful.”

“Is everything all right?” Ry calls up the ramp from outside the ship.

“Yes, we’ll be out momentarily.” Sophis smiles at Jadecan. “Suppose we should... we should go see the Fitura. When you’re ready, of course.” He chuckles, admiring the Akiko and cheiket’s relationship. “No rush.”

⊜ 18

The Akiko stands beside Sophis admiring the beautifully sculpted fountain and pond of the large courtyard in front of the Speran. It's a lot like Vyn in some ways, the greenery and all, not so much the white stone or pale metal of the building, although those did somewhat resemble the Olensi outpost. But it's the forest and flowing streams surrounding them, they're what reminds him of the planet. He observes the two black-armored soldiers before him, as the Flunari talks with their non-helmeted leader, a Grogan by the name of Untako.

"Things are good," Sophis says. "Been staying… staying busy."

"That's good," Untako states. "How's the Mez?"

"He's good, how are… how are things here?"

"Quiet," the Grogan answers.

Untako watches as Jadecan and Sophis are stood beside one another by one of the other guards at the complex's entrance. "All molecular technologies on or within your holo-system will be deactivated once inside the Speran. This is your last chance to retrieve anything you may need while within the complex," the officer explains, while the other one standing at his side hands him a Binox. "Do you understand?" the soldier asks Jadecan specifically.

"Yes," he answers.

"Good," the guard states, as the black box's projected screen appears and scans each of them in a wave of blue light. "Clear," he declares to Untako.

Untako approaches and directs them toward the building's entrance. "It's been nice chatting with you my friend, as always," he states to Sophis, whilst placing his hand upon the green screen next to the single-door entryway.

The door opens. "It has, I do appreciate our… our talks," Sophis says, nodding at the Grogan before walking into the Speran's main lobby in front of the Akiko.

Untako nods at Jadecan as he strolls past him, who returns the gesture while stepping through the entry after Sophis. The entrance closes as he sets foot onto the complex's main glass-like reflective white floor. He stares at the large beautiful clear chandelier sitting far above him as the Flunari makes for the Speran's check-in counter ahead of him. Jadecan glances back through the Speran's clear walls behind him at the Orphan soldiers outside the complex as he follows Sophis closely.

"Mr. Wonax," the odd looking representative behind the white counter of the front desk greets. "Of what do I owe the pleasure?"

"We are here to… to see the Fitura," Sophis answers.

The very strange dark purple skinned character peers at the blue screen before it. "I suppose this here is, Jadecan?" it asks, its orange eyes set on the Akiko as the tendrils on the corner of its mouth sway.

"Yes," the Flunari answers, and then introduces Jadecan and the representative to one another.

"Hello, sir," Valex greets the Akiko.

"Hello." Jadecan bows.

"Hope all has been well," the representative says to them both.

"As well as... as can be," Sophis states.

"Very good." Valex interacts with the projection. "The lift is now available, sir," he says, gesturing toward the elevator to the left of the check-in. "Good luck, sir."

"Thank you," the Flunari states, as the Akiko bows and trails Sophis who now waddles for the open lift.

They enter and stand side by side, and as the elevator's doors close, Jadecan states as it ascends, "He is interesting."

"Yes," Sophis agrees. "He's a... a Ventriku."

"I see."

"An interesting fact, he... he, like you is... is also from... from a moon," the Flunari says, as the lift's doors open.

They walk out of the silver lift and stand before a lavender skinned Yonalitu, who smiles at them from behind a colorless opal desk. Jadecan looks about the small blue carpeted corridor as its green eyes stare down upon them. To his right sits several potted plants of varying sizes while on his left, a white corridor ends at what he believes to be the Fitura's office.

"Sophis," the Yonalitu greets, her voice calm.

"Shea." The Flunari smiles. "We are... are here to see the Fitura."

"I know," Shea states, walking out from behind the white topped table. "If you would." She walks to the closed door at the hall's end, while asking Sophis, "How have you been?"

"I'm good," Sophis answers, as Jadecan walks at his side following behind the extremely tall white haired Shea. "How have... have you been?"

"I'm doing well, love," the Yonalitu answers, arriving at the door.

The entry opens revealing the Fitura, who is also a Yonalitu. She sits behind a black U-shaped desk. "Sophis," Natasha greets, heading over to the two of them. "And this must be, Jadecan," she states, once standing in front of the Akiko. "It's a pleasure to finally meet you." Jadecan nods in response, as she turns and saunters back toward the table, while loudly proclaiming, "Thank you, Shea." The Akiko and Flunari stroll into the clear walled room, as the Fitura's assistant strolls back to her station in front of the elevator. "I hope your trip here was good," the Fitura says, sitting behind the desk as the office's entry closes at their backs.

"Yes, yes it was," Sophis says, sitting with Jadecan in the red chairs across from her.

"Good, I am happy to hear that," she states, interacting with one of the white screens built into the dark table's surface before her. "Now, I hate to get straight to business, but time is of the essence. I hope you understand."

"Yes, of course, Ms. Fitura," Sophis says.

"Good, now Mr. Nix tells me you may know of a location on Niushki that contains a luminescent flora of sorts. Is that true?" Natasha asks Jadecan.

"It is."

"Would you be willing to guide one of our teams to it?" After a bit of silence, the Fitura explains, "I understand your hesitation, given the history of Niushki and those that have chosen to settle on it. I can assure you however, that we are not like the Balgorex or Reogki, in any way. We intend to only gather enough of the flora to sustain our city for the next couple of years, and then leave, that is all."

"What happens when you run out in a couple of years?"

"We'll be back," Natasha answers. "But again, only to gather enough of the material to sustain us for a couple of more years. I promise you, no harm will come of us, we'll take only what we require, and no more."

"It is not my place to allow it."

"Whose place is it?" the Fitura asks.

"You would have to speak to the Ruogjis of the area," he answers. "It is them you must ask. Only they can give you permission."

"Would you be willing to take a team to them?"

"No."

"Okay," Natasha says. "What do you want? Is there anything that I can offer you? What will it take for you to take us to these Ruogji?"

After a few moments, the Akiko looks over at the Flunari, and states, "I will take Sophis, and no one else. That is what it will take."

Natasha thinks long and hard, then pointing with a single finger says, "One soldier. You will take one of our militia with you, as well. You must understand my concern, considering how your last encounter resulted in the loss of his arm."

"Ms. Fitura-" Sophis begins, before Natasha sternly interjects.

"Sophis." She glares at the Flunari, quieting him. "Do we have a deal?" she asks the Akiko.

"We do."

A silver cylindrical object materializes above the desk in front of her. "Good," she states. "Sophis, this is your locator."

"Yes, ma'am," Sophis says, retrieving the device.

"Do you know what starship you will be taking?" Natasha asks them.

"We'll be... be taking his," Sophis answers.

"Fine, I suppose that is okay with you?" she asks Jadecan.

"It is."

"I will notify the militia to supply a volunteer to accompany you. You may leave as soon as you are ready." Natasha looks at Jadecan. "And at least try and disguise yourself, okay?"

⊖ 19

Well, everything after their meeting with the Fitura apparently went rather smoothly. Sophis and himself spent a good bit of time getting everything they would need for their mission in order. As well as informing individuals such as Lucius they'd be MIA for a while. It wasn't much, beyond a lot of running around really.

It's been a few hours since the two of them had arrived back at Sophis' place in Greenview Apartments. Not too long after returning, Sophis went off to sleep taking Mezrich with him, leaving the Akiko by himself. Which is fine, he could definitely use a bit of alone time. He now sits on the sofa in the darkness talking with Baby.

"Baby," Jadecan whispers.

Yes?

"How is everything?"

Well, Buddy is asleep, per usual. How are you?

"I am okay," he answers softly. "I am looking forward to being back home."

Remember, you are wanted by the Olensi. They will surely send hunters, Baby reminds him.

"Yes, I know."

Unfortunately, I do not believe Niushki to be safe any longer. I will elaborate on that more in a bit, but before that, there is a bit of information that I would like to share with you, that I found of interest.

"Like what?"

I am not sure if you are aware, but I was with you in the Fitura's office. I heard all that was said. It appears as if the access to your autonomic technology was all that was deactivated, preventing you from storing within it, or retrieving from it. I however, was still present.

"I was not, although I had assumed that was the case."

Indeed, it appears the holo-system's design was to be nothing more than an individual's own unique inventory system, Baby explains. *The inclusion of my Inner-Thought however, has modified it to be a bit more than that.*

"I see."

I have re-coded and reformatted the technology, there is no way to accomplish what we have achieved otherwise. It is almost as if we have been neurally-integrated.

"Explain."

Currently, I am a part of your holo-system, which allows me to interact with it as you would. The retrieval and storing of items, as well as neural-communication, are all basic properties of the technology. All of which, we share. True neural-integration however, would have me integrated directly into your neural network, making me a part of your consciousness. It would be a completely different experience.

"Interesting," Jadecan quietly states. "How different?"

Well, for one, we would become one single intelligence, although, we would remain as two separate entities. We would think, feel, and see as each of us currently already do, but we would also think, feel, and see as the other does, as well. You would become me, as well as stay you, and I would become you, as well as stay me. We would be one, but yet, still separate. Additionally, we would also share each other's memories.

"Really?"

Yes, with that, you would stay in control of your vessel, and I would stay in control of mine, as we are now. We would still choose and make our own unique decisions, however, we would both be aware of the other's, at the same time. We would each know what the other was thinking and intending to do, at the exact moment the other became aware of it themselves.

"Sounds complicated." The Akiko chuckles.

It does. But to go back to the topic of Niushki, I have been pondering a completely different matter as of late, and as I have put more and more thought into it, I have become increasingly concerned.

"What is this matter?"

It is the debris that we encountered upon our departure from Niushki. I have considered where it may have originated from, and its likely origins are also, out of all the possibilities that I have considered, the most concerning one.

"How so?"

It would seem, if I am correct, the debris was from one of the three Olensi starships that were orbiting the planet. In fact, I believe the fire that streaked across Niushki's sky, that signaled your return to the refuge, was that same starship.

"Why?"

Considering Sophis' trespass, the locator, and your bounty, I can not picture them leaving, but yet, that is exactly what we are faced with. What concerns me, if indeed the debris is from one of their starships, is that the Olensi are nothing to be trifled with.

"Elaborate, please."

The Olensi are a force to be reckoned with. Just one of their starships would pose a significant problem, and there were three of them. If I am indeed correct, someone or something, destroyed one of those starships, and sent the other two packing.

"Who could do that?"

A large enough force from anyone could manage it, but, they would likely lose the war that would surely ensue afterwards. I am unable to come up with a reason, or culprit, the entire scenario makes absolutely no sense. Also to note, whatever or whoever the cause of the debris was, left the scene shortly after, likely in pursuit of the two remaining Olensi cruisers.

"It is likely."

None of it changes the bounty however. The Olensi themselves may be otherwise occupied, but the hunters likely will not be. In relation to that, I was wondering if the Fitura and Orphan City are aware of the Olensi's departure from the area, and if so, do they know what happened? Whether they know, or not, I urge you to keep an eye on those that accompany you, especially the Orphan foot-soldier. Just a few things to keep in mind whilst carrying out the Fitura's bidding.

♀ Part Five: The Hunter

"What we wish, whether it be good or evil, will not always happen according to our desire." - George Fyler Townsend, *The Arabian Nights*.

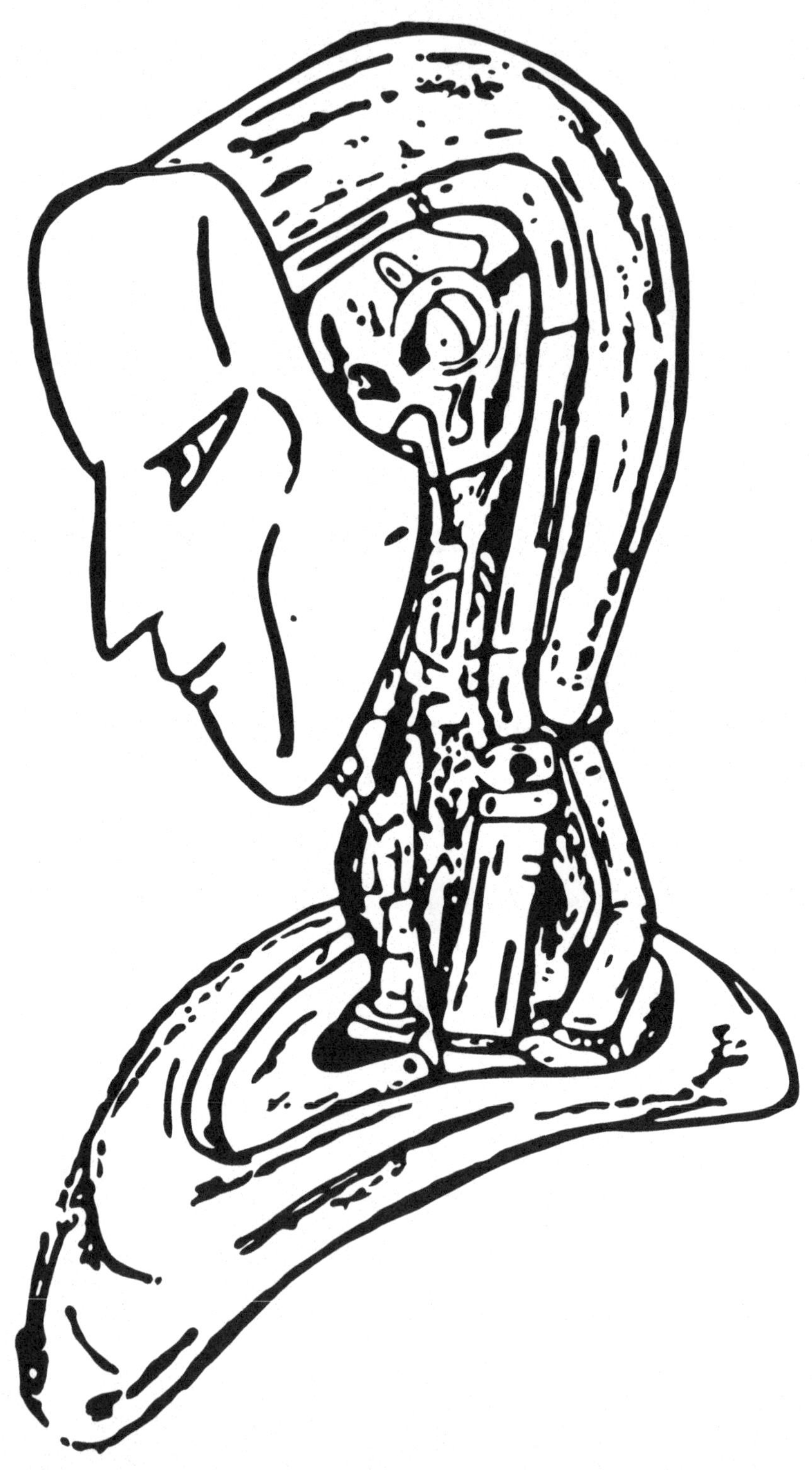

♀ Rough Start

⊖ 1

The black saucer settles upon the white dust of Niushki outside Ruogji Yano's village. Sophis glances over at Jadecan, who now dons a dark cloak and hood, his chosen disguise. It's really not too much of a disguise to be completely honest, but it'll work for now. The Akiko pets the cheiket dozing on his lap as the fully armored Orphan foot-soldier, Jayph, sits behind him. He's not too fond of the soldier, but it is what it is. Besides a sum of tongue-wagging, the flight here, for the most part, has been rather uneventful. They now sit in silence peering out at the desolate terrain whilst sitadoom fly in the distance. Strangely, no Kiwiwa are present outside the saucer. Where are they?

Smoke rises as usual but the fire in the village's center appears to be withering and dying. There's not a single Kiwiwa anywhere near it, not a soul's in sight. Odd. The sitting rocks are vacant, completely empty, not only that, but the entire village appears to be lifeless. Something is most definitely wrong. It's not like them to not be here to greet him. The Ruogji should be right there in front of the saucer, but he's not. Hastily, the Akiko departs the ship and heads for the village.

The closer he gets, the colder and more foreboding the scene becomes. A few Kiwiwa lie at the village's dismal entrance, unmoving. As he nears he slows ever so slightly, as more and more Kiwiwa become visible, lying scattered about the area, motionless, dead. His once quick pace turns into a crawl as he saunters into the harrowing ghost town. This was once the closest place he had to a home, but now....

It soon becomes apparent the Kiwiwa have been shot, young and old, every one of them slaughtered. Not even the juguke made it out alive, having all been killed in the exact spots they lain resting. Jadecan makes his way through the somber village and heads for the Ruogji's hut, bracing for the scene he is sure to find within. He stops for a moment at its uninviting entry and reaches for the green gem resting below his chin. Wallowing in guilt and shame, the Runuoscha enters.

Candles burn around the white bust of Caspa sitting upon the stone altar just inside. The medallion from the dungeon's pedestal glimmers in the candlelight whilst leaning against the small sculpture. What was once a heartwarming moment, the memory of Cassandra giving the amulet to the Ruogji as a peace offering from Oteniko, now plays in his head, thick in woe. He remembers how Yano's black eyes lit up as he held it within his small white hands and stared upon it in awe.

The Ruogji sits on the hard floor against his bed across from the table. Black blood oozes from two wounds on his chest, he's been shot, and is dying. A green gem, identical to the one around Jadecan's neck, faintly glows within one of the Ruogji's left hands. It's almost as if the jewel is sustaining him, but how? Yano looks up and smiles at the grief-stricken Jadecan.

"Runuoscha," the waning voice of the Ruogji calls.

"Caspa, Ruogji." Jadecan bows and slowly treads his way. "I am sorry, Ruogji. I have failed. I do not deserve the title of Runuoscha. Forgive me."

"Nothing to forgive, it is not your fault, Runuoscha," Yano says, to the kneeling Jadecan before him. "Nothing you could have done."

"What happened?" he asks. "Who has done this?"

After a moment, Yano answers, "A hunter came by, said they are looking for one called Jadecan. Said you are dangerous, could not be trusted. Told them, they are wrong, Jadecan, Kiwiwas Runuoscha."

"A hunter did this?"

"Hami." The Ruogji coughs. "Wanted to know where they could find, the Runuoscha. Told them, where they could find you. I sent them to Oteniko."

"I will find them, Ruogji," he states angrily. "They will pay for what they have done."

"Know you will, Runuoscha," Yano says, his voice weakening. "I know you will."

"I am sorry, Ruogji." His voice cracks. "I am sorry."

"I am here, always, Jadecan," the Ruogji says, placing one of his hands over Jadecan's heart.

The Runuoscha gently covers Yano's hand with one of his own and as they sit at peace, a tear streaks down Jadecan's pale cheek. The Ruogji tenderly wipes it away and smiles for the last time, as the glow from the gem in his hand fades. Emotions flood the Akiko, who stands and heads for the hut's entrance, with vengeance on his mind. He stops for a moment in front of the juguke hide covering the doorway, before pushing it aside and stepping out into the howling wind of Niushki.

The village's fire is now barely a flame at all and struggles behind Sophis, who watches as the Runuoscha leaves the Ruogji's hut and strides his way. Jayph is nowhere to be seen, he's most likely scouting the area as Meshel would have done in his place. Jadecan notices the Flunari's obviously heartbroken, but yet expresses concern and fright as he approaches. Rightfully so, he has every reason to be afraid, considering the look of anger worn upon the Akiko's face.

"I'm sorry, my... my friend," Sophis says to the devastated Runuoscha.

"I must honor the Kiwiwa's Ruogji, and send him to Caspa, by way of fire," Jadecan states. "It is tradition, and my duty as the Runuoscha, to see that it is done."

"I would... I would like to help, if I can," Sophis says.

"Sure." The Akiko stares off into the village's fire.

⊖ 2

Jadecan awakens to a Kiwiwa standing over him with a stone mortar and pestle grinding away. The small Kiwiwa's four hands work diligently taking lime green moss out of the stone bowl and placing it over top his wounds. The Akiko lies upon a woven rope bed on his back in pain. He watches as the Kiwiwa chants whilst grinding with the pestle and placing more of the lichen on him. This Kiwiwa's apparently a shaman of sorts, interesting.

The last thing Jadecan remembers, he was fighting with some Reogki and as usual, it wasn't going his way. If it wasn't for Stet's reliance on the Scuts however, things would have surely played out differently. The mission was simple, or so he thought. Leave it to some inept and incompetent Scuts to ruin it. What else would they be good for?

The Akiko groans and looks around as the Kiwiwa at his bedside continues to place chunks of the glowing moss on his wounds. The sound of a large fire rages whilst the voices of many Kiwiwa travel upon the subtle winds of Niushki. He knows exactly where he is, he's in one of the huts of a Kiwiwa village. The Kiwiwa's large white head tilts slightly smiling as Jadecan peers into its small pitch black eyes.

"Where am I?" Jadecan asks, as the Kiwiwa stares, silent. "Where am I?" he repeats.

No answer, typically was the case with the Kiwiwa. They are a silent and secluded species who rarely left their home village. Lately however, more and more have been wandering the wasteland, alone and dying. The Kiwiwa were not good at being solitary and more often than not, would die if separated from others of its kind. Ever since the Reogkis' arrival, lone Kiwiwa have become progressively more common. They aren't entirely defenseless, but for the most part, they're harmless. They are certainly no match for the Reogki raiding parties who frequently target them.

Jadecan grins at the tiny pale skinned Kiwiwa and then stares up at the dome ceiling of the hut. He's always appreciated their simplistic way of living. Life was usually rather peaceful within a Kiwiwa village. The Akiko winces in agony as the Kiwiwa places a mass of lichen on one of his severe wounds. He's apparently suffered quite the beating, he's more than likely lucky to be alive and has the Kiwiwa to thank for that. Jadecan's picked up a tiny bit of their language along the way, but not much, although he knows enough to know who he needs to ask for.

"Ruogji?" he asks. "May I see the Ruogji?"

A staff bearing elder of the Kiwiwa walks through the small hut's entry and heads for the Akiko. A couple of others stroll inside and stand at the entrance watching as the elder makes his way to the bedside. The old Kiwiwa places one of his hands upon the shoulder of the Kiwiwa who's been caring for Jadecan. The two stare at one another smiling and after a moment, the caring Kiwiwa nods at the elder and leaves the bedside.

"Caspa, Akiko." The old Kiwiwa gestures to himself, "Ruogji Yano. Pama hala?"

"Jadecan, Ruogji," he says back, he's pretty sure the Ruogji had just asked him his name.

"Jifefeno jukeunta, Jadecan?" the Ruogji asks.

"I do not understand you," he answers, sitting up. "Do you understand me?"

"Hami." Yano nods. "Hami."

"Suppose hami means yes."

"Hami," the Ruogji says.

"Well, that is a start." And after a few moments he nods gesturing to his moss covered wounds, and says, "Thank you."

Yano smiles then turns away, and beckons, "Geoth, geoth." He walks for the hut's entry and gestures with his staff for the Akiko to follow.

"Okay," Jadecan says to himself, standing and sauntering after the Ruogji.

He pushes aside the hide covering the huts open entrance and joins Yano, standing beside him outside. The village's fire bellows before them in the colony's center as dozens of Kiwiwa sit upon stones around it. The Ruogji slowly makes for the ring of seated Kiwiwa. The Akiko trails closely as Yano plods on with the help of his staff. The Ruogji places himself onto one of the stones and gestures for Jadecan to take the empty one beside him.

"Thife ol odfe Akikos jionta jakisu hioy," Yano says, as Jadecan sits upon the flat stone. "Loososha wu odfe omfe, padefusi hala ol nithu," he states, apparently happy to see the Akiko, likely glad to see they haven't gone extinct.

"Yea." Jadecan chuckles. "Same."

"Litaof, litaof," the Ruogji beckons.

A couple of Kiwiwa get up and tread off for one of the stone huts surrounding them. The Akiko observes as the pair disappear inside it briefly, before emerging with a tied up Reogki. They forcefully drag the bound, beaten, and terrified captive across the pale dust to Yano. Jadecan watches as the bloodied prisoner's violently thrown down before the Ruogji. The Reogki kneels in front of Yano, he's obviously been tortured to some extent. It's afraid and sobbing pathetically.

"Yaanze Reogki, onta defefe Reogki, Jadecan," the Ruogji says to the Akiko, while presenting him with a stone knife. "Sifegenosife."

Jadecan takes the blade from Yano's small light grey hand grinning. "I understand," he states, realizing the choice before him.

⊜ 3

It took a bit of time, but the Kiwiwa were all buried and the Ruogji was burned within the flames of the village's fire, as is custom. It was a somber moment, one of which the Akiko will always remember. The Kiwiwa had given him purpose when he felt as though he had none. Yano was like a father, a brother, his family, they all were. He'll miss them greatly. He feels so much more alone now, than he ever has before.

Sophis and Jayph sit quietly as Jadecan now flies for the Oteniko outpost. The cheiket lies comfortably upon his shoulder as usual, purring contently. Very few words have been spoken since their departure from the village and as they get closer to the Oteniko outpost it becomes clear, something is very wrong yet again. A central mass of ruins sit where the main complex would've been, as bits and pieces of debris lie diffused about the area.

Jadecan, it appears as if the outpost has suffered an explosion of some kind, Baby states.

"Are we sure that was the outpost?" he asks, as they near the pile of rubble.

Yes, I am unsure what may have caused it, but I do believe that what you see before you, is all that is left of the complex, Baby states.

"Wow... that does not... does not look good," Sophis remarks.

"It does not," Jadecan says, as the ship begins to land outside the main mass of debris. "Definitely does not."

I am detecting no lifeforms, nor no evidence of any organic material, Baby says, whilst making contact with Niushki's surface. *It is possible the Yonalitus did not perish here.*

"What... what happened?" Sophis asks, as the saucer powers down.

"It seems as if it exploded," Jadecan answers, as a large blue screen appears in front of the three of them.

"No heat signatures, no apparent bodies, radiation is minimal." Jayph reads off the projection. "Looks like a classic raid and capture. Any idea who may have done it?"

"The hunter, and if not him, then Reogki," Jadecan states, as the projection disappears.

"Works for me," Jayph says, eyeing Floating Rock within the craters center in the distance. "That's interesting."

"It is, indeed," Jadecan agrees. "That is Floating Rock."

"That it is," Jayph says to himself, as the Akiko walks to leave the ship with Buddy still perched on his shoulder.

The three of them step out onto the white dust in front of what was once the Oteniko outpost. Sitadoom fly high above them as they venture onto the silver terrace which once acted as a sort of porch to the complex. The pillars that once held up the second storey of the outpost still stand, although the storey is no more. Jadecan strolls to where the large door of the complex would have been, remembering when he first stood before it and spoke with Cassandra.

Floating Rock hovers a ways off, watching as Jadecan retrieves the badge Meshel had given him aboard the Cortnei. It wasn't all too long ago that he and Meshel had stood beside one another on the outpost's back deck where Jadecan told him of the Kiwiwa legend that tells of the large boulder's origins. He chuckles at the memory whilst admiring the blue Oteniko emblem on the badge's face.

"I am sorry," the black armored Jayph says to Jadecan, standing at his side.

"I appreciate that." The Akiko nods.

"Wonder if Oteniko was here because of that," Jayph says, gesturing to the Floating Rock. "It is quite the sight. What causes it to float, I wonder?"

"I do not know," Jadecan answers, walking back toward the saucer and putting away the badge.

Jadecan, hmm, that's strange, Baby says.

"What is it?"

My scanners had seemed to have picked up a heat signature. It appeared to be a life-form of sorts. I can not say for certain however, for it disappeared relatively quickly after its initial detection.

"So, what... what do we do now?" Sophis asks, as Jadecan passes by him.

"I must avenge the Kiwiwa, and deal with the hunter," the Akiko answers. "But as for you, I do not know."

"I... I will join you," Sophis states.

"Wait a minute, no. No, I don't think so," Jayph says to Sophis. "We are not here to hunt down and murder a hunter, no, we are not." He looks to Jadecan. "I'm not even going to try, and stop you. It would be a waste of all of our time, so I won't do it. Instead, what I will do is tell you that, Sophis and I, will have no part of it. None. None whatsoever. Considering everything that has happened, I cannot risk it." He pauses briefly, then turns to the Flunari. "I'm sorry Sophis, but we will not be joining him."

"You do not have to join me, I would rather go alone anyway," Jadecan states.

"So, what are we to do in the meantime?" Jayph asks.

⊜ 4

The decrepit L-shaped building of Taj's Fix welcomes Baby as she lands in front of it. The green glow of Taj's sign appears rather dim against the light rain falling upon the white dust of Niushki. Jadecan walks out of the black saucer and makes for the pale complex with Sophis and Jayph at his heels. A couple of juguke lie resting near the two garages on the repair shop's ell. They're probably quite enjoying the unexpected shower.

After a bit of thought and consideration, it was decided this was most likely the best place for the Flunari and the Orphan foot-soldier to stay whilst the Akiko tracked down the hunter. The only other option was Along the Way, but Jayph was more on the side of a Nudruk's place as opposed to a Drakon's, for whatever reason. All in all, it's not a bad spot. It's not where Jadecan would've chosen to wait, but he isn't going to be the one staying, now is he?

He strides along with Sophis and Jayph into the main office of the complex. Taj stands behind his worn down wooden front desk, same as always. The yellow light of the small room flickers, whilst a loud thunder cracks outside. The Nudruk watches worriedly as the Akiko approaches the faded counter with the Flunari and shiny black armored Orphan soldier close behind.

"Jadecan," Taj welcomes nervously. "Who um, who are your friends?"

"This is Sophis and Jayph."

"Hello, I'm Taj." The oval headed Nudruk waves as the Akiko introduces them. "Welcome to Taj's Fix." He chuckles uneasy.

"Thank you, it's ah, it's nice. What is it you do, exactly? If I may ask," Jayph asks, looking around.

"I'm um, well, I'm a technician," Taj answers.

"You... you fix things?" Sophis' eyes widen. "You're a... a tinkerer, like myself."

"Yes, he repairs hover-crafts, mostly, but yes, he is a tinkerer, like you," Jadecan answers, then stares at Taj. "I need a place for my friends here to stay, for a couple cycles. I was hoping they could stay here, if you of course, did not mind."

"Will you not be staying?" Taj asks. "Just the two of them?"

The light skinned Nudruk's small black eyes glimmer slightly. It's almost too obvious he's hoping for the Akiko to answer with a resounding, no, he would not be staying, and yes, it would just be his two companions. The Orphan soldier stands in the open doorway watching the storm rage outside while Sophis' large blue eyes wander about the messy office. Taj smiles eagerly awaiting the much anticipated Jadecan answer.

"I will not be staying," the Akiko states, after a small chuckle to himself. "It would be just the two of them."

"Yes yes, of course, of course they can stay," Taj exclaims. "A friend of Jadecan's, is a friend of mine." And after a brief silence, he asks, "And where will you be while they are here?"

"None of your concern," Jadecan states, dropping a few gold coins onto the wooden counter before the Nudruk.

"No, no, no," Taj says quickly, waving his hands before himself. "That... that won't be necessary."

"I insist," the Akiko states, and then walks for the entry.

"How do we know you won't just leave us here," Jayph asks. "What assurance do we have that you will return? That we'll finish the mission?"

"I will leave my ship," Jadecan answers.

"Hmm, okay," the soldier says. "I suppose that works."

"You are not to touch her," the Akiko adds aggressively.

"Fair enough," Jayph states, as Jadecan walks out into the pouring rain.

Are you sure this is a wise idea? Baby asks, as Jadecan strides for one of the garages. *You do not know how long you will be gone. It could be one cycle, or several.*

"Keep an eye on them, and look after Buddy."

Of course, Baby says.

"Have you found out anything in regards to the heat signature?"

No, I have not. I have not detected anything since, either. We appear to be relatively alone. It could have been nothing, a glitch of sorts, I suppose.

Jadecan turns the knob of the single metal door beside the two garages. It's got a few dents but pushes open easily enough. He walks inside the cramped grim box-like room and continues for the entry to the garages on its left wall. The door might as well be a duplicate of the one the Akiko had just walked through. He pushes it open and smiles at the few exo-crafts hovering in decent enough condition before him.

He strolls into the dimly lit garage as Niushki's wind howls out on its surface. The rain darts the now obvious metal roof of the garages which is surprisingly rather large, although not large enough for a starship of Baby's size to fit inside. They're clearly meant for more of a terrestrial vehicle, such as these hover-crafts. Jadecan looks over the three vehicles, he's sure Taj wouldn't mind if he borrowed one.

More often than not, they were stolen to begin with. It was sort of the Nudruk's thing, in fact it's what led to him on his knees before a few Reogki all those years ago. Lucky for him though, the Akiko was in the neighborhood and could use someone like Taj. It's rare to find an engineer as good as he is, and that very well could be an understatement. Unlucky for him however, the other two who accompanied the Nudruk were his brothers, and they, the Akiko did not need.

Jadecan jumps into one of the bike-like rust buckets and starts it up. It coughs at first, but starts after a few revs and runs just fine. It's probably been sitting for a long while. The door in front of him splits and slides apart, revealing the black saucer sitting before Taj's office. The Flunari and the foot-soldier watch as the cloaked Akiko speeds off, disappearing into the twilight of Niushki.

♀ By Happenstance

⊖ 5

The Akiko's been riding for quite a spell and although the rain stopped a while ago, the dust is still as damp as ever. His hover-craft is most likely going to need a top-off, so fuel is his current initiative. There's a cell station up the way, it was owned by Stet and run by O'an for a short time back in the cycle. It's as good a place as any to start, there's a good chance the hunter would have found his way there as well.

He knows the hunter had to have started at Stet's Place, it only makes sense. Anyone with half a mind would have gone to Skall's next, which would have led them to the Kiwiwa, who then sent them to the Oteniko outpost. From there, they'd be on their way to Shaw or Candenn, the towns nearest to Jadecan's birthplace within the black waters of the Achel Vein. The station, besides being a great place to pick up some rumors, is also somewhat of a halfway mark between the outpost and waterway.

The river was once a keystone to the Akikos survival, being the hub and lifeline of not only their civilization, but for most of the others as well. Jadecan was born only a few years before the first starships of the Reogki appeared. He witnessed the construction of the Reogki settlements and for a brief period, all was well. Now, not even a century later, he's the last of his tribe, and quite possibly, the last of the Akikos all together.

The cell station's white lights glow in the distance ahead of the fast approaching Akiko. The word Chelonan reads across the stop's fuel bay, weird, must have changed its name since last he was here. To be fair, it's been a while, and although its original name escapes him, it definitely wasn't that. Jadecan rides by a couple of holo-ads sitting outside the service area's entry and pulls alongside one of its four pumps.

He dismounts the bike and steps in front of the orange colored H_2 dispenser. The hooded Akiko watches a blue projection at the top of the pump around his eye level whilst hovering his wrist over the small screen at his waist. After a moment or two, the pump beeps and Jadecan removes the black hose from off its side. As he connects its nozzle to the exo-craft's fuel cell's compartment, a hover-craft of three Scuts pulls into the station and parks at the pump across from him.

The Akiko observes as two of the insects head for the main building while the remaining one begins to fill their vehicle. A click and the H_2 stops dispensing, his craft is full. He disconnects the nozzle and returns it to its place on the pump's side. A Niushki cool breeze rolls through as he makes for the small stone complex of the service area. Hopefully, the attendant inside can shed some light on what this hunter might look like and maybe, if he's lucky, who they might be.

Jadecan walks through the pale structure's glass front door. The two Scuts stand with holo-weapons in hand while chatting with the Reogki behind the counter. The clerk looks a bit unsettled by the two bugs in front of him. It's obvious the

Reogki is not fond of the pickle he's found himself in. He glances over at the cloaked Akiko and as the entry slides shut at Jadecan's back, the Scuts do the same.

"I hope I am not interrupting," the Akiko says.

"No, not at all," one of the Scuts answers.

"I was hoping someone here could help me with something," Jadecan states.

"Like?" the Scut asks.

"Like, where one may find a hunter, an Olensi hunter to be exact," Jadecan answers.

"You might try Shaw or Candenn," the Scut says.

"Any idea what an Olensi hunter might look like?"

"No," the bug answers. "I haven't a clue."

"I... I have a clue," the Reogki chimes in.

"Really?" The Akiko smiles.

"Yes, they're... they're usually wearing a set of armor and... and almost always are... are alone," the short-stature Reogki states, his eyes darting back and forth between the Scuts and Akiko. "Other than that, they're... they're heavily weaponized and... and will likely sport a red triangle, somewhere on them."

"Why a red triangle?" the Scut asks out of interest.

"It's the... the symbol of the Hunters," the Reogki answers. "It's a part of their culture. I don't know why, but... but they'll have one, somewhere."

"Interesting, I did not know that," the bug states, looking over at their companion. "Did you know that?"

"No, I did not," the other Scut answers. "Pretty interesting stuff though."

“Indeed, I will now take my leave.” Jadecan slightly bows and before turning to leave, says to the Reogki, “Thank you.”

“Are you... are you not gonna...” the olive skinned Reogki says nervously to the Akiko, as the door slides open, obviously hoping he’d help them with their current situation.

“No, I do not think I will,” Jadecan answers the frightened Reogki, then nods at the Scuts and leaves.

The Akiko strides across the white dust for his exo-craft, unsure of the fate awaiting the station’s clerk. The Scuts could be simply runners collecting the Balgorex’ cut out of the business, ‘tis true, it’s possible. For whatever reason though, this didn’t appear to be the case. Shame, the Reogki seemed to be a nice enough character. Too bad, that’s the way the cookie crumbles sometimes.

With that being said, he knows which of the colonies he’ll be going to, he’ll be heading to Shaw. Unlike Candenn, the city of Shaw’s not run by the Balgorex, it is instead owned and operated by the Reogki themselves and is but one of only a couple of places that are. For an individual such as the hunter, Candenn being operated by the Balgorex is most likely a deal-breaker. Considering his current employer the Olensi, and the Balgorex, aren’t fond of one another.

⊜ 6

Jadecan parks his exo-craft onto one of the holo-decks on the back of a terminal outside of Shaw. He jumps off the bike and heads for the spot’s blueprint kiosk. He activates the console’s blue projection and scans his wrist, storing the vehicle within its database under his holo-tech's unique signature. The craft is demolecularized by laser as the Akiko makes his way into the brightly lit complex.

These glass wall structures were built a very long time ago by the Olensi and were abandoned not long after their initial construction. Most of them are terribly placed and act as nothing more than glorified parking spots, being mainly built for starships. Some, a very slim some mind you, have become a kind of welcome center, like this one has, for the Reogki urban sprawls which still occasionally pop up on Niushki's surface.

The Akiko strolls through the automatic door of the terminal and walks for the ring of kiosks in its center. Besides himself, there appears to be a Nudruk and a couple of Scuts inside. These places never have been very busy. The hub's intelligence is quite useful, but the A.I. can be somewhat annoying at times and for the most part, unnecessary. As is the case here, for he continues right around it, having no need to interact with its hologram.

He meanders out of the terminal, having done basically nothing more than walk through the square building. White light illuminates the few landing pads in front of the complex, they were usually not occupied and rarely used. It's holo-deck though, is pretty popular. The majority of the moon's population may not have starships, but what they do have, is hover-crafts. Most of that current population is sadly now Reogki, as well as other outsiders.

Fun fact, it was the Reogki who first brandished the holo-system on the moon. It was the holo-weapon itself that made them dangerous, without it, they wouldn't have stood a chance against the likes of the Akikos. Jadecan spent a good many years without one, it was actually Stet who had suggested he have one installed, and so he did. Surprisingly enough, the process was relatively simple, being nothing more but a simple implant of sorts. The Balgorexes also paid for it, so why not. They claimed it would make the Akiko more effective, which arguably, it did.

What he remembered being a basic form of transfer from the terminal to the cityscape of Shaw, now looks to be a very sophisticated mode of travel. A large bus-like exo-craft, not too different from those of the Orphan, sits directly ahead in a pearly white color, awaiting him. He saunters down the railed walkway away from the complex toward the landing pads. His steps silent upon its steel as a cool wind blows, the Akikos have always been light on their feet.

The hooded Jadecan stops before the tiny ramp of the transport and glances back at the glowing terminal briefly as a droid greets him at its entrance. The robot appears to be an arm connected to the craft's ceiling by way of a rail. A large red eye at the arms end extends out of the vehicle and stares at the Akiko. It is apparently focusing rather intently, as its eye's circumference drastically reduces, by what can only be referred to as a metal eyelid.

"Identification," the droid demands.

The Akiko presents his blue holo-identification within his open palm. "I wish passage to Shaw," he states to the red eyed robot.

"Passage granted," the bot states.

If you wanted to enter into some of the more populated areas on Niushki, such as Candenn or Shaw for example, you would probably have to go through some sort of security. With Candenn, it was in the form of some armed Reogki outside its high wooden walls, while Shaw on the other hand, used a more modern style approach, having machines handling the bulk of it. Both have their advantages, to be sure, but anything non-organic is probably the better bet, definitely in a place like Niushki.

Jadecan boards the bus and places himself within one of its few rosy booths. The door slides shut and the craft pulls away from the railed walkway of the terminal. It's slow at first but quickly picks up pace, and as it does, the Akiko's eyes wander to the white dust outside the small window he sits next to.

⊜ 7

The empty dark terrain of Niushki passes by outside the circular window of the hover-craft. Jadecan sits watching as the cabin's only other occupant, the red eyed droid, observes the Akiko from the front of the bus. The moon's serene and beautiful, soothing his aura like always. A good feeling, it won't last, it rarely does.

The vehicle slows, coming to a stop, this is unexpected. The exo-craft's door opens, and five armed Ceruleans walk on board, they're definitely Olensi. One of them seats himself in the bench directly across from Jadecan, while the other four place themselves in the booth across from them. The Akiko glares as the bus' door slides shut and once again, the craft begins moving. The cabin bot never moved, staying locked in place at the head of the bus, watching.

The Cerulean's well-kept and rather formal in his appearance. He wears a lightly colored tan suit and tie. His moderately sized horns and skin tone nearly the same, all in all, he's a pretty decent looking fellow. Sitting quietly with his legs crossed, he scrolls casually through the blue screen of a datapad as the others watch from across the aisle. Their faces are a mix of concern and amusement. Jadecan readies himself for the inevitable fight that's fast approaching.

The Olensi looks up from the pad, and says in a relaxed kind of way, "Oh, no need to worry, Mr. Xtyct. I don't have the authorizations necessary to go that route. As much as I would like to, I sadly cannot." The Cerulean looks back at the droid. "You see that there, Mr. Xtyct? That'll act at even the slightest hint of violence. Hmm, so unless you feel like coming along peacefully, I suppose we're just going, going to chat. It's for the better of everyone, you understand."

"Are you Olensi?"

"Hmm, in a way, Mr. Xtyct," the Cerulean answers.

"Who are you?"

"You may call me, Mr. Sey, Mr. Xtyct."

"Why not get authorization, Mr. Sey?" Jadecan asks.

"Hmm, yes, that's partly why I'm here," Sey answers. "You see, not too long ago, an Olensi Cruiser, was destroyed while in the orbit of Vyn. Was rather unnerving to say the least. Would you happen to know anything about that? Anything at all, Mr. Xtyct?"

"No."

"No? Really? Interesting." The Cerulean chuckles. "Is it true you have one, Mr. Sophis Wonax, within your company, Mr. Xtyct?" Mr. Sey continues, after a few moments of Jadecan staring in silence, "I suppose that is a yes. Why did you depart Niushki, Mr. Xtyct? Some have speculated that you may have been staying within the Orphan City these last few days. What do you say to that, Mr. Xtyct?"

This Cerulean was certainly a bit different from any other of the species the Akiko had met. Although, to be fair, he really hasn't met all that many. Mr. Sey sits with a fixed smile worn upon his clean face, his bright gold eyes locked upon Jadecan. He clearly knew more than he was letting on, unnerving to say the least, indeed. And how did he know about Sophis? Had he been following the Akiko? There's something strange going on, that's for sure.

Jadecan glances from Mr. Sey to the group sitting across the aisle and then back, trying to wrap his head around everything. In all his eighty years, what happened? Life was rather simple at one point. Seems like ever since his finding of Amelia, things have escalated rather quickly. Or was it the death of Stet that set things in motion? Either way, they both go hand in hand.

"And what if I do, and have been?" the Akiko asks.

"Then you do, and have been, Mr. Xtyct," Mr. Sey answers. "It was but a simple question, requiring but a simple answer, Mr. Xtyct. Hmm, why did you murder the Olensi Operative, Hulikon, Mr. Xtyct?"

"I do not understand. What are you doing here? What is this? Who are you exactly?"

"I am no one, Mr. Xtyct," Sey answers. "I am but a humble Cerulean."

"Do you know who destroyed the Olensi Cruiser?"

"No. I do not, Mr. Xtyct," the Cerulean answers.

"Do you know which one of them was destroyed? Was it the Cortnei?"

"I am unsure, Mr. Xtyct," Mr. Sey states. "Is the black-armored character with you an Orphan City Militant?"

"Yes." Jadecan smiles at the Cerulean.

"Hmm, are you aware of any involvement the Orphan may have had? As to what part they may play in all of this?"

"I am unaware of any involvement they may have had, but I can not say for sure," Jadecan answers. "Do you believe them to be responsible?"

"Honestly, no, I do not, not directly at least. Although, I find it unlikely they are completely innocent."

"I see."

"Why did you kill the Olensi Operative, Hulikon, Mr. Xtyct?" the Cerulean asks again. "We know the Balgorexes were not fond of him. Did they perhaps have something to do with his execution?"

"In a way," Jadecan says. "How do you know about Sophis and the Orphan Militant? Have you been following me?"

"In a way, Mr. Xtyct, in a way." The bus comes to a stop and Mr. Sey stands. "I wish you luck on your quest, Mr. Xtyct," he says, stepping out of the booth behind the four other Ceruleans who head for the craft's now open entry. "I suppose you don't know what happened to the Oteniko facility, as well?" And after a few moments he fixes his tie, and states, "Hmm, suppose you would not, I'll be in touch, Mr. Xtyct. I hope Shaw's as nice as they say it is. Till we meet again, Mr. Xtyct, good day."

Mr. Sey follows the others off the exo-craft and as the door closes behind them, the vehicle yet again, begins moving. Jadecan returns to the scene outside the window he sits next to, smiling, as the beautiful landscape of Niushki stares back at him.

"I believe we may have found your heat signature," Jadecan quietly states.

You are more than likely, correct, Baby answers. *It would make sense, and does appear to add up.*

♀ Green Decay

⊖ 8

The bus-like hover-craft stops right before a smooth stone complex, known as a bulwark, and a couple of watchtowers sitting on either side of it. Shaw uses these as its main point of entry, they are pretty much bunkers and are heavily fortified. The city's outskirt's lined by the watchtowers forming a sort of boundary between themselves and the rest of the moon. Out of all the places on Niushki, this is probably the most dangerous. Not so much the town itself, but the barricade of security around it can be quite deadly.

Each tower's covered in blinking red lights and is armed with several fully automated sentry guns, they'll eliminate anything they deem worthy as a threat. The A.I. is apparently quite finicky though, it's rumored to kill not just the threats themselves, but also the city's own patrols sent out to confront them. As such, the patrols have been removed and replaced by small flying drones known as sentinels.

The cloaked Jadecan steps off the bus and heads for the bulwark under the watchful guise of the sentinels. Bright spotlights shine from atop the building, illuminating everything in front of the complex, including the Akiko and the drones following him. The lights are blinding and obscure most everything around them, even so, silhouettes of sitadoom can still be seen gliding in the dark sky. They circle high above, waiting to feast on the next unlucky soul who falls victim to Shaw's sentries. It happens a hell of a lot more often than you would think, even with the well known reputation of the area's sentry guns.

The borough glows some distance behind the bunker as the Achel Vein calmly flows alongside it. The waterways' reflective black waters appear even darker against the white lights of the city and terrain on either side of it. The Akiko stops before the reinforced door of the structure and peers up at one of the tall towers looming next to the bulwark. Its large guns are constantly moving and scanning the desolate dust as the red lights covering it blink every few moments in unison.

The solid steel entry before him is smooth and has no features to speak of. There is no handle, no door knob, no window, it's literally a blank slate. The sentinels hover around the Akiko coating him in a blue light as they periodically scan him. He waits, unsure of what else to do, someone's going to open it, right? It takes a moment but eventually, someone does. The heavy iron access slides open and Jadecan walks through into the empty lobby beyond.

He strolls across the silver metal floor for the purple counter and four white droids who await behind its glass barrier directly ahead of him. The automatons observe from within their own small booth-like cubicles separated from one another as he makes his way toward them. Red words flow across the top of the booths in a variety of languages, some of which the Akiko understands, but others he does not. The overall message was clear however, in order for him to progress any further he must first speak with the droids.

Jadecan approaches the counter, and as he stops before one of the automatons, it speaks in a robotic tone. "Identification." The Akiko presents his blue I.D. and as it spins in his palm, the droid states, "Jadecan Xtyct, Akiko, a native species of Niushki. Jadecan Xtyct is a known killer, runner, and affiliate of the Balgorex. Entry into Shaw requires threat assessment. Do you comply?"

"Sure."

"Assessing Jadecan Xtyct's threat likelihood and impact," the automaton states. "Jadecan Xtyct's threat likelihood is improbable, threat is unlikely to occur. Jadecan Xtyct's threat impact is tolerable, effects of improbable threat will be felt, but will not be critical. Jadecan Xtyct's overall threat assessment is low." The droid pauses briefly, before adding, "Low threat assessment requires the mark of subjects of low threat assessment who wish entry of Shaw. Jadecan Xtyct's entry of Shaw will require the mark of Jadecan Xtyct. Do you comply?"

"What mark?" the Akiko asks.

"The mark of Jadecan Xtyct," the automaton repeats. "Do you comply?"

"Fine, I comply."

A datapad materializes on top of the counter before him. "Carefully read the terms and conditions of Jadecan Xtyct's entry of Shaw," the droid states. "Return here when done and entry of Shaw will be granted."

"Seems simple enough."

He picks up the device and strolls away from the automatons while studying the lightweight silver datapad. It's normal enough, except for the small needle-like appendage on top of it. Jadecan looks around the relatively tiny empty area, there are no cameras, nor security, well, none he can see anyhow. There's sure to be some, there has to be, it would be ridiculous to think otherwise.

The Akiko looks at the blue screen of the device within his hand and reads. *Low Threat Assessments Terms And Conditions. L-I 1 Yellow.* He stores the pad within his holo-system and states, "You would probably be quicker."

Indeed, one moment. And after a few moments, Baby explains, *Well, to put it simply, if you are directly or indirectly the cause of any unrest whilst within the city limits of Shaw, you could face any number of consequences. They include but are not limited to, fines, injunctions, damages, imprisonment, and death.*

"What classifies as unrest?"

Unrest, in this case, is anything they deem as unrest. It is completely at their discretion, and by marking this, you also relinquish all rights you may, or may not be aware of having. Rights, in this case, is anything like a protection and/or affiliation, that may prevent the carrying out of these consequences. Of which, I believe you have none.

"What does it mean by mark?"

The mark is in the form of the subject's transport liquid, Baby explains. *For most organic beings such as yourself, it is commonly referred to as blood. You are to supply a small amount via the hypodermic syringe located at the top of the device. The blood will act as your signature, and you also, by supplying it, authorize them to use the liquid outside that, however they please. With 'they' being defined as simply, Shaw.*

"Interesting," Jadecan states, retrieving the datapad.

Indeed. The terms and conditions are also non-negotiable, and there does not appear to be any other way to safely enter into the city limits. If you wish entry, you must supply a sample of your blood, thereby agreeing to all of their terms and conditions. There is no other way. Also to note, whether you do or do not still wish to pursue entry after reading the terms and conditions, you must return the device before being allowed to exit the facility. Be it via transit rail to Shaw, or not.

"Transit rail?"

Yes, it seems as though there is a shuttle-like transit to and from Shaw. Most likely similar in function to those of the Orphan City.

"Sounds like fun." He pricks his index finger and returns the datapad to the counter before the droid. "Done," he states to the automaton.

"Thank you, Jadecan Xtyct," the automaton says. "Jadecan Xtyct may now board the transit to Shaw."

The Akiko nods as a door materializes on the wall to his right. He looks over at the entry and then back at the automaton who sits silent, still, and lifeless. Jadecan walks for the entry, away from the counter and droids behind it. The door slides open automatically as he nears and as it does another one directly behind it also opens, revealing the inside of what must be the transit. After a moment or two of standing before them, he strolls up a couple of steps into the short compact shuttle.

Five tiny red seats line either side of the narrow craft and beside each is a small square window. The Akiko takes a seat as both sets of doors close. A smooth metal-like grey wall stares at him from outside the window as the vehicle begins to move. The transit must fit perfectly into this space, there's seemingly no room between it and the walls slowly passing by outside its windows.

The shuttle picks up pace leaving its cramped parking bay as the white dust of Niushki replaces its silver walls. He's now behind the Bulwarks and watchtowers that wrap around Shaw. Sentinels can be seen patrolling the wasteland as a couple of towers fire upon some sitadoom flying nearby. The Akiko watches their bodies fall out of the dark sky as the transit speeds ahead for the borough awaiting it on the shore of the Achel's black waters.

⊜ 9

Jadecan steps off the worn gold rail-car onto a dark wooden platform before what appears to be a train station of sorts. He glances back at the transit as it rides away along its monorail. Besides a decently sized white number four towards the rear of its short rectangular body, it's rather dull and uninteresting. It's definitely one of the oldest things he's seen on Niushki in a while, and could probably use an upgrade. He turns his attention to the worn building sitting before him.

It's relatively small and is the same color as the boards of the deck itself. It appears to be a type of tollbooth, well, four of them to be exact, considering it's the number of windows facing him. They're vacant at the moment, in fact, there really isn't much of anyone here at all. Besides one Reogki who's seated upon one of the ebony benches that line the stage's edge, the entire station seems to be a bit of a ghost town. There is no one here. Several lamp posts run along the platform, their dim yellow lights barely doing anything, appearing to be more for show than anything else.

Jadecan looks over at the Reogki, who meets his gaze and smiles. It's a female, and a rather old looking one at that. Jadecan scans about, giving the area the once over, it's just the old lady and himself, no one else. She sits calmly with her hands atop a cane before her, it's almost as if she is waiting for someone. From the looks of things however, the Akiko is the first to arrive in quite some time. He strolls without hurry in her direction as the sound of the watchtowers sentry guns echo in the distance.

"Are you here with news of my grandson?" the old lady asks the approaching Jadecan.

"No, I am afraid not," he answers, sitting beside her. "Are you waiting for him?"

"Yes, I have been for a while now."

"How long have you been sitting here?"

"I've lost track of time, it goes by so much differently here," the old lady answers. "It's been a few years, I think."

"Where did he go?"

"He went looking for something, a purpose I suppose. He said he was going to go work for some Balgorex near Candenn and make something of himself." She lets out a small laugh. "I told him it was a death sentence, but of course, he didn't care. He just wanted out, saying there isn't any type of future here. He's right, you know, he's right. There isn't a future here." She sighs and smiles. "I hope he finds whatever it is he's looking for, I hope he finds it."

She sits with her faded green face focused ahead of her, staring into the twilight. It's pretty obvious she isn't worried about the Akiko, he is of no concern to her. A light wind sweeps as more gunfire echoes from across the terrain. The old lady scoffs and shakes her head, laughing to herself. The wooden stick her wrinkled hands rest atop looks just as aged and ancient as herself. Jadecan grins intrigued but yet confused by the Reogki. He's never seen nor spoken to one like this before. It's kind of nice.

"What brings you here?" the old lady asks.

"I am looking for someone," he answers.

"A Reogki?"

"No, not a Reogki. I do not believe so, anyhow, I suppose they could be. Although, I find it unlikely."

She looks over at him. "I know those eyes. I remember those eyes from when I was but a child. So, so long ago, over ninety years ago now. A lifetime ago, where has the time gone?"

"What happened here?" Jadecan asks. "Where is everyone?"

"The last of the first generation died a while ago," the Reogki answers. "I'm the oldest of the second generation, there are a few of us left, but not that many. Most of the third left, leaving us to look after their younglings. My grandson was one of them younglings." The lady pauses briefly. "I wonder if he's found them out there? Suppose I'll never know. Suppose most of us that are left, are just waiting to die from old age."

"I have to say," he states. "This is not what I was expecting to find."

"I suppose not." She smiles. "You'll find mainly old folks, such as myself here, there aren't very many young. Shaw over the years gradually became a… a kind of old folks home, I guess. A well fortified one, but an old folks home nonetheless." She laughs. "Who are you hoping to find here?"

"A hunter, an Olensi hunter. I was hoping they were here. Now that I am here however, I do not believe that they are."

"You are the first to venture here in quite some time," the Reogki states. "It's been a good many, many years since anyone has come here. They are probably not here, unless of course, your Olensi hunter is a very old Reogki, or a very young one."

"I believe them to be neither."

"I do as well," the old lady agrees. "I do as well."

"How does one go about leaving?"

"The sculler's skiff, across town on the river," she answers. "If you're looking to leave, that's it. It'll take some time, but nothing too extravagant. It usually takes around a couple of days or so to get approved."

"Approved?"

"I'm sure you have nothing to worry about. I can't imagine you'd face too much difficulty. The vast majority of those looking to leave here don't. It's the getting back inside part that's difficult."

⊖ 10

The Akiko walks beside the elderly Reogki, who moves slowly with the help of her cane. They venture down a wide dusty roadway through the center of several residential complexes. Each dwelling looks no different from the next one and are built of some sort of white stone. According to the old lady this is where she lives, within one of these small fenced-in homesteads. A couple of sentinels fly about scanning most everything while patrolling around the area. Other than the drones though, there is only Jadecan and the old lady, no one else.

The old lady had told Jadecan back at the transit station she'd help him with the whole leaving the city thing and that he could stay with her whilst waiting to be approved. A nice offer, one of which, he graciously accepted. Shacking up with a Reogki for any amount of time was not something he'd ever thought he'd do, but here he is, about to be doing that exact thing. Having said that, given his current situation he really doesn't have much of a choice. Besides, she has what he needs, and thus far, the Reogki has been rather pleasant.

The Akiko follows the old lady as she turns off the road for one of the abodes. While on the way here, she had explained to him what little of the departure process she knew and understood. From the sound of it, it was merely the basics, everything he would have already known and expected. Nothing new, nothing helpful, the obvious stuff. All of it she only knew because of her grandson, suppose leaving Shaw was never a thought that crossed her mind.

First things first, he is to fill out a departure request, and conveniently she has one inside her home. Apparently every resident of Shaw does, it's also evidently a rather simple application. Presumably, so long as you have a datapad and are a citizen of Shaw you should be able to pull it up, just as her grandson did. Secondly, you wait to be approved, that is it. The old lady says she doesn't know who's responsible for doing the approving, but if Jadecan were to hazard a guess, it's the automatons.

According to the Reogki things around the borough's done by the small flying droids and have been for quite some time now. In fact, the last leader of Shaw had up and disappeared, mysteriously, and was never replaced. Unless of course you count the sentinels and the automatons as a successor. Even so, the old lady is fine with it. Everything works and the whole community lives in peace, so what's to complain about? Suppose you could say, ignorance truly is bliss.

Jadecan trails closely behind the dull green skinned Reogki. "Well, here we are, this is where thy hangs one's hat," she says, walking through the open gate of the small white picket fence. "I've lived here my entire life, it's all I've ever known."

"It is nice," he states, as they head for the house's front door.

"Now, don't mind Norm," the old lady says, stepping onto the porch. "He's harmless, can be a bit annoying, but harmless."

"Norm?"

"Yes, he's one of those automatons as you've been calling them," she answers, opening the door. "Every homestead has one. Seems there are more of them, than there are of us these days."

The Akiko strolls after the Reogki inside and closes the wooden door behind him. A narrow flight of stairs sits ahead through an open entry as the pair stand within the foyer of the house. To their left is another open doorway leading to what appears to be a kitchen, or something of the sort. A couple of old square tables and a coat hanger populate the tiny landing area. The worn door closes at their backs and soon after, an automaton, presumably Norm, appears within the entrance on their left.

"Welcome home, Ms. Crinkly," the robot greets. "I see we have picked up a friend."

"Yes, Norm, this is Jadecan," the old lady says. "He'll be staying with me for a day or so, or until his departure request's approved."

"I see," Norm states. "Should I prepare some tea?"

"Yes, please," Ms. Crinkly answers. "If you would also, Norm, kindly bring our guest here the datapad."

"Yes, ma'am," the automaton says, and then disappears into the room.

Ms. Crinkly meanders through the entryway, the sound of her cane hitting the wooden floor resonating with each slow step she takes. Norm stands on the other side of a solid ebony island setting up two small cups onto a clean white saucer. A row of cabinets line the wall at the automaton's back running along the sink, stove, and countertop below them. Norm's glowing blue eyes observe as Jadecan and Ms. Crinkly mosey across the kitchen for the living room through the archway ahead of them.

An auburn couch awaits the two of them as they make their way into the room. Its russet colored carpet and walls are as old-fashioned as the room's faded wooden coffee table at its center. The little old lady gradually sits upon the sofa and relaxes while the Akiko places himself beside her. Several holo-images hang about the parlor with a couple more on top of the tabletop before Jadecan. He carefully picks up one of the grey frames and admires the few images stored within it.

The majority of the photos are of an older and younger male Reogki, presumably her husband and grandson. After scrolling through a few, he begins to question if he's seen the younger one before. The Reogki looks very familiar, but he's having difficulty pinpointing him. The Akiko's sure he's seen him somewhere at some point, but where? It doesn't take long for the revelation to hit. The young Reogki looks to be the very same one he killed outside the abandoned outpost. The very same one Jadecan savagely beheaded and left to be scavenged by the sitadoom.

"Who is this?" he asks, gesturing to the still shot of the young Reogki.

"Oh, that's my grandson, Isal," she answers. "That's a collection of him and my Angus, who passed on a few years ago, bless his soul."

"I am sorry," he says, putting down the holo-image as Norm walks into the room.

"Your tea, ma'am, sir," the automaton states, placing a small cup onto the table in front Ms. Crinkly and Jadecan. "The datapad, sir." Norm hands the device to the Akiko.

"Thank you, Norm." Jadecan nods.

"Yes, thank you, Norm. That'll be all," the old lady says.

"Yes, Ms. Crinkly," the automaton says, leaving the lounge.

Jadecan looks at the glowing blue screen of the device he now holds in his hands. "I trust you can figure it out," Ms. Crinkly states.

"Yes, I should be just fine, Ms. Crinkly, thank you," he says.

There are quite a few apps occupying the datapad's display. Each one's represented by a small logo or letter, with their corresponding names located beneath them. Most are pretty obvious as to what they are whilst others not so much. After a quick study of each though, it becomes apparent which one he seeks, the one labeled, Shaw's Proffer.

♀ Sapphire Docks

⊖ 11

Jadecan wakes up on the sofa to the sound of dishes and running water in the kitchen. The old lady had left him, retiring at some point during his filling out of the application. It was an easy process, like she had said it would be. A few simple questions as well as more terms and conditions, the normal stuff. After completing the request and paying for the sculler's skiff, which was also done via the app, he himself, also retired. All in all, it was an alright night.

He stares at the picture of Isal sitting upon the tawny tabletop in front of him. He's not sure how he should feel about it, or if he should feel any type of way about it, at all. In some ways it feels very similar to how he felt about the incident with Sophis, but in other ways it is different. The Akiko sits up as Norm wanders into the room carrying a bowl of oatmeal.

He places it down before Jadecan. "What would you have to drink, sir?" the automaton asks. "I could bring you some coffee or Achord tea, and of course there's water."

"Water, please."

Ms. Crinkly seats herself on the couch as Norm leaves. "Did you sleep well?"

"I slept fine, thank you. And you?"

"I haven't slept well in a while," she answers. "Not since my husband died."

"I am sorry to hear that."

"Oh, it's fine, but thank you." Jadecan nods, as she says, "Norm tells me your departure request has been approved. If you would like, after we eat, I could have Norm show you to the sculler's dock."

"I would appreciate that," he answers, as the automaton returns with a coaster and glass of water.

"If you don't mind my asking, sir," Norm says, setting down the coaster and glass on top of it. "Where will you go?"

"I am not sure." The Akiko spoons a bit of the porridge into his mouth.

"Might I suggest the Killum settlement, sir," the automaton says.

An interesting proposal. It's one of the most recent colonies to pop up on Niushki and suffers from what newly established urban areas commonly become ill with, an influx of wanderers, murderers, and thieves. Would be a paradise for one like Jadecan, 'cept for the majority of them are purposeless and shambolic. Not exactly an ideal environment, especially for one such as the hunter. Even so, it would make sense for them to have stopped by in their search for the Akiko.

Boroughs like Killum are usually chaotic and disorderly, only the truly deranged would dare call them home. Most newfound communities stay this way for a few years, in fact, Jadecan used to often jump from one to another when he was younger. They were merely a means to an end. Being full of work and opportunities, they're an easy avenue to earn some units. Those times of course, were a long time ago, way back before the time of Baby.

"How far is it from here?" he asks.

"Not terribly far, sir," Norm answers. "By boat, about a third of a cycle, or around a couple of hours, sir."

Jadecan's own voice emerges without warning and questions him, *What happened to the Seed?* He stops and cautiously peers around.

"Is everything okay, sir," the automaton asks.

It was his own thought, his own voice, but it wasn't him. "Did you hear that?" he asks, in complete disarray and looking up at Norm who stands at the couch's end.

"Hear what, sir?"

I did not, Baby answers. *Is everything okay?*

"Oh, well, it is nothing," he says to Norm. "I am just quietly losing my mind, nothing to worry about." The Akiko chuckles.

"That'll be all, Norm," Ms. Crinkly states. "Let our guest have his meal in peace."

"Yes, ma'am," the automaton says, and walks away.

"I apologize about him, he can be a bit rude sometimes," the little old lady says. "How is the porridge, my dear?"

"Very good, actually, thank you," he answers. "I appreciate everything you have done for me, Ms Crinkly. Yourself and Norm both, I cannot thank you enough."

"You are quite welcome," she says. "It's tremendously rare that we get visitors from the outside, it is nice to experience a change every so often."

"It has been a delight being here," the Akiko states, standing. "But regretfully, I must take my leave."

"Yes, of course, my dear." Ms. Crinkly slowly rises from off the sofa with the help of her cane. "I'll have Norm show you to the docks." She makes her way around the couch and strolls for the kitchen's archway, calling the automaton.

"Yes, ma'am," the automaton answers, appearing within the entry.

"If you would please, show our guest to the docks."

"Yes, ma'am. Will you be heading out as well, Ms. Crinkly?"

"Yes, Norm," the old lady answers. "I will be going to the transit station, to await my grandson, as I always have."

Jadecan trails Ms Crinkly who meanders through the arch into the kitchen behind Norm. The automaton strides for the homestead's front door a few paces ahead of the slow moving Reogki elder and Akiko. Norm opens the door as Ms. Crinkly enters into the wooden paneled foyer alongside Jadecan.

"I hope you find what it is you're looking for, my dear," she says, with her hand on his arm. "Have a good day, and thank you for stopping by."

"You as well, Ms. Crinkly." The Akiko leaves with Norm.

⊜ 12

The Akiko sits on one of the few bench seats of the sculler's wooden skiff as the sole passenger of the gondolier who stands near the stern of the boat. The galley slave is an automaton who dons a heavy black cloak and hood that's somewhat similar to the Faceless One's. Like the Faceless One, it looms in silence having not uttered a word the entire trip.

Jadecan looks away from the sculler toward the craft's bow as the faint yellow lights of Killum glow in the distance. The skiff moves ever so quietly towards it, gliding through the light fog resting above the Achel's dark calm waters. It wasn't all too long ago that he sped away from Taj's Fix, and although he knows Baby would have informed him if anything were to have gone wrong, he still worries. It's a newer development, a feeling he hasn't felt in quite a while, one which has only reared its head recently with the discovery of the cheiket.

"How is Buddy?" he asks, whilst Vyn watches from the star-rich horizon.

He is fine, Baby answers. *He has slept almost the entire time. It is rather surprising how much the creature actually sleeps.*

The Akiko smiles. "How are the others getting along?"

Well enough, I suppose. Jayph has vigilantly stood guard without rest ever since your departure and has also routinely scouted the area around the complex every couple of hours. Taj and Sophis on the other hand have remained indoors, and although I do not know it for sure, I am rather confident that they are getting along just fine.

"I suspect no one has stopped by?"

That is correct.

"Good."

The vessel comes to a stop at the end of one of Killum's short piers and as Jadecan makes his way out onto the dock, a few large sitadoom circle overhead. He continues across the planks of the wharf for the dismal dock house at its end. A

Drakon dock hand watches whilst the Akiko walks away from the sculler. If by chance the hunter ventured here by way of water, as Jadecan did, the town's harbormaster would surely know.

The Akiko walks past the Drakon seated upon one of the wharf's posts for the dully lit stained waterfront. It's a rather narrow building with a sand-colored door and window resting above it. Jadecan strolls up onto its small porch and after a moment or two of standing before the entry, he confidently knocks upon it. Within a short period of time, with almost no delay, the sound of footsteps are followed by the click of a lock and chain being undone. The door opens but a crack, just enough to peer through, revealing a Nudruk's sterling face who glares at the Akiko.

"Whaddya want?" the Nudruk asks in a demanding tone.

"Are you this dock's caretaker?" Jadecan asks casually.

"I am." The caretaker grumbles, staring at the Akiko.

"I am looking for someone and was hoping you may have seen them," the Akiko says. "An Olensi hunter, do you recall seeing one recently?"

"Hmm, I do recall seeing one," the harbormaster answers. "The bloke didn't stop by here though, you might try the Deura bar in town."

"Are you sure it was an Olensi hunter?"

"Had a red triangle on they left breastplate," the Nudruk states. "I pretty dang sure it was."

"Thank you."

"Ya welcome," the caretaker says. "I'd be careful Akiko, a hunter is nothin' to mess with."

"Noted."

"You ain't gonna easily dispose of 'em like you do them Reogki."

"Anything else?"

"Nope, nothing else," the harbormaster states, closing the door.

Jadecan eyes the dock hand who still sits upon one of the wharf's posts, whilst he saunters down the steps. The olive-brown Drakon observes as the cloaked Akiko strides up the slight hill for the borough of Killum at its peak. A couple of light posts inhere on either side of the colony's entrance up ahead, more or less illuminating it in a hazy saffron glow. He trudges on in between them and continues down the dust road running through the center of the tiny community.

A few ashen colored stone buildings line the sides of the roadway along with a few of the same light posts that welcomed him at the burg's entry. The town, if indeed it is big enough to be considered one, is very similar to that of Drakon Rock. They both have a distinctive thruway and are illuminated with opaque nebulous yellow lights. The two differ mainly in size, with Killum being noticeably smaller than Drakon Rock. Besides that, Killum also appears to be rather underdeveloped in comparison, and more than likely because of it, lacks any sort of significant population.

Unsurprisingly, one thing becomes readily apparent, there's no neon lit signs on any of the buildings. A rare occurrence, one that is unique, but common in places like this. No matter, for the location he's looking for doesn't need to advertise. The Deura is a bar, no different from any other, everyone who's anyone tends to find them pretty quickly. If you breathe, which is a challenge in itself on Niushki, you'll undoubtedly end up gravitating toward them, it's only natural. Jadecan of course, has no difficulty and sniffs it out with relative ease.

He strolls through the polished batwing entry of the hostelry and immediately notices its steward to be none other than the stereotypical Drakon. No surprise there, for what else would be running the joint? It's a fairly petite establishment having just a few tables, and the one corner bar the reptilian barkeep stands behind. A Grogan and a tandem of Nudruks sit at the tables whilst a Reogki is perched at the counter.

As he expected, there is no sign of the Olensi hunter. Odds are, they were here, and then they were gone, all within almost the same motion. Having been strictly here to only gather whatever intel they could on the Akiko before swiftly moving on, leaving this wretched place in the dust. To be honest, Killum so far doesn't seem half bad, but as with all things, appearances can and usually are deceiving. Jadecan makes for the Drakon with all eyes locked upon him.

"Welcome, cousin," the steward greets. "How may I be of service?"

"I am searching for an Olensi hunter," Jadecan answers. "They apparently bear a red triangle on their left breastplate. Have you seen them?"

"I have," the umber colored Drakon says.

"Do you know where I may find them?" The Akiko looks over at the Reogki who smartly minds his own business.

"I do not," the barkeep answers. "But the Grogan might."

"The Grogan?" the Akiko asks, glancing back at the obviously passed out Grogan at the table behind him.

"The hunter showed up and spoke a few words with the Grogan, then left," the reptilian explains. "They were not here all that long, although the Grogan himself, has yet to leave."

"What do you know of the Grogan?"

"Nothing."

"I see, thank you, cousin." Jadecan nods at the steward.

"You are always welcome here."

The Akiko paces for the Grogan's booth as the two Nudruks make haste and leave the Deura. He slides into the faded cyan pew across from the unconscious and now somewhat familiar Grogan, who snores loudly, completely dead to the world. The Reogki follows in the Nudruks footsteps and exits as Jadecan vigorously shakes the Grogan awake. The red fellow groans and rises up slowly, rubbing his head. He's clearly had a bit too much to drink and is currently suffering the consequences.

"Sadae?" Jadecan asks, pretty sure it's him.

The Grogan sighs. "It's you, great. What do you want?"

"I have reason to believe an Olensi hunter has spoken with you," Jadecan answers. "I just want to know what about and where I might be able to find them."

"You know, that's almost word for word what they said in regard to you," Sadae states, sighing while pinching the bridge of his blue nose and closing his eyes. "I don't know where he went, I told him you stopped by the Gloom to see Ternaan briefly and that you were annoying. That's about it."

"So the hunter is a 'he'?"

"Look, I don't know." Sadae throws his hands up. "They could be a he, or maybe they're a she or it, I don't know. What does it matter?"

"It does not," the Akiko states, then retrieves the extraction device Ternaan had given him from his holo-system. "Do you know what this is?"

"Am I supposed to know what that is?"

"I suppose not," Jadecan answers. "Ternaan had given it to me when we spoke at the Gloom, but did not really say what it was. I was hoping that he might have mentioned it at some point."

"Well, he didn't." Sadae lets out a small laugh. "I would say, ask him, but I'm afraid Jahrei probably killed him, so there's that."

"Why would Jahrei kill him?"

"I have no idea, and would you know it, I didn't ask. Is there anything else? I have a headache, and you're making it worse."

"No, I guess not." Jadecan smiles. "Do you know how one would go about leaving this place? Is there possibly some sort of shuttle or taxi service?"

"There is not. You leave the same way you got here, however that was." Sadae sighs yet again and scoffs. "It's been nice, but if you wouldn't mind, I'd like to be left alone, okay?"

"Very well," the Akiko states, with a slight nod, then leaves the Grogan and heads back to the bar.

"There is a ring out back, cousin," the Drakon steward says, as he pours a shot for Jadecan. "You may take it if you would like. I apologize, but that is all I have to offer in regard to transportation out of town. You could always leave by way of boat, as well."

"Did the hunter leave by boat?"

"I do not believe they did."

"Well then." Jadecan puts back the shot and places the small glass back onto the countertop. "I appreciate the offer and will gladly accept the ring, thank you."

"You are always welcome here," the barkeep states, as the Akiko walks around the bar and heads for the pub's back door.

Rings are one of the oldest types of vehicles on Niushki, and unlike the much more common hover-crafts of the Olensi that hover above the terrain, they are bound to it. They are unique in that they are operated by a lone rider inside a large unicycle wheel, and are pretty fast considering. The Reogki used them as well as other wheelers like them quite religiously back in the days before the terminals. Although they still have their uses, most of them are largely regarded nowadays to be nothing more than recreational vehicles.

Jadecan wanders out the back entry of the tavern and immediately spots the ring parked alongside its back wall. With its mauve fiberglass body covered in white dust, it's apparent the wheeler hasn't been used in quite some time. Apart from the dirt and debris that covers and surrounds it though, it seems to be in fairly good condition. The Akiko warily studies the endless dark terrain whilst trying to decide where the hunter may have gone in their search from here.

"Where did you go?" Jadecan quietly questions to himself. "Where would I have gone?"

He strolls over and inspects the ring's thick black rubber tire and dust filled command deck. After a thorough check of its wheel and body, he visibly finds nothing wrong with either, and climbs into its lone reddish-blue driver's seat. As usual, the means to start the vehicle stares him in the face on top of the ring's helm, abaft its steering wheel. A silver key sits within the bike's ignition, waiting to be turned.

It's a different mechanic, one that's usually only found on the Reogki wheelers. Jadecan's never been fond of it, preferring the Olensi's hover-craft's simplistic button method instead. Nonetheless, he turns the key, and almost instantly the ring comes alive. The bike's also extremely loud in comparison to the barely noticeable hum of the Olensi crafts. It's just another frequent feature of the Reogki vehicles the Akiko doesn't care much for.

⊜ 13

The Akiko's ring rapidly speeds across the dust with the Achel waterway on his left and the Despair Mountains to his right. The torch lined wall of Candenn glows up ahead on the other side of the river. After some deliberation, he left Killum for the most likely place for the hunter to have gone. The only place that makes sense is an old pawn shop known as the Unalome that sits on the river's shore. It, like Stet's Place, is a shop where Jadecan bought and sold items rather frequently, and with Stet now gone, it's probably just one of a handful of places left for the Akiko to go to make units.

The Unalome's small white sign glows as it spins slowly above the relatively tiny complex. The Ael Bridge sits beyond the structure in between the Unalome and Candenn. Jadecan smiles at the sight of it. He had thought he may have to swim across, forcing him to abandon the ring and travel by foot. Thankfully, that is not the case. A couple of sitadoom watch from atop the pawn shop as the Akiko parks the wheeler in front of the copper metal building and makes for its front door.

The Cerulean siblings who set it up about a decade or so ago are an interesting lot. They were allegedly exiled for, according to them, a misunderstanding, or so the story goes. That's apparently why the siblings' horns have been sawed off and filed down. It would seem it's the species custom when it comes to banishment. It's a strange look for a Cerulean, to be sure. The brother and sister duo has on occasion said they were once a part of the Olensi, and yet at other times, have also stated they were not. So yea, they're an interesting lot.

He walks through the automatic dull grey door of the Unalome and continues down the narrow short corridor inside. The sister of the two, De-ja, waits behind a pane of glass from within a small greeting area directly ahead of Jadecan. Her brother Ian observes through the large rectangular window of the Ceruleans' storage room on the Akiko's left. It's a very cramped space, as is the whole complex, to be frank. It's minuscule and compact, which are both attributes Jadecan despises. Nonetheless, units are an amenity for one such as him, and beggars can't be choosers.

"Welcome inside," the turquoise De-ja greets.

"Hello," the Akiko says, looking into her sapphire eyes.

"How can we help you, Jade?" she asks.

"Has anyone stopped by looking for me?"

"Actually yea, someone has."

"Who?" he asks, as Ian walks around the corner and stands at her side.

"Well, the memory is a little hazy," she states.

Jadecan drops a few gold coins onto the countertop between them. For these two, money talks, and unlike most others on Niushki, they are worth a few units. They're rather knowledgeable and can be quite helpful if you can afford it. As a side factor of their hustle, they often buy at higher rates and occasionally sell at lower ones. The Unalome is probably one of the best spots to buy and sell items, barring the fact they can't be trusted, of course.

"It's becoming a little clearer," she says, he drops a couple of more units. "Oh, yes, now I remember. It was a hunter, and they paid good units for information about you."

"You do not know anything about me worth any units," he states, as the money dematerializes from off the polished wooden surface in front of him.

"Yeah, but they didn't know that."

Jadecan smiles, shaking his head. "Where did you send them?"

"I don't remember," she says, with a small smile.

"Of course not." He chuckles and drops the extraction device onto the counter. "Is this worth anything?"

"Oh my," De-ja states, with wide eyes. "May I?" she asks, gesturing to the device.

"Indeed."

The large syringe vanishes and reappears before the sister on the other side of the glass pane. "Wow, I haven't seen one of these in a long while," she states picking it up.

"So, is it worth anything?"

"Definitely, we'll tell you what you want to know."

"Wait," Ian interjects. "It's been used." He points to the solid green light at the syringes end. "I'm sorry, but we cannot accept it," he states to Jadecan.

"I see," the Akiko says.

"I mean, we could if you were to empty its contents," De-ja says looking to Ian for confirmation, whilst returning the device to the countertop.

"Yea, if you were to empty it we could take it off your hands," the brother agrees, as the device rematerializes on top of the counter before Jadecan.

"And how would I go about doing that?"

"Um, well, by injecting its contents into something that is similar to what its contents are," Ian says as if guessing.

"What exactly is it?"

"An experimental technology that's meant to help with information retrieval," the brother explains. "It's a type of interrogation device, kind of. You basically imprison someone inside it, well, you store some form of them in it anyway, and release them at a later date into someone else. It's complicated."

"Okay, what do you mean by similar?"

"I'm not entirely sure to be honest," Ian answers. "I sorta know what it is and what it's used for, but I don't know at all how it works. I'm assuming that if there's a Drakon, for example, stored inside it, that you'd have to inject it into a Drakon, or a species similar to a Drakon, so to say. But honestly, I don't know, you maybe could inject just about anything with it, I really don't know. You could always try. One thing to note however, is that whatever species you decide to use as a test subject must be alive... in one form or another."

"Fine." Jadecan drops a few units. "How much will the information cost me? Where did you send the hunter?"

"How 'bout, we make it worth your while and sweeten the deal," Ian suggests, glancing over at De-ja.

"How so?" the Akiko asks.

"You go and empty the object, then bring it back here, and we'll pay you triple its value, and tell you where the hunter went, as well as, give you an upgrade of your choosing."

"What is its value?"

"It's an older model, but even so, it's still Oteniko tech, which makes it at least worth two hundred," Ian answers. "We'll give you say, an even one thousand, sound good?" Jadecan nods in agreement. "And as far as an upgrade, we have a few holo-system cards, and about one or two starship ones. You can have any one of them, free of charge."

"How do you suggest I empty it?"

"Just pop over to Candenn and pick a Reogki. I'm sure they'll work just fine," De-ja states.

"My sister is correct. That is probably your best bet, to have it done quickly anyway."

"Why do I feel like it is worth a lot more than you say it is?"

"You could go and get a second opinion if you'd like," Ian states.

"I feel I made a mistake by revealing it to you."

"Maybe, but not necessarily. It's a dangerous item and not one you'd want to be found with, especially if the ones finding it are Olensi," Ian smiles. "As it is however, it is what it is, and all in all, it's not that bad a deal. To be fair, I'd prefer killing you and taking it over paying for it, but... you're good business, and well, you're you, so we're paying for it. You could always keep it and find out where the hunter went yourself, and hope of course, that no one finds out you have such a device."

The Akiko chuckles. "Looks like I will be heading over to Candenn."

♀ Deathly Parasite

⊖ 14

The open shops of Candenn are busy as usual while Jadecan wanders down the town's main road. A constant moving crowd of Reogki surround the strolling cloaked Akiko, and like last time he was here, not a single one of them pays him any mind. 'Tis true, his capote hides his features but even so, a stranger is a stranger, and that alone should arouse some suspicion.

He stares up at the red Balgorex banners that wave in the subtle Niushki winds atop the dark wooden wall. It feels like forever ago that Stet and himself would meet up, party, and do business here. In the early days, Sycora was usually present during their get-togethers, if not for the simple fact she lived here, as Stet did, and was always around Candenn anyhow. Over time, the Drakon and Akiko grew rather close and formed a sort of bond, a kind of relationship. If he's learned anything from those times though, it's that you should never mix business with pleasure, it never ends well.

Jadecan slides off, out of the crowd, into a narrow alley in between a couple of stone buildings behind the merchants. He stops about three quarters of the way through and slowly sits against one of their hard walls. Most of the memories he's fond of revolve around those two. He once found a sort of happiness in the recollections, but now, it seems they're ridden with a haze of sadness and regret. Sadness and regret, seem to be the only constants in this long and painful existence. He gets up and trudges on to do what the Akiko does best, hunt down a Reogki and, more than likely, relieve them of this burden called life.

He heads for Candenn's ghetto, it's common knowledge, no one cares about what happens within the cheapside. Jadecan strides for the obvious target, the lone Reogki who pointed him to his friend O'an's abode. They should work fine, given the hut they retreated into was of course their own, and that they're somehow still alive. Both are factors that cannot be guaranteed, but fate would have it, they very well can be this cycle. For there they are, smoking, right outside the same hut, in almost the exact same spot. The Akiko observes from a distance as they enjoy the cigarette. It'll be the last time they ever smoke one.

After a few drags, the Reogki flicks away the stimulant and ambles back inside their homestead. A moment or two passes before Jadecan casually moseys over and knocks upon the worn timber door. The old entry creaks open and the familiar look of fear spreads across the Reogki's green face as they come to realize what it is standing before them. They're dressed in rags, middle-aged, and are as one would expect, extremely malnourished. The Akiko steps inside and closes the door as the Reogki back tracks.

The interior of the hut's unsurprisingly almost an exact duplicate of O'an's. The majority of the shanties are more or less the same. A small fire burns in the hearthstone of the abode's back wall as the Reogki gradually makes his way around the wooden table at the room's center. The Reogki shakes uncontrollably in terror and puts the table in between themselves and the Akiko looming before their front door. There's hardly enough space for the two of them with the table itself taking up pretty much the entire area. The room's meager and unfurnished, with its only light being a candle burning atop the table.

"Wha-wha... what do you want?" the Reogki stutters, stumbling over his words.

Jadecan walks 'round the diminutive table and stands for a moment in front of the green scared stiff alien. The Reogki's eyes somehow widen even more than they already were, as the Akiko retrieves the extraction device and stabs him in the neck with it.

"I don't want to die," the Reogki whines pathetically.

"No one wants to die," Jadecan states, as the device's light turns red, signaling it's now empty.

He activates his holo-weapon and removes the syringe whilst shooting the Reogki twice in the chest. The Akiko watches as the alien side steps and falls into the table, crumbling to the hard cement floor. The Reogki lays upon his back and appears to have a kind of seizure as he begins to randomly speak insensibly.

"He killed them! He killed them! He killed them!" the Reogki cries, spitting blood. "What am I saying? Why am I saying that?" They then yell at the Akiko, almost as if they were someone else entirely different. "I know you! I know you! No, no, no! This can't be happening!"

"Who killed them?" Jadecan asks, tilting his head in confusion whilst watching the Reogki breakdown before him. "Who is, them?"

"Kasper, Kasper, Kasper!" The Reogki screams in pain. "Please make it stop! Make it stop! Wait, what is, who is, who is, who is Hulikon?" They question, and then almost immediately answer themselves. "I am Hulikon," the Reogki shouts confidently, looking down at their bloodied chest. "You can not be serious! I've been shot again! Did you kill me?" they demandingly ask Jadecan. "Did you kill me, or is the other still alive? Did I die, Akiko? Tell me, am I still alive?"

It's now rather obvious what is happening to the Reogki. It appears as if Hulikon now occupies their body along with themselves, like a sort of parasite, compliments of the Akiko, of course. Unfortunately for the Reogki however, it's probable that after whatever it is that's happening to them runs its course, the host will wither away, leaving only the leech, Hulikon, behind. It also seems to be a rather painful process, for the Reogki anyhow. Although to be fair, he's been shot in the chest twice and stabbed in the neck with a relatively long needle-like device. To put it simply, they're not having the greatest of times.

"You are very much dead, Hulikon," he answers.

"No. No!" The Reogki shrieks. "Stet has a locator, Stet has a locator! My wife, my kids, I don't have a wife and kids. Why would he kill them? Why would he kill them? Nothing is real! Nothing is real! What is happening?"

"You think you're special." Hulikon laughs as blood pours out the corners of the Reogki's mouth. "You're not, this has all happened before, and it'll happen again. It'll happen again, and again, and again. You're nothing, Akiko. You always have been, and always will be, nothing. Zero, zilch, nothing. A means to an end, that's all."

"That, in itself, makes me something."

"Why? Why am I still alive?" The Reogki bawls, gurgling blood. "Please, please kill me!" He weeps, begging the Akiko.

Hulikon laughs as Jadecan activates his weapon and points it at the Reogki's head. "Did you know that when you die, which by the way, you will, you're still conscious long enough to know that you're dead, Akiko?" Hulikon questions, clearly suffering.

"An interesting statement to make in the face of certain death," Jadecan says. "But I am not the one who dies."

Hulikon chuckles. "Sure, Akiko, whatever helps you sleep at night."

"Please, kill me," the fading Reogki pleads. "I'm still here… I'm still here, please… please, kill me."

Jadecan pulls the trigger, putting a bullet in the center of the Reogki's forehead, killing both the Reogki and Hulikon instantly. He then deactivates the weapon and stands motionless, looking down upon the alien's lifeless body.

Are you okay? Baby asks.

"Yes."

Are you alone?

"I am."

That was odd, Baby states.

"Indeed," Jadecan agrees. "What do you make of it?"

I am unsure. I suggest you leave Candenn immediately and head back to the Unalome. I will work at unraveling this oddity in the meantime.

"As you wish. After all this, the siblings have better know where the hunter has gone off to."

⊖ 15

Niushki's breath howls as Jadecan departs the ring and strides for the Unalome. It's oval-shaped display hovers above the complex in almost the exact same way Stet's did. The rust-colored shack's as dull as it's featureless grey entry and as the Akiko watches the illuminated white sign slowly rotate, the door opens before him.

Ian observes from within as Jadecan wanders inside and strolls for him. The Cerulean's copper eyes gleam whilst he eagerly awaits behind the glass pane at the head of the small corridor. De-ja walks beside the Akiko alongside the large window on his left and after turning the corner, she stands next to her brother as Jadecan arrives at the counter.

"How'd it go?" De-ja asks.

"Well enough," Jadecan answers.

"Have you emptied the device?" Ian asks.

"I did," the Akiko answers. "Where did the hunter go?"

"I see," the brother states. "So that's how we're doing this. May I at least see it? I would like to know for sure that it has indeed, been emptied."

"Of course." Jadecan nods retrieving the device and showing it's now solid red light to Ian.

"Very nice," the Cerulean states, as the Akiko puts away the object.

"So, the hunter, where did they go?" Jadecan asks again.

"The White Claw," Ian answers.

"The White Claw?" Jadecan asks, somewhat surprised.

"Yea. To be honest, I had no idea where you may have been, but we weren't about to skip on a significant amount of units. So we pointed them to a spot that we thought, they may not have checked out. From there though, we have no idea where they may have gone. Suppose you'll have to go there to find out."

"I suppose so," the Akiko says, placing the device onto the polished wooden grain top of the metallic counter. "I have not been there in quite a long while. A smart play." He slightly bows. "Thank you."

"Not a problem, my friend," Ian says, as the object disappears from off the countertop. "As promised, the thousand units." A small plastic card materializes before Jadecan, who then retrieves and stores it into his holo-system. "De-ja, if you would please, show our guest what upgrades we have available," the Cerulean brother says to his sister, as he disappears around the corner.

Ian then reappears inside the storage room as a blue holographic menu manifests above the counter in front of Jadecan. He stares at the board's three options which sit in square boxes spaced horizontally apart from one another. Within each frame is a picture that corresponds to the associated text beneath them. They read: M.I., for molecular inventories, H.W., for holo-weapons, and S.S., for starship systems.

For the most part, the molecular inventory upgrades are primarily for increasing the user's storage capacity, whilst the holo-weapons are focused more on the damage, accuracy, stability, and fire rates of the weapons themselves. Neither of those the Akiko's in desperate need of, and he's already upgraded them both a couple of times as it is. Baby's systems on the other hand have yet to be upgraded, due to them being extremely expensive. Plus she was missing a few basic components and without them, she couldn't have been upgraded anyway. The energy cell was the last of those parts. Thanks to Amelia, it was installed, and for free to boot.

Jadecan chooses the starship systems category and is confronted with only one option: F.C.A. 3. "What is F.C.A.?" he asks the siblings.

"Flight control automation," De-ja answers. "It's pretty much an auto-pilot."

"Would that be useful?" he asks.

"Well, I mean, everything's useful to some extent," De-ja answers.

Yes, I believe it would be of value, Baby says. *I am fairly certain that Taj and/or Sophis could install it, as well.*

"I will take it," he states to De-ja, whilst selecting it.

De-ja calls to her brother who's busily rearranging items within their depository. "Ian, do you know where the F.C.A. is?"

The projection dissipates and a thin black hard drive of sorts materializes on top of the wood in front of Jadecan. "De-ja, he just has to select it, that's all he's got to do," Ian answers, as the Akiko retrieves the device from the countertop. "We don't have to do anything. If we have it, it should literally just come into existence before him."

"Oh," she exclaims, embarrassingly looking back at Jadecan.

He holds up the slim box for her to see. "Just out of curiosity, how much is an energy cell worth?" the Akiko asks, storing the device into his inventory.

"About forty to fifty, depending on its condition and so on," Ian answers, returning to his sister's side. "I'd let one go for thirty-five, if we had one."

"Figures." Jadecan chuckles to himself.

"Do you need one?" the brother asks.

"No, I was just curious." The Akiko turns away from the siblings and heads for the Unalome's exit.

⊜ 16

Jadecan parks the ring in front of the small stone building of White Claw next to a couple of hover-crafts. The complex's brightly lit blue sign sits fixed atop a steel pole on the side of the establishment, illuminating the entire area in front of it. The Akiko departs the vehicle and walks alongside the holo-windows that run down its face for the wooden door on its opposite end. He hasn't been here in a while, a very long while.

The last time he was at White Claw, he was in search of a Balgorex target. He naturally found them sitting at its bar, and of course, killed them. He not only killed them, but also murdered everyone else inside. Everyone else, including the couple of unfortunate allies who joined him on the mission. This is where, for the most part, the majority of the Akiko's problems lie. 'Tis true he's gotten better with time, but even so, the urge is still there, and at times, it's damn hard to ignore.

Needless to say, Stet wasn't happy but wasn't surprised either, for it wasn't uncommon for Jadecan to leave a trail of death behind him. It was expected, but usually wasn't appreciated. The bloodbaths were, according to Stet, generally bad for business, or so he said. The Akiko has not been back since, but there's not a specific reason why. The last time he was here has nothing to do with it. He just hasn't had a reason to come back, until now.

Standing at the Claw's faded timber entry, he peers through the blue windows at the backs of the few bar goers within. There are three individuals seated at the bar while poised behind its counter is a single barkeep. So, four in total, not too shabby. At first glance he thought the butler to be none other than a Drakon, as was usually the case, but upon a second look, it was definitely a Minorak, and a female at that. Strange, and unexpected, both of which are becoming more and more frequent on Niushki.

He grabs hold of the brass knob on the door and after turning it, pushes open the entrance and walks through. The interior's setup is very much like a bus with several bar stools following alongside a counter on either side of a narrow walkway. It's fairly long but uncomfortably tight. The stewardess and patrons observe as the cloaked Akiko wanders down the aisle for one of the vacant stools of the Claw's main bar.

Jadecan studies the few glass shelves at the barkeeper's back. They're filled to the brim with bottles upon bottles of liquor, of all types. He notices atop them a tattered black banner, and within it lies a simple threaded image of a violet crown. Odd, it's actually not too different from Kit's emblem.

The same one she etched into the wall of the Kurat that revealed the secret entrance into the Refuge of Keleth. Yea, that one. He peers up at the familiar symbol whilst sitting. The Minorak throws a hand towel over top of her shoulder and ambles over in his direction.

"How's the cycle so far?" the barmaid asks.

"Not too bad, considering," the Akiko answers.

"That's good." She smiles. "I'm Anya, and you are?"

"Jadecan."

"Is this your first time? I can't say I've seen you here before."

"No, but it's been a while."

"Well, in that case, welcome back. What can I get you to drink?"

"Anything neat."

"Will do," she says.

Jadecan watches her retrieve a small glass from underneath the bar and as she places it down before him, he asks, "Has an Olensi hunter stopped through here?"

"Yes," she says, turning to the shelving unit behind her.

She takes a clear bottle from off one of the top shelves and turns back to the Akiko, who asks, "Did they mention why they were here?"

"They did." The Minorak opens the bottle and pours a small portion into the glass. "Said they were looking for you."

Anya returns the bottle to the shelf as he sips the elixir, and asks, "Where did they go from here?"

"Oh," she answers, smiling and facing the Akiko. "I sent them to the mausoleum."

"Mausoleum? What? Why a mausoleum?"

“Why don’t you go find out.” She giggles, gesturing down the aisle beside her.

Jadecan looks to where the stewardess points and observes as a wooden door opens. It’s directly across from the White Claw’s timber entry on the opposite end of the bar. Weird, it wasn’t there before, or was it? He’s usually pretty good at attention to detail, and this one somehow, he didn’t notice? Granted the Akiko’s not perfect and has overlooked things before, but he couldn’t have missed something like a door. Could he?

The trio of drinkers seated upon the stools at his side are abnormally motionless. They haven’t moved, and stranger still, he hasn’t even noticed them. During his entire interaction with the barmaid, he has not once, felt their presence. He clearly remembers them watching him walk down the aisle, but can’t seem to recall their faces. In fact, he can’t remember much of anything about them, at all. The only thing he’s sure of is Anya, and as he turns back to the stewardess, she herself has disappeared.

“You can not be serious,” he says to himself in disbelief.

He shakes his head and takes a drink of the clear distilled spirit sitting before him, savoring it. He places the glass back down onto the countertop and gravely peers over at the three mysterious characters. They all look over at him in unison, their faces frightfully mangled, rotting, and in different stages of decay. They stare with their putrid eyes, cold and lifeless, as they begin to loathsomely groan. The repulsive undead-like beings begin to stumble out of the stools and stagger toward him. Their moans as harrowing as death itself.

Jadecan stands and faces the trio of clumsily advancing zombies. Their hands stretching out before them and lazily reaching for the Akiko ahead of them. Their festering torsos twist back and forth as they trudge slowly forward, painfully so. He activates his weapon and fires a bullet into each of the ghouls' heads, ending their miserable existence. As the dead crumble, he becomes unsteady. A bizarre feeling of dizziness washes over him, and after a few moments, he shakily attempts to walk, but faints after a couple of paces.

♀ Yellow King

⊖ 17

Jadecan comes to, lying face down upon a cold and dark hard floor. His vision is a blur, as an intense heat ignites his pale skin. Nearby, the sound of flames echo while the laden smells of burning wood linger in the musty air. A giant blaze gradually takes shape and rages within a colossal fireplace in front of him. The Akiko rises, wavering slightly, and stares into the inferno.

"Hey there, stranger," a loud monstrous voice bellows at his back.

Jadecan turns and lays eyes upon a pink-skinned one eyed monster, who sits within a massive stone chair glaring down upon him. "And you are?" the Akiko asks.

"What?" The huge Cyclops says, as if its feelings have been hurt. "I'm Tercal, the Bone-Breaker. Have you not heard of me?"

"I have not," Jadecan states, glaring at the shocked and dumbfounded half dressed titan. "What am I doing here?"

"You drank of mother's milk," Tercal says, as if surprised by the Akiko's question.

"And?"

"And you are to become my next meal," the behemoth answers, rubbing his massive stomach. "You are to reside right here, in my belly, for the rest of your days. That is, if you don't die immediately, like most of you do."

"I imagine you are going to try, and cook me?"

"No, no, no. That's barbaric, of course not." The Bone-Breaker laughs. "I am going to swallow you whole."

Jadecan peers about the enormous cobblestone blocks of the gigantic room. There aren't any doors, nor windows to speak of. It's a completely enclosed space and not too different from the dungeon he found himself in before his encounter with Wooden Face. To be honest, this entire scenario stinks of the Mistress' sorcery, but he knows this not to be true. Vulena is surely behind this, he's certain of it.

Jadecan chuckles quietly to himself. "No, I do not think you will."

The giant laughs manically, then stops after a few moments with a look of confusion and worry worn upon its weighty face. Tercal explodes out of nowhere, spraying blood and pieces of himself all over the moldy stone room. The Akiko, now drenched in the Bone-Breaker's blood and guts, looks to where the monster once sat. A skeleton, just as large, sits in its place.

The extremely tall skeleton dons a yellow robe and seems to be a king to some degree, considering its crown that's made of what also appears to be bone. Unless of course, it's just fond of the look, it would be quite the fashion statement. It glances about the blood-soaked walls whilst shaking its great skull. The Yellow King then looks down and somehow, appears to be smiling at the Akiko.

"I've never been a fan of my children," the skeleton states. "I find them rather, grotesque. You got a make 'em think the dog did it. Ya know what I mean?"

"Come again?"

"Are you really that dense?" the skeleton asks. "Whatever, never mind."

"And, you are?"

"Me? I'm Sh'lyn," the skeleton answers. "You know, good 'ol Fenric, the Great Prince of the Old Ones? The One Above All's main boy? You know? You know that guy, right?" Jadecan kneels quickly, bowing before Sh'lyn, as he speaks. "You know, come to think of it, I don't believe we've met. I could be wrong but, have we met before?"

"We have spoken, my Lord."

"Yes, yes, yes, but I don't think we've ever actually met. You know like, face to face," Sh'lyn says. "How does one hand pick an individual and never meet them? You know? Strange but, whatever."

"We have not, my Lord," Jadecan answers.

"You've met my trouble and strife." Prince Fenric chuckles. "Hell, you've even met my mistress. They're quite the pair, a combination of sensitive and savage. They're a couple of charmers, aren't they?"

"Yes, my Lord."

"You don't have to kneel, you can stand if you'd like." The Akiko nods and rises, as Sh'lyn speaks. "Most don't know how beautiful the darkness can be. How the light owes its existence to it, you know? You and I, we're creatures of darkness. It's where we're most comfortable, at our best." Jadecan nods in agreement, as the Lord continues, "The universe is full of monsters, as well as a good many friendly faces. It's sometimes hard to tell the difference." Sh'lyn chuckles. "I'm not sure which we would be considered. Suppose we're a bit of both. I suppose everyone is."

"I suppose so, my Lord," the Akiko states.

"You know, when I went in search of the Sight's Gem, I already knew what I was going to find. Same thing every time, three little ol' ladies." Sh'lyn sighs. "I despise them, I always have. After all is said and done though, destiny is what you are supposed to do in life, and fate, well, fate is what kicks you in the ass to make you do it. Three hags, that's what we're given, three little ol' hags. They get to decide the fate of the universe, and would you know it, it's never good. It's never, never good. Quite the concept, don't you think?"

"Indeed, my Lord."

"So, here I am. Who knows, maybe it'll change things, maybe it won't," the Lord states. "Nonetheless, at least we've met face to face. If anything, there's that. There is that. It's been nice, I really should do this more often. What do you think?"

"I think that would be nice, my Lord."

"I like you. I can see why, why the majority of us like you, and why, some of us don't. Suppose they go hand in hand. I think you'll do well, you always do. You have a type of feeling, a certain, certain aura about you. I like it, it's reassuring."

"Thank you, my Lord," Jadecan says, with a slight bow.

"Well, before I leave you, I suppose I should tell you where your hunter went. It's only a part of the reason I'm here," the Great Prince says. "She's on her way to Taj's Fix, and with that, happy hunting, J'dkyn."

The Lord of the Akiko disappears just as abruptly as he had appeared, and as he does, an open wooden door manifests at his back behind the large chair. "I guess that is the exit." The Akiko lowly chuckles.

The fire rages in the hearthstone as Jadecan walks for the worn timber entry. Oddly enough, as he casually strolls around the grand seat, he notices an old staircase, and a lone round eye upon one of its rotting posts staring back at him through the doorway.

The peculiar eye within the square newel keenly watches as the Akiko crosses the entry's threshold and the cobblestone room behind him dissipates. A solid wall now sits where the doorway once was, and at the top of the small flight of decaying steps ahead of him is yet another open rickety wooden entry. Jadecan glares into the mysterious eye as he traverses up the decrepit creaky steps for the quiet room at its summit.

Upon reaching the top of the staircase, he cautiously peers through the doorway into the empty and desolate tavern of the White Claw. A thick layer of dust blankets the worn and crumbling tap house, it appears as if no one has been here in a very, very long time. Weird, bearing in mind he's definitely without a doubt been here, and recently at that. But all things considered, it's far from one of the strangest things he's seen on Niushki. The Akiko glances back to look upon the bizarre eye for the last time, but now finds instead a brick wall at his back.

Sudden indistinctive voices resonate on a backdrop of soothing jazz-like music, as Jadecan glares at the solid barrier in front of his pale face. He slowly turns back toward the rundown hostelry, and lays eyes upon something else entirely. The White Claw is no longer broken and dilapidated, as it was, but a moment ago. It's now fit for the likes of a king, it's luxuriously swanky, and boisterously packed. A dark Drakon pianist plays in the club's corner as a female Minorak barkeep serves the several patrons seated at its golden counter.

"Anya?" he calls, unsure if it's her.

The steward stops, hell the entire place comes to a standstill, music and all. "What can we get you, Jadecan?" the whole bar questions him in unison.

"What?" he says somewhat curious, but worrisome.

"Would you like anything?" they ask again.

"I was just leaving," he answers. "So, no."

The music resumes as the barmaid speaks with a mischievous smile, and Jadecan hastily heads for the Claw's exit. "To each, their own. Safe travels, Akiko."

He has much more pressing concerns to contend with, and this peculiar bar scene isn't one of them. The Olensi hunter is apparently on their way to Taj's and at the moment, the Akiko's not there to protect them. Jadecan cannot say for sure what the hunter might do with the likes of Sophis and Taj, but as far as Jayph goes, the militant would most certainly be killed.

The Orphan soldier doesn't stand a chance against the likes of the hunter, it's almost too obvious a fact. Jadecan knows Jayph will be unable to fend them off for an extended amount of time. The militant will try, but ultimately, will fail. The Akiko's got to get back as quickly as he can. Having already fallen short with the Kiwiwa, he will not and cannot accept another failure. Their lives are in his hands, they fall squarely on his shoulders, they are his responsibility.

"Is there any sign of the Olensi Hunter?" he asks, marching out of the door and heading for his Ring with purpose.

No one has been anywhere near the facility, Baby answers.

"They are on their way," he states confidently. "They may already be there, waiting."

The White Claw's brightly lit sign saturates the white dust in a bluish tint as several sitadoom circle overhead. Vyn sits on the starless horizon as a cloaked and shrouded Vikerumu watches him board the circular vehicle. The Watcher lurks, observing unseen from a distance, as the unaware Runuoscha speeds off for Taj's Fix.

⊖ 18

The Akiko's saucer gleams within the twilight before the complex of Taj's Fix as he speeds hastily for it. A cloud of dust bellows from behind the Ring and as he nears he can make out a few sitadoom perched atop the building. They begin to flap their large wings and depart as the noisy craft passes by Baby. Jadecan parks the wheeler in front of the Nudruk's office and for a brief moment, all was calm.

His feet hit the dust as an arbitrary whistling sort of noise resonates throughout the dark landscape. He turns searching for its source, but before the Akiko's able to make heads or tails of the warble, he's upended and sent soaring into the air. The wheeler, himself, and the dust at his feet, erupt in a spectacular explosion. His back smacks the hard stone wall of Taj's Fix and with such a tremendous speed the impact nearly knocks him out.

Jayph's disembodied voice echoes, but is strangled heedlessly as Jadecan hits the ground and yet another explosion rocks the terrain. Dust, rubble, and the Akiko, are sent rapidly flying sideways away from the blast. For a few brief moments he's suspended in mid-air, amongst all the debris, before once again hitting the ground and sliding into the garage. A dense fog envelopes the entire area as pieces of what was once the ground rain down all around it.

A dazed and unstable Jadecan wobbly stands, leaning against the hard wall of the garage. A chain-like rattle swiftly follows the now barely standing Akiko. A piercing sensation emits from his shoulder. He drowsily looks down, laying eyes on a chain which quickly becomes taut and forcefully pulls him from off the wall. He falls like a stone onto his face and is dragged along the dust away from the garage.

Jadecan grips onto the aged chain-links as spurts of gunfire bursts forth from behind him. He looks over to see Jayph, who's bravely marching forward toward him. The Orphan militant no longer dons a helmet and his black armor's so heavily damaged, he might as well not be wearing it at all. The Grogan soldier's badly wounded and on his last legs. He, beyond a doubt, wasn't supposed to survive the initial onslaught. Guess they weren't banking on Jayph, nor his armor, to be as good and durable as they are.

The Orphan soldier fires ahead of him through the heavy fog at an unseen target. It's indisputable who Jayph's target is. He shoots at the culprit behind the destruction who's unequivocally the Olensi hunter. The Grogan militant's now only a couple of paces away and as Jadecan lies watching helplessly, another explosion detonates in the exact spot Jayph was standing. The Akiko's ears ring as he is covered in debris and for a split second, is unaware of what is happening as he is flung once again sideways. But this time he's attached to a chain and being dragged by it at the same time. Fun. He nearly loses consciousness, this by no means is looking good.

Silhouettes of Sitadoom circle overhead, barely visible through the haze as Jadecan tries to focus on where Jayph had been standing. A decent sized crater now sits where the Grogan once stood, and as the dust settles ever so slightly, the blurred outline of the militant can be made out in the distance. The soldier now lies a dozen or so paces away, outside the garage the Akiko once stood against. He observes the still body of the fearless Grogan whilst still firmly gripping the chain which relentlessly drags him away from Taj's Fix.

Miraculously, Jayph begins to slowly move but is almost immediately pelted with gunfire. The Orphan militant goes limp and lifeless, he would not move again. A warrior's chapter, which is irrefutably one of the toughest the Akiko has ever seen on Niushki, comes to a beautiful end. Jadecan nods in respect and turns his gaze ahead of him. He can only hope to die in such a prestigious and honorably righteous way. Only those worthy deserve such a noble death.

An approaching figure starts to take shape and before long the unmistakable symbol of the hunter bleeds through the fog. Just as the Killum dock master had claimed, there it is, engraved into the tracker's faded dark armor's left breastplate. The infamous red triangle of the hunter. The Akiko glares, still gripping the chain that's attached to an unknown source from behind the oncoming mercenary. Jadecan attempts to activate his holo-weapon but is for some unknown reason, unable to do so.

"Baby," he calls, to no avail.

She's been strangely quiet this whole time. It all now makes sense as Mr. Sey and his unit start to take form at the hunter's back. The humble Cerulean holds within his hands a device which steadily retracts the chain and mercilessly drags the Akiko towards them. A ship manifests within the starry sky as Jadecan arrives at the hunter's boots. The entire squad glances up as the Akiko peers at the feet of the red caped mercenary in front of him.

The Olensi hire looks away from the large vessel and back down upon Jadecan, before shooting the Akiko twice in the back. Three mysterious figures materialize near the rear of Mr. Sey and his squad as Jadecan goes in and out of consciousness. He lies there at the hunter's boots, barely able to keep his eyes open, but is somehow able to do so. With his strength waning fast he knows he'll soon pass out, as everything fades to black.

⊖ 19

The Akiko wakes to the sound of rattling chains and unhinged laughter. He lies with his vision a bit fuzzy as a wall of iron bars comes into focus before him. Slowly but surely, he rises from the hard torn mattress within a comfortless room. Jadecan sits on its edge and realizes he's being held within a tiny rusted jail cell. He must be a prisoner of the hunter's, it would only make sense.

He begins to wonder. *How long have I been out? Where am I?* The Akiko rubs his temples because of a splitting headache, and mutters, "Baby?" After a few moments of no answer he tries again, but this time a bit clearer. "Baby?"

A subdued and rather sullen chuckle echoes from behind the bars in front of him. "I see they have a new pet," a raspy voice says, in an oddly low and unbalanced tone.

It's unnaturally dark, but the outline of a figure becomes evermore into focus as Jadecan glares into the blackness. "I am no pet," he bitterly states.

Maniacal laughter's followed by its owner's hands gripping the bars and pressing their feline-like face against them, while staring crazily at the Akiko. "That's not what Korrine said. No, no, that's not what they said at all."

The Akiko's never seen this type of species before. Its face has some extremely clean-cut features, having distinctively sharp and edgy lines. The creature is very cat-like in appearance with its well-defined nose, slightly slanted narrow eyes, and pointy ears. It's definitely not like any other he's ever come across, and that's saying something. Jadecan keenly looks into it's deranged small pupils as it's smoke-darkened face lowers back.

"What are you?" he asks curiously.

"A Felxan," the bizarre character answers, with a mischievous grin. "And what are you?"

"An Akiko." He nods. "I am Jadecan."

"Itsune." The Felxan nods back.

"Who is Korrine?"

"She's the one who's been keeping me locked up in here," Itsune says quietly, gesturing for Jadecan to come closer. "You're locked inside here," he whispers, tapping his head as the Akiko slowly makes his way over to him.

"Where would 'here' be?" Jadecan says, with a small smile as he sits with his back against the bars.

"In here," Itsune answers, while looking at him and once again tapping his head.

"I am being kept inside your head?" the Akiko asks, glancing over at the Felxan.

"Yes, yes," Itsune exclaims.

"That makes a lot of sense." He chuckles, then gesturing to the surrounding cell, says, "So, you are locked in here." The Felxan nods in agreement, as the Akiko adds, "And I am locked in there." He points at Itsune's head.

"Yes, yes, you see?" The Felxan asks. "You understand now?"

"No. Not really," he answers. "Tell me, why would this so-called Korrine keep me locked up inside your head?"

"She's looking for something," Itsune whispers, glancing around cautiously. "I'm the only one who can find it for her."

"So, she keeps you in here," Jadecan says, looking around the cell. "So you can find what she is looking for inside here?" He gestures to his head referring to the Felxan's.

"No, no, well yes, but no," Itsune answers. "She keeps me in here so I can talk to those she imprisons, inside here," he states, gesturing to his head. "They have what she is looking for."

"Really? How long have you been here?"

"Too long," the Felxan states. "Much, much too long. I don't remember having a life outside here. So many have come and gone. I don't know if... I don't know if any of this is real."

"What is it, this Korrine, is looking for?"

"The Elder One," Itsune answers, with a hushed tone.

"Well, I do not know anything about the Elder One," the Akiko states.

"You must, you must know something," the Felxan says, seemingly pleading.

"What I know." Jadecan stands. "Is that I must avenge my family, and my friends. That is what I know. That is what I care about."

"If you don't know anything, then you will go away," Itsune states in fret. "You must know something, you must know something. Please, please, you have to know something." He then whispers fearfully, and with such a subdued voice the Akiko is hardly able to make out the words, "She's listening. She's here, she's always here. Listening, watching... please, you must know something."

"You are pathetic," the Akiko says, angry and annoyed.

Itsune lets out a demented laugh before apparently suffering a sort of psychotic breakdown. He absurdly begins to roll around on the cell's floor seemingly dying of laughter, while simultaneously screaming manically. Deliriously, the Felxan lets out an indistinguishable word here and there throughout the mad episode before coming to his knees, and after a moment or two, begins to cry softly.

Jadecan, now sitting on the edge of the cage's mattress, marvels at the scene, completely baffled by the nutcase who ostensibly resides in the hole next to him. Then steadily, as if in response to an unknown trigger, Itsune's entire upper body readily begins to rock back and forth as he kneels. The Akiko looks on as the Felxan bobs erratically, seemingly zoned out and oblivious to the world.

By all accounts, real or not, Jadecan for all intents and purposes wakes up, yet again. He blinks a couple of times and squints his eyes a bit, because of a blindingly bright light that's now all of a sudden present. He's no longer within the iron bar cage, and Itsune well, the Felxan has completely vanished. He's nowhere to be seen. Putting two and two together, it's probable the entire scenario never actually existed, being nothing more than an illusion of sorts. If indeed true, as does appear to be the case, it would give Itsune's claims to a degree, a bit of merit.

It soon becomes salient he's being held somehow suspended midair with his hands bound behind his back. Whatever the case, predictably the one thing that hasn't changed, is the Akiko is still apparently a prisoner. Whether it be within the confines of the iron bars of a jail cell, or cuffed and suspended within some sort of gravity defying field, he is surely someone's trophy. With that someone being surely the hunter, and if the deranged Itsune is to be believed, which is of course a dilemma in and of itself, his captor's known as Korrine.

Question becomes: is Korrine the mercenary he's been searching for, or is the mercenary working for this so-called Korrine, or better yet, could this Korrine be working for the mercenary? After all is said and done however, suppose it really doesn't matter, for he's going to have to endure the

Olensi first. He's decidedly aboard one of their vessels, and if not, surely will be relatively soon. At any rate, one thing is for sure, he will fulfill his duty as the Runuoscha. One way, or another, that is for certain, regardless of wherever he may be, unchanging.

"Hello, Jadecan," a strong feminine voice greets from in front of him. "How are you feeling? Did you come out okay?"

"He seems stable, your righteousness," another female voice says.

"Who are you?" He scowls, trying to focus on the blurred figures standing a few paces away from him.

A very Cerulean-like dark skinned lady gradually becomes clearer as the Akiko stares at the three silhouettes before him. He peers into her bright green eyes as the two fully armored female soldiers on either side of her, stand attentively. This is clearly not a Cerulean considering her lack of horns which in turn means she's definitely not an Olensi. She, like Itsune, is of a species unknown to him.

That said, this has to be either the hunter, or at least a mercenary of the same faction as the one from Niushki. Even though she's not wearing a cape and there is no red triangle present on her left breastplate, she has got to be one of the same, just another hired Olensi mercenary. Her thick lightly colored dreadlocks flow out from underneath a fancy headdress and over top of her broad shoulders. She looms confident, she's clearly the one in charge.

She smiles. "I am Korrine."

"What do you want?" he asks, demandingly.

"I want, in a way, what you want," she answers, taking a couple of steps forward.

"And what is it that I want?"

"To find the Seeds, of course," she states. "I, however, am in search of the one responsible for their planting."

"I know of no Seeds," he retorts.

"Oh, but you do," she says, as the glowing orb he found within the Reogki dungeon forms within her palm. "These are what you're looking for, are they not?"

"Where did you get that?" he demands.

"Don't worry, it's not the same one you foolishly gave away," she states, as he angrily glares at her. "I had nothing to do with their little facility's destruction."

"Am I supposed to just take your word for it?" he asks.

"Obviously, you really don't have much of a choice, do you?" The orb disappears from out of her palm.

After a small sigh, he asks, "What is this place?"

"You are aboard my ship."

"And the Flunari? Where is he?"

"He is here, too. Unharmed, of course."

"And my ship?"

"It is where you left it," Korrine answers. "Untouched, along with the Nudruk, back on Niushki."

"Where are we?"

"Currently, in hyperspace, on our way to Solarius."

"Interesting, what do the Olensi want with the orbs?"

"Sh'lyn wasn't kidding, you really are quite dense," Korrine states. "I am no Cerulean, as I'm sure you can attest, nor do I work for them, or their Olensi. You'll find that they, and I, have very little in common, if anything at all."

"Even if you are not one of their hired mercenaries, you are still, but a hunter," he sneers, disapprovingly.

"I am not. But believe what you will, it matters not."

After a few moments he scoffs, and asks, "Who is it you are looking for? Who is the one responsible for planting these so-called Seeds?"

She tilts her head with a bit of a worried expression as if taken aback by the question, and answers, "The Elder, the System Lord."

After a long moment of silence, he asks, "And they are?"

Korrine lets out a disappointed sigh. "Kasper."

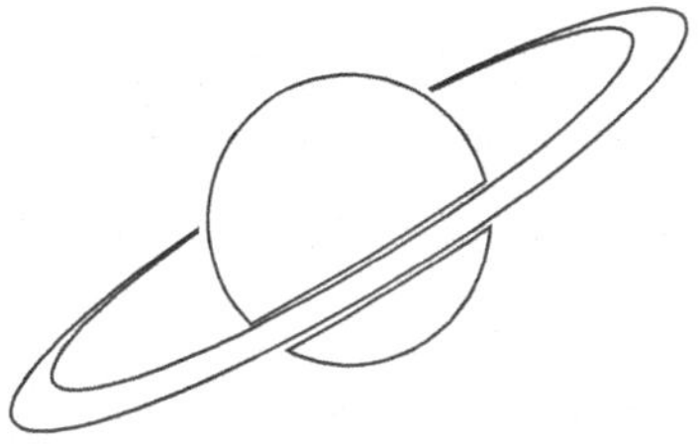

Acknowledgments

First and foremost, I would like to thank my beautiful wife, my co-author, and my parents. For without them, I wouldn't even have a novel to be writing any acknowledgments for. I would also like to thank a couple of close friends for the work they did to evolve the first part of the story, The Watcher. I would also like to thank, our proofreaders, editors, and anyone else I may have forgotten. Your contributions in feedbacks, comments, and critiques helped shape this into a better story.

I would like to give a nod to all of my co-workers, past and present, for the majority of the characters, places, and items within these hundreds of pages are named in one way or another, after one of you, so thank you.

Thank you, thank you all. I am forever grateful and humbled by all that you do, thank you.

From the Authors

The System Lord tale is a story I've been wanting to tell for over a couple of decades now. The concept itself actually came to me in a sequence of dreams over the course of my younger years. They heavily focused on another character - not Jadecan, and that book will be written at a later date - but with that being said, the overall account itself is directly a part of the same universe. I never planned on writing a novel. I suppose that's the beauty of it all. I have always imagined it playing out on the big screen in one fashion or another, but upon looking back at all the different avenues I've dabbled in (of which, there are many), this is by far one of the most enjoyable and fulfilling exploits I have ever taken on.

I've always found enjoyment in learning, and firmly stand by the popular statement, "knowledge is power". As such, I spent just as much time researching, as I did the actual writing itself. And as with most works of fiction, there are countless cultures, mythologies, religions, and ideas that I've woven within these pages.

Notably, most of the god-like beings in this novel are heavily influenced by the entities of the H.P. Lovecraft mythos. Such Lovecraftian Gods as Azathoth, Nyarlothotep, and Shub-Niggurath, as well as Hastur, from Robert W. Chambers, *The King In Yellow*, are of just a few that immediately come to mind. Others worthy of mentioning include the Slavic Baba Jaga and Leshy, the Moirai of Ancient Greece, and Oscar Wilde's, *The Picture of Dorian Grey*.

I would have to say, writing is something that I have always done, and thoroughly enjoy. My writing process itself, in a nutshell I suppose, is what one would call, "writing by the seat of your pants". Whilst I did have a vague outline, I tended to stray from it relatively frequently, with the bulk of the story more or less writing itself. I often had no idea where the tale was going. Surprisingly, that was probably single-handedly the most exciting part of it all. I would find myself amused by most of the situations that Jadecan would find himself in, and would be just as perplexed to see how he would ultimately deal with them. It was certainly a wild ride, and one that I will without question be getting on again.

I find myself wondering at times how this overall experience has changed me, and if I have grown in one form or another as a writer. There are a slew of other questions as well, but hmm, it is difficult to say. It's undeniable that my writing evolved to an extent over the course of the manuscript, but considering this is the first book I've written of any format, I suppose that is to be expected.

I would like to think that I've changed and grown in some way as a writer, but I'm just not sure. One thing is for certain though, this venture has brought an old friend and myself much closer, and that in itself has changed my life, for the better, as a whole.

So... hmm. Thank you for tagging along. I hope you've enjoyed this adventure as much as I have, and maybe, just maybe, we'll see you in book two, of the System Lord saga. With that, be thankful for all that you have, whether it be something small, or something grand, or quite possibly something in between. As always, I wish you a legendary day, and that you achieve all that you set out to do. Life is a beautiful thing, so go out there and live it.

Kody Killam

Kody Killam is not exactly what one would call normal, and his space operas are no different. Whether it's in his lyrics or his manuscripts, he enjoys the unhinged and telling a story that's much the same. His tales are often a complex labyrinth of science fantasies meshed into a web of weird horror fictions. Having been living alongside aliens for most of his life - on a little planet called, Earth - Kody's stories are uniquely otherworldly, and his debut novel, Benign Dystopia, is no exception. He was born somewhere out there in the cosmos, far from this planet, but would eventually find his way here in the year of 1986. On the 28th day of September, he would land under the cover of darkness on the outskirts of Houston, Texas, and around thirty years later, the author Kody Killam, would be born.

Aaron Harvey

Music, art, math, language, and science have always been a part of life for Aaron Harvey. A couple of decades later he became connected to what his fate would be, allowing him to see his potential and sentinel the changes needed. Perceived as weird by many, he has been a helping hand for those uniquely unaware of the guidance given where place meets time. Throughout it all, he has been an artisan to troubleshoot the shape and composition of ideas made manifest by allies. What will come to pass can be determined by rearranging the visions located in his dreams. Residing in that stormy mind, lives a perplexity that many cannot understand or relate to. This simplicity comes from complexity, but that ambiguity sprouts chaos that designs the future.

Made in USA - North Chelmsford, MA
1317132_9781957195001
06.08.2022 0928